# A Certain Fall

Robert W. Chapman

PublishAmerica
Baltimore

First printing



Author Photo Credit: J.L.C.
Cover Art: Watercolor - "Sunset Marsh" by Gene R. Fuller - *works in watercolor* www.generfuller.com

ISBN: 1-4137-5284-5
PUBLISHED BY PUBLISHAMERICA, LLLP
www.publishamerica.com
Baltimore

Printed in the United States of America

*To JANIS ~ my wife,*
*whose initials are carved in*
*those high school bleachers alongside*
*of mine, somewhere in time.*

# Preface

The first story was written last. In fact, the book revealed itself in this manner, i.e., as individual stories, not in any particular sequence. Originally, I had intended that the stories not be sequential but be placed in the order that they were written—or even a random placement throughout the book. Because—it is a truth that when this kind of story is disclosed by individuals it almost never comes out in any organized way.

This book is a collection of stories—since that is what the larger story is—an anthology of narratives that describes fortitude, resilience, and treachery, inside one impoverished family. These stories were written as individual short stories, so it does not matter how the book is read. Yet it seemed reasonable to place them in time...so, if read from the beginning to the end, they have a sense of time for the events in the main character's life.

I have interviewed hundreds of children and adults in my career, and I have found that when they tell the stories of dysfunction and abuse in their families they usually reveal them in vignettes, a little at a time—over long periods of time. And much, very much, is not told, ever—to anyone. So I suggest the reader consider what is not written here, as well as what is.

The first short story that I wrote about this family is not included in this collection. When I wrote that first short story, I thought that I might be able to write others, and maybe attempt to write a collection of stories, not love stories, but stories about what love is. Instead, I found in the telling of these stories, that I had ended up writing about what love is and what love is not. Evil? Well, evil is not the opposite of love; evil is the absence of love. And it does the greatest damage to humankind when it is absent in a child's life. There can be no greater betrayal than the betrayal of a child by their parent.

~ rwc
Upper Range Pond
June, 2004

"Come—see real flowers of this painful world."

~Matsuo Basho, 1644-1694

# Contents

# palace of cold

She had never done anything like this before. The young woman stood looking at her reflection in the pane of glass in the porch door. She put her right hand up to her left cheek, dipped her head to see herself in the window pane, and tucked a loose strand of hair behind her left ear.

Last night she had colored her brown hair with a reddish tint. It had not come out auburn, like on the package. It did not look the way she had planned for it to look. Now, she regretted the impulse. She had gotten through the entire day and not a soul at work had mentioned anything. She thought that was not a good sign. She heard footsteps and then a voice.

"Just a minute," a woman said from inside the apartment.

She shifted her feet. She tried to peer through her reflection to see into the apartment. She moved her head at different angles, but the glare from the pane of glass was too bright. She gave up and looked around at the porch landing she was standing on.

Last night her mother had said, "That's not a good neighborhood. I don't think you should go over there. Not alone, anyway."

She had responded that it was part of her job. Her father had looked around his newspaper and shook his head, indicating he agreed with his wife. She ignored them both. She had graduated college a year ago.

She knew that many people assumed she was still a school girl. She appeared far younger, even than her actual youth, partly because of her petite stature. This annoyed her. She tried to change herself in different ways to modify her appearance...to look older. But, this often resulted in having the opposite effect. *Like now,* she thought, and smirked at her reflection, then caught herself.

"Hold on," the woman said.

The young woman heard the television from inside the apartment, then—thumping sounds and footsteps.

*"What time is it, boys and girls?"*

She leaned sideways to look through the other window on the porch. She could see the television. It was not coming in well. The black and white picture was snowy and rolling up the screen.

*"It's Howdy Doody time!"* said Cowboy Bob.

The music played, and a chorus sang along with Cowboy Bob: *"It's Howdy Doody time, It's Howdy Doody time…"* She could see Clarabelle the Clown, squirting his seltzer bottle at someone, running around in circles, and honking the toy horn on his belt.

She looked down at her dress. The small purse matched the printed blue dress. She carried a canvas bag that contained papers she would be looking over tonight at home. She sat the bag on the floor of the porch, placed the purse in the bag, smoothed out the front of her dress with both hands, looked at herself in the pane of glass again, then picked up the bag, and stood waiting. She looked over her shoulder into the dooryard—then the porch door swung open.

"What! What do you want?"

The young woman looked at the woman in the doorway. The woman was short. She looked older than herself but not by much. She stood waiting, staring up at this younger woman who was standing on her back porch stairs.

The woman in the printed blue dress started her prepared introduction, "Hello. I'm Miss Coburn. I teach at your daughter's school…"

"Hold it. Hold it right there, girly."

The young woman flinched at the term "girly." She looked around herself to see if there was something wrong.

"I don't have no damned daughters. Take a look behind me, sweetie…you see any pretty little darlin's runnin' around in there?"

The young woman dutifully looked over the woman's shoulder. Four young boys were tackling each other on the kitchen floor. The larger one, no more than eight years old, took off into the living room, the other three followed in pursuit with toy guns and a large stick. The household rang with their screams.

"*Cowabunga!*" the Indian on the television said, walking toward a bleacher full of children. The television blared, "*…and the Peanut Gallery.*"

“I’m sorry. I am looking for Jenny’s mother…Mrs. Merchant?”

“Upstairs,” the woman said, and slammed the door.

When the young woman knocked on the upstairs door, there were no sounds from inside the apartment. She could still hear the boys downstairs and the faint voices of Cowboy Bob and Howdy Doody from the television. The door opened and a familiar little girl—thin, with brown eyes and wavy brown hair that had been cut short, the bangs uneven and too short—peeked out at her.

“Oh. Hello, Jenny.”

The little girl did not answer. Her eyes darted across the woman’s face. She looked past the woman and behind her, and then back to her face. She left the door open and disappeared inside.

A dark haired woman opened the door wide. She was slim, except that she was visibly pregnant. It was difficult for the younger woman to assess her age; she seemed younger than she appeared. She stood about the same height as the younger woman. She wore a light gray dress, the material too heavy for the warm weather. The dress was large, it hung in a distorted manner—snug around a bulging middle, but loosely on the woman’s wiry frame. Her thin, fine hair was pulled back in a loose bun that was coming apart in every direction.

“Yeah?” she said to the younger woman.

“Hi. Mrs. Merchant?”

The woman did not answer; she nodded.

“Hi. I’m Mrs… I mean, Miss…Miss Coburn…Jenny’s kindergarten teacher.” She held out a hand.

The woman took it—a brief touch—and dropped it. The younger woman put her dropped hand to her side. She shifted the canvas bag to the dropped hand to cover the awkwardness of the gesture.

Inside, the young teacher sat at the kitchen table. There were three, mismatched chairs around the table, but the little girl’s mother stood at the sideboard smoking an unfiltered cigarette. The young woman waited for the mother’s response. The room was silent. She could hear the boys downstairs.

Finally, when it was apparent the woman was not going to speak, she said, “So…we at the Longfellow School are a little concerned for Jenny.”

“Hmmm,” the woman said, exhaling smoke in the direction of the table.

“See…the stuttering and the…the…aloofness…I mean the…”

“I know what aloof means.”

The teacher nodded.

"So...what do you want me to do?"

The young teacher paused and looked around the apartment—it was sparse, but clean. "Well, I am interested in what you think of Jenny's...um...behaviors?"

"What about them?"

"Are you worried?"

"About what?"

The young teacher struggled with a sputtering agitation toward this woman. She smiled and looked into the next room. She could see the little girl's head behind an overstuffed chair. She said, "She is such a quiet girl. A good girl."

The mother waited, smoking her cigarette.

The teacher continued, "I am worried about what might be causing her to be so..."

"Aloof."

"Withdrawn. Mrs. Merchant, Jenny's behaviors are not typical of other kids in the classroom. It may be that she has...troubles."

The woman leaned across the sink, turned on the faucet and ran water over the cigarette butt. She tossed the soggy butt into a paper bag sitting beside the sink. She turned to the young woman. She looked her over. She took in the pretty, blue printed dress, and the funny looking coloring to the young woman's hair. Then she said, "Troubles?"

"It just seems that..." the young teacher swallowed and then started again. "She has no friends, Mrs. Merchant. She can hardly speak. She's polite, but sits by herself at recess, and in the classroom too. When I do speak to her, she seems almost paralyzed...afraid. It takes a lot to get her to smile. It shouldn't take so much effort to get a child to smile. The stuttering..."

"She puts that on a little, you know."

"What do you mean?"

"She exaggerates that little stutter."

"Whatever for? Why would she do that?"

"Attention."

The young teacher stared at the mother. "Mrs. Merchant," she said, and held back a sigh, "this little girl goes out of her way to *avoid*...attention."

"That just started after her..."

"Something happened?"

The teacher waited.

"Nothing happened. She has nightmares. That started the stuttering.

That's all."

"What started the nightmares?"

The mother took a crumbled package of Pall Malls from her pocket and extracted a broken cigarette. She said, "Are you a teacher, or what?" She put the broken piece between her lips and lit the cigarette with a paper match that she ripped from a small, nearly empty book of matches. She threw the empty Pall Mall package onto the kitchen table.

Suddenly a boy came barging into the kitchen from the porch. He slammed the door behind him. He stopped, looked at the young woman sitting at the table, and then proceeded into the other room.

"Hey!" The mother started toward the room, following the boy. She held one hand under her belly. "What the hell are you doing home?"

The boy ignored her.

The young teacher guessed that he was Jenny's brother. He looked to be about twelve or thirteen years old.

"Hey, Buster Brown, don't you ignore me when I'm talking to you," the woman said, following the boy into the next room.

"Leave me alone," the boy said. He opened a door to another room and slammed it behind him.

"Open this door."

There was no response.

"Goddamn it, Kicky...you open this door right now or you'll get your ass blistered when your father gets here."

The young teacher leaned forward across the table to see into the living room. She could see the mother standing in front of the door to the boy's room. She looked around but could not see Jenny. It was quiet; the mother was listening with her ear to the boy's door.

The teacher was about to stand up and prepare to leave when someone knocked at the kitchen door. She looked out the window and saw a police officer.

He knocked again.

"Mrs. Merchant," the teacher called into the living room. "There is a policeman at the door."

Mrs. Merchant stormed into the kitchen. She mumbled, "...little bastard..."

She crossed the kitchen to the door and opened it.

The man wore a uniform, he did not remove his hat. The badge and a patch on his left shoulder declared: Portland City Police Department.

"Sorry, Mrs. Merchant. Gotta talk with you and the boy...again." He looked around the apartment, glanced at the young teacher, nodded at her, then looked back at Mrs. Merchant. "Your husband home?"

"Later. He'll be here later," she said. "Can we do this later on? I'm busy with my daughter's teacher right now."

"Nope. This is serious this time. We gotta talk, Mrs. Merchant."

The teacher watched as the police officer took a small notebook from his shirt pocket. He flipped through some pages. He looked up at Mrs. Merchant.

He said, "I can wait for your husband if you wish. But, I am not leaving here. Is your son, Chester—is he in the apartment?"

"We call him Kicky. He's in his room."

"Is there any way out of there?"

"There's a window. He can jump two stories if he wants to bad enough."

"Okay," he said, shrugging, "let's just skip all the history here. You know what that is about."

She looked past the police officer and out into the dooryard.

"He's here. My husband's here."

The police officer and the teacher turned to watch as the man pushed the door open and staggered into the kitchen. The smell of whiskey arrived just ahead of him. The man stood in the kitchen.

He was a short man, thin to the point of being gaunt. His dark, wavy hair stood up on his head. It should've been a crew cut, but it had grown too long. This made his features appear exaggerated, especially his large nose. His disheveled clothing and unshaven face added to a comic, hobo appearance.

He smiled and saluted the police officer. He turned toward his wife, started to speak, and then noticed the teacher at the table. He smiled and gave her a wave.

He looked at his wife. "Who's she?"

"Thomas Merchant?" The police officer stepped forward. "You remember me?"

The man looked the officer over and started to nod his head. He said, "Yup. I sure do."

"We need to talk with your son again. Your wife, you, and myself. We all need to talk to your son. He's in some serious trouble this time."

"Okay. I can handle that." The man looked back at his wife. "Where is he?"

"In his room."

The husband walked toward the living room. He bumped into the side of the table. It scraped across the floor. The teacher stood up and moved toward the porch door. She stood just outside on the porch with the door open, watching the events inside. She looked around for the little girl. She saw her standing in another doorway, with the door open, only her face peeking out.

The man kept moving through the living room. When he reached the boy's closed door he tried opening it. When it did not move, he stood back, and with a quick kick, he broke the door open.

"Hey!" the boy yelled.

The man came out, dragging the boy by the hair on the top of his head.

"You stupid little shit," the man starting hitting the boy around the face and head.

The boy protected himself by placing his arms around his ears, his hands clasped behind his head. Then the boy grimaced, gripping both of his hands onto his father's hands to support his weight, as his father continued to drag him with one hand by his hair; the boy did not defend himself and did not speak. The slapping went on. The police officer watched this for a minute and then stepped in and grabbed the man's arms.

The policeman said, "Hey. Enough. Let's talk."

When the teacher left, she waved to Jenny at the door. Jenny waved back at her. Now she sat on the sofa in the living room. She watched her parents and the police officer talking at the kitchen table. The officer's hat sat on the table beside of him. Kicky stood by the sink.

The police officer said, "And now these kids have formed gangs. Your son is a part of that."

The little girl's father took a chrome flask from his back pocket and started to unscrew the cap. The police officer took it away from him and placed it on the table beside of himself. He said, "You've had enough. Listen to what I'm saying to you."

Her father kept his eyes on the flask beside the officer's arm.

"Let me tell you two this much," he said, addressing the parents. "You have not kept any of the agreements we have made in the past. He still runs the streets. We pick him up almost daily. He is not in school. He is in trouble. This time the trouble is on an adult scale and we are not inclined to do any favors. But, he's the youngest in this gang, and I have spoken to Judge Pickens."

He paused. He looked at both parents, one at a time. The father glanced up at the officer, then back at the flask.

"Here's the deal." The police officer leaned across the table, making a point of getting the eyes of both parents on him. "And it is not negotiable." He looked over at the boy, then back at the mother. "If you don't get him out of this city, he's going to the Boy's Detention Center in South Portland. And...he will stay there until the judge feels like letting him out. Probably until he's eighteen years old. Or...longer. He can do that, you know. The judge...he can keep him there longer than that, if he chooses to." He looked over at the boy and held eye contact with him. "You understand what I'm saying, kid?"

The boy nodded, but did not look away.

They all sat in silence—a long silence. It seemed almost as if the police officer had decided to wait them out—that they must speak next. As if there were unfinished business, and the parents needed to make the next move. The silence filled the entire building. And still, in silence, the officer sat looking back and forth at the parents and the boy.

The little girl looked back and forth at the grownup's faces. She put a hand up to her eyebrow, and using her little finger, she played with the little hairs. She looked at the gray sky outside the living room window.

A pigeon sat on the cable that ran between the poles along the street outside. His head bobbed. He cooed.

She did not think about anything except that it was very quiet in their apartment. Then, suddenly, the police officer's voice, baritone and loud, filled the room—the little girl jumped.

"So...I'll be back at the end of the week." Then, nearly in a whisper, he leaned toward the parents across the table from him and said, "He better be gone."

He pushed his chair back, scraping the floor, and stood up. He took his time, looked into the living room at the girl, looked back at the parents at the table, over at the boy, put his hat on, and then he left the apartment.

They all sat listening to his footsteps going down the porch stairway. Jenny got down from the sofa and went to her room. The father reached across the table and retrieved the flask.

Jenny awoke. She looked over at Harry, her eight year old brother, who shared a bed with her. His light-brown hair, cut close to his head, made the spread of freckles across his nose seem more prominent. As he slept, there was a small trickle that drooled down the corner of his mouth. He opened his eyes, looked at her, then rolled over.

She heard loud voices in the other room. She put a hand up to her left ear. It hurt.

She threw back the sheet and climbed out of her bed. She looked over at her sisters, Kelly and Missy, who were asleep in the bed that they shared. She went to the bedroom door, opened it, walked into the living room, and across to the kitchen. She stood by the door frame in her t-shirt and underpants, holding onto her left ear.

"...with the Coopers, in Otisfield. They need the help. They're getting old, you know," her father said.

Kicky sat at the table. He smoked a cigarette with his father. They passed it back and forth. Her mother sat listening to her husband. She smoked also. They all had coffee mugs in front of them.

"What do you want?" her mother asked, looking at her child in the doorway.

"My ear hurts."

Her father said, "Come here."

She walked over to stand beside of his chair. He picked her up and sat her in his lap. She started to lay her head against his chest, but he held her head close to his mouth, cupping his hands over the ear she had been holding onto. He blew cigarette smoke into her ear. "There." He put her down.

Her mother said, "Get back into bed."

She walked into the living room, crawled up onto the couch, and put a pillow over her ear.

"He can use the bathroom on the first floor," the elderly man said.

The boy was still looking around the inside of the shed. A small cot stood against the further wall next to the only window in the one room shed. A folding table sat beneath the window, its surface warped and stained, a wooden, folding chair was slid under the table. A light hung on a wire from the middle of the ceiling. It did not have a shade.

"Hey," the boy's father said, giving his boy a push on his shoulder, "you listen to Coop. You can use the bathroom on the first floor."

The elderly man, Coop, waited for the boy to look over at him, then pointed in the direction of the rear of the farmhouse. "Through that door. Don't be usin' the front door. Ever. Just that door there."

The boy watched the old man. The man was bent forward far enough so that he looked down at his own feet. He could barely look up at them when he talked.

"Now…" the old man started, "Thompy, you got any rules for your boy here?"

Thompy looked at his son. "Kicky's thirteen years old. He can take care of himself."

"Well, I've got some rules for you." The old man took a step toward the boy. His posture made it possible for him to look at the boy without having to make any adjustments. "This is where you live now. This little house."

The boy looked around the shed again. There was a small woodstove in the corner. A rusted stove pipe ran up and out the wall to the brick chimney outside.

"I expect that you work days. Starting at 7:30 in the morning. When school starts, I'll have a list for you to do each morning, before you leave for school…besides your regular work. You get Sundays off. You can come inside for your meals and to use the bathroom. I'll pay you every Friday, but I deduct your room and board.

"I do have a telephone, unlike most folks out here, but you can't use it. So…don't touch the phone. Except in emergencies, in which case you come see me and I'll call for you. We'll know if you do—Midge Potter's on our party line and she knows everyone's voice. And, don't be coming into the house when you're not supposed to be there.

"And, I don't have one of them damned telly-visions. There's 'lectricity. You can have a radio out here, but I don't want to hear it. My wife and I are sort of deef, so that shouldn't be a problem."

Thompy looked at his boy. "You got that? You can have a radio," he said.

The boy looked at his father. He didn't own a radio. He said, "I don't have a radio."

"Well, then, that's the first thing. You can save up for one. Mr. Cooper here is gonna give you some money each week."

"Ayuh. After I take out the room and board," the old man said.

They started to leave. The old man stopped and turned. The boy could see the man's face, his eyes were on him. He said, "There ain't no screens on that window, boy, and this is black fly season, so if I was you, I would keep that window closed. Those little pricks will eat you alive."

They walked toward Uncle Lenny's black 1947 Chevrolet sedan parked in the driveway. Each of them slapped at mosquitoes. A shower earlier that morning left the grasses wet and the air moist. The boy's torn sneakers were wet through and he had grass between his toes.

The sun came out from behind a dark heavy cloud. He noticed his father wiping sweat from his forehead with a red handkerchief. His mother stood beside the front fender of the Chevy, smoking a cigarette. Uncle Lenny was behind the steering wheel with his windows down.

The boy walked behind his father and Mr. Cooper. He looked around the farmyard. He knew that the village was down the road—a considerable distance away. They had driven through the village shortly after crossing Route 11. This area was not unfamiliar to him.

He had been here before, Aunt Ethel, his mother's sister, and Uncle Lenny lived near the village. But, out here it was all woods, there were no other houses in sight—only a sprawling field across the dirt road and then just the forest.

The lawns were not mowed. A large garden had been started on the other side of the front lawn. There were several cows in a fenced area beside the barn. The forsythia splashed a bright yellow against the weatherworn barn boards and a large lilac bush nearly covered the front of the small, cape farmhouse; it was blossoming and gave the air a perfumed sweetness that contrasted with the manure from beside the barn.

The boy stood in front of his mother. She reached into the window of the back seat of the black car and pulled out a duffle bag. It was a pea-green canvas bag with U.S. Army printed on the flap. He recognized his father's pack. He took it from his mother's hand.

"What about bedding?" the old man asked.

"Ain't got any bedding," his mother answered.

The old man thought for a minute then said, "We'll come up with something."

Uncle Lenny had come around the side of the car and put an arm around Kicky. Kicky withdrew and stepped back from him.

Uncle Lenny said, looking away from the boy, "Nice place you got here, Coop. Looks like it could use some work."

"Ayuh. That's the idea. This young man can earn his keep. We'll feed him and give him a place."

"That's a deal if I ever saw one," Lenny said, looking around the yard.

The boy said nothing.

Thompy had walked down the driveway and stood next to the mailbox, looking across the road to the fields. The boy watched him. His father stood there. Suddenly, his father's head tilted back as he took a swig from his chrome flask. Then he stood there for a while longer, looking across the road.

Lenny said, "Addie..." he spoke to the boy's mother, "...get Thompy's ass up here. We gotta get going. I got things I gotta do after I drive you two back to Portland."

As they drove away, the farmer walked back toward the farmhouse. The boy watched him, he thought that this old man was probably the slowest human being he had ever seen in his young life. He wondered how he could see where he was heading.

"Supper's at six o'clock. Get that shed cleaned out. I'll have Ada pull some bedding together for you."

The boy stood watching the man walking away from him.

"I'll be docking that bedding from your first pay," the man said.

Jenny looked out the window and down to the curbing in front of the apartment building. She waited. She could not remember what it was she was waiting for, but she stayed there and watched out the window with her left hand touching her ear. She turned and looked at Harry sitting on the couch, turning the pages of a book. She looked over at Kelly and Missy playing with a deck of cards on the floor. Then she turned back to the window and continued to watch the street. She cupped her left ear in her hand.

A car pulled up and stopped. It had a light on the top and the letters: TAXI. The back door opened onto the curb and her father climbed out. Jenny smiled. Then her mother came out from the interior of the vehicle as well. She was carrying something.

The little girl watched her mother step onto the sidewalk. It started to rain. Her mother pulled a blanket up over the bundle she had in her arms. Her father leaned back inside the vehicle and did something, then returned to help her mother. The vehicle drove off. Her parents both walked toward the back porch stairway.

Once inside the apartment, Jenny watched her mother go directly to her own bedroom. Jenny stood outside the doorway. Her brother and sisters stood there also. No one spoke.

Her mother leaned over the thing with bars on it and put the package inside this odd piece of furniture. Jenny had seen this furniture in her parent's room for a while now. She did not know what it was. It looked like a small bed with bars around it.

"Come here, Jenny," her mother said.

Jenny did not move.

"Get over here."

Jenny walked over to her mother. Her brother and sisters followed.

"Look at your new baby sister," her mother said. "Her name is Sophy."

Jenny looked at the mysterious thing in the crib. Her mother moved the small pink blanket and Jenny saw a funny-looking face. The baby slept; her tiny lips pursed, then moved in a sucking gesture. Jenny backed away from the baby in the small bed with bars around it. She left the room.

The older nurse handed the bedding to the younger nurse who took it and placed it in a large, cloth bag. She looked down at the young girl in the bed. The girl slept.

The older nurse waved the younger one toward the door. Outside in the hallway they looked back in at the child. There was another child in the room who was also sleeping. The two children were about the same age. This other child's parents had just left to go home. They would be back in the morning.

"How long has she been in here?" the younger nurse asked.

"Which?"

"The little Merchant girl."

"About six days now."

"Tonsils?"

The older nurse nodded. "And, a mastoid infection of the ear. Pretty far gone...I guess it was a mess. Had to open it up."

They carried the bag of laundry down the hallway. The early evening shift had just begun. The older nurse prepared to go off duty. She let the younger nurse take over the laundry task to complete by herself. She had done her share of laundry duty over the years and was eager to pass it along.

She also knew that when she arrived home tonight she would be doing the family laundry. She knew that the younger nurse still lived with her parents. And, she knew who did *her* laundry.

The younger nurse stood at the station, the laundry sitting on the floor, still looking back at the girl's room. There were only about four children in the entire ward.

The younger nurse asked, "She had any visitors at all?"

"Nope."

"They live far away or something?"

"Nope. Just up the road a few streets, on Lincoln Street I believe, according to the chart." She shook her head. "I read to her tonight. She likes books. So if you see her awake later, finish that one." She pointed toward a book on the nurse's station desk. "She hasn't spoken much since she got here." She closed one of the charts, opened another, and jotted down a note.

She said, without looking up from her work, "Stutters like crazy. Poor kid."

There were boxes all over the apartment. Jenny and Harry stood beside the kitchen sink. Jenny still had a small bandage covering a scar behind her left ear. Every once in a while she would reach up with her hand and touch it. Her ear felt better. But, she could not hear well with it.

She watched her mother scurrying around the apartment. Someone knocked at the door. Her mother opened it. Her Uncle Marty and Aunt Ethel stood in the doorway. She knew that this was important because these were her mother's brother and sister. They had never been for a visit together before.

Aunt Ethel had been here, but only with her husband, Uncle Lenny. Never with her brother, Marty. She wondered whether Uncle Lenny was downstairs. She went to the window to look outside. She did not see him or his car. She walked back over to stand beside of Harry.

"The girls ready?" Ethel asked her sister.

"Kelly! Missy! Get out here now. And bring your bags."

Kelly and Missy appeared in the kitchen, each with a small suitcase.

Uncle Marty said, "What about Harry and Jenny?"

"They're all set. I've taken care of them."

Jenny looked up at her mother. Her mother looked over at Uncle Marty.

Marty said, "Addie…they can come with me too. They're no problem."

"I have arrangements for them. They will be fine."

"You sure?"

"Marty. Drop it. For Christ's sake, I said that I got them taken care of. Okay?"

Marty reached out and took the bags from the two older girls. He turned, "Hey…where's Kicky?"

"He's fine. He's living at the Cooper farm."

"Coop's place? In Otisfield?"

"Yeah."

"What's he doing there?"

"Jesus, Marty, what are you, a detective or what? He had to go someplace."

"Addie, I told you that Prissy and I could take all of them. I don't see any need to separate them."

Addie shrugged and continued to pack things in the cardboard box. "It's already taken care of."

Marty looked at his sister, Ethel, and then back at Addie. He looked over at Jenny and Harry. Then he said, "Can I see Sophy? The baby?"

"She's in there. She's going with me to Ethel's and Lenny's." Addie nodded toward a blanket wrapped and lying on the sofa. Marty and Ethel went into the living room. They stood over the baby. Marty said, "She's a little doll, Addie. She's a real pretty baby."

Addie continued to put things in boxes.

Marty came back into the kitchen. He looked back over at Jenny and Harry. He seemed hesitant. He did not prepare to leave.

Kelly and Missy stood by the door.

"Addie," Marty said. "The girls are leaving now."

Jenny watched her mother. Her mother looked up. She said, "Goodbye."

"Addie," said Marty, "what about Thompy?"

"What about him?"

"Have you heard anything?"

"The sonofabitch! He did it again." She slammed a picture frame into a box. It shattered. "I'll kill the bastard when I see him...I swear to god...I'll kill him." She stood and looked at her brother. "No. The answer is no. I have not heard anything for weeks. He just did what he does...he left."

The afternoon sun came in the kitchen window. Harry sat on the floor dealing cards for solitaire. Jenny dozed, lying on her right ear, her head on a folded blanket. The voices woke her. She looked over at her brother. He stopped playing cards.

"Oh. They're adorable," the strange woman was saying.

"Harry. Get Jenny up."

Harry looked down at his sister. She sat up, rubbing her eyes.

"Let's get your things," the woman said. She walked over and picked up a bag of clothing that sat beside Harry on the floor. "Grab your sister's bag."

Harry picked up Jenny's smaller bag and looked at his mother.

His mother said, "You remember Shirley."

It wasn't a question, so Harry did not respond. He looked at the strange woman. She was large and moved around almost like a man. There were small hairs above her upper lip. She wore a white cap on her head.

"The milk lady. Stupid. Shirley delivers the milk here."

Shirley smiled at Harry and Jenny. Harry's mouth was open. He looked back to his mother.

"You're going with her for a while."

Harry stared at his mother. He did not make a move. "For how long?"

"Shirley...here's $10.00. I'll send more." Addie turned to the two children. "You two behave yourselves or you'll get a good thrashing from Shirley here. You better mind too."

Shirley smiled at the two children. "I bet that they are going to behave just fine. Right kids?"

Jenny put a hand up to her ear. She looked at her mother. Her mother was smoking a cigarette. She reached down and grabbed the small blue blanket. She folded it under her arm. She and Harry left with the milk lady.

Outside, they climbed into the cab of the milk truck and then, with instructions from the milk lady, they climbed into the back through a narrow opening that allowed entrance to the milk storage area. It smelled of stale milk and a cool dampness.

Harry and Jenny sat on the floor beside of each other and leaned against the milk crates. There were two small windows in the back doors and one small window on either side of the truck. The bottles rattled as the truck pulled away from the curbing.

The house could not be seen from the road. When the milk lady drove up the dirt driveway, she stopped at a mailbox, reached through her open window, and retrieved some envelopes, setting them on her dashboard. Jenny and Harry stood up, holding onto the sides of the small doorway that opened into the cab where the lady sat driving the vehicle. They weaved and bobbed unsteadily as she continued up the driveway.

They came to an unpainted ranch fence. The rail fence had a faded white archway that rose up and over the entrance. It gave Jenny the feeling that she was entering another world and leaving the one she knew. She looked around at the fields and the woods. As they passed under the small archway, little Jenny thought that maybe this was a kind of palace.

A man waited outside the house. He sat in a rocking chair, that barely contained his overweight size, on the porch of the small house. When they pulled up and the milk lady shut the truck's engine off, the man did not move to get up. He sat rocking.

The woman got out of the truck and opened the back door. Jenny got out first, Harry followed. Then the man stood, watching the two children. Jenny noticed how short he seemed. He wore farmer's jeans but had no shirt on underneath.

Harry took Jenny's hand.

# dark-blue lullaby 2

It was an Indian summer. Above the trees, the sun possessed the blue sky. Below the trees, on the soft floor of the woods, it only cut through in places. The way the wind stirred the leaves made the woods appear to be moving in little gestures, and the soft shushing sound they made offered a soothing effect for the creatures of this sylvan chamber.

Other than the gentle motion of her small finger playing with one eyebrow, the young girl did not move. Stretched out on her back, she stared up through the tall oaks, firs, and the white birches. Sunlight sprinkled through the swaying trees, fluttering across her face and eyes. The earth smelled of pine and a dry, leafy sweetness.

Slowly, she moved her head to the side to look at her brother. The boy, also on his back, turned his head away from her. She watched his breathing, but he did not turn toward her. She lifted her head and looked around her. The man was gone.

She trembled. The shaking intensified. She put her head back down on the leaves and pine needles; looking up through the trees for glimpses of blue sky, she waited for her body to be still. She resisted the tears. When she had lived at home, her sister had taught her a song that she sang with her at night in bed. Now, she hummed the melody in a broken, shaking whisper.

Then she said to her brother, "He's gone."

The boy stirred, then sat up, holding himself erect with his palms on the ground behind him. He picked up his clothes from the ground near his feet, then picked up his younger sister's clothes and laid them on her legs. He wiped tears with the back of his hand, leaving smudges across his cheeks. He did not look at her.

Both children dressed without speaking, and then, with the boy leading, they left the woods and went to their hideout. Later, before dark, before suppertime, because there was nowhere else to go, they returned to the house where they lived with those people.

# momma

The doctor walked into the kitchen. He was a slender, tall man. He was not an older man, but he was not young. His dark hair had shadows of gray above his forehead and ears.

His wire-rimmed eyeglasses hung from the flare of his nostrils. He frequently pushed them up to be tucked on top of a rather, large bump in the middle of a long nose. This position worked well until he began to sweat. Then the glasses would slip. He wore them only for reading and close work and because of his work he kept them on most of the time.

He pushed the glasses up as he came into the kitchen. He walked directly to the refrigerator. He opened it up and studied the interior. It was nearly empty. He then went to the cupboards and opened them one at a time. There were some bulk items of food. Otherwise, the cupboards were sparse.

Finally, he turned and looked at the mother. He figured the woman to be a couple of years younger than himself. He knew her and her husband. They moved frequently, around the area; he had been to their home in the past to see their children.

The previous time he had been called by Mrs. Packard, who worked at the school, she had heard that the young boy in the home was very ill—this was last December. The doctor had visited the family that night and found the young boy to be delirious with a high temperature. He had pneumonia.

The father was gone, a common circumstance in the family, and the mother had neglected to contact the doctor. He had given her a strong lecture for not seeking medical care for the child. She gave a string of excuses which he refused to accept. He had responded, "I live down the street...," "I've told you before, I don't need to be paid," "You know when your child is sick, if they are burning up!" "This is the 1950s...we have penicillin."

The doctor lived in a house not far from this place on the way to the village. He knew also of the domestic fights in this home. They lived in a small community. Most folks had a telephone by now, though some did not, and they were on party lines, sharing phone lines with their neighbors. It was difficult to keep secrets in a small town, in fact impossible with the party lines.

"I want to see the other children," he said to her and walked to the nearest bedroom.

He opened the door and stepped in. The boy was awake. He checked him, touching his forehead and speaking to him in a quiet voice. He came back into the kitchen. The woman was standing by the table.

"Where is the oldest boy?"

She said, "He moved out, when we left Portland."

"Moved? Where?"

"Some people in Otisfield."

"Relatives?"

"No."

"He's just a kid. Why did he move?"

"It's easier. He didn't get along. He kept getting into trouble with the law where we lived in Portland."

The doctor shook his head. "Well." He did not finish his thought.

The woman took a long pull on her cigarette. "So...?"

"Your little girl has a severe ear infection. It has gone into the mastoid bone behind her left ear. That's what the swelling is. It's serious. You should've contacted me a long time before this."

The woman smoked her cigarette and watched the doctor.

"She has a perforated ear drum. She's going to have hearing loss."

"Yeah. I know. She's been to the hospital before. What do I owe you?"

The doctor looked at her.

"You have enough food for these kids?"

"We get surplus...peanut butter, flour, powdered milk...we're okay."

The doctor took a brown bottle from his bag. He opened it and spilled it onto the kitchen table. He sat down and counted each of the pills. He put them back into the bottle and took a pen from his jacket pocket and wrote on a small piece of paper.

"I am giving you instructions for this medication. Give it to her," he looked up at the girl's mother, "exactly as I have written this. I mean, exactly. You cannot skip a dosage...you must do this exactly right."

He pushed away from the table, leaving the pill bottle and instructions on the table top, and walked back into the girl's bedroom. The sick girl's two older sisters sat up in their bed when he came into the room. He smiled at them and went over to the youngest child—she was asleep. He put a hand on her cheek. Then he walked around to the other side of this bed and sat beside of the sick child.

She rolled over and looked up at him. Even in the dim light of the bedroom, he could see the flush in her face; her brown eyes were bloodshot.

"I gave your mom some medicine. You will be better in a day or so, but you mustn't get out of bed for a few days. Maybe by this weekend you can go out and play, if it's nice out."

He put a hand to her forehead. He had done this a couple of times. He had already taken her temperature, but he felt a need to somehow comfort the child.

"How old are you, honey?"

The little girl made a soft noise and rolled back over onto her side, facing her younger sister. She did not move. Then she whispered, "Seven."

The doctor stood and looked down at her. Then he left the room and went back into the kitchen.

"I can't pay you anything..."

"I have told you before, I will treat the kids for nothing. Call me. Your pride is not nearly as important as the health of these kids. Because of your pride, that little girl will lose some hearing in that ear." He shook his head and looked around the kitchen. "Where is he?"

"I don't know. He's been gone for a few days."

"Look...I know it's not easy, you can let a lot of things go, but you cannot neglect your children's medical needs. There are no excuses...none. Do not avoid calling me because you have no money. We have had this conversation in the past. I have other families in similar situations...they do not neglect their kid's health. I will not stand for your pride, or whatever it is...I will not accept your excuses. You must take care of these kids."

The doctor sighed. He looked around the kitchen one more time, hesitating. "When he gets home, I want to talk with him," he said, picking up his bag. He nodded toward the paper on the table. "Do you understand these instructions?"

She nodded, crushing her cigarette into an ashtray.

"I'll be back to check on her in two days. She should be feeling a lot better."

He left, closing the screen door behind him. The evening was hot and the humidity left him instantly weak. He removed his jacket. His glasses slipped to his nostrils. He reached up, took them off, and slipped them into his shirt pocket. He walked toward his car. He swatted at the mosquitoes. He took a deep breath. He was glad to be outside.

He thought, *Her house is clean. The kids are clean. But, it's…well…I don't like being in that house.* This thought bothered him. The doctor prided himself on his house calls. These days more and more doctors were expecting their patients to come to them, even in these rural areas. This made it possible to see more patients, of course, and make a better income. But, a lot was missed not seeing them in their homes.

He threw his bag on the front seat, started his old Studebaker, and drove down the road to his own home.

Thompy reached into his jean pocket and pulled out a handful of change. Brushing toast crumbs and a crust onto the floor, he spilled the change onto the kitchen table and sat down to count it out. Harry and Jenny sat across from him. They watched him count the money.

Jenny had her chin cupped in both hands, her elbows on the table top. Every once in a while she would put her left hand up to her ear and touch it. She winced. She looked up at her father's face, watching his dark eyes. She lowered her head and leaned to the side to get a better look at his expression.

He had told her she had his nose. She touched her nose and looked at his nose. It was big. She wondered if she had a big nose. She liked that he was sitting at the table with them. She was glad he was home again.

She looked over at her brother. He was watching the coins. She looked back at her father. She made a small smile at her father, but he was not looking at her.

"Okaaaay…let's see now," he said. He leaned back in his chair and took a drink from the Black Label beer. He gave an exaggerated burp. The kids snickered. "I think we've got a small fortune here. Yes. You kids are in luck today."

Jenny watched her father. He ran a hand through his wavy dark hair. She wondered what he meant by the word "fortune." She looked at her brother. He seemed pleased also. She looked back at the coins on the table.

"Now, I have this for you…" Thompy said and scooped up a handful of coins, handing them to Harry, "and this for you, young lady." He gave some of the coins to Jenny.

She held them in both hands. She looked at her father. She couldn't recall him ever being so pleased and excited. She smiled. She liked it that he was happy.

Thompy went to the refrigerator and opened it. He drained the beer from the bottle in his hand and took another from the refrigerator, putting the empty on the sideboard. He reached for the key chain hanging from his belt loop. Using the bottle opener that hung there, he opened the beer.

"I want you two to go to the parade today and to the carnival tonight."

Harry looked at Jenny and grinned.

"You don't sleep here tonight, though. Go to Lenny's and Aunt Ethel's," he said.

Jenny whispered to Harry, "I don't wanna go to Aunt Ethel's and Uncle Lenny's."

Thompy heard her. He said, "Don't be coming back here. You better damn well go to Aunt Ethel's." He drank from the bottle. "Your mother has Kelly, Missy and Sophy with her. She won't be back until Sunday night."

Harry asked, "Where'd they go?"

"What do you care? She's gone. So go have some fun." He looked at Jenny. He said, "She went to New Hampshire to visit her sisters, and Uncle Marty…alright?"

Harry and Jenny started toward the door.

"Hey! Wait." Thompy grabbed a small brown bottle from the counter top and tossed it at Harry. Harry missed it and it fell to the floor. The cover came off and the small white pills spilled across the floor.

"Jesus Christ," Thompy said. "Pick 'em up, asshole. Queer-ass kid can't catch worth a shit." He looked over at Jenny. "Take one of those pills later on. And take another in the morning sometime."

Jenny helped Harry locate as many pills as possible and put them back into the bottle. She put the bottle in her pocket. Then they left; the screen door slamming behind them.

"And remember," Thompy was saying, "you don't come back here tonight. You stay with Lenny and Ethel. Got it?"

Outside, the sun blinded Jenny. Harry said, "We ain't gonna stay at Uncle Lenny's. Don't worry about it. I got a plan."

Jenny followed her brother down the hill toward the village. At first they ran, but it was too hot. They stopped and sat on a stone wall. They panted.

Harry took out his money and counted it.

"One dollar and ninety five cents."

"Is that a lot?" Jenny asked.

"Are you kidding? It's almost a fortune."

"What's a fortune?"

Harry stood up and put the money into his front pocket. "Let me see yours."

Jenny shoved her right hand into her pants pocket and pulled out the change in her fist. Harry took it and counted it one coin at a time.

"Seventy nine cents."

"Is that a fortune too?" Jenny asked. She studied her brother's face.

"Almost." He gave the coins back to his sister. "Whooopie!"

Harry rolled backwards off the stone wall into the fields. He rolled down the hill. Jenny watched.

"Harry. That's poison ivy." Jenny stepped backwards away from the stonewall and the grasses growing behind it.

"No it's not."

"Yes it is."

"So...?" He grabbed a handful of the shrub and rubbed it all over his face and head. Then he wiped his arms with it. "I ain't allergic to it." He held up his arms and said, "See? Do you see any rash? No. 'Cause I don't get poison ivy."

"I do."

"Well...I wouldn't touch it then if I was you," Harry said.

They continued toward the village. Jenny kept her right hand in her pocket, gripping the coins in her sweating palm.

People milled through the streets in the village. A wagon, filled with hay, pulled by two large horses, came down the middle of the street. There were no cars allowed on the main street during the parade day.

Jenny and Harry moved out of the way of the horses. Jenny stared up at them as they passed, then down at their hooves: *clop-clop, clop-clop, clop-clop...* She watched them as they swished their tails and she jumped when they snorted. The outside horse looked down at her with a glare that startled her.

She turned and found that Harry stood in front of a booth. She moved over to stand beside of him. He put a nickel on the counter and the man gave him three balls. They looked heavy. Harry threw the balls at some wooden milk bottles. He missed. He missed again. And missed with the third ball. He stood there scratching his head.

Then he turned and said, "I'll get warmed up and come back later." He walked off and Jenny followed.

Later, the sun hung low over the woods behind the Ferris wheel. Jenny and Harry were sitting on the grass near the Fun House, eating cotton candy. Both of them watched the crowds. They counted their money again. They had only spent thirty cents apiece so far this afternoon.

Harry nodded and said, "That's good." Then he sat up, looking across the field filled with people. "Listen…it's the parade. It's starting."

They bolted toward Main Street and squirmed their way through the crowd. Jenny lost her cotton candy; a dog picked it up and ran with it. She followed Harry. They reached the curb in time to see the majorettes. Jenny watched them toss their batons into the air and drop them.

One girl—Jenny thought she was about her own age—got hit by her own baton and started to cry. A woman, who must have been her mother, came out of the crowd and comforted her; she put an arm around the girl, picked up her baton and handed it to her. The woman hugged her, kissed her head, and sent her back to the majorettes with a pat on her bottom. The girl kept going.

Jenny watched this. She held her breath and her mouth stayed open. The majorettes passed. She watched their backs as they disappeared around the corner by the Grange Hall. Jenny thought, *I want a baton.*

Next were the fire engines, the men and boys hanging off the sideboards and sitting on the top. They blared their horns and sounded their sirens. Jenny covered her ears. Her left ear throbbed.

After they passed, there was laughter and people were hooting and yelling. Jenny looked across the street and saw the doctor in the crowd. He glanced over at her and then waved his fingers at her. He had a little boy on his shoulders and a younger girl holding onto his right hand. They both had candy apples. She watched them with their father.

"Jenny. Look." Harry grabbed Jenny's shoulder. "It's Daddy."

Jenny looked back at the parade. She saw some boys with bikes that were decorated with colored crepe paper. They darted and veered their bikes in the center of the street. Some of the bikes had large wads of cardboard attached to the bike frame, positioned to strike against the spokes as the wheels turned to create the sound of a motor.

And she saw a man, nearly naked, wearing a giant diaper with large pins. Barefoot, pale, hairy legs and chest, holding a whiskey bottle with a large nipple attached to the end, he walked past the crowd, pushing an empty baby stroller. The crowd roared.

It was daddy.

She started to say, "*Hi, Daddy.*" But she did not speak. He did not look at her or Harry. The crowd roared and applauded. They jeered. Daddy staggered and drank from the bottle. Jenny looked around her at the people in the crowd. They were having fun.

After he passed, the crowd quieted; some still stared after Thompy, but they were now silent. Jenny and Harry stood beside of each other. They did not say anything.

Jenny looked across the street. The doctor watched her. He smiled. He waved to her, again. She waved back to him. He continued to watch her for a few seconds, and then, his own little girl tugging at his arm, he walked into the crowd.

Mrs. Geraldine Packard worked at the village school. She did some secretarial work and some janitorial work, if Hank was not well enough to do it. Hank was her husband. He drank too much. Sometimes he was not well enough to go down to the little school house and sweep, clean the bathrooms, and mow the small lawn out front.

Mrs. Packard also raised the flag outside each morning. She knew most of the children and their families. She knew Jenny and Harry's parents.

"Doctor," she said, touching his arm.

The doctor took a mouthful of hot dog. Mustard squirted onto his chin. He looked over at Mrs. Packard, nodded, and grabbed a napkin.

"Mmm…?" he mumbled.

"Did you see that man? Thompy Merchant?"

The doctor nodded and chewed. He wiped at his chin with the paper napkin.

"Did you see his children?"

He nodded and chewed. A group of children ran by, screaming and laughing, chasing a dog that had a paper bag in his mouth.

"Well?"

The doctor chewed, swallowed, and chewed some more. He looked over at his own two children, sitting nearby, eating French fries. He looked back at Mrs. Packard's face. Then he let his eyes roam across the crowd. He knew what she was getting at. He looked back at her. He swallowed hard.

"I'm sorry…what is it, Mrs. Packard?"

"You saw that man. He's a drunk. Those kids are still here and they are not with an adult. It's getting dark out."

The doctor was familiar with this role. In this small, rural village, there were few authority figures. One was the town constable, who was also the town clerk, Asa Hackett was somewhere on the grounds tonight. The doctor had seen him earlier, sending some young boys away from the girly-show tent.

Often, people in town went to the school teachers, or himself, when they couldn't find Asa. The doctor thought of the little girl. He had seen her touch her left ear.

"Yes, Mrs. Packard. It is shameful."

She stood watching him.

"Mrs. Packard..." the doctor looked past her, then back at her face, he sighed. "I...okay...I'll look around for them."

"You send those kids home, doctor. And speak to that father..."

"Have you talked with Asa about this?"

"Asa is too busy driving the boys away from that filthy girly show. They flock around that tent like...dogs," Mrs. Packard huffed.

"Mmm." The doctor pressed his lips together and furrowed his forehead in concern. He took a white handkerchief from his jacket pocket and wiped his brow. It was hot tonight, but he wore his sports jacket at all times when in public. He dressed as his father had dressed...as a doctor would dress. His short dark hair clung to his damp forehead. He did not have his glasses on. Mrs. Packard stood silent, waiting.

"Umm...Mrs. Packard. I will find the children. But first, I have to take care of my own two. I will be back."

She stood for a few seconds. The doctor smiled and turned to watch his son and daughter sitting on the ground near him, eating the last of the French fries. When he looked back for her, she had left and was headed toward the tent in full stride, her green wicker purse dangling from her right forearm. He guessed she was headed to where she had last seen Asa.

His son had fallen asleep and was sprawled across his shoulder and on top of his head. He walked for a ways but needed to stop. He moved his son from his shoulders and held him across his chest, with his head against his neck. He handed his little girl the remainder of the candy apple that the boy still clutched in his hand.

"Helen, put this in the trash over there."

His daughter ran to the trash container, dropped the apple into the receptacle and ran back. "I run fast, huh, Daddy?"

"You certainly do. Like the wind."

They walked toward a booth. There were three women in the booth. The booth displayed a variety of quilts, blankets, and knitted goods. The sign that hung on the booth read, "Methodist Ladies Goods."

The doctor walked up and stood in front of his wife. She was talking to Mrs. Stevens and knitting. He waited.

He admired his wife's pretty face and red hair. She was a large woman but attractive. Her pale, glowing complexion pleased him. When she turned and saw him, she stood, immediately reaching for her son. She and her son had matching hair and complexion. Her daughter looked more like her father.

"He has been busy," the doctor said, passing his son over to her. "I need to do something. The kids will need to stay here for a while."

"Is everything okay?' she asked, handing her knitting to her little girl.

"Fine. I am looking for a couple of kids. The Merchant children."

She sat and snuggled her boy. She nodded and smiled. "We'll be right here." She touched her girl's hand and said, "Do you want to try working on that? Remember what I showed you."

The little girl sat beside her mother and arranged the knitting in her lap. Her father walked off. The doctor's wife watched him. His height made him visible for sometime in the crowd. Even before he got out of her sight, a family had stopped him, and he was kneeling down to look at their little one. Then he stood, spoke to the adults, and disappeared into the crowd.

Harry and Jenny were hiding. They walked behind the House of Mirrors. The smell of grilled sausage, and burgers, mingled with popcorn and the sweet scent of cotton candy, made Jenny hungry. Her stomach growled.

It was dark behind the booths. The sun had gone down and the sky was slate gray. They were peering into the midway between booths. The midway was bright with lights and the noise of people. They had seen Uncle Lenny. So they had walked around the outside perimeter of the midway in the shadows of the booths and tents.

Now they came to the pony rides. The woman was putting the ponies away for the night. They watched her walking the ponies back and forth to the small, fenced-in pasture that had been set up for them. Harry stepped his foot in something.

"Yuck. Pony poop," he said, lifting his foot to look at the bottom of his tattered sneaker.

"Hey...that's Daddy." Jenny pointed to the large tent in the field behind the Ferris wheel. There was noise from the tent—men yelling, laughing—and light came from the tent's open doorway that faced away from the rest of the carnival.

Jenny and Harry ran the distance to the tent. As they approached, an older man, wearing farm jeans and no shirt, pulled the flap of the tent closed.

"You kids get the hell outta here." He started toward them, waving them away with wide sweeping motions of both arms.

Jenny and Harry ran around the tent to the backside just in time to see their father duck under the tent on his hands and knees while two other men held the bottom of the tent up. Then the two men each ducked under, one at a time, while others inside held the tent for them. The man in the farm jeans came around the rear of the large tent. He had not seen what had just taken place.

"Hey! I told you two to get outta here. Now scram, you little shits."

Harry grabbed Jenny's hand and they ran back towards the Ferris wheel. They stopped in the dark field behind the Ferris wheel and sat in the deep grass. Then they both spread out flat on their backs, panting and coughing. Jenny itched from the sweat and the grass weeds against her arms and face. They stayed like that, looking up at the sky that now was completely dark.

They watched the Ferris wheel, lighted up with blue, green and red lights, turning one way, and then the other as it took people on, gave them short rides, and let them off. When the wheel stopped, the people at the top would scream or yell...laughing when their seat swung.

Jenny smiled at them. She wondered how far they could see from way up there. She looked up at the night sky. Jenny saw dim stars appearing. She looked away from a place in the sky, and then back again, and another star appeared. She thought that it was like the opposite of fading away—the stars actually faded into sight.

Her stomach growled again. She could smell the pony poop on Harry's shoe. The moon, half full, hung low on the eastern horizon, across the town's village square that now contained most of the carnival and community booths.

She turned her right ear up toward the sky and could hear crickets. She turned her other ear, the sore one, to the top, but could not hear the crickets, only some dull noise from the carnival. She turned her head back and forth like this several times. She reached up and touched her left ear. It hurt, but the swelling behind the ear was not as bad. Then she remembered her medication.

She stuffed her left hand into her jean pockets and felt the pill bottle.

"I need something to drink," she said, sitting up.

Harry sat up. He said, "Me too, I'm dying..." He collapsed and made choking sounds, putting his hands to his throat. "I think I only have little time...left... to...live." He gagged and then went spread-eagled, flopping onto his stomach.

"No. I mean it, Harry. I have to take my pill like the doctor said," she said, hitting him on the back of the head. She stood up. "C'mon."

Harry did not move.

"I'm going, Harry." She started to walk away. "I mean it. I am going over there and get a drink...right now. By myself. I mean it."

Harry still did not move. Jenny watched his body. She started to turn to leave but looked back and stood with her hands on her hips. She watched to see if he was breathing. She could not tell—it was too dark.

"Harry?"

No response. Jenny walked over to where he had spread out...he was motionless. "Harry?" Suddenly she realized that he was not breathing. She reached down and touched his back. "No...Harry?" She pulled herself up and backed away from Harry. Then she turned and started running toward the crowds and the line standing by the Ferris wheel.

"Jenny!"

She stopped and turned. Harry was sitting up, grinning.

"Fooled ya." Jenny stood looking at him. Then she stomped her foot and turned, walking away toward the crowd.

Harry caught up to her. He said, "Hey...are you mad?"

She stopped and looked at him. Her eyes filled with tears, her bottom lip trembled. She started to speak and stopped herself, then she turned and walked away from him again, in the opposite direction.

Harry ran around and stood in front of her. "Jeeez...I'm sorry Jenny. I thought you'd think it was funny."

She blurted, "It's not funny, Harry."

He was quiet. He looked around. A few people passed by but ignored them.

"I was just..."

"I don't care. Don't do that again."

"Okay."

She walked, slower this time, and Harry caught up to her, falling into step. They walked a few feet without speaking. Then Jenny stopped and turned to her older brother.

"You're the only one I have, Harry…the only one that…"

Harry shrugged. He looked at her face and said, "I didn't know it would scare you. I didn't mean to."

Jenny walked back to the fields and sat down in the grass. Harry followed her. He sat down next to her. They listened to the sounds of the crowd and the music from the carousel. Jenny wept without making a sound.

Then Harry said, "What did you mean?"

She looked at him. Her cheeks were smudged from crying.

Harry said, "When you said I was the only one? What did you mean?"

"You know…"

Harry shrugged his shoulders, "What?"

She looked at his face, his short hair, the light sprinkle of freckles across his nose…she looked away and said, "The only one who knows…what happened…"

"What?"

"What happened to us?" She looked back at his face. He looked at her and then away. "Harry…"

Harry moved his shoulders up and down a couple of times and continued to look at the crowds just outside the darkness of their place in the field. He did not say anything.

The doctor saw the two Merchant children near the Ferris wheel. He started towards them, moving through the crowd. When he arrived at the spot where he had seen them, they were gone.

He looked around. His height was an advantage in the crowd. He turned himself in a full circle several times, looking through the arms and legs of people walking or standing in lines. He could not see them.

He moved toward the House of Mirrors, stopping to buy an Orange Crush at the burger stand. He stood watching the people moving around the midway, the field, and into the street. The doctor walked over to one of the improvised street blockades and leaned against it, sipping on his drink.

He took out his handkerchief and wiped his face, stuffing it back into his pocket. He became lost in thought and somehow hypnotized by the cacophony of the scene. Some folks walked by and spoke. He smiled and said, "Howdy."

He saw Mrs. Packard walking in the crowd, still in full stride, her purse swinging from her arm. *A woman with a mission,* he thought. He decided to move along. He slipped into the crowd and walked back toward the Ferris wheel.

And there they were. They stood on either side of a man. The man was bent over, speaking to them. The doctor recognized the man but did not know his name. He lived in town near the lake with his wife. They had no children.

When he approached, the little girl looked up toward him. She pulled her hand from the hand of the man and stepped sideways, away from his reach. Her gesture caught the doctor's attention. An unpleasant feeling stirred at the back of his mind—a shadow of a thought really.

"Hello," said the doctor. He was looking at the girl.

"They're with me," the man said.

The doctor looked at the man. He was not a clean man. He was skeletal and tall—balding. The man smelled of body odor and stale cinder and ash…as an abandoned cabin with a damp, neglected fireplace would smell. It was difficult to know his age, but he was not a young man. The doctor nodded, then looked back at the girl.

"How are you? Feeling any better?" he asked, leaning down toward her as he spoke.

She nodded her head. She had her left hand in her pocket.

"How's the ear?"

"Okay," she answered.

"You're out-and-about too soon. You taking your medicine?"

The man let go of the boy's hand and reached toward the girl. She backed away, one step at a time. The man finally stood still. He turned toward the doctor.

"I'm their uncle. My wife had supper ready for them. We're taking care of them while they're mother is away. We've been looking for them for a while tonight."

"I see," the doctor said. He looked at the boy. The boy looked at him and then away. "This little girl has a pretty serious infection in that left ear. Is she taking her medication?"

The man hesitated, then said, "Of course."

The doctor kneeled down in front of the little girl. He put a hand up toward her ear. She flinched.

"Is it still sore?"

She moved her head up and down.

"May I touch your cheek, child?" the doctor asked.

She nodded.

The doctor touched her cheek with the back of his hand. Then he moved his hand to her forehead. He shook his head.

"You still have fever," he said, standing.

"I'll take her home, her Aunt Ethel will be taking care of them tonight." The man started to move toward the little girl again. She backed away...again.

"Just a moment." The doctor moved between the man and the child. He looked the man in the eye. "Why are these children here tonight? Were you not watching them? This child is sick. I think maybe they should go home with me tonight."

Jenny looked up at the doctor then over toward her brother. He looked at his sister but made no expression. She looked back at the doctor.

"I told you, I am their uncle. They'll go home with me." He started to move toward the doctor.

Asa was out of breath. He spoke to the two men as he approached. "Hold on," he said. A small group of people had gathered. The doctor looked around and then over to the little girl. He moved closer to her and knelt down again.

"Have you taken your medicine tonight?"

She shook her head. The doctor did the same, moving his head in unison to hers. He said, "Why not?"

The girl pulled the small brown bottle from her pocket.

The doctor reached out and took the bottle from her. He looked at it and then at Jenny. "What are you doing with these?"

Asa said, "Doc?"

The doctor turned toward the constable. Asa wore a dark-colored t- shirt, a badge flopped from the sagging pocket.

"Asa."

"What's goin' on here?"

"I've been looking for these kids."

"They're with me," the other man said. "I'm..."

Asa said, "I know who you are."

"The kids are staying with my wife and I while their mother..."

"Yup." Asa turned toward the boy. "Is that so? You staying with Lenny and Ethel?"

Harry looked over at his sister. "I guess so..."

Asa looked at the doctor. "Ran into Mrs. Packard. She said they were here alone. I guess she was wrong."

The doctor did not say anything. He looked at the little girl and back at the boy. He looked at the man and then back at Asa.

"This man says he's their uncle."

"That he is," said Asa. "His wife, Ethel, is their mother's sister."

The man started toward the little girl. He reached out and gripped her hand. He looked at the boy. "Come along, boy." He did not look at the doctor. He left the doctor and Asa, walking away with the two children.

"Hold it." The doctor caught up with the man—Asa followed.

The doctor knelt down and gave the little girl his Orange Crush. He opened the bottle of pills and gave one to her. She opened her mouth, allowing the doctor to place the pill on the back of her tongue. She swallowed it, drinking the remainder of the orange soda, the sweet tang of orange lingering in her mouth. The doctor stood and gave the pill bottle to the man.

He looked him in the eye and said, "I'll be around to check on these children tomorrow morning."

The man turned and left the carnival with Harry and Jenny.

Aunt Ethel, small and slight, with thinning hair, held her hands out to Harry and Jenny. "You two look like rag-a-muffins," she said, taking each of their hands and leading them closer to the center of the kitchen. Jenny did not like the way her aunt's house smelled. It smelled like the woodstove—Aunt Ethel had been cooking on it—and old garbage. Jenny noticed that trash was piled behind the kitchen door. The house was hot...hotter than outside.

Ethel looked at her husband. "What are they doing here?"

"I ran into Asa. He told me to take the kids in tonight. Thompy's drunk." He pushed the kids forward toward the kitchen table in the center of the room. "I told him I didn't mind at all. Said that you would be happy to take them in for the night. I told him we'd feed them." He reached into his pocket. "Oh yeah...and Doc said to give the girl these." He handed the bottle back to Jenny.

"What are they?" His wife watched Jenny put the bottle into her pocket.

"She got some infections. Needs the pills."

Ethel turned back to the children. "Well...are you hungry?"

Jenny watched her uncle's face. She didn't answer her aunt. They had not eaten a meal in several hours.

Harry said, "Yes."

Aunt Ethel started preparing something on the stove.

Lenny said, "You kids run along to the other room. You...girl," he looked at Jenny, "are sleeping in the little bedroom, and you, boy, you sleep on the porch."

Aunt Ethel turned. She looked at her husband and then at the children. She said, "Lenny? I think that they both should sleep on the porch. It's hot tonight."

"I want the girl in the house."

Aunt Ethel smiled at Jenny. She said, "No. Not this time, Lenny. I want them both on the porch."

Lenny looked at the woman. He said, "Ethel...the girl sleeps in the house."

Harry looked over at his sister. Jenny studied her aunt's face, her small hands clenched into tight fists.

Ethel said, "Lenny," she moved toward her niece, "if you want that, then I will be sleeping with her."

Lenny glared at his wife. He made a noise and walked out of the house.

"It will only take a second. I will make some oatmeal." She put a pot on the stove. "Do you kids like oatmeal? So...how long is Momma gone for? Did you have a nice time at the carnival? Is your daddy going away tonight?" She had her back to the children. "I know it's hot out, but I only have oatmeal. I will fix you a big breakfast in the morning." She hummed and stirred the oatmeal into the pot of hot water.

Harry and Jenny did not move. They stood watching their aunt as she prepared the oatmeal.

Later that night, after his wife fell asleep, when Lenny went out onto the porch—he found the two children gone.

"What happened to you?" Jenny was staring at her brother.

It was morning. They were on the back porch of their own home. It was early. The morning air already hung heavy with humidity. Sunlight came through the rusted screens and landed on her face. She rubbed her eyes and sat up on the cot. She watched her brother scratching himself with a fury.

"I don't know," he said.

Jenny moved toward him. "You're all red." She stared at the swollen red skin on his face, neck and arms.

Harry was scratching his head and his neck. His arms were developing small spots of blisters. "I can't stand this..." He started to cry.

Jenny started to touch his shoulder, but he pulled back.

"Let's show Daddy," she said.

"No! Don't go in there."

"Why? He's not drunk now. He's sleeping."

"Don't go in there."

But, Jenny was already inside the door and headed toward the bedroom. She pushed the door open. Harry came up behind her and pulled her back into the living room. The bedroom door swung open.

"Shhh—" he said, still scratching himself.

Jenny whispered, "That's not Momma."

She and Harry returned to the back porch. Harry scratched. Jenny sat in silence. Then she lay back onto the cot and stared up at the ceiling. There were several spiders, with well developed webs, clinging in carefully selected locations, housed in the beams and eaves of the ceiling. She watched them. They did not move.

Something had woken Jenny. She looked over at Harry, on his side, scratching himself with his eyes closed. The sun had moved up and was no longer in her face. A car door slammed. Then another car door slammed. Jenny sat up. She heard voices. She peered over the sill.

"Harry..." Jenny moved to touch her brother. He opened his eyes.

"What?" He scratched at his neck and face.

"Momma's here."

Harry sat up. He looked out into the doorway. The car was pulling away. In the dooryard stood his mother with his three other sisters. Kelly was holding Sophy. His mother picked up a suitcase, handed the other to Missy, and they all started walking toward the back porch door.

"Uh-oh," Harry said, forgetting to scratch for the moment.

His mother stepped onto the porch. She put the suitcase down. Kelly, holding Sophy in her arms, and Missy stepped onto the porch and stood staring at Harry. They glanced over at Jenny but looked back at Harry.

"Jesus. What in hell happened to you?" Addie asked her son.

"I don't know," Harry answered.

"Well, something happened."

Harry shrugged. He looked over at Jenny.

His mother moved closer but did not attempt to touch him. "Looks like poison ivy to me."

Harry dug at his head. "I don't get poison ivy...I'm ah-mune to it."

"Hmmph," his mother grunted. "You ain't immune to it now." She swatted his hand. It stung him. "Stop the goddamn scratching."

Harry continued to scratch.

"Where's your father? Is he sleeping?"

Harry said, "I don't know."

"Well, is he home?"

"I don't know," Harry said.

"What does that mean? You don't know. Is he or isn't he?"

Harry didn't answer, he scratched instead.

His mother started toward the kitchen. The kids remained on the porch. Kelly and Missy still stared at their younger brother. Kelly started laughing.

"It's not funny," said Jenny.

Kelly laughed louder.

Jenny said, "It's not poison ivy. Harry doesn't get poison ivy. He's 'mune to it."

Kelly continued to laugh. She said, "You two are so stupid." She was laughing hard now. "Immune. Ha! Look at you."

Missy said, "Harry. Let's go in and put some calamine on it. It will help the itching."

There was a loud banging from inside the house. All of the children jumped.

Then, "Get out!"

More banging and pounding. A loud thump.

The kids gathered around the screen door and looked inside.

Their mother had a naked woman pinned to the floor. Their father, also naked, dragged Addie off from the woman. Addie pounded at the woman's face. Then she turned on Thompy. She dug at his face until he bled.

"You fucking bastard! Yougoddamnsonofabitchinbastard!" Her voice cracked. She moved as a vicious animal, seemingly all over him at once.

Then, stillness—except for some grunting sounds, as Addie struggled with Thompy on the floor. The naked woman stood and pulled at Addie's left leg, her own large breasts hung, flopping back and forth. She was not an older woman, she was younger than Addie. She made no sound as she crouched to pull at Addie's leg.

Addie turned and grabbed the woman's hair. She pulled at her until the woman screamed. "Stop. Let me go!" The woman started to cry. Addie did not release her. Thompy picked up his head and bit on the forearm of the hand that gripped the woman's hair.

Addie turned on him and spit in his face. She screamed. She let go of the woman's hair and attacked Thompy's face again.

Thompy swung a fist and caught her on the left cheek. Addie fell sideways. She grabbed a lamp that had fallen to the floor. She swung it, slamming it into the side of Thompy's head. He moaned and fell over.

Addie went for the woman again, but the woman had grabbed an afghan blanket from a chair, and running past the children on the porch, wrapping herself in the afghan, she ran into the dooryard and continued running until she was out of sight. Addie sat on the top step of the porch and panted. She stayed there for several minutes. Then she returned to the inside of the house. Thompy was gone.

Harry sat still in the chair. He and Jenny were in the room that they shared. He touched his face. Jenny sat looking at him.

She asked, "Does it feel funny?"

Harry nodded his head.

"You look funny," she said.

Harry was covered in calamine lotion. Every inch of visible skin was covered with the dried light-pink lotion. He wore only his bathing trunks. They were too large for him and sometimes fell down around his hips, exposing his buttcrack.

"Do you think Daddy will come back?" Jenny asked.

Harry thought, then shook his head.

"Me neither. Not for a long time this time."

Harry mumbled something.

"Huh?" Jenny leaned towards him.

"...thirsty."

"Well, I'm hungry."

Jenny passed him her glass of Kool Aid. He sipped at it. He was hungry too. They both knew there was no food in the house—they had already looked. Earlier, when their mother was outside explaining events to Asa Hackett, they each had snuck a spoonful of greasy peanut butter from the large surplus can supplied by the town's welfare office.

They didn't talk for several minutes. Harry was sitting motionless. He had a book open on his lap but did not look at it. It was from the library. It was a well-worn paperback book, filled with pictures of other places, other countries. Harry liked books about other places. He sat looking out his window.

They heard their mother in the kitchen. Her anger still hung throughout the house.

"Jenny!" she yelled at her daughter. "Get away from your brother. You wanna catch that shit?"

Jenny looked at Harry and stood to leave the room.

"She's still mad," Harry said. His expression, even through the calamine, was strained.

"Gotta go."

Jenny left the room and went into the room she shared with her sisters while her brother recovered. They were not in the room. They were outside somewhere. There was no door, but a blanket was hung with nails, and closed her off from the rest of the house. She sat on her bed. She listened to her mother slamming around in the kitchen. Then she heard a door slam.

"Open the door, Harry," her mother said.

Jenny listened.

"Open the damned door, Harry! Open it."

She heard Harry's muffled voice, "You're gonna hit me."

"Open the door."

Jenny moved to open the blanket a crack. She saw her mother standing by Harry's door. She had a strap in her right hand. Jenny wondered why her mother was going to hit Harry. She couldn't think of any reason.

"I'm not gonna hit you," she said. Her mother's voice took a softer tone. "Just open your door so I can talk to you."

Harry unlocked his door. His mother burst inside his room. Jenny could not see them well, only through the crack of Harry's door.

Harry yelled. Momma swung the strap. It was a strap she took with her every time they moved to another house. She had gotten it from Uncle Lenny a long time ago. She told them once that he had used it on her, when she was younger, when her mother had left her to be babysat with Lenny and Ethel for days at a time.

Jenny went back to her bed. She listened as her mother swore at Harry.

"That's for getting this goddamned poison ivy. Pain in the ass. You must've rolled around in it. You deserve it. And...this is for lying. You knew your father was home. You were trying to cover for him, you little bastard." The strap swung through the air with a whistling sound.

Then it stopped. Jenny waited. Her mother came into the room. She was out of breath. She looked hot and tired.

She walked over to Jenny and swung the strap. It hit Jenny on the shoulder.

She cried, "No, Momma. Don't hit me. Please...Momma." But Addie swung the strap. It struck Jenny on the neck and on her arm. Jenny fell onto her stomach on the bed and covered the back of her head.

She was quiet now. No crying. No pleading. Quiet. Addie struck her daughter's buttocks and the backs of her bare legs. She looked down at her child. The strap had left large red welts across her little girl's bare skin.

Then it was over. Addie, panting, gasping—left the room.

Jenny buried her face in the sheets of her bed. After several minutes, she curled up into a fetal position, clutched a pillow to her, and let the pain subside. Her left ear pounded. She did not cry.

The town, still littered some from the carnival and parade day, lighted only by a couple of streetlights, was quiet, as the doctor drove home from a late house call. He had all of the windows in his old Studebaker rolled down.

He enjoyed the summer nights in his small village. He liked the quietness of the town after everyone retired. A scent of lilacs came to him as he passed the town office building.

He knew it would be a couple of more days before the place completely recovered from the parade day. His wife and her church group had collected a sizable fund from their booth. Other towns often attended their event. In fact, many folks from Cold Brook Mills, the next town over, attended. It was only a short drive for those folks with automobiles.

The doctor had met up with Doc Williams, who had a practice in Mechanic Falls, not far from Cold Brook Mills. They had talked for a while on Sunday morning at the closing events. Doctor Williams and his wife had bought a quilt from his wife's booth.

Tonight, as the doctor drove through his village, he thought of Doc Williams and his wife. They were a little older than he and his wife. He thought that perhaps they should invite the Williams's over to their home for dinner some night. He liked talking to another doctor. They had met up several times before, and he always enjoyed their professional discussions.

They both agreed that things were changing. Doc Williams had confessed that he saw most of his patients in his office now. A few…poor or elderly…or very rural homesteads, he still visited at home, if called. The doctor told Doc of the events the other night with regards to the Merchant children. They agreed that certain families were problematic and needed something more than just medical attention.

Tonight, hot and humid, quiet, and filled with the scents of summer grasses, wildflowers and lilacs, the doctor decided to drive past the Merchant house. He glanced at his own home as he continued up the road. The lights were still on. He knew that his wife would be working on those curtains until she was too tired. She would leave one light on for him in the kitchen when she retired for the night.

As he approached the Merchant home, he puzzled over the automobile in the driveway. Luggage hung off the back bumper and from the roof. He stopped at the roadside to watch. The lights were on in nearly every room.

Then, abruptly, it became dark inside the house. Adults and children came out of the house into the darkness of the night and piled into the car. The doctor made a decision. He pulled his car into the driveway and drove up behind the other car, blocking it from backing further out of the yard.

He pulled on his handbrake, leaving his engine running, and he put the gear into neutral. He walked up to the driver's side window of the black Chevrolet. The windows were all down.

"Howdy folks," the doctor said, looking into the back seat, and then at the two adults in the front seat. There was a toddler, a girl, on the seat between the man and the woman in front.

"What do you want?" Lenny asked.

The doctor looked at him then at the woman. "Evening, Mrs. Merchant."

Addie did not speak to the doctor. She looked out the windshield.

The doctor leaned into the back seat window. He looked at the children crowded into the back seat, sitting in each other's laps. He spotted the little girl.

"Hello," he said.

"Hi," she said, glancing at the back of her mother's head. She clutched a small toss pillow.

"How's the ear?"

She shrugged.

The doctor smiled at her. "You okay?"

The little girl nodded.

"You're going to have to move that car," Lenny said, "we gotta get going."

"In a hurry?"

"Just move. It's late."

"Where you headed? Moving out?"

Lenny did not answer him. The doctor looked over at the woman.

"Mrs. Merchant...?"

She glanced at the doctor, then away from him. The strong exhaust fumes moved to the front windows. She said, "We're just going over to New Hampshire to visit family. Comin' back in a couple of days."

The doctor looked into the back seat. He looked at the boy. The boy was painted with calamine.

"What happened to him?'

Addie did not move. She replied, "Poison Ivy."

The doctor nodded. He looked one more time at the little girl. He watched the girl but spoke to her mother. "Be sure she takes her medication, Mrs. Merchant." Then, to the little girl, "Take your pills, child."

She nodded to him.

The doctor backed his car out of the way and watched as Lenny moved his car down the driveway and into the street. When Lenny shifted to go forward, the car stalled. He cranked it.

The moon gave some light. The doctor watched the little girl through the window in the back seat of the car. She watched him. He waved his fingers at her. She waved back. The car started. They drove away.

The doctor sat in his car for a few minutes. Then he drove up the driveway, shut off his engine, got out, and went up to the porch. He walked up to the door.

The screen door screeched when he pulled it open. He tested the doorknob. It was not locked. He pushed the door open and stepped in.

He found the light switch and flipped it on. The house was empty. Some trash remained in the middle of the floor. The kitchen chairs were overturned. No curtains hung from the windows. A broom leaned against the kitchen sink. Cupboards were open and empty.

He left the house, got into his Studebaker, and drove home.

# down back

The older boy walked past young Harry Merchant and hit him on the back of the head with an open hand. Harry's cereal and milk spilled into his lap and onto the table where it dribbled to the floor. He watched his brother walk out the screen door, he looked at his mother standing at the sink, then looked over at his younger sister.

Jenny, eight years old, two years younger than her brother Harry, shrugged; she stared at the little bit of cereal still left in his bowl. Jenny scooped some of her cereal into his bowl then continued to eat her own cereal. They were both hungry. There had been no dinner last night.

When she finished, she went over to the door and let her dog into the kitchen. She glanced at her mother to see if she would say anything. Her mother was smoking a cigarette and looking out the window over the sink. She ignored Jenny and the dog, but Jenny knew that she had seen her let the dog in.

Jenny went over to the other side of the refrigerator and looked up at the cookie jar. There was not a lot of food, but her mother was able to bake with the surplus flour given to them by the town. Her mother could not see her from where she stood at the window. Jenny stretched up to the cookie jar, reached into it, and removed two oatmeal cookies. The dog went over to the table and helped Harry clean the floor.

"Jenny!" Her mother did not look away from the window. Jenny stopped. She believed her mother had eyes in the back of her head, under her hair somewhere. "We can't afford to feed that dog. Your father hasn't been around for three goddamned months. So don't be giving away any food to that stray."

Jenny went through the living room and into her bedroom and ate one of the cookies.

Harry came into the bedroom.

"What are you eating?"

"Nothing."

She looked at the dog that had followed Harry into the bedroom.

"C'mon, Bullet. Up..." She patted the bed.

The dog jumped up onto the bed and began licking Jenny's face. Jenny gave him the other cookie. The dog swallowed it whole and drooled on the bed cover.

"Daddy's coming home today." Harry watched the dog drool.

"How do you know?" she asked.

"'Cause he is. That's all." He sat on the side of the bed that he shared with her since Kicky had moved back home. Kicky had taken Harry's place, sleeping on the sofa. "Momma's watching for him. He's been gone the longest this time. She's really mad."

Jenny patted Bullet with both hands, one following the other, down his back. As her hands neared his tail, one of his legs started pedaling back and forth, his ears lay back, and he made a face that Jenny thought looked like a smile. She shook the shedded hair from her fingers onto the blanket and made a face. Harry picked up Jenny's doll and held onto it.

Kicky stood in the doorway. He looked at his younger brother.

"Hey, you little queer. Get your ass out here and help me clean up the car. If you're ever gonna ride in my car, you're gonna help clean it out...*Haaawwie*. Or would you rather play dollies with your little sister? Wouldn't Daddy love to see this?"

Harry looked over at Jenny, dropped her doll onto the bed, and got up to follow his older brother. Jenny got off the bed and went over to the doorway and stood watching as Kicky pushed his brother outside. She went over to the kitchen doorway and saw her mother leaning against the back screen door. She looked into her mother's bedroom, off the kitchen.

Kelly and Missy were still in the bed that they were sharing with their mother. They were pretending to be asleep. Missy stuck her tongue out at Jenny.

"Momma?" She looked at her mother's face. Jenny thought her mother looked like one of those porcelain dolls that Missy used to have. She was going to ask her where Kelly and Missy would sleep when Daddy got home.

"Momma?"

"Jesus H. Christ...what?!"

Jenny turned and left the kitchen.

That afternoon, Jenny and Harry walked through the woods to the shore of Coffee Pond behind their house. Harry told his sister to wait on the beach, where she was sitting with the dog. He walked off toward one of the camps. Jenny and the dog watched him walk away. Then she sprawled out flat on her back, looked up at the blue in the sky, and wondered what made it blue.

She rolled over onto her belly and almost rolled onto Bullet, who jumped out of the way. He sat back down beside her. He watched a mother duck and ducklings on the pond. Jenny watched them with him.

The mother duck quacked two times, and the little ducks followed her. Jenny watched them and made two quacking sounds. Bullet ignored her.

Jenny sat up and crossed her legs. She closed her eyes and put her face toward the sun. It made her face warm. When she squeezed her eyeballs tight behind her eyelids, she could see streaks and spots of orange and red, mostly red.

She could smell the lake and the water lilies that were near the shore. She remembered that Missy had told her it was against god to pick water lilies. She could smell the woodsy sweetness of the balsams, the pines, and the junipers. She could smell Bullet...she liked the way he smelled...soft, comfy, and friendly.

Jenny thought it was a long time for Harry to be gone. She thought that he might leave her there and not come back. Then, later, when she got home, she would say he left her and he would say "No, sir." Then she would get into trouble and he wouldn't. Then she would get mad at him and he would say, "What's the matter? Can't take a joke?" And she would swear she would never trust him again. But, she would. And he would trick her again.

"Hey. Jenny."

Jenny opened her eyes. Her mouth opened while she stared at him. She asked, "Where did you get that?"

Harry struggled to row the small blue boat. The oars were flailing around him. One came close to hitting him in the head when it came out of the oarlock. But Harry kept right on rowing as though he had done it a hundred times before.

"C'mon!" Harry said.

"What?"

"Get in."

Jenny took off a pink and a blue flip-flop, the blue one was a little bigger than the pink one and wouldn't stay on her foot anyway. She made a face at the blue flip-flop and threw it across the beach where it landed near the pink one.

The pond was warm. Jenny felt the mushy bottom of the pond ooze between her toes. She waded out as far as her shoulders, parting the lily pads with her hands. She still had on her slacks and t-shirt. The t-shirt was too large for her and she kept pushing the sleeves up over her shoulders.

She stood on her tiptoes. When she got close enough, she grabbed the side of the boat and tried to pull herself in. The boat tipped and took in water. Jenny lost her grip and went under the surface. She came up and Harry grabbed her short, wet brown hair and one of her arms. She pulled herself up on the side of the boat and fought her way into it.

She was gasping and spitting up water as she spread out on her back in the bottom of the boat. Harry proceeded to row. Jenny ducked around to avoid the oars that would not stay in the oarlocks. Bullet swam alongside and dodged the same oars.

"Let's go over there." Harry waved the oars around and seemed surprised when he hit the water with them.

"Where did you get the boat, Harry?"

Harry jerked his head toward the direction they had come from, which wasn't that far back Jenny noticed. "Mrs. Leighton let me use it."

"Oh." Jenny thought Harry was lying. Harry was known to tell a lie.

Jenny saw the ducks again. They moved fast, away from the boat and the oars. She looked back at the shore. Bullet was doing well keeping up with the boat. He didn't seem tired. Jenny remembered that Missy had told her dogs could swim good and go a long time before getting tired, because they had four legs instead of just two. Jenny thought that was odd because dogs have four legs but people have two legs and two arms and they still couldn't swim as long as a dog could.

"Mrs. Leighton told me to take it and you and I could go for a ride in it."

"Harry. You're gonna get in trouble."

"No, I'm not."

"You are so. Momma's gonna blister your butt."

Harry kept rowing. They were not going very far, but the boat was moving. They moved out toward the middle of the lake. Harry's face was red and he was panting. He stopped and sat with the oars up in the air.

They drifted toward a swimming raft. Jenny sat as far back in the boat as she could get. The oars could not reach her. She had one hand trailing in the water, and Bullet was keeping up with it, his nose sometimes touching her fingers.

They had reached the swim raft. It was floating, anchored to the bottom of the lake and riding high on some old metal barrels. Jenny tried to look underneath it to see if there were any big turtles.

"Get out on the raft." Harry bumped the boat sideways against the float.

Jenny climbed out, holding onto the raft, and jumped onto it from the boat. She was glad she was not in the boat anymore. She left wet spots around her where she sat on the raft's dry surface. Harry started moving the boat again.

"Hey, Harry. Where are you going?"

"I'm coming back, don't worry. I just want to practice rowing."

Jenny sat down with her feet dangling in the water and watched Harry banging the oars around. She laughed once when he dropped an oar into the lake and almost fell out of the boat trying to fetch it back. He retrieved it and started his wild rowing again.

Jenny stood up and walked around on the raft. The smooth, wooden surface was warm on her bare feet. She looked at her wet footprints and tried backtracking onto the same prints. She walked to the edge of the raft and sat down to watch Harry...he was close to the shore.

Jenny cupped her hands to her mouth and yelled, "Harry. Come back and get me now."

"I can't right now."

"Harry!"

"Jenny. You gotta learn to swim sometime. I can't come back right now, it's too hard and I'm too tired. What do you think I am anyways?"

Jenny watched as Harry flopped around in the boat and finally hit the shore. He left the boat and walked off. Bullet was following him. She yelled again and then yelled some more for Harry to come back and get her.

Then she started crying and couldn't yell. She sat down on the raft and cried some more. She was hot and thirsty. In fact, she thought she might die of thirst. Jenny thought how bad her momma would feel when she found out that she was dead of thirst and wouldn't be coming home anymore.

She sprawled out on her back and stared up at the sky; the sun warm on her body. She imagined the scene—Kelly, Missy and Kicky would all cry, and they would beat up Harry, and Harry would be sorry, and then Daddy would come home and they would all have a cookout and drink some beer and they would miss her a lot.

She knew that Bullet would miss her the most. He liked her a lot. She knew that, because he lapped her face, even when she didn't have stuff on it.

It wasn't dark yet, but the sun was getting low and it was still hot. Jenny, lying on her belly, smelled the warm, wooden surface of the float and listened to the water lapping against the sides. She peeked through the crack between the boards trying to see snapping turtles. She heard some sloshing water sounds and sat up.

"Are you okay, sweetie?"

Jenny couldn't see well because her eyes were hot and sleepy.

"Have you been out here long?" Mrs. Leighton handled the blue rowboat much better than Harry had.

Jenny blinked and peeked sideways through squinted eyes, her left hand shielding her face from the sun.

Mrs. Leighton pulled up to the raft, got out onto it, and tied the boat to the hitch on the raft. She turned and sat down cross-legged next to Jenny. She was wearing a white one-piece bathing suit. She held a bottle in her hand. "Want some Kool-Aid?"

Jenny took it. It was not cold, but it was a big bottle and it was orange Kool-Aid. Jenny took a long drink and wiped her mouth.

"You have orange mouth," Mrs. Leighton said and smiled at her. Then she put her hand on Jenny's forehead and wiped the moisture and sweaty hair away from her eyes. "But, it looks good on you. With those pretty brown eyes. Tell me why you are here." She stroked Jenny's cheek.

Jenny watched her face. Mrs. Leighton did not look old like her momma, she was older than Kelly, and she was pretty. She had brown hair that was short. She also had brown eyes, and Jenny thought she was nice.

Jenny told her all about how she and Bullet had watched the ducks and how she had not even thought about picking the water lilies. She told her about what a good swimmer Bullet was because he had four legs, instead of just two legs. Jenny also told her about Harry getting the boat and taking them for a ride. She said that Harry had told her she had to learn to swim sometime.

Mrs. Leighton asked her if she could swim. Jenny said she could swim under water, but just a little bit. Mrs. Leighton asked Jenny if she would like to learn to swim. Jenny nodded. Mrs. Leighton helped Jenny take off her slacks and t-shirt, and with Jenny just in her underpants, she brought her into the water with herself, and they swam.

Jenny learned to float on her back and back paddle and swim a couple of strokes on top of the water. Then Mrs. Leighton returned her to the shore and they dried off with Mrs. Leighton's giant yellow towel, then Jenny dressed and started home barefoot, carrying the mismatched flip-flops in her hands. Then she stopped, turned, and ran across the warm, sandy beach, back to Mrs. Leighton's camp and knocked on the door. Mrs. Leighton came out and smiled at her.

"Yes?"

Jenny, panting, looked behind her into the camp. It was like a library. There were books on the walls, and lots of open windows. The white curtains billowed with a breeze. There was music playing—the kind that didn't have voices, only the music. She saw no one else inside. She looked back at Mrs. Leighton. Mrs. Leighton was still smiling at her.

"Thank you," Jenny said, hopping down the steps. She turned to wave one time at Mrs. Leighton who stood watching from her porch door, and then she headed home, barefoot, on the pine needles, through the mossy pathway, past the junipers, pine and fir trees, and up the hill into the woods.

She saw Harry standing at the back of the house as she came up the Coffee Pond path. He was looking down the other field. She went into the kitchen. Her mother was smoking a cigarette and watching her from her chair at the table.

"Come over here," her mother said.

Jenny walked over to where her mother was sitting. She still held the blue and pink flip-flops, dangling from her fingers.

"Closer." Jenny took another step to stand in front of her mother.

"How many cookies did you take?" Her mother squinted through the smoke from her cigarette.

"Huh?"

"Don't you 'huh?' me, little missy! How many cookies did you take?"

"One?" Jenny whispered.

"Liar." She slapped Jenny hard on the left side of her face. Jenny's face stung and her eyes welled up. She put a hand to her face. Her cheek felt hot. Her ear made a ringing sound. She turned and walked outside.

Standing behind Harry, who had not seen her, she held onto her face. Her eyes blurred with tears, she saw Kicky and her Daddy with Bullet. Kicky had Bullet at the end of his belt that he had looped around the dog's neck. Bullet was walking between them, his tail wagging.

"Daddy!" Harry yelled but did not move. "Daddy! He's not a stray, he's

Jenny's dog, Daddy. Please. He doesn't eat much food, only the leftovers."

Jenny walked up to stand beside of Harry. They watched quietly as Kicky and Daddy, carrying the rifle, walked out of sight with Bullet, his tail still wagging.

She recalled how Mrs. Leighton had touched her face, brushing her wet hair from her eyes and forehead. Jenny thought Mrs. Leighton's hand was soft, and she had long, pretty fingers. She had watched as Mrs. Leighton carefully and deliberately folded her clothes, like they were special things, and placed them neatly on the raft. She had ignored the holes, and the frayed cuffs of the slacks, and Jenny's faded and worn t-shirt that was stretched out of shape by Kicky when it had been his.

Mrs. Leighton had put them on top of each other and patted the t-shirt and pants and had said to Jenny, "There. Now let's swim, pretty miss." Jenny thought that Mrs. Leighton was not poor.

She was suddenly drawn back to the present and she jumped a little when she heard the gunshot. She looked over at her brother, who was crying. She felt as though a small door that had been opened by Mrs. Leighton this afternoon had just closed someplace.

*It felt like that*, she thought, *like a door closing.*

She looked back down the field where Bullet had walked off, wagging his tail, and she decided that she would never walk down back again. Instead, she would only go down the other path.

*It was an in-between time. One of those times in life that are easy to miss and that are easy to live. Such times are not always good, but when they have passed and are reflected upon, people recall them as good times.*

*Prosperous and without war. Not true, of course, not everyone is prosperous, and there is always aggression somewhere else, toward someone else. But this is often forgotten during these times in small towns when the quiet, busy days follow one another and become winter, spring, and then summer.*

*Autumn comes to the southern part of Maine in a different way than it does in the other parts of the state. The people from northern towns refer to two Maines; economics defines this but so does the climate and the shape and force of the seasons. October of 1960 was especially warm and it was true of both Maines.*

*The town's people of Cold Brook Mills enjoyed the long, sunny summer, and being of the southern part of the state, they expected the extended summer, and sprawled out on their lawns with their charcoal grills, and horseshoes, and transistor radios, to delay the onset of the fall. The economics of Cold Brook Mills was driven by their paper mill—they thought of it as theirs—which was driven by the Little Androscoggin River and the waterfalls that divided their small town in half.*

*The mill employed hundreds of people, nearly all from within the town limits—neighbors and friends. It ran twenty four hours a day, seven days a week, in three shifts. This pulpy, throbbing creature did not shut down for any reason. It sometimes would become injured or ill, and the men—they were not yet called engineers—would anxiously seek out the injury or illness and cure it.*

*The mill workers were busy with overtime. The weekends were non-existent for those who were prepared to take on the hours. It was a good time for the mill. The mill hummed through the nights and the days. And when the train came through town, as it did several times a day, and during the night, picking up and dropping off pulp and paper, its long, beckoning whistle harmonized with the hum of the mill and the falls of the river.*

*The train, the river, the mill, and the people worked together, and together they composed a melody, an adagio, an organic song of their lives. It would be nearly twenty years before the town would feel the death of this mill. It would not come suddenly, but in a series of shutdowns and startups and different owners.*

*People who started work in the mill while still attending high school; people who put on snowshoes and hiked into work in a blizzard; people who climbed through every nook and cranny of this complex network of pipes, pumps, machines, and generators, searching for breakdowns, sweating and swearing over broken steam pipes, slowly going deaf from the constant, roaring, pulse of the paper machines; people who picked paper pulp from their hair and fell asleep with the sweet, damp, cottony smell, and the sound of the mill muttering and breathing in their dreams; these same people would slowly disappear from the interior of these brick and mortar dungeons and caverns.*

*And the mill would sit, dead and silent, no longer harmonizing with the river and the train. But this was twenty years away from this autumn's summer-like days. And the town's people did not know that this was an in-between time.*

*The war had been over barely seven years, and they had forgotten that there is always another war, another tragedy; they had forgotten that for some, there is never a time in between. In fact, they had been lulled into thinking that nothing else was ever going to happen...except to get up in the morning and go to work. Or, at the end of a shift, to go home, or, if you were a child, to play or go to school. They knew it was true, of course, that more things were going to happen, they had just forgotten.*

# the emerald bird fell from the sky

The rain stopped, the sun came through, and it seemed that the clouds were all at once blown away to the east—only the blue of the sky remained. Young Danny Cummings walked past Kelsey's Village Store. He saw Dummy James sweeping leaves from the gutters in front of the library.

Dummy was the town sweeper. He was tall and skinny. Danny couldn't decide Dummy's age. He seemed old, but his movements were strong and deliberate. Danny made eye contact and nodded. Dummy was a deaf mute. He made a grunting noise in return.

Danny crossed the bridge and passed Merrill's Market and turned down Water Street. He stopped. He set the school books on the ground and pulled the navy-blue sweatshirt over his head and tied the sleeves around his waist. He had put it on this morning because it had been cold and drizzling when he left for school. The afternoon felt more like August than October. He now wore only a white t-shirt. He picked up his school books, which he knew he had no plans to look at, and continued home.

His parents were both working second shift at the mill. His dog Jack met him when he came in the door. Jack jumped around, whining and panting. He licked Danny's hand at every opportunity. Danny kneeled down and allowed Jack to lick his face.

He said, "Good dog, Jack," and rubbed Jack's head and scratched his ears.

Danny went into his parent's bedroom, opened the closet and took out the Stevens 16 gauge, single shot, shotgun. It was new and smelled of gun oil. His father had given it to him for his fourteenth birthday. He had polished and oiled it numerous times over the past two weeks.

Last night his dad teased him that if he didn't stop oiling it and polishing it, he wouldn't be able to hold onto it. Danny took the cloth from the top shelf and wiped the excess oil from the barrel. The oil on the stock had been absorbed into the wood and was dry and shiny.

He reached for the box of ammunition. He removed two handfuls of the bulky, green shells...number sixes, and stuffed them into each of his jean pockets. He went into his own bedroom. He slipped a red flannel shirt on over his t-shirt. He rolled the sleeves up above his elbows and left it unbuttoned.

Every time he put his hand down, Jack licked it. He smiled and patted his dog's head. He left the house with Jack walking beside of him, the dog running ahead, his nose to the ground on the side of the road, occasionally looking back at Danny.

Mill Street was just outside the village. The only cemetery in town was on Mill Street. They passed the cemetery and continued past Ted Walker's place without seeing a single car or person. They walked across the small, cement bridge that crossed Cold Brook. This was the end of Cold Brook Mills's town limits.

Danny walked past the old, unpaved road that went into The Point, a favorite fishing hole for some local people. It was called The Point because it was where the Little Androscoggin River joined up with Cold Brook.

Danny thought there might be some partridge on the road in. He remembered his dad saying he should be alert for mallards or geese that used the quiet parts of the brook to rest on their flight south. He had hunted other game with his father, but not ducks. And this was his first solo hunt.

He carried the shotgun, held in the crook of his right arm, so that the barrel pointed to the ground in front of him. He looked down at his gun. He had the barrel broke open, the chamber empty but ready for a quick load.

He decided to go up to the fields and circle around, crossing Cold Brook near the shallow sandbar, then going out the old road. He figured that he had a couple of hours before dark; it always gets dark in the woods first. He gave himself an hour and a half to make the complete hunt.

The sun settled low on the western horizon, but it was still bright and warm on his face. The sky was now entirely blue. There were no clouds.

Danny Cummings came to a halt in front of the fields behind the Verrill Farm. He loaded a single shell into the chamber. He liked handling the shotgun. He liked the way the barrel of the gun made a snug click when it broke open; he liked the seedy, sweet smell of the gun oil and the way the shell fit just right into the chamber. He closed the barrel—a tight "*tunk*"—

and he rested his right thumb on the ridged surface of the hammer.

He liked the serious feeling of responsibility that came over him. He and the gun had changed the spirit of these fields and the forest. He became alert to the sounds, colors, and movements of the scene. As he walked into the field, all of the creatures he saw, he now looked at differently. He knew that these were the same creatures he saw each day, squirrels, a blue jay, a chipmunk—all beings that shared his world. But, it was different now. The gun made it all different.

He walked slowly around the edge of the large field. He took deliberate steps. His dog was just ahead of him but invisible in the deep grasses and goldenrod and Queen Anne's lace.

The boy did not call him. He could see the movement the dog made, moving through the grasses, or he would catch a glance of him, now and then, leaping, his ears and tail up. Sometimes he could hear him whine or snort, but he did not bark. Jack was an intelligent dog and he knew it was a hunt. But, Danny now wondered if he should have left the dog home.

He strolled half of the circle of the field. He walked with the barrel of the shotgun held in the crook of his left elbow, holding the grip with his right hand, his right thumb resting near the hammer. The sun was hot on his back. He could smell the balsam firs, the soft, earthy scent of the fields, and the junipers. He scanned the edges of the field.

The trees—yellow, green, red, and orange, flamed against the blue sky. The white birches stood out against the dark firs. He looked down at his feet; there were grasshoppers everywhere. He stooped to pick one off from his boot. He held it up in front of him and studied it. They studied each other...then he put it down on a tangle of purple vetches.

A mourning dove cooed from across the field at the edge of the woods. He could see the rooftop of the Verrill's barn above the trees to the east; the silhouette of the funny pig they had for a weather vane was not moving.

Then, from the brook to his right on the opposite side of the field, he heard them. Ducks. They came up out of the cove by the brook and flew at tree level; gaining altitude noisily...*kwek, kwek, kwek,* they began to form into a V-formation. Danny raised his shotgun, pulling the hammer back until it clicked into a deep, taut, recline...ready to fire.

Danny took sight on the lead duck, remembered what his father had taught him, and moved the sight out in front of the duck, leading it, allowing for the time it would take for the number six BBs to reach that distance. A glint of bright green from the duck flashed against the blue of the sky, as the lead mallard banked away from the sun.

Just before he fired the gun, Danny thought how beautiful this colorful bird was, and he knew he would kill this creature. His heart thumped. Danny had the odd sensation that he could not see anything except the duck and the sight at the end of his gun barrel, but that simultaneously, he could see everything on the periphery of his vision—the grassy fields, the gleaming October trees, his dog, and all the other creatures who had paused to witness this act.

He squeezed the trigger.

The lead mallard continued to fly for a while—a proud leader. Danny watched the duck fly. He thought that he had missed. His father had told him once that he was a natural, good shot with a gun. And he was. The duck wobbled, floundered, and then fell, wings flapping crazily, to the ground.

Danny remained motionless. He still looked down the barrel of the gun, pressed tightly to his shoulder, he held his breath—his vision unexpectedly blurred.

When Danny reached the spot where the mallard had fallen, his dog Jack was already there, poking the duck with his nose. He crouched, tail wagging playfully. Danny noticed that the duck was still alive. He kneeled down and pushed Jack away. The dog immediately came back and continued to sniff and prod the duck. Danny pushed the dog away again.

The mallard was a male. Like all drakes, he was colorful: an iridescent green head; a narrow, white band around his neck, with purple patches on his wings, also bordered with white; a chestnut breast, and a gray body; a white tail, and small, delicate black tail feathers that sort of furled forward. The duck glared at him.

The boy reached down and lifted the duck with both hands, his left hand supporting its head. He looked up to the sky. The other ducks were re-forming and a new leader emerged. They continued to bank toward the south. He looked back at the duck in his hands; a moment ago, he was their leader.

The duck's feet fluttered, and Danny knew he had to finish the kill. He used his leg to hold the dog back, and laid the duck back down on the ground. His dog whined and looked at the duck. Danny picked up his shotgun, and using the butt end, he struck the duck in the head.

He carried the duck by its feet, hanging from his left hand, his shotgun held by the barrel over his right shoulder, and he walked toward the brook. When he came to the shallow sand bar and the large, oak tree that had been felled across it for a bridge, he stopped and sat on the water's edge. His dog came up to him and sniffed the duck, but this time he sat down and watched Danny.

Danny said, “Hey, Jack.” But he had a cool, hollow feeling in his gut.

The dog’s ears came up, and he tipped his head.

Danny looked down at the duck. He laid the shotgun across his lap. On the other side of the sand bar he could see a large rock. He stood and picked up the duck and his gun. He started across the oak tree bridge, balancing himself with the duck in one hand and the gun in the other. Jack followed, diving into the water, walking as far as he could, then swimming the rest of the way.

When they got to the other side, the dog shook vigorously from head to toe, shedding the excess water. Danny went over to the rock. He searched around the area and found a sturdy branch. Using another rock for a brace, he levered the larger rock with the branch until it moved. He dug a shallow hole, using the branch, and placed the duck in it. Rolling the large rock onto the makeshift grave, he kicked dirt around the edges and stood back to look at his work. His dog had sprawled out on the ground, his chin on his front paws, still watching the boy’s every move.

Danny found a dry, grassy spot in the sun and sat for several minutes on the brook side of the shore. He stretched out on his back and put his arms under his head. He looked up through the trees at the blue sky. He looked over at Jack who was sniffing around the rock where he had buried the duck. Later, he and Jack hiked out The Point road to the paved Mill Road and walked home.

# a certain fall

Danny Cummings stood nude in the brook with his best friend Dennis. They stood staring at Alex who was holding a fishing rod in one hand and a tackle box in the other. Alex MacAllister was the town's only policeman. It was his day off.

"Beautiful day—Mr. Cummings...Mr. Witham," he said, nodding to each boy, then gazed up to scan the blue sky. "Cutting school?" he asked, setting his tackle box down.

The boys nodded.

"Well, boys...I guess you know I'm going to have to tell your folks," Alex said.

Alex recognized both boys, but nodded again to Danny. They knew one another; Alex was a friend of Danny's uncle and came by his home occasionally. As the boys, still wet, pulled on their jeans, Alex walked over to the other side of The Point and stood on the riverbank.

He stood watching the thick, white foamy stuff that was floating on top of the water. The Point was located in a remote part of the woods behind the paper mill, downstream. It was the point where Cold Brook met with the Little Androscoggin River. The foamy stuff only came in from the river side...the side the mill was on. Cold Brook, where the boys were swimming, was clean and clear .

"Looks like dirty marshmallow," Danny said, walking up to stand beside of Alex.

"Pollution." Alex nodded up river. He looked at Danny, the boy's wet hair matted to his head, his t-shirt on backwards and already wetting through. He looked away, smiling.

"Comes from the mill, probably. And all the other mills up river."

"What's pollution?" Danny asked.

"It isn't good."

"Is it poison?"

"Probably make you sick if you got enough of it in you."

Dennis walked over and joined Alex and Danny by the river.

The two boys stood on the river bank with Alex, watching the foamy stuff float by in patches.

"The government is looking into it," Alex said.

Danny looked up at him. "What'll they do?"

Alex stood quiet. Then he said, "I don't know. Make a law, I suppose."

Alex told the boys to go home…and to stay there. Then he picked up his tackle box and walked toward the shallow sandbar, crossed the brook on the old oak tree that had been felled as a bridge, and disappeared into the woods. The boys put on their sneakers, got on their bikes, and peddled back into town.

They separated, and Danny went to his grandmother's mobile home, next door to his parent's house. He stayed with his grandmother most of the time now, since his grandfather died nearly four years ago. He figured it would be a better place to be when his father got home this afternoon. His mother would not be home until late that night.

First, he put his and Dennis's cigarettes into the hiding place he had out back of his grandmother's home. It was a White Owl cigar box wrapped in a plastic bag, placed under the skirting that went around the bottom of the home. Then he went inside to wait for his father. He opened his algebra book on the kitchen table and sat watching his grandmother making bread.

The truck was loud when it pulled up out front. His father got out, slammed the door, and called Danny outside.

"You're grounded for the weekend," he said. He removed his work shirt.

Danny noticed the familiar splotches of dried paper pulp all over it. His father lifted his cap off his head, shook it, and with his other hand, ran his fingers through his hair, wiping some of the pulp out. He sighed. Then he shook his head slowly, put his cap back on, tipped it back on his head, turned, and started toward his pickup truck. "You do your paper route in the morning and come straight home."

Danny watched as his father kneeled down on the ground and crawled under his truck.

"C'mere. Give me a hand with this." His father tossed him an empty beer can. "Take these," he said, reaching from under the truck, he handed Danny the tin snippers. "Cut that can up the middle and cut out the top and the bottom."

Danny did this, and scootching down, he handed it to his father under the truck.

"Dad?"

"Hmm…"

"I was wondering…?"

His father grunted. "Hand me those two radiator clamps on the front seat."

Danny stood up and looked in the window on the driver's side of the seat. He spotted the two clamps, opened the door, picked them up, then closed the door carefully. He got down on both knees and looked under the truck. His father was sweating. He held a beer can that was slid on over one end of the tail pipe. Danny handed him the clamps.

"Well…?"

Danny looked at his father. He was peering back at Danny, his chin pushed down to his chest to see under the tail pipe. He was holding the pipe and the beer can together with his right hand.

Danny asked, "Did you ever…cut school?"

His father made a snorting noise.

"I was just wondering."

"Don't do it again, Danny."

His father started pushing out from underneath the truck. Danny moved to give him room.

Sitting up, wiping his hands on his work jeans, his father paused and looked at his son. Danny saw fatigue in his father's face, his blue eyes were not clear. He knew his dad kept the mill running. The mill called him for every breakdown at any time of the day or night.

"Danny…"

Danny was quiet.

"You remember when you built that raft and took it down the river?"

"Huck Finn…"

"Just listen, Danny…you never mind the books…remember the shotgun out the bathroom window? You scared the shit out of your uncle upstairs. He drives a truck all night. Come to think of it, you were supposed to be in school *that* day too. I never did get what you were thinking. Anyways, all I'm trying to say is that those things are fixable, mostly, if you don't blow your head off or drown."

He looked at his boy, shook his head, and looked away. He lowered his voice. "I dunno...you just started high school last week. This is not a good start. You can't go back to high school when you're all grown up to fix whatever you did wrong. You can't...you have to go to school, Danny."

"I do."

"Not just when you feel like it. You know what I mean." He glared at his son.

Danny nodded.

His father continued to stare at him. "As a matter of fact, I did cut school. Look, Danny...I work at the mill. I practically live there...now, you go to school. Just...go to school. Okay?"

"Okay. I will."

"And do your homework."

"Okay."

"I mean it, Danny. Your mom and I can't keep up with you. Things are really busy, and your grandmother lets you do as you want. I expect you to be more responsible."

His father slid back under the truck. "Damn it. Give me that glove. This pipe is still hot."

Danny retrieved the gloves from the ground beside his father's feet and passed them in to his father.

"What do you have for homework tonight?"

"Algebra."

"What?"

Danny spoke louder, "ALGEBRA."

"Well, your mom can help you with that. I was never any good at math."

"Me neither...I hate it."

"Yeah. But you're gonna do it."

Danny nodded, then said loud enough so his dad could hear him under the truck, "I will."

At three thirty the next morning, Danny, Dennis and Alton, another friend with a morning paper route, stood in the dark beside the drug store. They planned a small revenge. It was warm. The swashing of the falls, and the dank smell of the river filled the night air.

They were still...intensely observing Alex's blue Ford Galaxy parked in front of Spike's Garage. When Alex dozed in his car, Dennis snuck over and placed a small cherry bomb under his rear tire. They waited in the shadow of Mac's Drug store for Alex to wake up and drive off, exploding the cherry bomb, and flattening his tire.

"He told on us," Dennis whispered.

Danny and Alton nodded.

"He could've just warned us." Dennis sounded like he was talking to himself.

Danny said, "He sort of has to tell our parents, though. It's the legal thing to do."

"So...what are you saying? You wanna go get the cherry-bomb back?" Then softer, "It's only gonna give him a flat."

"I know."

Danny watched the traffic light go from green, to yellow, to red, over and over again...in an empty street. A bat darted around the streetlights, diving for insects. Danny looked across the river and thought he could make out the outline of the mill chimney looming up into the night sky.

There were lights coming from inside the mill. The third shift was busy. His dad was working in there right now... and then suddenly, Alex's car started up. Danny jumped. He was worried that maybe he was becoming a juvenile delinquent.

"Uh-oh," he mumbled.

Alton put his hands over his ears. Dennis patted his thighs with both hands. After a few minutes, Alex shut the engine off, opened the car door and got out.

Danny said, "Uh-oh...he knows."

Alex walked to the front of the car and opened the hood. He stuck his head under, fooled around with something, and then got back into his car. Danny let out a sigh. Several minutes went by. Alton fell asleep sitting with his back against the building.

Dennis said, "This is boring." He handed a paper bag to Danny. "You want a donut?" Danny's stomach growled. He looked at the bag of donuts that they had stolen from the drop-off box at Merrill's Market earlier, before Alton had arrived with the cherry bomb. He chose a jelly donut and began to eat it. It was warm and chewy, the sweet jelly gushed from the donut to fill his mouth.

"I don't like this," Danny said. He thought of the jelly donut he had just finished and added, "I think we shouldn't be doing this."

"Too late now," Dennis said his mouth full of donut.

Alton snored. Danny and Dennis both looked down at him. Then they looked at the bag in Dennis's hand, there was one donut left.

Alex's car started up again. Dennis kicked Alton. Alton did not move. And then...Alex drove off. He drove right over the cherry bomb, did a sharp u-turn, and speeding under the railroad overpass, headed out of town. The waterfalls continued to fill the night with soft, gurgling sounds.

In the distance, Danny could hear the train coming. Soon it would sound its whistle as it came to the crossing on Elm Street. But, there was no bang...no explosion. He and Dennis looked at each other. Dennis kicked Alton again, he moved, opening his eyes.

"C'mon stupid. Alex just drove off." Dennis walked across the square toward Spike's garage. Danny followed.

"What if it goes off now?" he asked.

Dennis stopped. Danny bumped into his friend. They walked slowly toward the place where Alex parked his car. There it was...the small, round cherry bomb. It sat there—still round and undamaged.

"What do we do with it?" Dennis asked.

Danny did not answer. They looked at it, walked around it, and finally Danny picked it up and threw it down the banking on Water Street.

It was the following Monday that Danny met the new boy in their class. He had seen him around the school before this day. Danny thought Harry was an odd kid, with a funny voice and heavy-framed glasses. But he was friendly. Today he sat next to Harry in Mr. Conroy's algebra class.

Danny whispered to Harry, "This is stupid."

"What do you mean?"

"I haven't even learned to do math with numbers. Now they change it to letters? Stupid."

"The letters are symbols for numbers, that's all."

Danny made a face.

"Mr. Cummings," Mr. Conroy said from behind his desk. "Do you wish to share anything with the rest of the class?"

"No."

"Then keep your eyes on your own paper."

Danny put his eyes back onto his algebra book. He made another face at his book.

"Hey..." Harry whispered without lifting his head, "I'll help you later."

After school, Danny and Dennis walked home with Harry. They stopped at the parked boxcars on the railroad tracks. Dennis climbed to the top of one of the cars, using the ladder on the side, and walked around the top, hooting. He lighted a cigarette and allowed it to dangle from his mouth.

"Hey," Dennis yelled down to Harry, "Danny and I are gonna take off one of these days. We're gonna jump into one of these boxcars and go to Canada."

Harry looked at Danny. "What are you going to do in Canada?"

Danny shrugged. "I dunno. Maybe California, too."

"When are you leaving?"

"Haven't decided yet. Probably quit school and bum around."

Harry did not say anything.

"You know…" Danny said, "like Jack Kerouac."

"Or Jack London."

"Yeah."

Danny held out his pack of cigarettes to Harry.

"No thanks." Harry shook his head. He was watching Dennis start down the side of the boxcar. He said, "They were both drunks."

The three boys continued up Park Street. At the top of the hill they could see the house where Harry lived. Harry said he had sisters and brothers, older and younger than himself. They lived in this apartment on Elm Street. Danny knew the place, and he thought that it must be crowded.

Harry said, "I'm going to go over to the elementary school to wait for my sister."

The three of them turned left and continued walking up Elm Street toward the elementary school, a short distance from the apartment house where Harry lived. They waited for a few minutes outside of the school.

"Here they come," Danny said.

"These kids really look young," Dennis said.

"Did you guys go to school here?" Harry asked.

"Yeah," Danny said.

"When?"

"Last year," said Dennis.

Danny kept his cigarettes in his pocket because he saw Mr. Wheeler standing by the parking lot where some of the older kids parked their bikes. Mr. Wheeler always stood there during class dismissal. He waved to the boys, and they waved back.

Danny liked Mr. Wheeler. He thought Mr. Wheeler was a good teacher. In his science class, he had taken a whole week to explain about electricity and then taught them how to read the electric meters outside their homes.

Danny noticed a girl with short dark hair, wearing a red skirt and a white blouse, walking toward them. He watched her, ignoring all of the other students coming up the sidewalk. He watched her as she came up to Harry.

Harry asked, "You've got homework?" The girl did not answer. She was holding a book close to her chest. They started walking again, back toward the apartment house.

"This is Jenny," Harry said, walking beside of her. "Jenny, this is Danny and Dennis."

Harry watched his sister. "Hey...say hello...what's wrong...what's the matter with you?"

"Hi." Jenny looked briefly at Danny and then looked away.

"Hi," Danny said. He watched her brown eyes. As the four of them walked down Elm Street, he kept stealing looks at this girl Jenny. But he knew he was way too old for her. She was only in the eighth grade.

When they approached the apartment house, Harry said goodbye. As Harry and Jenny crossed the street and entered the side door, Danny noticed Alex's blue Ford Galaxy parked in the driveway.

Jason drove down the wooded road, *Mostly a path,* he thought, and still the best damned parking spot around as long as it was dry and solid. *It's so late Friday night that it's actually Saturday morning*, Jason thought.

They had left Mortons Dance Hall and had been looking for a private place to make out. He hoped Barbara was still interested. He left the Desoto's headlights on. He came to the wooden gate and turned right just slightly off the path into an opening. His headlights caught somebody's taillights just as he switched them off. He didn't let on to Barbara. He was afraid she would back out on him.

He wasted no time. He slid across the seat and put an arm around Barbara, pulling her toward him. They kissed. He put his tongue in her mouth. Barbara pulled back a little.

"Easy, Jason." She shifted to give herself some room. "Let's put some windows down. It's hot."

"Yeah...it *is* hot."

"I meant...you know what I meant."

They rolled down the windows and began kissing again. This time Barbara did not pull back. Her kisses were wet and her tongue was in his mouth. After several minutes of heavy breathing and fondling, Jason started to remove her blouse.

"Jason!" Barbara whispered.

"Hmmph..."

"Shhhh..."

Jason lifted his head from her breast and looked at her. "What?"

Barbara was tense, sitting bolt upright. "There's someone else in here."

Jason's shoulders dropped. "Okay, so what? C'mon..."

"No." She pushed him away, pulling her bra down and searching for her blouse. "No. Stop. Shhhh...Jason." She rolled up her window and locked the door. "There's something wrong."

Butchie O'Brien watched his friend breathe on the chrome flask, polish it on his shirt, and put it into his jacket pocket. Then he folded his jacket and set it on the seat between Butchie and himself. The whiskey was warming Butchie's belly and insides all the way down to his groin. He could feel the heat of it behind his eyes. He continued to drive along Route 11 toward Cold Brook Mills.

"You know that bastard shorted us, don't ya?" Butchie asked his friend.

"Yup."

"Think we should do something about that?"

"Like what?" The man turned to look at Butchie. "Beat him up?"

"No. You got us into enough fights...'Stompy.' You and your big mouth usually got the shit kicked out of yourselves."

"Don't call me that."

"Hey...I didn't give you the..."

"Don't ever call me that again. That whole crew was assholes."

Butchie was quiet. Then he said, "We should've been paid at least another hundred or so. We practically built the damned house by ourselves. Half the crew was gone on the other project most of the time. We spent a bunch of weeks down there and we got screwed."

"Yeah...well, join the club."

Butchie looked over at his friend and looked away again to the road. He decided to drop it, knowing that Thompy was drunk and probably would be asleep in a couple of minutes. He poked his friend in the shoulder and said, "Hey."

"What?" Thomas Merchant did not lift his head from the car window and he did not open his eyes.

"We're almost to your place."

"Yeah? So?"

"Well, you can't pass out yet, Thompy."

Thompy kept his eyes closed and did not respond.

"How about another drink?" Butchie suggested.

Thompy did not move.

"How about it?"

"What?"

"Another drink, shithead."

He handed the flask to Butchie without opening his eyes or moving his head. Butchie took a drink. He looked at the monogram on the flask. He had pissed off Thompy before about this. Now he wanted to keep him awake.

"Whose initials are these anyways...they ain't yours."

"Told you before...I got it in the service."

"Yeah...I bet you did." He took a drink and handed it back to his friend.

"Screw you, Butchie."

He stood unsteadily, leaning against Butchie's Studebaker, looking at the house. He turned and stuck his head into the passenger side window. He asked, "Second floor?"

"Yeah," Butchie answered.

"And..." Thompy said, shaking his head, "what day is this?"

"Tuesday. Does she even know you're coming home?"

He didn't answer.

Butchie drove away.

Standing in the dark, narrow hallway, he tried the doorknob and then decided to knock. He felt in his pocket for the flask but did not take it out. He heard steps and then, "Who is it?"

"It's me, Addie." He smiled his little boy smile and started to open the door. He heard a flurry of noises. The door was locked.

"Addie?"

"Go away."

"Let me in."

"Go away!"

"Addie..."

Silence.

He pushed on the door. It would not budge. He bounced on it with his shoulder.

"C'mon, Addie...I've missed you. Let me in." It sounded familiar to him, this statement. He tried something different, "And I have some money this time. I made some good money. I know you all need this with the move and all. I spent all this time working my ass off. Are you going to let me in?"

"You're drunk. I can smell it through the door. Go away. I don't want to see you." Then, "Leave the money in the mailbox."

Thompy stood, sweating and breathing heavy, but quiet...waiting. Then he turned and started down the stairs. Halfway down, he stopped. He turned and ran back up the stairs and crashed into the door. But the hallway was narrow and the stairs were steep and the door was at such an angle at the top of the stairs that his inebriated momentum only made him stumble as he hit it. It did not move.

From inside the apartment, he heard Addie mumble, "Jesus H. Christ!"

"Let me in, Addie, or I will break the goddamned door in!"

The door opened. Addie walked back toward the kitchen sink. She turned and looked at him with her left hand on her hip. She was smoking a cigarette. She squinted at him through the cigarette smoke. "You're not staying. I don't wanna get thrown out of here, so keep it down."

He looked around the apartment. It was neat as usual and clean. But also, it was bare and lacking furniture. It occurred to him that perhaps this was one reason that Addie always seemed to have a neat place...she had so little.

"Nice," he said.

"Mmm."

He took a step toward her and put his arms out. He wobbled. "C'mon, Addie..."

"Just get out!"

"Jesus, Addie, don't make me go through this whole damned routine again," he said. "I'm tired..."

"You're drunk."

He reached into his pocket and pulled out his chrome flask. "Want to get a couple of glasses?"

"No."

He put it back into his pocket. "Don't you want to know where I've been?"

She waited.

"Butchie and I got a job in Massachusetts. We've been there building a couple of houses with this crew...bunch of assholes..."

"Humph. Nice of you to tell me...two months later."

"I had to..."

"I ain't interested." She looked him up and down. "So...where's this money?"

"I got it. Don't worry…I'll take care of things now." He sat in one of the three chairs at the kitchen table. They were all different sizes and styles. He looked up at her and pulled out a crumpled pack of Lucky Strikes, took the last cigarette, tapped each end on the tabletop and then put it between his lips.

There were matches on the table. He picked them up and lighted the cigarette. Shaking the match, he dropped it in an ashtray. He exhaled and looked at Addie with his boyish grin.

"Don't bother."

"What?" he asked.

She smirked and moved away from the sink toward the kitchen window. It was open. She looked out over the back dooryard and saw Kicky talking to Rick, the kid next door.

"Kicky!" She leaned toward the window and yelled again, "Kicky, get over here!"

Thompy got up and went over to look out the window. She moved out of his way, but not away from the window.

Thompy said, "What is he doing here?"

"He lives here."

Thompy looked at the car behind Kicky, who was now looking toward the house. It was a black Ford Fairlane. "Whose car?"

"Ours!" Addie said. "Well…Kicky's…but, ours…"

"I thought he was in the goddamned Air Force. What happened?"

Addie shrugged, took a pull on her cigarette and said, "He's out now."

Thompy looked at her. "I bet he is. He got out sorta early, didn't he?"

Addie looked up at the ceiling and blew cigarette smoke at the kitchen light. "Whatever…"

"Where are the kids?"

"What do you mean, 'Where are the kids?' They're in school, you asshole." She dragged long on the cigarette, still squinting at him. "Kelly and Missy moved out this summer…with their boyfriends…the baby's asleep…if you were ever around, you'd know that they have a life…like I am supposed to have a life, too!"

She slammed her palm down on the sideboard. Then she grabbed a pan and swung it at his head. He moved, but not quick enough and it glanced off from the back of his skull.

He whirled around and grabbed her arm, twisting it and pulling the pan away, throwing it across the room. He did not let go of her arm but continued to twist it until he had her in a half-nelson, one forearm around her throat the other pushing her arm up behind her back, forcing her hand up to her shoulder blades.

Kicky came through the door, did not stop, went straight across the kitchen floor, and from behind his father, he put a hand across his face and with his other forearm against his father's throat, he pulled hard and twisted his father's head until he let go of Addie.

They struggled and fell to the floor. Thompy was on top briefly, on his back, with Kicky strangling him from behind and under him. After a few minutes of rolling around on the floor, they both stopped and separated, sitting up and looking at each other, breathing hard and sweating. Kicky got himself into a kneeling position facing his father.

His father spoke first, one hand rubbing his throat and neck, "What are you doing home?"

"Yeah? What are *you* doing home? Nobody wants you here. Get out."

His father shook his head slowly, "I ain't leaving, Kicky. Get used to it."

"We're all 'used to it,' and we're all sick of it."

"You're an asshole." Thompy pulled himself up into a chair.

Addie was standing by the sink again, her hand at her throat. She looked at her left arm where the cigarette had burned her. She ran it under the cold water tap, then turned and looked at Kicky and Thompy. Kicky was now also sitting at the table.

Thompy took out his cigarette package. It was empty. He crumpled it up and threw it across the floor.

Kicky retrieved a package of Camels from his own pocket and handed them to his father who removed one and tossed the pack back across the table.

Kicky also took one out and they both sat there, still panting and smoking cigarettes.

"Nice car."

"Got it last week from Sammy's"

"What's 'Sammy's?"

"Car sales guy here in town. Across the bridge, behind the Depositor's Trust Company."

"What'd you pay for it?"

"Couple hundred or so—"

"Not bad. Run?"

"It's hot. Rick and I are soupin' it up a little." Kicky smiled, "He's a hot shit. Knows motors and cars. He's just a kid though. He's only seventeen."

Thompy sucked deep on his cigarette. "So how come he ain't in school?"

"He dropped out last year. He's cool...he'll do okay...probably run his own garage someday."

Addie said, "I got your stuff packed. It's in the back room."

They both ignored her.

Kicky was silent. Smoking his cigarette, he watched his father reach into his jacket pocket and take out his flask. He passed it to Kicky who took it, unscrewed the cap, letting it dangle on the small, linked chain, and took a quick drink. Lowering his head and exhaling hard, he passed it back to his father, letting the cap dangle.

He watched the flask as his father drank. He admired the flask. It was an impressive way to drink whiskey.

He said, "Cool."

"You legal yet?" His father wiped his lips and slowly, deliberately, screwed the small cap onto the top of the flask. He polished it on his shirt and slipped it into his jacket pocket. He saw his son watching him.

"Almost."

"Yeah." He smiled. "You been 'almost' for a long time now."

Addie spoke, "You're not staying here."

"Shut up, Momma," Kicky said.

"Don't talk to your mother that way," Thompy said, pushing his chair back.

"Yeah...right..."

Addie was quiet.

"What the hell is that supposed to mean?"

Kicky stared at his father.

His father said, " I told you...you, 'Do as I say, not as I do.'" He took the flask out of his pocket and drank again. He did not offer it to Kicky.

It was quiet in the kitchen. From the window over the sink, they could hear Rick clanging tools around his dooryard. Frankie Avalon was singing, "Why" on the car's radio. Rick spoke loudly to someone, "Can't...it's the distributor cap...cracked..."

Kicky spoke, butting his cigarette out in the ashtray, "So...Daddy, you want to see that Ford or what? I brought it around."

Thompy looked up at his son. "Sure."

They both stood up and moved toward the door. Addie started to speak. Kicky glanced at her. "I'll be back."

It was hot outside, and the sun was bright in Thompy's face as they walked toward the black Ford Fairlane in the driveway. He staggered and stopped abruptly; he pulled himself up straight. He continued to follow Kicky across the driveway where he had stopped in front of the car.

"Rick is working on his dad's piece-of-shit Chevy. Later on, he and I are gonna put some straight pipes on this baby."

Thompy was trying to stand still. He stood with both hands in his pockets, his legs spread, swaying. His eyes were drooping. He put a hand up to shade his eyes from the sun. His face was red. He wiped the sweat from his forehead on his shirt sleeve. He said, "...pissashit..."

Kicky looked at his father's drooping, bloodshot eyes. Then he opened the driver's side door and proceeded to give his father a tour of the inside of the car. He got into it and started the engine. It roared.

"I got the muffler off. Rick and I are..."

"Yeah. Pipes...later...gotcha."

Kicky shut off the engine, got out and opened the hood of the car. He propped it. His father slowly moved around to the front of the car, started to lean against the upright hood, missed, and fell into the engine.

"Jesus...be careful of that...you'll frig up the plug wires or somethin'..." Kicky grabbed his father, pulled him up and sat him down on the ground beside of the open car door.

"Hey." Thompy tried to stand. "Let me borrow thish for a while."

"Yeah. Sure."

"Really?"

"No. To begin with, you're drunk as shit. And besides, the muffler is off. I won't have it fixed until later today."

Thompy slumped down and then stretched out on the driveway.

"You gotta leave."

"Mmmmm...later."

"No. Right now." Kicky pushed his father with his foot. "Either you leave or I'm calling the cop."

From the ground, lying on his side, Thompy asked, "They got a cop?"

"Yeah. This town's got a cop."

Thompy did not move.

After a minute, Kicky tried picking him up. He was deadweight. He dropped him onto the driveway and went into the house. At the top of the stairs, he looked out the small shed window and saw his father stagger down Highland Avenue, barely staying on the pavement. Kicky shrugged and went into the apartment.

As Alex drove beneath the railroad overpass, he glanced into his rearview mirror and saw the Cummings boy and the other two boys behind Mac's Drug store, watching him drive away. He shook his head slowly. He recalled that Dickie Merrill had asked him to speak to the boys about the bakery drop-off box.

It seems that the boys were helping themselves to a donut each and then sometimes forgetting to close the box. This attracted and allowed either 'coons or dogs to get into the box and pretty well devour the remainder. Dickie was okay with the boys having a donut; he was a little annoyed that they couldn't close the box.

Alex smiled to himself. That would have to be some other time. He continued out of town. The trucker who had radioed—sounded like Larry Gagne to Alex—sounded upset. Said that he had stopped for a young couple and something was wrong out on old Burp's place. Actually, Burp and his wife had both passed on sometime ago and left their place to their only son, Butchie.

Alex knew Butchie. Not a bad guy, but he hit the bottle and often got too much attention drawn his way at times. Butchie's biggest problem, as far as Alex could see, was that he had too much time on his hands. The only income he had was the little bit of money he made selling his produce on the roadside stand, what meager produce the farm put out these days.

It was still the honor system that old Burp had set up: a box with a note that said, "Leave what you think its worth." People used to get some high quality vegetables during the summer, and Burp did a fine, seasonal business. But, Butch had not kept up the quality or the volume, and the box reflected that in low financial returns.

Butch did do some carpentry and was gone for periods of time. He just didn't pay attention to the time of the year. A lot of the produce would just rot in the ground until Butchie returned from building a house or some other structure.

Alex turned on the interior light and looked at his wristwatch. It would be dawn in a couple of hours or so. He would have to see what this call was about and then head home. He yawned.

Driving slowly, he reached into his lunch box, took out a donut and started munching on it. His wife had been taking the donuts out of his lunch box lately and he had been sneaking them back in. She told him he would never be able to catch any crooks if he didn't lose a little weight. He smiled and told her he knew them all anyway, so he could just go pick them up at their home later on if he needed to.

Alex had not intended to become the local police officer. He had, in fact, wanted to be a minister. But he didn't know how to go about that. He had worked in the mill for a while and then this job came up. He applied and was surprised when they hired him. He had been the town's only police officer now for about five years.

He liked the job. He liked helping people in his town. He also had some reservists he could call on if the need ever came up. He used Cal Strong as a back-up when he needed time off. Cal was reliable and semi-retired, so he could be available almost anytime. Problem was, Cal was getting up in years and he had this cancer now that probably would kill him off soon.

Cal told Alex he should be looking for someone else to bother when he wanted to go gallivanting. Alex wasn't sure if Cal was serious or just trying to remind Alex of his condition. Alex ignored it pretty much.

When they were at Kelsey's for coffee, sometimes Alex would just watch Cal real close to see if there was any change. He couldn't see any. Cal had always been a skinny guy. And he smoked. So did Alex. Until he had quit last month. He counted on his fingers, lifting them slightly from the steering wheel. One month and seventeen days...well...this was really Saturday morning, so...eighteen days. He had quit once for over a year and started again. No reason. Just picked up a cigarette one day, put it in his mouth and smoked it. Now here he was...quitting again.

He continued driving past Sunset Lake and toward Burp's old farmhouse. As he passed the farmhouse, he made note that Butchie's old Studebaker was parked in the driveway. In fact, parked rather well for Butchie, *Must have been an okay night for him,* Alex thought.

The farm was pretty run down. The barn was caving in and there were still an assortment of several dead-and-dying, motorized vehicles on the property. Alex was always impressed with the amount of rust a machine could accumulate and still stand erect. He thought this each time he passed the old farm.

Alex had told Butchie once, as paternal advice while driving him home one night after stopping him on the road, driving drunk, that he ought to put some of those carpentry skills of his into his own place.

Alex continued a short distance and came to the little pasture road that led to the back of Burp's farm. He saw some people in the road and an eighteen-wheeler pulled over, lights on, and what appeared to be the trucker leaning against the front bumper.

A young man and a young woman were also standing on the side of the road a little distance from the truck. In his headlights, Alex could see that the young woman was being held and comforted by the young man. His headlights captured the scene. Alex felt a tickle in his solar plexus, like on the Ferris wheel at the carnival when he would come to the top and start to fall.

The trucker had his arms folded across his chest. He said, "Hey, Alex."

"Larry. Thought that might be you."

Alex walked toward the truck. He looked around the area as he approached the trucker.

"So, you getting back from down South?"

"Ayuh. Got an empty truck."

Alex looked over at the young couple. The lights from the truck reflected off the woods behind them. There were crickets sounding off from the woods. The CB radio in the truck was turned down but occasionally made noises.

"You gonna be around for a while?"

"Nope. Gotta haul for the mill next week. Goin' right straight back down the same damned route."

"Didn't you used to do all the haulin' for them?"

"Yup. Well…me and a few uhtha boys. Not as much business, though. Must be a slow period. So…I been hauling for other businesses too."

"You folks okay?" Alex had not taken his eyes off the couple for several minutes.

The young man had been watching Alex ever since he got out of his car. Alex did not wear a police uniform, and he used his own vehicle when on duty. The town was not interested in purchasing a cruiser. Alex did have a small red flashing light to put on his dashboard, but he rarely used it; the last time he had turned it on was for the Homecoming Parade last July. And he had a badge somewhere in the car that he sometimes pinned to his shirt. The young man didn't respond.

"This here's Alex. He's our town cop," Larry said.

Alex walked over to the couple. He said, "You okay, young lady?"

The young woman had her face in the young man's chest. Her hair and clothing were disorderly. Alex was wondering if the parking had gotten a little out of hand and now they were all made up and ready to go home…or continue the parking.

Alex did this when getting into new situations. He would run a series of hypotheses through his head, keeping an open mind. He believed it gave him a little edge. It usually did. In his little town, the possible scenarios were simple and scant.

"So, young fella, what's your name?" Alex turned to the young man when the girl did not speak.

"Jason."

"Jason what?"

"Jason Wheeler."

"You Jake Wheeler's boy?"

Jason nodded.

Alex relaxed a little. The Wheelers were good folks. Alex knew they had a home in the next town over. Mr. Wheeler was a schoolteacher at Whittier Elementary in Cold Brook.

"So, Jason, what's going on here?"

"Out there. You need to go out there."

Jason was gesturing with a nod of his head to the pasture road behind him.

"Alex." Larry was starting down the road. "He's right. You need to see this. But I don't think these young folks need to be seeing it again."

They started down the road.

"That young lady okay?" Alex was watching where his feet were going on the dark pathway. He stumbled and caught himself.

"Nope. I mean...she ain't hurt or nothin' if that's what you mean. But she got the bejesus scared outta her."

Alex walked carefully. He did not speak again. He fell behind Larry for a while and had to move quickly to catch up. Alex was thinking about Burp and his farm. Alex had worked summers for Burp like a lot of young people did back then to earn spending money. Doing odd jobs. Mostly picking produce and loading it onto the trailer behind the old tractor...the same one that was now rusting away beside the barn.

Burp had been the one to put the idea into Alex's young head that he could go into the ministry. It always puzzled him why Burp had ever brought that up to him. Burp had not been a man of many words. He had rarely spoken to the people who worked for him. He had been aloof, taciturn, and sometimes damned grumpy, but for some reason, folks had not feared him. Burp had become something of a sage around these parts. Alex always thought him wise and kind.

"The old place is really run down." Larry was breathing hard.

"Yup."

"I used to work summers for old Burpie," Larry panted.

"Yeah. So did I." Alex stopped and took a deep breath. "So...what's out here, Larry?"

Larry kept walking, pausing for breath. "Gotta see it...for yourself...Alex."

They came up to a green Desoto. Larry said, "This here's the Wheeler boy's car."

"Jesus. What's that smell?"

Larry started walking further up the pasture road. Alex followed. He could make the outline of the other car in the dark. Suddenly Alex switched on a flashlight.

"Well, for chrissakes, Alex. Where the hell were you hidin' that!"

Alex ignored Larry. He was looking at the car parked in the middle of the path. He walked past Larry, who had stopped.

Larry mumbled, "Town make you buy your own batteries too?"

Alex had his hand cupped over his nose and mouth. He stepped toward the car, his light directed to the license plate—there was none—then moved the light over the vehicle. He did not recognize the car.

Strangely, Alex knew what the smell was...it was oddly familiar, one of those dark, subliminal memories that may have nothing to do with a personal experience but are known to humans in the same way that humans understand how to mate or recognize fear or know danger. The last time Alex had experienced this odor was in Korea.

"Addie!"

She stood by the sink, smoking a cigarette. She ignored him.

"Addie! It's late. I gotta sleep somewhere!" He was yelling. Addie did not move.

She was not looking at the door. She was alone in the kitchen. She stood staring at the ceiling and blowing the cigarette smoke up toward the light. From the living room she heard Kicky swearing. Little Tommy came out into the kitchen.

Addie said, "Go to your room."

The little boy turned and walked to his room. He left the door open and sat on the bed beside of his sister, Sophy. Sophy was playing with a doll. She was three years older than her brother.

"Daddy's here," Tommy said.

Sophy put the doll down and got off from the bed. She walked to the living room and into the kitchen.

"Momma..." she started.

"Get back to your room."

Sophy turned and ran into her older sister's belly. Jenny put an arm around her little sister's shoulder and looking back at the kitchen door, she led Sophy to her room. She passed Kicky on the sofa that also served as his bed. He did not look up from his car magazine.

As she passed, she looked into the bedroom that Harry and Tommy shared with Joey, the baby. Harry was doing homework. He looked out at her and shook his head slowly. Jenny took Sophy to the small bedroom that they shared.

Tommy was still sitting on his sister's bed. Jenny sat on the bed with them. She reached over and passed Sophy her doll. She looked out the door toward the kitchen that was directly across the living room. Sophy pretended to play with the doll. Tommy sat cross-legged on the bed beside of Jenny. She put a hand on his leg.

When Kicky yanked the kitchen door open, Thompy fell flat on his face on the floor. He said something.

"What?" Kicky asked.

Thompy tried to sit up. He pulled his legs under him. "I said..." he weaved on his knees. "somethin'..."

Addie walked across the kitchen floor and sat at the table. She used her cigarette butt to light a new cigarette and then crushed the butt out in the ashtray. She still did not look at Thompy or Kicky. She smoked her cigarette.

"Addie!" Thompy slurred, "I gotta shleep. I'm beat...whew...really beat."

"You ain't staying here." Kicky picked his father up and leaned him against the wall beside the door. "You don't live here. Leave."

Thompy tried to focus his eyes on his son. He gave up.

"Addie."

"Never mind Momma. You ain't stayin'."

"Addie!"

Kicky started to push and roll his father toward the doorway. Thompy put his hands on his son's shoulders and pushed back, but it was a weak shove. Kicky pushed harder and Thompy slumped to his knees. Then he fell onto the floor again.

Kicky stood over his father and looked over at his mother. She sat smoking, not looking at them. Kicky shook his head. "What do you want to do?" he asked his mother.

She shrugged one shoulder, "Whatever..."

Thompy lifted his head from the floor. He looked up toward the living room. He saw Sophy, Tommy and Jenny…with her hands on each of their shoulders. He said to Jenny, "Hi, Princess…"

Jenny spoke so softly that, many years from this night, she would doubt that she had spoken at all, "Hi…Daddy."

Kicky reached down and pulled his father up. Thompy pushed off from Kicky and stood on his own. His nose was bleeding. The blood ran down his mouth and chin. "You little shit." He swung a punch at Kicky, but missed. He said, "You wanna fight…I'll whip your ass!" He lunged toward his son.

Kicky stepped aside and swung a fist into his father's face. It opened a slash on Thompy's left cheek. Thompy surprised himself when he did not fall. The blow actually put him back a little on his feet. He swung again at his son. He missed.

Kicky punched his father in the gut and then on the side of his head. This time Thompy fell backwards. He hit the door frame and bounced back into the kitchen, falling to the floor onto his knees. Kicky used his foot to push his father backwards into the hallway. Thompy climbed back into the kitchen on his hands and knees.

Grabbing his father by the back of his shirt collar, Kicky dragged him backwards onto his back and pulled him into the hallway. He dropped him and walked back into the kitchen. He tried closing the door but his father's feet were in the way.

As he pushed his father's boots out of the doorway, Thompy sat up and rolled over onto his hands and knees. He pushed himself up, and quicker than Kicky expected, he stepped right back into the kitchen again, grabbing Kicky by the front of his shirt. They pushed and pulled at each other for several minutes.

Then Kicky kicked his father in the groin with his knee. Thompy doubled over. Kicky then shoved him, but he did not lose his balance, so Kicky hit him in the face again. Thompy stumbled backwards and fell into the hallway.

From a sprawled sitting position, he looked up at Kicky. He was bleeding from two cuts on his face and from his nose. He sputtered something and blood spattered onto his shirt from his mouth.

Kicky was puffing, "Get the hell outta here." He was breathing hard and he did not take his eyes off from his father. "We don't want your drunken ass around here anymore. You think you are a father? You think that? You're not! You're just a useless drunk. You have never…never…" he walked out into the hallway and stood over his father, his voice so loud that it was breaking up, "ever…been a father. You're never here anyway, until you run out of other places to go…wherever the hell that is…so what difference do you think it makes to us? Huh? What's your answer, Daddy?! I'm waiting!" Kicky was spitting as he screamed. He wiped a hand across his mouth.

Before Kicky grabbed his feet, Thompy looked across the kitchen at his kids, standing just inside the living room. Sophy, Tommy and Jenny. His eyes fell on Jenny. She was crying. Her lips moved. He couldn't hear her. He tried to focus his eyes. He watched her lips…she was trying to say something…

Kicky dragged his father down the stairs on his back. He reached the door and pushed it open with his rear end, dragging his father out onto the porch. He continued to drag him until he reached the driveway. When he stopped, he looked down at his father; he watched to see if he was breathing. He pushed him with his foot and Thompy made a noise. Kicky made the same noise back at his father.

He was trembling. He looked around him. It was dark. The people in the downstairs apartment were looking out the window at him. They did not move when Kicky looked back at them. Then he turned and walked into the house.

Jenny was awake. She turned her head on her pillow and looked at Sophy, sleeping with her fingers in her open mouth, and her chestnut hair, smelling of the shampoo that Jenny had given her earlier, askew on the pillow.

The window was open. She could hear a cricket outside in the grass; she rolled over so that her good ear, the right ear, could pick up the sound. She could hear her little sister breathing. No one had talked about her father.

After Kicky had come back upstairs, her mother had gone over to the refrigerator and taken out a can of beer. Kicky had gone directly into the bathroom. He stayed in there for a long time. Harry had never even come out of his room. She had helped the younger kids get ready for bed.

Now, Jenny turned onto her other side facing her window. It was a warm night. She had slept earlier. She was awake now and was not tired. She worried that her dad had no place to sleep. She wanted her mother to let him come home.

She was mad at Kicky. Jenny had not seen her dad for a long time. She wanted to maybe talk to him and ask him about where he goes when he goes away. Maybe she could sit on his lap while he talked to her about where he went and what he did.

She remembered one time she did sit on his lap. She liked that and thought about it sometimes. She wondered if he thought about her, ever. She was sorry he could not come home.

She heard someone pound on the kitchen door. She got out of bed and stood in her bedroom doorway. She stood looking through the living room into the dark kitchen. She heard it again. She looked at where Kicky was sleeping on the couch. He did not move.

She looked at her mother's room and saw that the door was open. She could make out her mother standing in front of her bedroom window, and she saw the glow of the cigarette in the dark. Then it was quiet.

Butchie opened his eyes. He did not move, but in the stillness of his dark room he began to think that he was feeling peculiar. Then he realized that he was not hung over. He closed his eyes again.

He smiled at the thought that he had just had…he would have to remember that one and tell it the first chance he got. He opened his eyes again. There was a noise outside. He listened and recognized it as an engine idling.

He sat up slowly and rubbed his hands over his face. He sat on the side of the bed and looked out the window. It was not quite daylight, but the horizon was lightening up some. Then he heard the sound that had awoken him. Someone was knocking at his front door. He got up and walked over to the stairwell.

"Yeah?!" he called down the stairs.

"Butch? It's Alex. Alex MacAllister."

*Alex…*? Butch looked down at himself. He had no shirt on but was still wearing his dirty jeans. He started walking down the stairs, trying to remember why he was wearing these filthy jeans. Not that he had never slept in his clothes before, but these were pretty dirty. Then he recalled he had been in the pasture all day the day before, mowing and hauling hay.

He unlatched the front door.

Standing on the porch, Alex was alone; his blue Ford was idling in the driveway behind him.

"What's up, Alex?"

Butch noticed that Alex was looking him over. "There's a car on your property, Butch. Down by the back pasture. I need you to help identify it."

Butch screwed his face up. "They all park there…the kids, I mean."

"Yeah…well…I need you to come down to take a look, Butch, that's all."

Butch lifted his shoulders. "Okay. Let me get a shirt."

They were silent on the brief drive down the road to the back pasture, Alex had the car windows open. It was already warm.

"Gonna be another beauty today," Butch said. He rubbed his face with his left hand and looked over at Alex.

"Yup." Alex glanced at Butch, then he looked back at the road.

As they drove past the back pasture, Butch caught the sweetness of the freshly mown fields. He looked to see how much he had completed, but it was still too dark. Alex asked when he had gotten back in town.

Butchie answered, "Just last Tuesday. Why?" Alex did not answer.

When Butchie looked back at the road, he saw a truck and three people standing alongside the pasture road. In the headlights, he recognized Larry Gagne. He did not know the young couple.

"What the hell's goin' on, Alex?" Butch asked, looking straight ahead at Larry and the young couple standing in front of the trailer truck.

Alex led the way into the pasture road. Butchie was next. Larry turned off the truck lights. He found his own flashlight in the truck, and catching up with them, he spread it out in front, sharing the cone of light with Butchie. Jason and Barbara stood by the truck, watching the three men disappear down the wooded road.

This time Alex had his flashlight on as he walked in silence. As they approached the Desoto and moved passed it, Butchie made a gagging sound and stopped. Larry paused, and when Butchie moved to catch up with Alex, Larry shared his light again.

Alex stood on the driver's side of the vehicle. He let the light from his flashlight roam over the car. He said, "You know this car, Butchie?"

Butchie had his right hand over his face. "What the hell is...?"

"The car, Butch. I don't think I've seen it in town. Do you know it?"

Butchie looked the car over as Alex moved his flashlight across it. "No," he said and shook his head. "What is that smell? Alex...what...?"

Alex put a hand on Butchie's shoulder and brought him up to stand next to him. He put the light into the driver's side window. But Butch was looking at the rear window. Something stuck all over it...stuck in the window. It was a rig of some kind. Tape...some kind of hosing...he looked in the front seat where Alex's cone of light was focused. He yanked himself out of Alex's grip and stumbled backwards, tripping over a log, he fell onto his rear end in the middle of a grassy spot.

"Holy shit! Holy shit! Jesus Christ, Alex, what the hell is that?" But he knew now that it was a man. It didn't look like a man, but he knew that it was.

Alex kept the light in the car and inspected the interior. The body was severely bloated and the man's face, cracked and twisted, was smeared with a whitish fluid. There was a wristwatch on his left wrist; because of the swelling, it looked imbedded in flesh. The man's shirt was stretched and ripped.

Alex put the light onto the backseat. He had not looked this closely the first time. He saw some of the hosing spread out on the floor.

"Larry...do you know who this guy is?"

Larry was on the other side of the car. He was letting his light shine into the front seat and he explored the floors and the man's clothing. He spotted something on the floor beneath the man's feet.

"Nope. God ahmighty, Alex, his own mother wouldn't recognize him." Then he whispered, "Poor bastard."

"Butch? Can you take a look?" Alex did not turn toward Butch. He was still looking inside the car. "I need all the help I can get here. Looks like this fella's been in here a few days."

Butch was sitting upright. He pushed himself to his feet and stood staring at Alex's tall form bent over the car. He took a step and stopped. Then he walked over to stand behind of Alex. He said, "Okay." Alex jumped and hit himself in the face with his flashlight. Butch said, "Sorry, Alex."

While Butch studied the thing in the car using Alex's flashlight, he held his hand over his nose and mouth. "You think we could catch anything?" he asked, moving his head slowly from side to side. He handed the flashlight back to Alex.

Alex stood silent.

Larry opened the door on the passenger side, opposite from where Butchie was peering into the car. He reached into the car and picked something up off from the floor from beneath the man's feet. Butch watched carefully as Larry retrieved the shiny item.

Alex said, "Hey...Butch...do you know this car...or the guy?"

Butch was quiet.

Larry, from the other side of the car, said, "I don't know his name, Alex, but his initials are J.W.T."

Butch stepped back from the car, his hand still over his nose and mouth. He took Alex's flashlight and passed the light across the car again. A black Ford Fairlane. He put the light back into the face of the disfigured, swollen head that was sprawled across the steering wheel.

"No. Those ain't his initials."

Larry came around the car, and using his red handkerchief, he handed the chrome flask to Alex. Alex looked at Butchie. "You know this guy?"

Butchie nodded, he held the flashlight on Alex's hand. He stared at the flask, stained and reeking of vomit but still shiny. After a long silence, he realized Alex could not see him nodding, so he said, "Uh-huh...I think so."

Walking back up toward his farm, Butchie looked over the horizon to the east. The sun was coming over the treetops and beginning to shed light on his back pasture. He had told Alex he wanted to walk home. He decided to walk into the pasture, and he stepped off from the pavement.

In the deep grasses on the edge of his fields, he paused. He smiled at the pleasure the sweet, mowed field gave him. He looked around the edges of the field where there were tangles of purple vetches, goldenrod and a bounty of Queen Anne's lace.

Butchie stepped into the mowed field. His boots and pant legs were wet from the damp grass. He remembered how his father would smell of the fields when he came in late for supper. He would lean over and give Butchie a stiff hug, rumple his hair and sit down to eat.

Butchie couldn't remember his father's voice. His father didn't speak often. He wondered if his father had even loved him. He thought that he probably had.

Butchie faced east and stood quietly for several minutes. In the distance, he heard the dull rumble as the train moved slowly through Cold Brook Mills. Then he heard the muted whistle. He waited as the train thundered through the town and headed north toward Canada. This was not a stop today. In fact, it seemed to him that the train did not stop as frequently as it used to when he was a kid.

It was quiet now. Suddenly, the sun came over the trees and fell directly on Butchie's face. Looking down at his boots where the sun was splashing into the mowed grasses, he saw dozens of grasshoppers popping and jumping erratically, almost playfully.

He turned back toward the sun, and closing his eyes, he put his face directly into its warmth and its light. It poured down on him. He accepted all of its brightness.

Down the hill, toward the village, a dog barked. A strong breeze hushed through the trees. He took a deep breath and held it. He thought, "*I will not die...*" His eyes welled up. Then quietly, but out loud, his eyes closed, the sun warm on his face and the sweetness of his pasture in his head, he spoke, "I-will-not-die."

Jenny opened the door and walked into the apartment. Dropping her red jacket onto a chair, she stepped into the kitchen. Her mother and Kicky were sitting at the table with a man. She looked at the man and then at her mother. She continued toward her bedroom.

"What are you doing home?" her mother asked.

"I just came home for lunch. The school is close and I didn't have any lunch money."

Her mother and Kicky were smoking cigarettes.

"Cigarette?" Kicky offered the man a pack of Camels.

The man stared at the pack for a second. He said, "No thanks. Trying to quit." He had a small, pocket-sized notebook opened on the table in front of him. He glanced at Jenny then back at the notebook.

Addie said, "Well, get something and get back to school. We're talking here."

The man stood up and pushed his chair back. "I can finish this later. No problem. And thanks for coming down to the hospital morgue Saturday." He closed the notebook and put it into his shirt pocket.

Jenny noticed that he had a badge pinned on his shirt…it was crooked and sort of flopping on his shirt pocket. She looked back at his face. He looked tired…weary.

He spoke to Addie, "I know that was not easy. We just had to be sure." He moved toward the door. "By the way, I have a few things you should probably have. They were things we found in the car…the trunk, too."

"I'll give you a hand," Kicky said.

Addie did not stand up, but Kicky did.

When they returned with two boxes, Jenny was standing by her bedroom door. Her mother was standing by the sink.

Kicky dropped his box on the table and took the other box from the man. He started going through the boxes immediately, removing items and putting them onto the table. There were some shirts and pants that had been stored in the back shed. There were some tools and an envelope. Addie walked over and opened the envelope. It had money in it.

The man said, "It was in his wallet. There is about a hundred and fifty dollars there."

Addie sat at the table and opened her purse. She put the envelope inside and snapped it shut.

"Oh…and there was this." The man reached into his back pocket and took out a chrome-plated flask. It had the initials "J.W.T." engraved on the front. He set it on the table. It shined.

The room was silent. Then Kicky picked up the flask. He held it in his hand and turned it over a couple of times. Then he unscrewed the cap and smelled it. It had been cleaned. He screwed the cap back on and then breathed on the chrome and polished it on his shirt. He put it into his back pocket.

Jenny watched this and did not speak.

Then the man walked over to where Jenny still stood near her bedroom door. He bent down. He put a hand out to her. She took it, and they shook hands.

The man said, "I am very sorry about your dad."

Jenny watched his lips, she said, "What?"

The man stared at her. He said, "I'm sorry...but you look like someone I know." Alex MacAllister was thinking of his own daughter who was barely fifteen years old. He wondered how this child was handling this news. "I said I'm sorry about your dad."

Jenny whispered something. This time it was Alex who did not hear. He kneeled down and said, "I'm sorry, honey...what did you say?"

Jenny repeated, "What about my dad?"

Alex looked at the girl, and then turned to the two other people in the kitchen. He looked back at Jenny. He studied her face for a while. "Well...I guess...I should be getting back," he mumbled.

"Jenny—get your lunch." Addie started toward Jenny.

The girl walked briskly to the kitchen, picked up her red jacket, walked to the door and left. She did not look back.

Alex stood watching the door. He looked down at the floor and then, for some reason, at his hands. Then he turned to the woman and her son. "I...ah, didn't realize... I'm sorry..." Then, "You hadn't told her?"

"No need to tell the kids about this stuff," Addie said.

Alex looked back at the doorway. He turned and moved toward the kitchen table. He started to say something and stopped. Then he looked at Addie and back at Kicky. Kicky was still rummaging through the boxes. He stopped and looked up at Alex.

"You know...if you want, I could come back later and talk to the kids for you," Alex said to Addie. He looked at Kicky and then back at Addie. "I mean, if you want." He waited, then he said, "Ma'am...they need to know about this."

Addie looked at him. "Whatever...but make it this afternoon. And it'll have to be before supper."

As Alex started to leave again, Kicky said, "So when can I pick up the car?"

Alex said, "Well, I guess...anytime. It's down at Sammy's, in back of the Depositor's Trust Company. You know the place?"

"Yeah. I bought it there. From Sammy."

Alex nodded, "Son...you know, that car is probably...well, not much good now."

"What do you mean? It still runs doesn't it?"

"Oh...yes, it does still run. But...well, go check it out. See what you think." Alex decided that it was time to leave these people.

Jenny spent the afternoon at school in a daze of thoughts. She knew that he was dead but she wondered how he had died. She knew that her mother and brother had known it. She didn't think that Harry did...he would've told her.

Mrs. Mills spoke to Jenny twice, to see if she was okay. But Jenny only smiled and kept working on her paper. Mr. Wheeler stopped her once in the hallway and asked if she was feeling well. She smiled and nodded.

After school, Harry was waiting with two other boys. Harry looked at her funny...he asked if she had homework. She did not respond. She had absent-mindedly brought her English book home with her. She clutched it tightly to her chest. She said, "Hi," to the two boys after Harry spoke to her, and she smiled at one of them who seemed nice, except that he kept staring at her with those blue eyes.

She just wanted to go home, go into the bedroom and stay there. Just stay there.

When they arrived at the apartment house and Harry said goodbye to the two boys, she saw the policeman's blue car in the driveway. She did not hesitate. She followed Harry up the stairs. She wondered what Harry was going to do when he found out that Daddy was dead.

Danny Cummings chased his dog around the inside of Red's chicken pen. He was hot, tired and losing his patience. A chicken flopped from the dog's mouth. The dog avoided Danny's clutches.

"Get over here. Now!" Danny used the demanding style instead of the chasing style.

His dog stood on the other side of the pen. The dog seemed oblivious to the frantic, panicked, squawking chickens, running, flying and bouncing off from the chicken-wired pen. Danny knew that in a few minutes Red would be coming home and he would be in trouble...again...this was not the first time that Jack had gotten into Red's chickens.

"Jack! Drop that chicken! I mean it. Right now!" Jack did not move.

Danny wiped his forehead and spit out dust and chicken feathers. The chicken was alive and apparently well in Jack's mouth. Danny could see his eyes move, his feet fluttered periodically. Jack seemed to be holding him lightly. There was hope. Danny did not want to disturb this situation and have Jack get violent with this chicken.

Lately, Red had been keeping count of his chickens. He would miss this one. Danny moved toward Jack. The dog crouched playfully but did not move. Danny got closer. Jack stood still. The chicken's eye rolled around...then fixed on Danny. The other chickens were settled now, strutting around the pen, giving a wide berth to the dog, clucking, tipping their heads and glaring at the situation.

Danny lunged, Jack bolted around him to the other side of the pen. Again, every chicken in the pen went flying. Danny landed on his knees. He pounded the ground with his hand. Dust and feathers flew up around him. Danny threw his head back and stared at the gray sky.

A car pulled into the driveway. Danny stood up quickly and looked over at Jack, then out at the road. It was Alex, the cop. Danny dropped his head and looked at Jack. "Now you've done it. You'll be lucky if you survive this time."

He started walking toward the gate. He opened it and walked over to Alex's car. Alex had a smile on his face that he got rid of before Danny got to his window.

"I'm sorry, Alex. I was trying to get him out of there," Danny said.

"Well...he's out now."

Danny turned as Jack went trotting across the road and into the fields...the chicken flopping in his mouth. Danny shook his head. "Dad's gonna make me get rid of him this time. He's given Jack a bunch of chances. So has Red."

Alex watched the dog disappear into the deep grass. He turned to Danny. "I'm sorry, Danny...anyway, I just spoke to your mom and dad. I need you to come up town with me. Okay?"

"I guess," Danny sighed, watching the field where Jack had vanished.

As they drove down the hill on Water Street, Alex cleared his throat and said, "Hey. I have an offer for you."

Danny turned toward Alex in his seat.

"I need someone to wash this car once a week. I'll pay him two bucks if he does a good job. You interested in the job?"

Danny said, "You bet." He was thinking that the money would come in handy for the movies and he wanted a book at Mac's Drugstore. It was a paperback and it was one his parents probably would not buy for him—*Peyton Place.*

Alex pulled into the parking lot behind Merrill's Market. Danny suddenly understood what was happening. Inside they waited for Dickie to finish at the register. Danny stood beside of Alex behind the meat counter. They both were leaning against the cooler and watching Dick as he moved up back toward them.

"Hello, Alex." Dick nodded at Alex and looked over at Danny.

"You know why you're here, son?"

Danny nodded. His stomach was turning over on him. He said, "Yes sir."

Dick looked up at Alex then back at Danny.

"The other boys...? That would be Dennis and that Alton kid?"

Danny nodded. It occurred to him that being a real juvenile delinquent was probably not much fun really. It would mean going through this kind of stuff all the time. Besides, he had just caved in quickly on his two best friends. He doubted this would qualify him for juvenile delinquency. He recalled James Dean's tortured determination to rebel against authority. He glanced up at Alex and dismissed the idea.

"Okay. Here's the deal." Dick Merrill paced in front of Danny a few times. Alex stood with his arms folded across his chest. "Your father already knows about this. So does your mom. They're good folks...you know that?"

Danny nodded. He did know that. And he was expected to be "good folks," too.

"I don't give a hoot about the donuts, not really. You guys can have one apiece. That's it. But, damn it...close the box when you are done. The dogs or 'coons or whatever..." Dick stood facing Danny now, "they are getting into the box and eating up every last baked item that Jake leaves me. I can't afford that."

"It won't happen again, Mr. Merrill. I promise."

Dick paced a couple of more times. He looked at Alex, who was avoiding his eyes. Then the door at the front of the store opened, the bell jingled.

"Customer," Dick said. "That's it. Alex? You got anything?"

"Nope."

"That's it then."

Danny looked up at Alex. Alex said, "Well, Danny, you're free to go."

As Danny started down the aisle, he saw Harry's sister Jenny at the register, waiting behind some people. She had picked up several items and had them on the register and in her arms. She did not see Danny. He stood by the aisle, watching her.

Alex walked by her and said, "Hello, Jenny."

She smiled at him and said, "Hi."

Alex looked over at Danny, and then he left the store.

Some other people came into the store, the bell over the door ringing with each entry and exit.

After several minutes waiting on the lady in front of Jenny, Dick Merrill turned to her and started ringing in her items. As he got to the last item, he turned to Jenny.

"That'll be $12.79."

Jenny said, "My mother just called down here and she was going to…put this on a slip or some kind of voucher?"

"Your mom?"

"Yes. She just called you."

Dick looked around the store to see where his other customers were. He had some time. He turned back to Jenny. "I don't think your mom called here. Maybe Samson's Market?"

Jenny was shifting from one foot to the other. She had a small purse on her shoulder. She took it off and looked inside, she only had a small package of tissues inside. She snapped the two small silver clasps at the top closed and then looked at the stuff she had on the register. Dick Merrill waited.

"Umm…" Jenny started.

"Tell you what," Dick said, "give me your mom's phone number. We can straighten this out, don't you worry."

Jenny recited the new phone number that they had only put into the apartment a few days ago.

Dick got on the phone and dialed. After talking for a few minutes with Jenny's mother, he turned to Jenny. "Miss…your mother wants to speak to you."

Jenny took the phone. "Hi." She was silent for a long moment. "I did." She looked down at the floor. "You didn't tell me that. I didn't know that." She was quiet. Then she took the phone from her ear and looked at it. She handed it to Dick.

Dick took the receiver from the girl, put it up to his ear, and then hung it up beside the cash register. He waited.

"I'll tell you what we're going to do," he said as he bagged the last of the items and pushed both bags toward Jenny, "you take this on home, and I'll work it out later. Okay, miss?"

Jenny looked at him, scooped up the two bags and started out the door.

"And, miss? Thanks for shopping here. I want you to come back."

"Thank you," Jenny whispered.

Outside, Danny caught up with Jenny. He fell into stride beside her.

"Hi," he said.

She did not say anything.

Danny realized she had not heard him. He said, louder, "Hi, Jenny."

"Oh…hi." Jenny was struggling with both bags. They walked almost to the bridge before Danny reached over and took the bags from her.

"Thank you."

Danny smiled at her and they walked halfway across the bridge and stopped. Jenny leaned over and watched the waterfalls. It was a cloudy day, but it was still warm outside. Danny set the bags on the sidewalk and looked over the side of the bridge with her.

They were quiet for a while. The noisy waterfall was hypnotizing. The mist dampened their faces.

"I just got in trouble, too…again." Danny thought he would just talk about it with her—for something to say.

"What happened?"

"It's my dog Jack. He keeps getting into our neighbor's chicken pen. He's already done in a bunch of chickens. Today, Alex caught him red-handed…well, red-pawed, so to speak."

Jenny looked him up and down. He glanced down at her gaze. The front of his shirt and pants were covered in dust, and chicken feathers clung to the material.

Danny said, "I couldn't catch him. He had a chicken in his mouth when he got away. Alex saw the whole thing."

Jenny snickered, then she laughed aloud and put a hand over her mouth. She laughed a little too long for Danny's comfort. But then he laughed also and started brushing himself off. The feathers caught in the breeze and drifted around them almost like a light, drifting snow.

Then Danny heard sounds from the other side of the bridge.

"C'mon," he said, grabbing her hand. He looked both ways and they crossed to the other side of the bridge together. Jenny looked back at her two bags. Danny reassured her, "They'll be okay. Nobody will touch them."

On the other side, they looked down into the water. Rick Larabbee was doing stunts in his small motor boat. Turning tight, fast circles, he scooted under the bridge toward the waterfalls, disappeared, then came racing back out. Rick's stunts made it look more daring than it actually was.

"I know him," Jenny said, looking at Danny. "He lives next door to us."

"Yup. Rick has a really fast car. A white '53 Chevy."

They watched Rick for a while, then crossed the bridge, picked up her groceries and started back up Elm Street.

They walked past the small library. They stopped briefly to look into the windows at Kelsey's to see if they knew anybody in there. They saw some older kids sitting at the soda fountain. Danny knew who they were, and he told Jenny what each of their names was and who was going out with whom.

"Someday I'll buy you a cherry coke." He was thinking of the money Alex would give him if he washed the car this week.

"That sounds nice."

Danny showed her the tall statue of "The Unknown Soldier" in the small park across the street from Kelsey's Village Store. "See how the soldier sort of leans backwards? See...?" He brought her to the side view of the statue. Jenny looked up at it. "Rick did that. One day he climbed up on it...we were all watching him from Kelsey's. He sat on his shoulders and waved at all of us. Until Alex pulled up and told him to get down. It's been leaning ever since. Probably always will."

When they came up to the railroad crossing, Danny said, "Hey. I got an idea. I'll put your bags down over there and let's go across the railroad trestle. It's neat."

Jenny hesitated. She shook her head, "I'm afraid of heights."

"It's okay, there's a railing," he said, putting the bags down and taking her hand.

Jenny looked down the tracks. "What if a train comes?"

He shook his head. "Nope. I know the schedule. I've lived here all my life. No trains today. C'mon...and don't look down."

They proceeded down the tracks to the middle of the trestle. Jenny looked down to make each step from one railroad tie to the next. Between the ties she could see the long drop to the river below. She gripped the boy's hand tighter and moved one step at a time. Finally they stopped and looked over the railing, across the river toward the village and the bridge, where they had stood watching the waterfalls only minutes ago.

It was quiet. Jenny shook and took a deep breath. The scene across the river to the village enthralled her. She became still.

Together they watched people crossing the street near the traffic light. Cars stopped for the light—then started again. Some went straight up the hill, some turned and went down the street beside of the market where Jenny had just come from. Some cars parked in front of the stores, the people got out of their automobiles and walked the sidewalks, entering and exiting the shops.

A truck pulled into the mill parking lot and had trouble backing out. The driver climbed in and out of the cab several times, checking the traffic and the clearance behind the truck. In the distance, they saw Rick pulling his boat onto the shore behind the fire station.

Danny watched her face.

"Neat, huh?" Danny looked at her wide brown eyes.

"It's like a silent movie," Jenny said, her voice almost a whisper.

They stood by the railing, watching the activity in the village square. The only sound came from the distant waterfalls.

"Who is that man? The one by the drug store?"

"Oh...that's Dummy. He sweeps our streets."

"How come?"

Danny shrugged. "I don't know. But I see him everyday doing that. He's always done it...my whole life."

"How come they call him Dummy?"

"'Cause he's deaf and dumb."

Jenny watched the figure as he made sweeping motions by the street leading to the bridge that they had crossed a few minutes ago. She thought about this man who could not hear anything. She touched her left ear. She wondered why he could not talk.

"But he's nice anyways," said Danny, watching Dummy push his broom.

Again they stood without talking, watching the silent activities of the village across the river. Along the river banking, near the area where Rick had pulled his boat onto the land, a mother duck, with her young ducklings following single file, swam toward the opposite shore. They passed directly beneath the railing where Jenny stood. She looked down and watched them move past, making little duckling noises. She smiled.

She looked up at the village in the distance. *I live here now,* she thought. She looked over at the boy that had become her friend. He was watching the ducks. She looked back at the village.

"What's that?" Jenny asked.

"What?"

"That..."

They both felt a rumble beneath their feet.

Danny listened and then turned toward the tracks they had just walked up. He recognized the sound.

"Run!" He grabbed her hand.

But, it was too late. The train came on fast. Danny and Jenny pinned themselves to the railing. The train roared past, inches from their faces—the whistle blowing. The wood and steel trestle shook violently. In their terror, they did not feel the sting of the flying dirt and dust.

It seemed like the longest train that Danny could remember going through his small town. When it had passed, he turned to look at Jenny. Her left hand clasped over her ear; she returned his stare. He could see her shaking. Her lips were pale. He shuddered.

He released the grip he had on her hand. She rubbed it. They brushed themselves off and walked back toward the grocery bags. Neither of them spoke.

They stood trembling by her bags. "Uh...I'm sorry...about the train thing," Danny said finally.

Jenny was quiet. Her face and lips were still pale.

He said, "Kinda scary, huh?"

Jenny's laugh trembled, "No train today, huh?"

Danny smiled and shook his head. "Dumb. I'm sorry."

Jenny gave him a little hit on his shoulder. "Lived here long?"

Danny rubbed his arm and smiled.

They continued up Elm Street. Danny carried the bags. "My mother was born in town. On Pleasant Street. I've always lived here."

"I was joking."

"Oh..." Danny said. "Where did you live before you moved here?"

"Lots of places," she said. She looked at him and smiled. "We've moved a lot."

"You like it here?"

Jenny said, "It's nice here. People are friendly."

Danny smiled. He looked over at her while they walked. Then he said, "I heard about your dad. I'm real sorry."

Jenny did not say anything for a while, then she said, "That's okay...thank you."

As Danny walked home, after leaving Jenny at the top of Elm Street, he thought about the way she had smiled at him. He liked the little hit she gave him on the shoulder. He liked her voice; he thought it sounded special when she spoke directly to him, using his name. He liked her dark eyes. He liked the way she walked. Heck— he liked the way she stood still. In fact...he liked a lot of things about her.

He decided that he could probably run really fast right now—so he did. He ran across the bridge, through the village, past Dummy, who turned to watch him go by, then he turned the corner by Dick Merrill's Market and ran down Water Street. It surprised him how light his feet were. For a second, he believed that if he pushed off with his right foot...just so...maybe...just maybe he could...

The streetlight on the corner was humming and giving off a dim, flickering blue light. The man limped into the driveway. He watched the house closely. He went up to the car and looked into the driver's side window. It was not locked. The keys were in the ignition.

He walked around to the rear of the vehicle. He inspected underneath. Satisfied, he went back to the driver's side, opened the door, shifted it into neutral and pushed the car out of the driveway into the street and down the hill. He jumped in, and after a short, silent ride, he popped the clutch and started the engine. It was loud.

He drove through the soft evening, his windows down, and the radio on. He listened to country music. Patsy Cline sang "Crazy." Hank Williams sang "Cold, Cold Heart." He sang along with Jim Reeves. He took the car out Route 11 and all the way to Casco. He drove the familiar back roads of the little country village where he had spent so much time before and after the Army.

He drove past Mortons Dance Hall. Later, he drove back toward Cold Brook Mills. He passed his friend's farmhouse. He kept going. When he came into Cold Brook again, he pulled up Highland Avenue and parked the car on the side of the road.

Taking the flashlight he had found in the glove compartment, he limped across the street and into the stairwell of the apartment house. Upstairs, he pounded on the door, but there was no response. Turning around, he found the shed door behind him unlocked. He went inside.

He took some clothes in a box. He also took some tools. He found some old hosing. He took that, also. He searched through the entire shed until he found the other item he was looking for...he took the tape and put it into the box with his clothes.

Back in the car, he continued to drive around. After nearly two hours of back road driving, the man pulled into a small pasture road, drove in as far as a gate and then turned the car right, into a small grove of young pine trees. He shut off the engine and sat there smoking a cigarette. He was humming Hank Williams's "Cold, Cold Heart." He dozed off.

When he awoke, he got out of the car and urinated beside of the front fender. Then he opened the trunk of the car. He removed the hosing and the tape. He looked at the clothing, put it back into the box and closed it in the trunk. Then he took one end of the hose and crawled under the rear of the car, and lying on his back, he put the end of the hosing on the pipe. It was too small.

He took out his pocketknife, split the end of the hose and forced it onto the pipe. Then he wrapped several layers of tape around the hose and the tail pipe. He folded the knife and put it back into his pocket. He was still humming Hank Williams' song.

He pulled himself up and went to the front of the car to the driver's side window and rolled it down. He put the other end of the hosing through the window and carefully sealed it into place with the tape. The man got into the car and sat down behind the steering wheel.

He left the door open and smoked another cigarette. Then he smoked another one and sat in the quiet of the night. He could hear the crickets making their music.

Then he started the engine of the car and closed the door. When he did that, the hosing pulled out of the window, pulling loose the careful taping he had done. He opened the door and got out. He pissed again.

Then he fit the hosing back into the window, allowing some slack from the exhaust pipe. He got back into the car and closed the door. He started the engine.

The exhaust came into the front seat with too much force, so he shut off the engine and got out. He put the hosing into the back seat window, installing it as he had in the front, using a lot of tape. This time he got into the car, closed the door, started the engine and reached for his flask. He took a drink from it, shook it and thought there was plenty left.

He sipped from the flask. He polished it on the front of his shirt. He did not feel drunk. In fact, he felt more sober than he could remember. He thought he was clear and sharp and alert. But...tired. He decided to have another cigarette. Instead, he fell asleep:

*He looked across the room at his daughter...she was crying...her lips moved, but he could not hear what she was saying...she was trying to say something...he focused his eyes and watched her lips closely. He smiled...*

# dark-blue lullaby

When Jenny was eighteen years old and I was nineteen, we drove to New York City to pick up Harry. It was November. Harry was near the end of his first semester at Newport College. He was not supposed to be in New York City.

We were all from Cold Brook Mills, Maine...Jenny, Harry and myself. Being from Cold Brook in those days meant being from a town with one policeman who didn't carry a gun and didn't have an office, never mind a jail. It meant a town square with two traffic lights; and it meant if you cut school, the whole town knew before the end of the school day.

This was in part due to the fact that most of the town's people worked together at the paper mill. Those who didn't were the town's merchants...and, of course, the school teachers...but the point is that word of anything spread fast in Cold Brook. Harry's current, strange circumstance was already news.

In those days, as far as I knew, no one from Cold Brook Mills had ever been to New York City. Newport College, only an hour's drive from Cold Brook Mills, was a much smaller college then and not part of the university system as it is today. Most of the college's student body were from Maine.

It was a curious thing then, a mystery even, that Harry had somehow ended up in New York City and that we were on this adventurous journey to find him and bring him home.

When I picked Jenny up early that morning, she wore jeans and a white hooded sweatshirt, and she still wore rollers in her hair. We drove down Interstate 95 in silence, except for some talk about having to borrow my dad's car, knowing that my car would never make the trip.

Jenny smiled. She asked me to thank my dad. Jenny's family did not own a car.

Harry and I had just graduated together in our class of forty-seven seniors—Harry being the brainy one. We all expected great things from Harry. He was the only one of the guys to go straight on to college. The rest of us had done things differently.

Some had gone to work, some married and some had just moved away. Some of us were getting close to a place in southeast Asia but just didn't know it yet. In less than a couple of months, I would be saying goodbye to Jenny and going into the Army. Later, I would ship off to Europe. I would marry Jenny before leaving though. And Harry would be right behind me, only he would not end up in Europe.

On this day, Jenny was a quiet navigator. She consulted the map and traced her index finger all the way down to New Hampshire and then changed maps and continued through Massachusetts. Her finger kept going until she had to change maps again.

On the car's radio, the Beatles were singing "It's Only Love."

"Well…I don't think we are actually going to have to go into New York City. If this is right and the man gave me the right directions, we should be able to go a little ways around the city, and this place is really not in the city exactly." Jenny was still looking at the map. "And it's not far from the Interstate. It must be a little suburb or something." Then, "Oh shoot…I forgot my purse!" She began searching under the seat. "Nope, I got it."

"You okay?" I asked.

She shook her head. I glanced over at her, then back at the road. She looked straight ahead out the windshield. "Harry never drinks. You know that," she whispered. "He has never been in trouble like this before. I just don't get it."

I did not say anything, but I did agree. Harry always seemed to have trouble just slide off from him…even while he stood in the middle of it.

"Do you know what happened?"

She was quiet again. I watched the road and waited. We were just passing Portland and it was nearly seven in the morning. I was thinking we had started a little late.

Dad's little Buick Skylark was a sporty little car, and I felt good about having it for the trip. I glanced over at Jenny, she was looking out her window.

Jenny had a lot of brothers and sisters. She always said that she and Harry had been through a lot together. She was the one who had taken care of the younger kids growing up. As their older sister, she parented them—she became the one who mothered them.

Harry was a year older than Jenny. He was the one she practiced the new dances from "Bandstand" with, and he was the one who got her into the older kid's crowd at school and at the teen center on Saturday nights, where they showed all of us the newest dance. Harry and Jenny had even managed to get on the Dave Morrow Show, a local version of the "American Bandstand" show. This helped them achieve a minor celebrity status with the teen center kids. And Harry was the first in their family to go on to college.

"He did something really stupid," she said. "Momma told me to ask you if you would take me down to get him. I didn't really want to ask you, but I didn't know what else to do. We don't have much money and we don't have a car. Kicky's car is ruined...again. He got drunk and smashed it up...again. And even if he hadn't, I mean, even if he still had a car, he would never let us use it to get Harry, and he sure wouldn't go and get him. They never got along."

She tried folding the maps but they didn't cooperate, and so she just folded them into a square and stuffed them into the glove box.

I nodded. Kicky was the oldest brother and he picked on Harry constantly. I did not know their father, he died before I had met them, but from what I had learned, Kicky got most of his coaching on harassing Harry from his father. I had heard him often, giving Harry a hard time. Harry never talked back to Kicky. Never.

I knew that Harry was a lot smarter than Kicky and I suspected Kicky did too. Kicky had left home at thirteen to live with family friends or something. It was a peculiar situation that led up to that, and I never got that straight. He did move back in sometimes, whenever his father was away, which was often, and Jenny found out later on that he had been in trouble with the law in Portland during that time.

"You know...my father never believed that Harry was his kid."

"I didn't know that. How come?"

She looked straight ahead out the windshield. It was a cloudy, cold morning. "'Cause, he just found him in a crib when he came home from the Army. Mom had never told him about the baby. She swears Harry is Dad's son. But, he never believed it. Harry doesn't look like any of us, either. He just looks like Mom's side of the family."

"Kicky know this?"

"Of course he does. We all do. They fought about it all the time. In front of all of us. Even Harry. Harry always just shrugged and walked off. He used to say, 'I haven't got a father.' Harry disowned Daddy. Just like Daddy disowned him."

She reached up and started removing the curlers from her hair. Then she reached over and pulled the rearview mirror around and started fooling with her brush to fix her hair, puffing it up with both hands on each side of her head. Jenny had short, wavy dark hair that she fussed with and worried about. She looked at herself in the mirror one last time and then pushed it back where she thought it belonged. I adjusted it.

"So, is this why Harry and Kicky never got along? Because of this thing with your father? I always thought that Kicky and your father never got along. Didn't they have some really bad fights?"

"I don't know. Yeah, I guess so. But, I don't think that was the only thing." Jenny put her hand on my shoulder and moved closer to me on the seat. "Can I ask you something?"

"Sure," I answered.

"Do you think Harry is a queer?"

"A homosexual?" I looked at her. "Why?"

"Because Kicky always calls him a queer."

"That's Kicky." I was going to stop at that, but I didn't. "Well...to be honest, Jenny, I think Harry is a homosexual."

"Why would you say that?" she asked.

"Uh..."

"He's not, you know. He has a lot of girlfriends. He was a great dancer and had a lot of girlfriends and you guys were always just jealous of him." She put her hand in her lap. "And Kicky is just an asshole. He never liked Harry because Daddy didn't like him and Harry was smarter than both of them..." She paused, "...put together!"

I was quiet. "Well, you know, Harry is smart. And he does have a lot of friends that are girls. And, I like Harry, we are friends, you know that. But all the guys know that Harry is a homosexual. We just know that, Jenny. We can tell."

"How? How can you tell?"

"It's just something about being a guy...a guy does certain...or acts a certain way..." I thought for a minute. Jenny was not saying anything, but she was waiting for me to answer her question. "I don't know. Maybe I'm wrong. You know, I don't know."

"I want you to tell me. How can you tell?"

"Well, I can't prove it. So...probably, I shouldn't say anything at all. But, just so you can be thinking about it...it might be..."

Jenny started playing with her hair, then using her little finger, she did this little twirling thing with her eyebrow. She did this and went into a little daydream. It was a habit she had when she was upset. She would single out a small eyebrow hair with her little finger and just sort of move it around at the end of her small finger... and drift away.

I drove and waited. It was looking like it could snow. This trip could take us all day and all night. I was nervous because I had never driven into New York before and the one time I had driven into Boston, I had gotten lost. Seriously lost.

I had borrowed some money from my parents, in case we had to spend the night somewhere. It wasn't a lot of money, and Jenny and I had never really, officially spent the night together...anywhere, except for the times we would fall asleep holding each other on the sofa at my house...my dad would get up in the morning and wake us and send Jenny home. In fact, we were both a little surprised that my parents didn't say anything about this. Then again, we had plans to marry.

I ducked my head and looked up at the sky through the top of the windshield. Dark, heavy clouds were moving fast from the northwest, but there were some lighter clouds that were brightened from the other side by a cold sun.

I turned the radio up, thinking that we were a little closer to New York and might be able to pick up Joey Reynolds's show. He played all the latest hits. He was different. A little while ago, he had had some little drama going about his disappearing or something. The disk jockey would be talking about how Joey had just gone away, disappeared, and they would be asking for help looking for him. Or, begging him to come back. "Come back, Joey Reynolds!"

Clues would be mysteriously called in and checked out. We all knew it was him. But, he kept it up for quite a while. Naturally, the kids all tuned in to get the latest update. But on this day, the static was bad, so I turned off the radio.

Getting out of Maine can take a long while. Even driving at 55 or 60 mph. From Cold Brook to the New Hampshire border was a couple of hours. Maine also has this problem with moose crossing the highway. They are so huge and long-legged that when they appear on the side of the road, you don't have any time to think, they can take just a couple of steps and be right in the middle of the highway. My imagination started up, and I scanned the sides of the road carefully.

"You know, he probably has a really good reason." Jenny was still looking out the side of the windshield, avoiding my face.

"What?"

"Harry. He probably has a good reason for being that way."

"You mean homosexual?"

"A lot of things have happened to him. They weren't nice things."

"Did he tell you about this?"

"No."

I thought for a second then asked, "How did you know about it?"

"I was there, too." She looked out the front windshield, "Most of the time. There were times when we weren't together and bad things happened to him…and to me."

"You think that those things made him homosexual?"

"Maybe," she said, lifting one shoulder a little and letting it drop.

Once, when I was a small boy, probably in the fourth grade, I had missed the bus and was late for school and had to walk. It was late in the spring, almost the end of the school year. It felt like summer. It was quiet on the way up Elm Street.

A few minutes before, the sidewalk would have been busy with kids walking to school. But this day I was dilly-dallying, as my nana would say. Now I was the only one on the sidewalk, and just before the railroad tracks, across the street from the Congregational Church, a car pulled up beside of me. A man leaned across the seat and rolled down his passenger side window. I stopped, taking a step backward away from the car.

He invited me to get into the car. He said that he was a friend of my father's, and that my dad had told him to pick me up and drive me to school because I was going to be late. Cold Brook Mills was a small town, and this man was not familiar to me. I declined and quickly walked away.

I never told my parents about this. I'm not sure why I didn't. I knew that this was one of those bad things that happen to kids, and I never forgot it. I was only vaguely aware of what the bad things might be, but I knew that it was dangerous.

Perhaps I thought I was protecting my parents from their fears for their children. Or maybe I just didn't want to lose the fantasy of the innocence of my little town's life. When Jenny talked about things that had happened in her childhood, she left much of it to my imagination. Maybe she thought that I could guess the rest. Or maybe she was protecting me from my fears, or perhaps she was hanging on to her own slim fantasies about childhood.

As we entered New Hamphshire and paid our toll, I noticed that it had begun to clear up a little, and although the sun was no where to be seen, it was a little brighter and the clouds were higher and not so threatening.

Harry had never mentioned anything to me about his or Jenny's childhood. Harry and I were not really friends, we were friendly. He was the brother of the girl I was going out with and probably would be marrying. Harry never complained or showed any signs of being a troubled kid. He was, instead, funny, easy to talk to and always a good student. The teachers liked him. Most of us liked Harry.

But there was another side to Harry that was not apparent unless you looked closely. He had no real friends, no real loyalties. He always seemed to land on the right side of things, never putting himself at risk or in any compromising situations. Things were always going just fine with Harry.

When things did not go fine, when something did happen, well, somehow nothing stuck to Harry, he would walk away looking good, rarely admitting that anything could be really wrong, and if there was, he certainly had nothing to do with it. Consequently, Harry came across as someone who didn't want you to really know him, and so nobody did. And Harry, in spite of his popularity, was really quite alone.

"I 've got to use the bathroom," Jenny said.

"Me too. There's a rest stop just ahead. "

We pulled into the parking lot. There were only two other cars and a trailer truck parked in the picnic area. Jenny and I went to the rest rooms. When we returned to the car, Jenny got into her picnic basket and pulled out a thermos. She poured me some coffee into the small red plastic cup that came off the top. The coffee was sweet and had evaporated milk in it. She also unwrapped an egg salad sandwich and passed it to me.

"Coffee's good. I didn't know that I was this hungry," I said, chewing.

"Don't talk with your mouth full," Jenny said.

"I don't want to stop for long. It's a long trip."

"Don't talk with your mouth full, Danny." Jenny smiled and wiped some egg salad off the side of my mouth. I opened my mouth and pretended to talk, making noises and sticking out my tongue. "Cut it out," she laughed, putting a hand to her mouth.

I swallowed. "You know, Jenny, you have never really said much about what you mean when you say that you and Harry went through a lot together."

Jenny was quiet for a while and then said, "You know what he did?" She folded her sandwich back up in the wax paper and carefully placed it back into the basket. "He left the college on Thursday and drove to New York City with some other boys. They got drunk. Can you picture Harry drunk?"

I had never seen Harry drunk, but I could picture it.

"They were up all night, driving around in this boy's car, drunk, setting off fire alarms all over the city." She shook her head, slowly. "Dumb. Just dumb stuff." She was still shaking her head, only harder, and said, "The cops caught them, of course...and now the college has said that they cannot return to school. Harry, it seems, has been flunking out! God. I can't believe this is happening. To Harry!" She whispered, "He was supposed to make it."

I was holding my sandwich and looking at Jenny. She looked at my face. I searched her eyes and wondered what she had not told me.

"He took a bunch of pills," she said softly.

"What do you mean?"

"Harry...he took a bunch of drugs. I guess he had been on some kind of medication for a while, after starting college, and he took the whole bottle." Jenny put her left hand up to her eyebrow and started that little twirly thing again.

"Hey...what did Harry do?" I asked, still holding my sandwich.

Jenny put her hand down, looked at me and then looked away. "They put him in jail after he came out of the emergency room. And, we are going to get him at this jail."

Jenny fooled with the radio dial. It was not turned on, but she kept turning it and going back and forth from one end of the dial to the other, the little needle was zipping back and forth. Then she opened the car door and got out. She closed the door and stood outside.

I sat with the sandwich still in my hand. I looked at it and took a bite. I looked out at Jenny and could see her breath in the cold morning air.

The trailer truck let out its air brakes and the noise startled both of us. Jenny's head turned quickly toward the truck. It started up and slowly began to move out of the parking area to the highway. I put the rest of the sandwich into my mouth, set the coffee on the dashboard and opened my door.

I got out and walked over to Jenny. I put both of my arms around her. I could feel her trembling. I held her for several minutes like that. We didn't speak.

Later, as we were leaving Massachusetts, Jenny slid over onto my side of the seat and put her head on my shoulder. I put an arm around her and we rode like that for a while.

"When we were really young, Harry and I had to go live with some people."

I waited. Jenny did not continue for several seconds.

"Maybe I was six or so…Harry was about seven." She adjusted her head on my shoulder. "We were just given to them by Momma. We didn't know who these people were. We didn't know them."

"Did your mom?"

"Well, years later, she said that the woman used to be our milk lady…she delivered the milk."

"So they were friends?"

"No. She was just the milk lady."

"So…why did you have to go there? I don't get it."

"I don't know for sure. Momma never said anything to us about it. She never tells us anything. But, we were poor and Daddy was always leaving home and going away somewhere. She gave us to that woman. I can't remember her even saying goodbye. She didn't cry or anything. She didn't say, 'I'll be back to get you.' Nothing…we just left. Harry and I were scared. We didn't know if we were ever going to go home again."

Jenny sat up straight. "Just before Missy died last year, one night, we were all sitting at the kitchen table, and Momma was fixing supper, and Missy said something to Momma. I don't remember what it was, but all of a sudden, I realized that when Harry and I went to this home to live, all of the other kids, Missy, Kelly and Sophy, had all gone to stay with family people, and they were already back home when Harry and I finally returned. They stayed with our aunts and uncles…but, for some reason, Harry and I were just given to these strangers."

"How long were you there for?" I asked.

Jenny shrugged and thought. "I don't know. I've tried to remember, but…I do know that I went to school while I lived with those people. Because I remember that one day, on the school bus…I had…messed my pants. I didn't want to go back there. But the bus was taking me there and I couldn't stop it from happening. I would have to go there. I was so scared of those people."

"Were they mean to you?"

Jenny nodded. She looked down at her lap. "Harry and I used to go down to a grove of trees and hide until supper time." She started to say something, stopped—then continued, "Then she would come out and yell for us. We didn't dare to not get up and go back. We were scared."

I drove and waited for Jenny to speak again.

"The man raised rabbits. They had cages full of them. He made Harry and I go out back with him, and he would take a rabbit out of the cage, make us sit on the ground with him holding the rabbit, then he would kill it in front of us." Jenny was a long ways away. "He cut their throats. But, before he cut them, he would...hurt them. He stabbed them with a sharp stick, in their cages. He squeezed them and sometimes just...broke them." She shuddered. "He made them cry. They sound like human babies when they cry—rabbits do." She squeezed her hands in her lap. "Then, we would..." She put a hand up to her face and then put it back down into her lap. "We would have it for supper that night."

"Did he make you kill the rabbits?"

"No. He killed them."

"Why? I mean, why did he want you guys to see him do this? Did he make you watch?"

"Yes."

I turned to her. "But why? What was the point?"

"He wanted us to be afraid."

"You mean he wanted to scare you?"

"Yes. But...he wanted us to be afraid..."

"Isn't that the same thing?"

"No."

"I mean, he wanted to scare you so that you would be afraid of him?"

"Yes. He used to make us sit at the table a long time before we could eat. He just made us sit there without moving an inch. Like we were frozen. We couldn't move or speak until he told us we could."

I shook my head slowly. Jenny wept. I drove and watched the road. It was quiet in Dad's Buick, except for the heater fan that hummed in the background. Jenny continued to cry.

At first, she was quiet about it, trying to keep me from noticing, but then she started to sob and tried to talk, but couldn't...so she just cried more and sobbed harder.

"Harry tried to protect me." Then softly, "He tried...but he was just a little boy."

I pulled over to the side of the road. There was not much traffic. I put my arm around her and held her.

She said between sobs, "These…people…were evil…"

"It's okay," I said, because I didn't know what else to say. I turned the heater down and held her and waited.

After several minutes, Jenny spoke about when she and Harry had lived with those people.

# alex

He watched the deaf mute walk toward his car. Dummy James was the town's street sweeper. Alex MacAllister often shared his thermos of coffee with Dummy before getting off the overnight shift. Alex tried to recall Dummy's real name—Alfred James. But no one called him Al, or Alfred, he was known only as Dummy.

He knew that Dummy lived alone and was alone most of the time. This was so, even though Alex also knew the rest of Dummy's family lived right here in his small town. They were good folks but simple...*No, basic*, he thought.

He never saw them with Dummy. He never saw them stop to talk to him or wave or go into his apartment at the top of Water Street. In fact, he never saw anyone go into Dummy's apartment except Dummy. The kids in town picked on Dummy. Not all of them. There were a few though, that just had the bully in them and picked on him. Alex had no patience for those boys.

On one occasion, a couple of years ago, he had caught the Carver boy pitching snowballs at Dummy from the steps of Kelsey's Village Store. The Carver boy was a bully. He had a younger brother and a sister, who were not like him. They were polite and never had problems in town. But Rusty Carver was trouble.

The Carver family lived in a small house across the street from the rear entrance to the paper mill. Their father had died a young man of a heart attack when his kids were still just youngsters. Their mother had raised them alone.

Rusty, the oldest, was angry and hard. Alex had known their father. He and Alex were close in age and had both worked in the shipping department at the mill. This was before Alex had returned from Korea and took the job as the town cop in Cold Brook Mills in the summer of 1955, just over 10 years ago.

Carver had been a heavy drinker and rarely worked. His then young wife, Esther, often showed up for work in the toilet tissue department of the mill on Monday mornings with bruises on her face, her lips swollen and cut. She wore considerable makeup on these days, so heavy at times that the effect would have been cartoonish, if not so sad.

At these times, she did not take her paper bag lunch with the others to the small dining room in the basement, but instead, ate alone at her workstation until the buzzer sounded, bringing everyone back to start the machines and finish the day.

The school had spoken to Mr. Sawyer, the town manager, because sometimes young Rusty would show up for school after the weekend and sob at his desk. He would become angry, throwing tantrums in class. The teachers did not want the young boy in their classrooms. They sent him home frequently, where he spent his day unsupervised.

Until one day, when he was in the eighth grade, he just stopped going to school. He told people he quit school. He told this to his teacher, who told Rusty he was too young to quit school. He told his teacher he quit anyway—and he did.

About two years ago, on a day off, Alex had been driving past the Village Store, headed for the town office to turn in a report he had finished at home and had witnessed Rusty and three of his younger friends—Rusty's friends were always younger than he was—slamming snowballs at Dummy from the steps in front of Kelsey's. He pulled up and they ran.

Dummy was an older man. He was timid, even childlike. He had not defended himself but had simply turned his back on them and stood still while they pelted him with snowballs; he had been through this before.

Alex had brought Dummy across the street and put him into the front seat of his car. Dummy sat quietly for several minutes, and after warming up, he had gotten out and started walking across the bridge toward his apartment. Alex found Rusty at home later that day and had brought him outside to his car to provide him with what he hoped was an impressionable threat of ending up in the Boy's Dentention Center in South Portland.

But, he had threatened the boy with this for years. He was hardly a boy at this point, and he knew as well as Alex that he would not be put in prison for throwing snowballs at Dummy James. Rusty had remained nearly as mute as poor Dummy had been in his front seat earlier that day. Alex had wondered over the years, if Rusty's father had lived, would Rusty have been worse? Alex believed that Rusty was like his father, and his father was like his father. Bullies are not born—they are made.

On this bright summer morning, Alex leaned across the front seat, opened the door to his old, blue Ford Galaxy and let Dummy into his car. Dummy slid his tall, stooped body in and closed the door. Alex handed him a cup of warm coffee. They sat sipping from their cups, watching the town square. The town was quiet.

Alex had re-set the traffic lights so that they no longer blinked. The lights were cycling through red, yellow and green in preparation for what traffic would be coming through for this day. They saw a young boy come down the hill on Pleasant Street, alternately coasting and pedaling fast on his bike. He was the morning paperboy, finished with his route.

He passed their car, waving as he went by, crossed the bridge, passed Kelsey's Village Store and Norton's Market and continued up Elm Street. Parked in front of Spike's Garage, Alex could see across the village square, the bridge, and all the way up the hill on Elm Street. This was another new paperboy. They had changed a few times recently.

Alex recognized this boy as Hank Piper's kid. No more than thirteen years old. Good kid. Alex thought that it did not take too much effort to raise a good kid. But it took some time and attention. And, to make a kid turn bad? Well...it took the reverse of this...and something extra—a little meanness. Alex also had come to believe that some folks came into the world with a little something of their own that sort of factored into this whole mix of good and bad.

He glanced over at Dummy. They looked at each other. Alex nodded and smiled. Dummy never smiled; but he nodded in return. After several minutes, Dummy made a grunting noise and a sound that was almost a word. He lifted his cup to Alex and nodded. He put the empty cup on the seat.

Dummy got out of Alex's car, closed the door, walked across the street, picked up his large broom and began sweeping the gutters. A car came across the bridge, and even though there were no other cars in sight, it dutifully stopped under the traffic light beside of Mac's Drug Store where Dummy, stooped over his broom, was sweeping the sidewalk.

The driver waited for the light to turn green, then drove past Dummy and past Alex, still parked in front of Spike's Garage, and went up the hill on Pleasant Street. Alex watched all of this. Later, he started his Ford and turned up Pleasant Street, headed home for breakfast with his wife and his dog. And a good morning's sleep.

His dog did not move; he was snoring in Alex's ear. Boots now slept with them since Phoebe had gone off to college. He was a big mutt and took up a lot of the bed. Phoebe had spoiled him and sometimes even ended up on the floor with her pillow and blanket, to give Boots her bed.

Alex had his eyes open when his wife came into his room. Actually, he had been listening to the scanner in the kitchen. Annie usually kept it turned down, but his ear, trained to listen to its every sound, picked up bits and pieces of information even as he slept.

"You awake?" she asked.

"Yup."

"Bud called. He says he tried to handle this himself, but it's turning into something else, he said."

"Okay." He threw the covers back, nearly covering his dog. He looked at Boots, who had opened one eye and was watching Alex. "Sleep well, Boots." The dog made a noise and closed his eye. He stretched and sprawled across the space where Alex had been on the bed.

"He's in front of the mill in the park across from the Village Store."

"I heard Dennis Witham's name."

"Yeah. He's been hurt." She started to mention Dummy James's name.

"And Dummy?" He was pulling on his pants and buckling his belt.

"He didn't mention that he was hurt. Just Dennis." She handed him a shirt. Alex did not own a police uniform. She tried to make sure that his shirts were presentable, pressed and neat. He had a badge that he sometimes pinned on his shirt. "And that Carver boy. He's involved."

Alex was nodding.

Annie followed him out to the car. It was warm and muggy; the early morning sunshine now covered by a few clouds.

"What if it rains?"

Alex said, "I'll drop by later and get a jacket or something."

He turned the key on and nothing happened. He turned it off and tried again. The engine turned over fast. It did not start. He shut it off. He could smell gas. He put the pedal all the way to the floor and held it there while he turned the engine over again. After a long grinding effort that he feared would drain his battery, it kicked in. He looked at his wife and shook his head.

"Town's finally voting on buying me a cruiser. Hope my old Ford will hold out a little longer."

"Be careful," she said and leaned in his window to kiss him on the cheek.

Bud Hemmings was standing over Dennis Witham when Alex walked up to him. He turned to look at Alex. He looked up, always surprised at how tall Alex was. There were a few kids from Kelsey's Village Store and some folks from the mill standing around on the lawn of the small park.

Bud was an on-call auxiliary police officer for the town. He was one of two, part-time backups that covered for Alex when he was on vacation or off duty. They also were on-call when Alex was off his shift. The other was Doug Stevens.

Doug worked days at the mill and usually took an afternoon shift if something came up. Bud had replaced Cal Strong, who had died five years ago in the winter of '61 of cancer. Alex missed Cal, but the truth was that Bud was a better cop.

"You left your car runnin'," said Bud.

"Yeah. Afraid it won't start again. Gotta charge the battery." He looked down at Dennis who was sprawled awkwardly across the grass at the foot of "The Unknown Soldier" monument.

Dummy was standing beside Bud. Alex smiled at him and looked him over with a quick glance. He looked fine to Alex.

"What happened to you?"

"That bastard Carver." Dennis was in some pain.

Alex looked at Bud.

Bud said, "I called for an ambulance." He shrugged, "We don't have one, so we have to wait on the one from the city."

"We could just take him in."

"Well…they made those new rules, Alex."

"Yeah. So that Action Ambulance can make some money."

"Now you know better. It's about the patient, Alex." Bud made a face.

Dennis said, "Who gives a shit…this hurts…I don't care to listen to you two argue."

Alex looked down at Dennis. "Tell me what happened."

Dummy made some grunting sounds and pointed across the bridge.

Alex watched him then looked back at Dennis. "What's Dummy trying to say?"

Dennis attempted to sit up, winced, and leaned back on his elbows. "Rusty went home. Bud told him to go home."

Bud said, "Rusty was being a pain in the ass. So I told him to get home and that you'd deal with him later."

Alex waited.

"He kept coming back and arguing...so I put him in my car and drove him home, took him inside and that's when I saw the other stuff."

Alex nodded and said, "C'mon Bud...spit it out."

"Bunch of kids in there smoking weed."

"Weed?"

"Pot. Mary Jane."

"Who?"

"Marijuana."

"Oh," said Alex. He looked back at Dummy and Dennis. "So...I still don't know what happened here."

By now, Dennis was flat on his back, moaning. His right leg twisted into a strange position.

"Rusty Carver was harassing Dummy. And Dennis...who was getting off work and leaving the mill, saw it and intervened." Bud pointed at Dummy. "When Carver started punching on Dennis, old Dummy here got involved." Alex glanced over at Dummy and back at Bud. "Yeah...I know...doesn't sound like Dummy, does it?"

Dummy started making noises again and got excited. Alex held up a hand to Dummy. He spoke low but moved his lips for Dummy to read, "It's okay, Dummy. Just getting the story straight."

Bud continued, "Well...somehow or other, Dennis ended up with a busted leg. Look...you can see the bone..." He leaned down and showed Alex where he had cut back the pant leg.

"OW! Damn!"

"Sorry, Dennis," Bud said. "And when I got here, Dennis was like this...Dummy was on the ground with him, and Rusty was standing around ranting that Dennis had started a fight with him."

"Got any witnesses?" Alex looked around at the people watching them.

"Got some names written down."

"What about the kids at Rusty's place?"

"I sent them home. I know who they are." He looked toward his own car. "And I grabbed most of the stuff off the kitchen table. Plastic bags full of shit." Bud lowered his voice. He said, "A couple of those kids there were pretty young."

"Okay." Alex stood looking around, then he turned to look down at

Dennis. "Hey…Dennis…think you can make it if we help you into my car?"

"Yeah. Just get me up." Tears rolled down Dennis's face.

"Let's get this fella to the hospital." Alex turned to one of the men in the crowd. "Art...give Bud and I a hand here."

On the way to the hospital—Dennis sprawled on the back seat, releasing a stream of curses in a monotone as he groaned at his pain— Alex kept his radio turned up. He had sent Bud to tell Rusty to stay put today. He would be back to interview him later. He passed the ambulance headed toward Cold Brook Mills with its red light flashing. He waved.

"What was that?" Dennis groaned from the back seat.

"Action Ambulance—on their way to get you."

"This is gonna screw me up."

"How's that?"

"I was going into the Army next month. Gonna fight those Commie bastards."

"Wanna go to Viet Nam, huh?"

"Bastards."

At the hospital, Alex waited in the office of the nurse's station while the doctor took his time with Dennis. He had taken a few minutes to contact Dennis's family, and then he started jotting down some notes. He decided that after he spoke with the doctors and talked some with Dennis's folks, he would head back to interview Rusty…and figure out what to do about this drug business.

This was new to Alex. *Things are changing,* he thought. He knew Bud dreaded going to the homes of those kids. Bud was good at that though. And people in town trusted Bud. He would do okay.

"There's someone here to see you," the nurse said.

It was the driver of the ambulance.

"You're supposed to wait for us," the young man said to Alex. He wore a dark blue uniform. It was starched, pressed and creased.

Alex thought this boy would do well in the military—not that he would wish that on anyone. He looked down at the young man's shoes—spit-polished black leather. His name was pinned on his shirt. STEVE.

"Well, Steve…you took too long."

"My boss'll be talking to the town manager about this."

"Yup. I'm sure he will."

"There are…"

"Rules. I know…now run along, son." The boy looked like he might have graduated high school last year. Alex turned back to his small notebook and continued jotting down notes. The young man left.

When the nurse returned with a cup of coffee, Alex was dozing, his long legs stretched out in front of him, his arms folded, his chin resting on his chest and a little noise coming from his throat. He peeked at her. She set the cup down on the table and left the room.

Korea had surprised Alex. As he got older, some things that he learned about himself had surprised him a lot. He was surprised that he had ended up a cop. Especially in his own hometown. And, he was surprised that Annie had fallen in love with him and married him. She was too pretty for him. He had always thought that he never stood a chance with her. That was a nice surprise.

When he was in Korea, he thought at times that his heart was being damaged by the constant cramp he felt in his chest…he missed her so much. And, he was surprised, when he returned from Korea, that he could no longer hunt. He had always enjoyed the challenge and sport of hunting. He was not hypocritical about this…he did not feel that others should not hunt…he just had no taste for it after Korea. He still enjoyed fly-fishing, though.

But Korea had surprised him more than anything else in his life had. He had entered the service just about a year and a half before the war had ended. Infantry. He had been in his late twenties when he went overseas. In Korea, he had learned that, under certain circumstances, he could kill people.

He wondered if Dennis Witham had thought about killing people. He doubted that Dennis was more than twenty years old. Still a kid really. Alex remembered Dennis as one of the paperboys in town. It seemed like just a short while ago.

"There's someone here to see you," the nurse said.

Alex opened his eyes. He looked around for the ambulance driver.

"Alex MacAllister?" A Maine State Trooper about Alex's age stood in front of him.

"Yeah."

"Can we have a word with you?" He turned to include a man in a sport coat and tie. He looked at the nurse. "Alone. Please."

The nurse left the room.

Alex sat up straight in his chair. He rubbed his eyes and yawned.

"Sorry to bother you," the trooper said.

"It's okay."

"We have a problem."

"Uh-huh?" Alex yawned again. "Sorry. Haven't had much sleep."

The trooper waited.

"Dreaming…I guess…" Alex sighed and rubbed his face with both hands. Still in a reverie, he thought about his dad teaching him how to cast on Swift River when he was about twelve years old.

It was a late spring day. Cool, and the wind blew, moving the trees in a heavy way, swaying them back and forth. The roaring of Swift River nearly drowned out by the wind rushing through the forest. It had been difficult to cast that day. They had gone home early. Fly-fishing had been his closest times with his father.

Now his father and mother lived in a trailer park in Florida. He rarely saw them. He wiped his right hand down his face and looked at the trooper.

"We heard about you from Ned Francis."

Alex knew Ned. He was a state trooper who covered their area and lived not too far outside of Cold Brook Mills.

"Ned says you're the best damned shot he ever knew."

Alex studied the trooper and the man in the coat and tie.

Rusty Carver paced the kitchen floor. His mother's car drove in the driveway. When his mother came in the kitchen door, he sat in a chair at the table. They did not speak. Another car drove into the driveway. It was Bud Hemmings. Rusty got up and left the room. Esther went to the door.

"Sorry to bother you, Esther." Bud watched as Esther placed some bags on the floor. The bags contained empty beer bottles. She continued to pick the bottles up from around the kitchen and put them into paper bags. Bud could smell the sour odor of beer.

"What can I do for you?" She looked at the badge pinned to Bud's plaid shirt pocket. He was wearing Levi jeans.

"Rusty home?"

"Rusty!" Esther yelled.

Bud waited and watched the door to the living room. He could see the stairway from where he stood just inside the kitchen entrance. The furniture was sparse and in rough shape. There was only the sofa in the living room, and a television, the "rabbit-ears" antenna askew on the top.

The television was on. He recognized a rerun of *Sea Hunt*. Lloyd Bridges, in black and white, with a snorkel and mask hanging around his neck, was having a conversation with a young woman, maybe Tuesday Weld or Sandra Dee or one of them blonde starlets. There was no sound. Bud shifted his attention back to the stairway.

Rusty came down the stairs and into the kitchen.

"Yeah?" He acted surprised to see Bud.

Bud smiled, shaking his head, he said, "Remember me, Rusty?"

"Yeah…so?"

"Alex said you are to stay here until he gets done at the hospital. Don't be going anywhere. Got it?"

Rusty smirked and made a noise out of the corner of his mouth.

"What's this about?" Esther looked from her son to Bud.

"Well…he's not a minor anymore; so technically, I ain't supposed to say anything. But…he's in a bit of trouble, Esther."

"What now?"

"Want to tell her about it, Rusty?"

"I don't know what you're talking about."

Bud looked over at Esther.

"Rusty…" Esther moved toward her son.

"Get away from me," Rusty said.

"He needs to stick around, Esther." Bud put his hand on the doorknob and looked at Rusty. "If you aren't around when Alex gets here, you will be in much worse trouble. Be here."

After Bud had driven out the driveway, Rusty left the kitchen and went back up the stairs. Several minutes later, he came down carrying something in his hand and went into the bathroom. Esther stood with her back to the sink, watching the bathroom door. She did not hear the usual gurgle from the toilet that he made when he urinated.

Rusty stayed in the bathroom. She heard him flush the toilet a number of times. He came out empty-handed.

"I'm going out."

"Bud Hemmings said you were not to go anywhere."

"Yeah. Screw Bud. I'm outta here."

"Tell me what this is about, Rusty. I want to know before Alex MacAllister shows up here later looking for you. What kind of trouble are you in now?"

Rusty went to the refrigerator and took out a bottle of Black Label beer. He opened it on the edge of the sink, allowing the bottle cap to roll across the floor. He drank from the bottle. Then he took the last four bottles from the refrigerator and put them in a paper bag.

"Give me some money."

Esther looked at her purse on the kitchen table.

"I need a few bucks," said Rusty.

She went to her purse and picked it up. She clutched it to her chest, briefly. Then sat down at the table and opened it. She took out a five dollar bill and handed it to him.

"I need more than that."

She gave him her last ten dollar bill and closed her purse.

Rusty looked at it and then back at her. "That's it?"

"I bought groceries. That's the end of the money, Rusty."

He stuffed the money into his front pockets, finished his bottle of beer and left. She heard the car start up and she bolted for the door. She stepped outside. The door slammed shut on her fingers. She yelped, pulled her fingers loose and ran out into the driveway, holding onto her hand. She cried.

"Rusty! No...don't take the car..." And then, softer and weaker, to nobody in particular, "I need the car."

But he backed into the street and screeched the tires, driving toward the village square. He was gone.

Bud was a little younger than Alex. Not by much, but he couldn't shake the feeling that he knew most folks felt, being around Alex. Didn't matter, your age. He sort of made you feel like you were one of his kids. Bud guessed the word was paternal. You felt like he should be your father.

He knew that Alex was a good man. The kind you could not help trusting. He had a certain decency about him. He knew, also, that Alex had attended some college when he returned from overseas. And even though he had not finished, he was regarded by most folks as intelligent—a bookish sort of man.

As Bud sat in Alex's kitchen, he watched Annie's face and eyes following Alex's every move. Bud was certain that this was not a good thing for Alex. This kind of thing had BAD written all over it.

He said, "You want that I should look around for Rusty?"

"Nope. He'll show up." Alex went into his bedroom and shut the door.

Annie stared at the door. She turned to Bud.

"What's going on, Bud?"

Bud thought for a moment, then he said, "Annie, I don't know what I should say. In fact, I don't know too much anyway."

"He must've told you something. He came home in a rush. Said that he was going to be gone for the rest of the day, maybe real late."

"Yup. The state police spoke with him today. They got something for him to do."

"What? What do they want him to do?"

Bud was silent. He looked at Annie and then at the bedroom door.

"It's not dangerous, is it?"

"Well..."

"Bud...?"

"No. It shouldn't be dangerous for him."

Annie sat quietly, holding onto her hands, wiping them occasionally on her apron.

When Alex had arrived home from Korea, he had used some of his savings to buy this rifle. It was a Remington and the scope was the best they made at that time. Clear and quick to sight on an object. Especially effective for moving targets

He had planned to use it for hunting, but never had. He had, instead, done considerable target shooting with it. He liked to shoot. In fact, he liked the Remington a great deal. It had a smooth action and it was lightweight. It was slim and compact, not bulky and bony like some bolt action rifles could be. The .30-06 made it a powerful gun for almost any game, had he ever used it for that purpose, or any purpose, other than target shooting.

He removed it from the case. It was like new. The barrel still had a light film of oil on it. He kept it maintained. The stock was a blond walnut, smooth and polished. He sat on the edge of the bed and placed the rifle across his lap. He stroked the stock with his right hand. He picked the gun up and held it with the butt of the stock against the inside of his upper right thigh.

He opened the bolt, checked the chamber and closed it. Then he opened the chamber again, held the trigger in and removed the bolt. He then held the gun up to look down the barrel, with the butt-end facing the window for the lighting.

The barrel glistened with oil, the rifling deep and twisting. He placed the rifle down on the bed, replaced the bolt and reached into the closet for the ammunition. He took out the three green boxes—Remington Ammunition—.30-06, 180 grain—printed in yellow lettering on the side. He placed them on the bed beside of the rifle.

Then he stood back and looked down at these items on his bed. They had offered him a rifle. He declined, choosing to use his own. He was familiar with this rifle and scope, even if the new ones were supposed to be better. He knew this rifle.

When Alex put the gun back in its case, he slipped the ammunition into his small gym bag. He had a handgun that was issued to him that he kept locked in the glove compartment of his car. He took it out only to oil it and target shoot. He had never needed it for anything job related.

*Strange*, he thought, *I end up using my own rifle after all. Just like I use my own car. The one thing the town gave me to use on the job...my pistol, a .38 Colt, I have never used.*

Alex came out of his room and walked through the kitchen, carrying his rifle in the case and the small gym bag. He sat the gym bag on the counter top. Annie stood up, walked over to the screen door and held it open.

"Thanks, Annie," he said, and walked out to his car. He placed the rifle on the back seat. He returned to the kitchen.

"Are you going to need something for later? Sandwiches? Coffee?" Annie asked.

Alex noticed that his wife's eyes were teary. He said, "Sure. That would be great, Annie. I may be a little late."

Annie went to the stove and started a pot of coffee.

Bud watched this in silence.

"Bud. Get a hold of Doug and tell him what's up. When he gets out of work later, he can plan to take my shift tonight. I'll be on-call tomorrow."

"I'll cover the on-call tomorrow, Alex."

"Okay. That would be fine. Thanks."

Alex went to the refrigerator and took out some bologna and mustard. He took out the bread and slapped several pieces of the cold cuts onto four slices of bread, took the yellow jar of French's mustard, removed the cover, and using a table knife, he spread large scoops of mustard onto the meat. He covered them each with another slice of bread and wrapped them in wax paper. He put all of this into a paper bag with an apple and scrunched up the paper bag noisily. Annie gave him a thermos with coffee.

Alex gave her a kiss on the cheek. He grabbed his gym bag.

She said in his ear, "You want some cookies?"

"Nope," he said. "The apple is fine."

He started out the screen door and turned. "See you tomorrow, Bud."

He left.

He could not recall The Speedway not being here. It had to have been built during his lifetime. He did remember when they put in the new bleachers. That had only been a short time ago. The stock car races had not been an attraction for him.

He had only attended but a few races over the years. The track was not large. The short, cyclic activity of the cars—the track was so short it always seemed to him that the cars were in a continuous circle—and the loud, jarring noise of the vehicles simply did not appeal to him as a form of entertainment.

As frequently as he passed The Speedway, only a few miles out of Cold Brook Mills, he rarely gave it more than a glance. It was sometimes a problem if he came through as a race was ending. Traffic would come to a near halt, and the short drive to Cold Brook could turn into a long, frustrating traffic jam. Most locals had learned to take other back roads at those times.

There was a breeze this afternoon; the sun was in and out from behind large, drifting white clouds. It was warm. Alex had made himself comfortable at the top of the empty bleachers. No race today. He was the only person in the entire complex.

There were some pigeons on the top railing a few feet to his left. They cooed, bobbed their heads, and tipped them sideways to see him better. The only other sound he had identified was the clinking of the metal clips on the ropes to the flagpole as the breeze moved the cord.

He turned and looked back down the rows of seats. He looked away, back at his hands and the equipment that he had spread out on the bleacher seat. It surprised him that he had become so winded climbing the narrow steps to the top row. It was obvious to him that he had to lose some weight. His height often disguised his being overweight. But, Annie noticed.

Alex made a vow to exercise more, starting next week. And to stop sneaking pastries into his lunches. Annie kept taking them out and he would sneak them back in. He turned and looked down into the parking area. It wasn't too bad if he didn't look straight down at the ground. He had never been good at coping with heights. That was one reason he had stayed out of the airborne units in the Army.

Now, from the top row of the bleachers, he avoided looking straight down and, instead, would only acknowledge to himself that he was high up. There were no cars in the lot, of course, and his view to the main road, Route 26, was completely unobstructed for perhaps as much as a half-mile in each direction. That seemed like a lot to him, but the distance was considerable.

It was a straight, direct route past The Speedway on Route 26. No traffic lights. No homes. No shops or stores. No roads coming into Route 26, except for the entrance and exit to the parking lot. Nothing but The Speedway and lots of woods on either side of the road.

He rested the rifle barrel on the folded blanket he had placed on the top seat of the bleachers and, one more time, he sighted quickly to a small notice tacked to a tree across from the bleachers. He could read the print. "*LOST MY KITTY. GRAY TIGER, FEMALE ONE YEAR OLD CALL JAN AT 5884.*"

He moved the rifle to another point he had singled out further back, to the south, on the road. It was a small, hand-printed sign that said "*ROLARSKATING*." He knew that the small rollerskating rink further down the road had been cleared out and shut down.

Then he swung the rifle quickly in the opposite direction, to the north, focusing on a yellow fire hydrant. He stopped and took a deep breath. He experienced a feeling of lightheadedness. For a second, things didn't seem...well, real. He thought, *Who am I? What am I doing?*

In the war, he had been designated a sniper. He was quick and extremely accurate with a rifle. He had not realized this skill had any purpose other than making him an exceptional hunter when he was a young man.

The Army, of course, had noticed it quickly though. He had been encouraged to practice frequently and given special time for this. At first, he had enjoyed the extra opportunity to shoot. He liked guns and he enjoyed the skill, even talent, which he apparently possessed. So taking more time to target practice was a privilege that he had appreciated. It also had taken up his spare time before being sent overseas, and this helped with the homesickness he felt for his family and new wife. But, that had all changed.

The first man he ever killed was a Korean soldier of course. He had been scanning a ridge of rocks from his perch and had spotted him vividly in the rifle's scope. He could still see him today; he did not need to close his eyes.

He recalled that when he had seen him, through the scope, remove his winter cap (it had been one of those strangely warm, winter days) this man looked like a boy. He could not have been a day over sixteen years old. He had not a doubt that he would kill him. He had known that it would happen, after all...they were both in a war...they were enemies. But, he had watched him in the scope for several seconds.

The young Korean had worn thick spectacles. He was a little walleyed. Alex had smiled a little, thinking of the boy as the geek of his class maybe. Then he had squeezed the trigger.

He had tried over the years to remember making that decision—to pull the trigger. Had he really made that choice? He could not recall being cognizant of any sound the rifle had made—could not remember feeling the punch of the stock against his shoulder. But a small, black spot had appeared on the boy's forehead, just above his right eye.

The thick spectacles had flown off his face. Alex had continued to watch the scene in his scope. A surprised look had flickered across the boy's face—his mouth opened wide, his nostrils flared, his eyes rolled up, and then he had crumbled like a puppet whose strings were cut from above. His head had snapped a little, but he wasn't flung backwards, he hadn't grabbed himself and collapsed, rolling in pain like in the movies, he had simply crumbled. And, like a gruesome halo, the white snow turned a brilliant, dark red around the boy's head.

There were times when he wanted to tell Annie about this. One time, just a short while ago, sitting in the living room, he and Annie were still laughing as the credits to *The Jack Benny Show* were rolling, and they heard Jack say, "Rochester!" He had almost blurted it out: "*Annie...I shot this boy in the head. I killed him.*"

Another time, when his parents were up visiting and his daughter Phoebe was teasing to return to Florida with them to spend the remainder of the summer and start school late, he had said that she couldn't. She argued valiantly, a well-spoken, beautiful and convincing child, even at fourteen.

He had just finished that sad case in Cold Brook Mills, around 1960 or so, in the autumn of the year, where the father of several young children had committed suicide. The young girl in that family had been about Phoebe's age at the time. It still bothered him; the poverty...the poverty of emotion the parents in that family had for their children. The father abandoned them in the most abusive way possible. Their mother was cold and hard. He had clung to his daughter for months following that case.

Alex's parents had tried to plead Phoebe's case with him, also. He had wanted to say yes. He had wanted to give his parents and his daughter the joy of the moment... "Yes! Go! Enjoy being with each other, the ones you love." Instead, he had flatly stated, "*No. You are not going. —Because...once, I shot this boy in the head and killed him. I took away his life. Forever.*" He had *nearly* said this. He had not. But, it had nearly fallen out of his mouth as he finished saying that she could not go to be with the grandparents she loved so much and saw so infrequently.

This day, now, sitting on the top row of these bleachers, Alex still wished he could do that over. That he could say, "*Go. Be together.*" And to his parents, "*Love Phoebe; spoil her, while she is still a child.*"

Suddenly it occurred to Alex that he could just walk away. Take his rifle and go home. He could curl up on the sofa with Annie, a good book and a cup of coffee. He would tell her about this day and about the boy he had killed in Korea. Simultaneously, he knew that he would not leave. He knew that he had to do this.

What was it that kept him from telling Annie...or anyone for that matter, about what he had done in Korea? Was it shame? No. He did not feel shame. It was something else...more like...fear. It was a fear that was so deeply rooted in his psyche that it was not always understood as fear.

It was a certainty that a sin had been committed. A sin that was not forgivable, in the sense that it could never be reversed. That entire generations, entire family histories, had been impacted by this one act. This single act of sin.

He prayed, *God. Help me understand what I am about to do.*

Alex watched as the truck pulled into place and the crane tipped and dropped the trailer onto its side in the middle of the road. It had begun. Again, he had the sensation that this was not real, that this was happening inside a space of time that was not within his control. That, in fact, *it had already happened.*

Abruptly, he had an insight that deja vu was not a recognition that something had happened before...but, that it was already here...that it had always been here; that this was the nature of time and space and that, in a fleeting second, he had somehow stumbled upon this familiar moment, this point in time, and simply recognized it.

The man pulled into the grove of birch trees and sat quietly. He smoked a cigarette. He waited. He could see the road from here. A few cars and some trailer trucks went by. No cops. He waited. He finished the cigarette and threw the butt out his open window.

He reached up to the rearview mirror and adjusted it so that he could see her face. She looked back at him. Her eyes were red and her cheeks tear-stained and smudged. He had taken the tape from her mouth because he wanted to be able to see her face. He liked looking at her.

"We lost 'em," he said. He looked at her as if he expected her to be as pleased as he was about his cleverness.

She did not respond. She moved on the seat.

"Do not sit up! You stay down," he said. He turned in his seat and reached over to check the cords that tied her hands and feet. He touched her. She closed her eyes tight and pressed her lips together.

He smiled at this.

"Hey!" He squeezed her nose hard. "Hey!"

She opened her eyes. He was holding a hunting knife inches from her face. She made a noise and squirmed on the seat. He grinned…it excited him. *They always do that when I use the knife*, he thought.

There was a .38 Smith and Wesson revolver on the seat beside of him. He put the knife down. He picked up the pistol and waved it at her.

"Stay down. In a couple of hours, we'll be in Canada. They won't cross over. Hell…they won't even know where we went."

Last night in Pennsylvania, when that cop had pulled him over, he had been dozing at the wheel. He thought, *Good thing I got stopped, might've had an accident. Not so good for the cop though.* When he came to the window, he had simply shot him in the face. He thought, *God—it was so damned easy.*

But, it had not killed him quickly as he had thought it would. He had had to get out of the car, drag the cop over to the ditch and shoot him in the eye. The cop had been conscious through the whole thing. He had begged him not to kill him. Said he had a kid and a wife.

The man was amazed that the cop was still awake after shooting him in the face; he was bleeding from the head wound. The man had shrugged, then he took the cop's own pistol from his holster, pointed the gun point blank at the cop's eyeball, and pulled the trigger.

The girl had screamed. That was when he had put the tape on her mouth. But he liked looking at her, so he took it off later and had sex with her in a parking area, somewhere just outside of Pennsylvania. They had had sex a lot over the past several days. She was pretty. He liked her. But he knew he would have to kill her. That was okay though, it could be fun, if he took his time and didn't have to rush it.

He had gotten through two separate roadblocks. At one, he had run right over the trooper who had tried to get out of the way. *Not quick enough*, he smiled. That was in Massachusetts and New Hampshire. Now he was nearly in Maine, headed to Canada. He had not seen a single cop for a while now. He had been pulling over and hiding in different places. He decided he would get onto Route 95 in Maine and then onto Route 26 and head straight up to Canada. There were remote places where he could cross the border. He would drive slowly and not draw attention to himself.

He checked the young girl in the back seat, started the white Dodge Charger, the powerful engine rumbled, and he pulled out into the road. The girl started crying.

"Shut up," the man said.

It was getting late. Alex began to think that maybe they had made a mistake. Perhaps the man was not going to come this route at all. Maybe he was not headed for Canada. He picked up the binoculars and scanned the road to the south. No vehicles in sight.

He wondered if the man would think that was odd. No cars on the road, and a truck overturned in the middle of the road. It seemed too obvious. He scanned up the road, past the overturned trailer truck. He could see a couple of troopers in the woods with rifles. Further up, he knew that there were four cruisers waiting, but he could not see them.

Alex yawned and put the binoculars back down on the bleacher seat. He glanced down the road one more time and saw the car. He grabbed for the binoculars and knocked them over. They fell off the bleachers and to the ground. Alex watched them as they hit the dirt and made a small burst of dust.

He reached carefully for his rifle. He brought the scope up to his eye. Pointing the scope toward the road, he picked up the car. It was the white Dodge Charger. He noticed that it had slowed nearly to a stop. He focused on the driver. He could make him out, but not clearly.

He watched as the Charger moved slowly toward the overturned truck. As the car approached nearly in front of Alex, he looked for the girl. He could see feet in the back seat, and legs...but he could not tell if it was the girl. He also knew he could not waste time trying to positively identify her. He put the sight back onto the man.

The man had light hair and a short crew cut. An almost shaved head. He also had a light-colored goatee. This was the man. Alex put the cross hair of the scope on the man's temple. Almost casually, the man looked over at the bleachers...directly at Alex.

The man's glance, magnified in the scope, startled Alex; he blinked into the scope. And suddenly the Charger lurched forward; the man yanked it to the rear and into the ditch behind the truck. Dirt spewed and spun behind the Charger as it twisted sideways and emerged, skidding, from behind the trailer. The man was having difficulty getting back onto the pavement. The car banged and bounced around.

Alex struggled to find the man in his scope. He stayed calm, doing his best to hold the scope on the interior of the car. Then, for only a second, the man's head appeared in the crosshair and Alex fired.

Alex met Bud at the front door. Alex was holding a cup of coffee and was still wearing the same clothes he had on when he left the day before.

"Morning, Bud."

"Alex."

Alex opened the screen door and Bud walked into the kitchen.

"Morning, Annie."

"Bud. Seems like you were just here."

Bud smiled. "Yes. Guess I'm bein' a real pest."

Annie smiled back at Bud, glanced over at her husband, then poured Bud a cup of coffee. She added one sugar and a little cream.

"Thanks, Annie. Alex," Bud said, "glad you were around yesterday." He looked at Annie. "A lot of folks feel the same way."

Alex was quiet. He had been lost in thought all morning. He looked up at Bud. He was thinking of something he had read somewhere…Hemingway maybe.

Bud said, "Put that guy out of all of our miseries." Bud looked over at Annie and then back at Alex. "And the girl is safe, Alex. Back with her folks. Thanks to you."

Alex sipped his coffee.

"He was an evil guy, Alex."

Alex nodded. "He was that." He leaned back in his chair, then sat forward, leaning on the table top. He looked up at the clock and back at his coffee mug. His eyes were burning, he rubbed them and sighed.

Unable to remember Hemingway's exact words, he said softly, "But, just being against evil doesn't necessarily make you good."

Bud watched Alex. He had not tasted his coffee yet; he sipped on the mug. It was quiet. They listened to Boots snoring in the next room.

Then Bud said, "Got some bad news for ya."

Alex put the cup of coffee on the table and looked over at his friend. "What's up, Bud?"

"Ricky Larabbee was killed last night."

Alex shook his head. He didn't speak.

"Car crash on outer Main Street. He was speeding, went into that sharp corner before the little cement bridge and lost control. Car turned over, threw him out, landed on top of him." Bud added, "We decided to let you sleep...you know, after yesterday and all. Besides, there was nothing you could've done. Doug did the paperwork. I covered the rest."

Alex was still shaking his head slowly. "Just a kid... Anyone else hurt?"

"Well," said Bud, "the Coolidge boy and his cousin Jeff Garner were in the car. They were not seriously hurt, but pretty bunged up." He watched Alex's face. "Thing is, we think there was another car involved. The Garner kid said something and then shut up."

"What did he say?"

"He mentioned Rusty Carver's name. Said they were drag racing."

Alex pushed his chair out from behind the table. He stood up quickly and walked into the bedroom. He left the door open. Bud saw him change out of his dress shirt and put on a dark t-shirt. He came back out to the kitchen.

"Annie. I'll be back later."

He went out the door into the driveway. Bud followed.

"Where is Rusty now?"

"I'm not sure. Home...probably."

Alex got into his Galaxy and closed the door. Bud strolled over to the other side and climbed in. Alex turned the key. Nothing happened. He tried again. Still no sound. He sighed and slammed a hand on the steering wheel.

"Well, Bud. How about your car? Are you gonna offer or not?"

"Depends. What are you gonna do?"

Alex thought for a second. "I don't know. But first I'm going to find that little shit."

They pulled into the driveway and Bud turned off his engine. They walked to the side door and knocked. Rusty opened the door.

"Where's your mother, Rusty?" Alex asked.

"Working."

"You alone?"

"Yeah."

Alex pushed past Rusty and into the kitchen. Rusty turned and Bud grabbed his shoulder and led him into the kitchen.

"Sit." Bud pushed him toward a chair.

"I don't feel like sitting." Rusty leaned against the sink.

Alex walked over to stand directly in front of Rusty. He said, "Sit in the chair, Rusty."

Rusty hesitated, then moved around Alex and sat in the chair at the kitchen table.

"Alex..." Bud started. Alex ignored him.

"Where were you last night?"

Rusty did not answer.

"Were you racing with Ricky Larabbee?"

Rusty was quiet.

Alex leaned over and put his face in Rusty's. Their noses nearly touched.

"Listen, you little..." Alex stood up straight. He ran a hand across his face and rubbed his eyes. "Rusty, I'm going to ask you some questions, and you are going to answer them."

"I saw Ricky last night," Rusty blurted.

"And...?"

The kitchen became quiet. The faucet dripped into the sink, *tunk, tunk*. Alex waited. Bud watched Alex and did not move. He stood beside Rusty. Alex stood up straight. He repeated, "And...?"

Bud looked at Alex. Alex did not take his eyes off from Rusty.

Bud said, "We took a look at your mom's car at the mill parking lot. We already know, Rusty."

"Am I in trouble?"

Alex pulled a chair up and sat facing Rusty.

"Son," Alex started, "Ricky is dead. I need to know what happened last night."

"Am I gonna in be in a lot of trouble?"

"Probably."

Rusty hung his head and looked at his lap. His left leg was bouncing on the ball of his foot. He started to move his head from side to side. He said, "We got some beer from Bucky. He gets us beer sometimes."

"Yeah. I know that." Alex looked over at Bud then back at Rusty.

Rusty was talking so quietly that Alex had to lean over toward him. "Billy Coolidge came over to Rick's...he had Jeff with him. We drank some beer. We didn't have that much. None of us had any money and we have to give Bucky some for buying the beer." He stopped. "So...we didn't have that much. We listened to 45s but the damned records kept skipping...Ricky never took care of his records...so we turned on the radio...Rick's dad is deaf as old Dummy...so he didn't care."

Bud still stood beside of Rusty's chair. Alex was leaning forward, his arms folded on his thighs. "Go ahead, Rusty," he said.

Rusty was silent for another long minute. Neither Bud or Alex made any comment or movement. They watched Rusty.

"Ricky…" Rusty whispered, "He was my friend."

"I know, son." Alex put a hand on Rusty's shoulder.

"I…I'm sorry, Alex." Rusty started to cry. Alex kept his hand on his shoulder. And then Rusty leaned forward, put his arms around Alex's neck and sobbed.

Several minutes went by. Alex held onto Rusty in an awkward position, and then re-positioned himself so that he could hold him closer. He held Rusty as he would a young child. Rusty wept for a while and then became quiet. Alex continued to hold him.

Alex thought about how Ricky had always been in his dooryard working on some old clunker. He had quit school years ago. Just as Rusty had done. Usually the cars he had were never roadworthy, even after he worked on them. They were just junks that he picked up to tinker with. Probably not that good of a mechanic even, but it gave the boy something to do, when he wasn't running his little motor boat up and down the river that is. He was never in any trouble.

His dad was old, nearly blind and hard of hearing and never left the house. Ricky's mother had died a long while ago. Ricky was a motherless kid before he ever knew he had a mother. She had been mentally ill. Folks said she was retarded.

Ricky and Rusty had one thing in common that made Rusty think that Ricky and he were friends…they were both going nowhere. But the difference was that Rusty had been headed in a different direction his whole life: trouble. Alex wondered what had happened today…yesterday really. Something was changing this town. He had been noticing this for a long while.

Alex stretched out. He lay quietly. He listened. The scanner was not making noises. Alex thought, *This is nice.* He had made up his mind about some things.

He looked over to the other side of the bed. Boots was not there. Then he remembered that Phoebe was home for a while. He rolled over and sat up, rubbing a hand through his hair. He pulled on his khaki pants and walked into the kitchen. Annie was sitting at the table reading the paper.

"Good morning," she said, glancing over the top of the page. "Coffee's on."

He looked over at the coffee pot on the stove. He walked over and poured a cup. Then, holding his cup, he walked over to Phoebe's bedroom door and opened it. He looked in. Phoebe was on the floor with a pillow under her head and a blanket thrown over her. Her bare feet were sticking out. Her toenails were painted purple.

On the bed, Boots sprawled out across the entire middle of the mattress. He opened one eye, picked up his head and looked over at Alex. Then he made a noise, dropped his head back onto the bed and went back to sleep. Alex smiled.

"So..." he sat at the table and looked over at his wife. "So..." he said again.

No answer. Alex waited. Annie read. Alex did not read the paper often. Hardly ever really. He was mildly annoyed when she did this.

"So..." he said. "What are we up to today?"

Annie pulled the newspaper down just a little and looked over at him. "Reading the paper...?"

"Besides that."

She put the newspaper down on the table. She recognized something in her husband's face.

"How about we take Phoebe over to the lake? We could grill out and do some boating. Maybe fish. You want to do that? I can take a book along and you two can fish."

Alex smiled. He liked that idea. Phoebe was a better fisherman than he was. He always got a kick out of that. He looked out the kitchen window. The sun was shining and it was a warm day. *These kinds of days*, he thought, *are hard to come by. Gotta take advantage of them.*

# perfidy—dark, simple

It was early afternoon, and everyone spoke of the beauty of this day, an early June day that previewed the summer. A purple scent of lilacs filled the air, and the women who did not work in the papermill worked outside in their flower gardens, or sat sipping cool lemonade in their summer lawn chairs that they dug out of their sheds to set up on their lawns, and in their driveways.

Their men, the ones who waited to go in for the second shift, tinkered with their lawn mowers or napped under the trees before work. The blue sky was cloudless. People did sweat on these first summer days in New England, but for now, they did not mind. Winter is long and summer is short. Later, in August and September, some of these same folks would curse the heat and humidity and wish for an early fall.

The two women sat on a blanket on the banking of the lawn in front of an apartment house. They wore shorts and blouses without sleeves. They sat directly in the sun. One of the women leaned back on her hands, her head turned up, her face into the sun.

They were at that age that young people reach, as adults, when they still thought that being old was a long ways away. They wanted to be tanned like the young women in the magazines who lived in California, the same ones who were dressed for summer everyday of the year.

"There's that girl," said the woman with short blonde hair.

The other woman, who was not blonde but had her brown hair pulled up in a bun, said, "Who?"

"That woman's daughter."

"What woman?"

"You know..."

The young woman opened her eyes and looked at her friend. She squinted and covered her brow with one hand to shield her eyes. She followed her friend's gaze to the young girl walking down the hill in front of them. She said, "I don't know who you mean."

"Her mother is the sister of Pete's wife...on the hill."

"Which hill? The whole town is hills."

"Across the bridge...right over there." She pointed across the river.

The woman shrugged, leaned back and made a noise. Pete was one of the shift supervisors at the mill. She did not like Pete. She closed her eyes again. Then she opened them and watched as the young girl walked past them.

There were two boys walking close behind her. She recognized one of the boys, he was in the eighth grade. He lived near her place.

"She never has any girls with her, just boys."

They looked at each other and raised their eyebrows.

The woman with the brown hair that was up in a bun continued to watch the girl and the two boys walk down the hill. The other woman leaned back and closed her eyes.

"Where does she live?"

The blonde said, "Well...not far from you. Her mother moved into the apartment above the Bolduc's." She added, "Boy...she's a piece of work that one."

"What about her?"

"Just moved up here with her kids, from out of state. Rumor is...to be near family, I guess." She stretched out her legs. "No husband. But she really likes the younger men." She raised her eyebrows and pursed her lips. She made a slight nodding motion toward the young girl as she passed.

Her friend glanced at her and looked away. She found this facial expression to be annoying. It made her friend's face look puckered, and it accentuated the lines around her mouth.

She glanced at her friend's legs stretched out in front of her on the blanket. She did admire those legs though. She looked at her own. She studied them and compared them to her friend's. She asked, "What about the husband?"

"How the hell do I know that?"

The woman with brown hair watched as the girl and two boys disappeared around the street corner onto Birch Street. She stared after them. Then she said, without turning toward the other woman, "What about her kids?"

"According to Diane, she's got a brood...this girl's brother hangs out with a bad crowd. She has some other kids, but they're older. They don't live around here." She added, "The family's poor."

"Yeah…who isn't?"

"Their mother doesn't work."

"There's plenty of work at the mill."

"Yeah. I know."

"She's pretty. The girl, I mean." She was still staring at the corner where the girl had turned onto Birch Street.

"Yeah."

"She better be careful though."

"What do you mean?"

She was thinking about the way the girl dressed and the way she had moved her body as she walked past them. She thought that the boys noticed too. "You know…" she said.

"Yeah. Like her mother. She had better be careful too." The blond raised her eyebrows and pursed her lips again.

Her friend looked over at her and stared at the lines around her mouth. The blonde woman caught her gaze, and her friend looked away but with a gesture that was too smooth and took too long. The blonde looked down her nose toward her mouth. She raised a hand and touched her face at the corners of her mouth. Then she wiped the back of her hand across it and looked at her hand. She looked back at the other woman, but her friend now sat staring at a place somewhere across the street.

They both leaned back on their elbows and put their faces into the sunshine.

The woman with blonde hair said, "It's hot." She kept her eyes closed.

"Yes."

"Andy working today?"

"Yup. Second shift."

"Wanna come over for dinner? Ralph is cooking out. We're having chicken."

"Sure. I'll bring the beer."

They did not talk. They sat in the sun. The woman with her brown hair in a bun thought about the cookout. She thought, *Andy is working a double. Ralph is going to be there.* She thought Ralph had said last night that he was working this afternoon. He would be surprised to see her. She would like to be at the cookout without Andy. She would help Ralph with the chicken.

She reclined onto the banking and stretched her arms out above her head, running her fingers into the thick, uncut grass. She wanted to tan—instead, she would get a sunburn.

A streetlight right outside her shadeless window and some light coming beneath her door from the kitchen made it possible to see things in her room at night. She stared up at the ceiling. She had the covers down. She wore only her underwear and a t-shirt.

The cracks in the ceiling plaster made designs, which she studied and attempted to form into patterns or sketches. One area of ceiling was sagging. She wondered if it would crash down on her floor during the night.

The girl heard them coming up the steps outside on the porch balcony. Their apartment was on the second floor. She hated that her bedroom window was on the balcony.

The day after they had moved here she had told her mother she hated her room and wanted her brother's room on the other side of the apartment instead. Her mother ignored her. Her brother slept like a rock. He would never hear people outside in the parking lot, or on the steps, or outside his window. But he would not change rooms with her either. They had fought. He had told her, "Tough shit."

Now she looked out the window through the rusted screen. She watched her mother kiss the man. They both wobbled and nearly fell off the steps. Then her mother laughed and hit him on the chest. The girl looked at the man, his face visible from the streetlight. She did not recognize him. A new one.

He did not look young to the girl, but he did look younger than her mother. He had a badly pocked face. Nearly bald, he had his hair pulled back into a skimpy ponytail. His belly was big. He made a loud flatulence, and they both laughed. A familiar, sour beer odor came through her window. She rolled over and pulled the covers up to her chin.

At school today she had talked with Morrie, the cute boy she liked. He had asked her to go to the school dance. She had told him no. She had just smoked a joint with Billy and Junior out back of the teacher's parking area and had felt really stoned. Her mother had said Morrie was a Jew. Her mother said she knew this because his family had money and he had a big nose.

The girl pointed out that her mother had a big nose. Her mother had said that was because she was part Penobscot Indian and reminded her daughter that they were the first Americans. The girl didn't care. She hoped Morrie would ask her to the dance again. This time she would say yes.

Whenever she saw him at school, he would smile. Morrie was in high school...a grade ahead of her. But he seemed shy. She was not shy. She knew that the boys at school talked about her. They said things about her that made the other girls look at her and talk about her. Some of them wanted to hang around her because the boys wanted to be with her and they wanted to be around the boys. But most of the girls did not want to be around her and they would stop talking when she walked by them.

She knew she was pretty, and her young curves were flattering, so she dressed in tight jeans. She fought with her mother to buy her more clothes, she hated being poor. Sometimes she would go into the department store and try on clothes and steal them. She figured this was okay because she needed them. She also wore her blouse unbuttoned almost to her small, young breasts. The boys liked that and paid a lot of attention to her.

Morrie was different. He looked at her breasts, like the other boys, but he was nice to her. He did not act stupid. He just acted like he liked her.

Mr. Gorin—the kids called him Mr. Groin—had spoken to her in the hallway today at school and asked to see her in his office. When she had walked into the school office, Betty Bryant stood in front of the files, her arms full of folders.

Betty, a senior, was an honor student in the commercial course. She could type fast. She got to work in the office at the school two afternoons a week, for the experience. She had long red hair, and except for some acne, she had a pale beauty...and she had big boobs. She was poor also, like the girl, but the girl thought that was no excuse to dress so pukey...she dressed dumb.

Betty wore long skirts and sweaters, like ladies wore...even in June when it was hot out. And she kept her blouse buttoned all the way to the top. Betty liked to push her boobs out when she was around boys, but she didn't unbutton her buttons for them to see anything. The girl thought that if she had big boobs, she would show them off.

Everyone knew that Betty looked up all of the kid's files and spread rumors about what the teachers wrote about them in their private records. Betty had turned to look at her when she entered the room, and she did not look away, but watched her walk all the way across the room to the principal's door. The girl had just glared back at her.

"You can go in now," Betty had said.

"I know that," the girl had said back to her and continued to glare at her, trying not to look at those boobs. The kids talked about that...how hard it could be to talk to Betty without looking at those boobs. Especially the boys.

It proved to be an impossible challenge for the boys. They had fits of laughter over it. Some were just shy, and when Betty would corner them to talk to them, those shy boys would just blush until it looked like their faces would burst into blisters. Betty pretended not to notice. But she had a smile on her face all the time when she talked with the boys.

In Mr. Groin's office, she had sat in a chair that was placed beside of his desk. He had looked up from his work, glanced at her, then looked back at the papers on his desk. He had a pencil stuck behind both ears. She had snickered and almost laughed at this. Traces of marshmallow lingered around his mouth, *Probably from his bag lunch*, she had decided. He had looked very important and busy.

"Do you know why you are in my office, young lady?" he had asked.

"Nope." She had tried to stop a smile that creeped across her face. She had to look away from him. She had chewed her gum as obviously as she could manage and still talk.

He had turned to look at her. His eyes moved down her face to her chest. "You need to button up."

She had watched him. He had not looked away from her chest. She had continued to smile. She had felt stoned as she sat in that chair. She had felt nervous too. But that did not interfere with the smooth feeling the dope left her with. It had bothered her that he kept looking at her. But she sort of liked it too.

She never wore a bra and the white blouse was very loose. She did not have much to show. She was too young and too small, but he had kept looking, and she did not say anything.

"I said," he finally had looked up at her face and then back at her chest, "you need to button your blouse up. I have had a number of complaints."

She had looked down at her blouse and buttoned it up to her neck. She had thought, *I bet it ain't the boys...probably Betty Boobs.* She had said, "Whatever."

"And lose the gum." He had gone back to his work. "You can leave."

But when she had glanced back at him from the door she caught him looking at her. At first he had not noticed her watching him. Then he had fumbled for a pencil and discovered that he had two, one behind each ear. One of them had dropped onto the desk and rolled to the edge, falling to the floor. He had ignored it and looked down at his desk and papers.

This had given her a strange feeling in her belly. She liked that men and boys looked at her, but she didn't like it very much.

Now she could hear her mother in the kitchen opening the refrigerator and laughing. She heard bottles making clinking noises. The table scraped across the floor. A chair fell over. The girl had to go to the bathroom. She did not want to get up and walk into the kitchen to go past the living room doorway to the bathroom. She did not want to have to see the man in the light. She did not mind if he wanted to see her in her underwear. She just didn't want to have to look at him.

The television blared. The newsman on the television talked about the war. He talked about how many boys had been killed today, the names of the places were strange but becoming familiar: Da Nang; Pleiku; Khe Sahn...

Some older boys she knew had gone away into the military. She didn't know about this war. She didn't care. She did want to know about whether Morrie might go away. She thought he was too young right now, but he might have to go later. She would talk to her sister about this.

Her sister was gone, though. But she would talk to her when she saw her again. She thought she missed her sister. She wasn't sure if she missed her. She wasn't sure if she missed anyone, really.

She wasn't sure if she missed her father. He was dead, and she didn't know for sure how he had died. Nobody talked about that. She didn't know him and she didn't care that she didn't know him.

She had seen a picture of him once. It was in a box under her mother's bed. She had found it one day when she was home alone. It had surprised her that he was so young-looking and skinny.

The visor of the military hat had covered some of his face, like it was too big. He was smiling. He wore a uniform, but she knew he did not ever go to a war; he did not die in a war. The picture was black and white. Although she had never asked her mother, or anyone else, she did wonder what color his eyes were. She didn't care...just curious. She didn't care much about anything, she thought—she was just curious about some things.

She no longer heard sounds from the kitchen. She got up, cracked her door open and peeked out. They sat on the sofa in the living room with the television on loud and the lights out. She watched as the man groped at her mother. Her mother kept pushing him off of her and laughing at him.

The girl crossed the room to the bathroom. She sat on the hopper and urinated. In her jacket there was a joint that Junior had given her after school. Actually, it was more like a big roach, since they had smoked most of it on the way home from school today. She decided to save it for the morning, before going to class.

She thought of the man in the next room with her mother. She wondered if she could see them from her room. She went back to her room and climbed back onto her bed. She listened to the noise from the next room: the television; her mother's pretend, girlish laughter; the man's moaning sounds; and outside, the sounds of occasional cars passing by the apartment house; some boys going by on the sidewalk, talking loud and vulgar...her mother's laughing, taunting voice...the girl dozed off.

It was quiet when her bedroom door opened. No television sounds. No light came from the kitchen. She saw her mother's figure come through the doorway, followed by the man.

"Shhh..." said her mother. The door closed. They undressed.

The girl moved over to the far edge of the bed and made room for them. Her mother had the man get into bed first. Her mother got in after him and pushed the sheet down.

Her mother whispered, "It's too goddamned hot."

The man pushed up against the girl's buttocks. He reached out a hand in the darkness and touched her back. He made a noise. He said, "What the...?" Then he was quiet and still. The girl pushed against his buttocks with hers. He moved to give her room. Minutes passed. The girl sighed out loud.

She heard her mother snore. Then her mother said, "Get off me..."

The man groaned. Her mother kicked her feet at the man. "Jesus. Leave me alone..." The bed moved abruptly. Her mother sat up. "I can't sleep in here." She left the room, closing the door behind her. She went into her own bedroom.

No sounds came from the next room or from the streets. The man did not move for several minutes. The girl rolled over onto her back. The man cleared his throat, then put a hand on her belly. He did not move his hand. She did not say anything.

Then he moved his hand under her t-shirt. He caressed her belly and moved his hand to her chest. He made a deep, trembling noise in his throat. The girl thought, *Men are really simple. Now, mom can get me those jeans at The Mart. If Morrie doesn't ask me to the dance, then I will ask him.*

Sometimes these men talked to her. Sometimes they didn't. She didn't care one way or the other...she was curious, though, if they knew who she was...if they cared who she was...she didn't care who they were though. They all smelled the same—the men that *she* brought home and brought to her room.

The boys didn't smell like that. Sometimes they smelled like beer, or pot, but they didn't smell like these men. Boys smelled...sweeter. These men brought the dark, coppery scent of strange, dangerous animals. It was not that she didn't like the smell of men, the scent was oddly appealing in a way that was not really pleasant. The threat of the force that they possessed frightened and excited her.

Cool, empty streets, quiet neighborhoods and the lateness of the night...all of this appealed to the girl's sense of liberty...lack of restrictions. The acrid odor of sulpher from the papermill hung strong in the night air. It burned the back of her throat. She thought that this mill was different than the mill in the other town they had lived in. That mill had no nasty smells.

She walked up the hill. She put her hand in her jean-jacket pocket and found the roach that Junior had given her. She took it out, found matches in the upper pocket and lit the roach up. She inhaled deep and held it. She looked up at the streetlight that was buzzing and flickering. She exhaled.

The sweet hemp smoke filled her with a pleasant amusement for the world. She hummed, walked, and thought that she felt pretty good. She wasn't sure she felt pretty good, but she thought that she did.

When the man had finished with her moments ago, he had been sweating and panting, sprawled on his back, she thought he was going to have a heart attack—he had thanked her. He had mumbled, "Thanks."

She didn't say anything back to him. She thought that it had been okay. Not great, it was never like that, but it was okay. She wondered when she did it with Morrie if it would be different. The thing was...some of the men, even when she was a little girl, would be nice to her, and some of them were just mean. It didn't seem to matter what she did or didn't do for them.

She didn't really care, though, that the man had thanked her. She had ignored him, rolled over, tried to find her underpants in the dark, gave up, pulled down her t-shirt and pretended to go to sleep. She had waited until he snored, then she had dressed and left the house.

She continued to walk up Birch Street. *Probably,* she thought, *Morrie and I will get married some day.* She thought about having children. They would have children, for sure. The girl wondered what it would be like to be a mother.

# surface of the moon

She knew that she would die tonight. Looking out of the window from the rear seat of her friend's car, she looked up at the night sky. The moon was full. A silent sky and a silent moon. Inside of the car the people were loud. They were all drunk. On the radio, Paul McCartney crooned his tune "My Love."

She looked at the man sitting beside her. Her friends had introduced her to him. She knew he was much younger than herself. She liked that.

She looked at each of her friends. They were all younger than her. Her nausea passed. The pain continued. But the pain had been there for a couple of days now and had gotten no worse. Just like a tooth that throbbed quietly, threateningly, and you just knew that when it came on…it would knock you onto your ass.

Her doctor had described to her how it would happen—what she would feel. He told her this so that she could get help, he had said. But she thought he was just trying to scare her into giving up her smoking and drinking.

He had told her for a long time now to stop smoking and drinking. She smoked and drank each day. She liked cigarettes. She liked beer. She saw no point in stopping the things that she enjoyed. After all, life is short. *You're gonna die of something eventually,* she thought.

She said this to her doctor. He had replied, "What about your kids?" She hadn't understood the question; she had asked him, "What about them?" He had just looked at her strangely and said nothing. Whenever she left his office, she would light up a cigarette and pick up a six-pack of beer. She would go home, drink, and sit there wondering why she kept going back to him.

He asked her questions and tried to make her think about things. But there was nothing to think about. It did make her think about needing a cigarette and another cold beer though. She had told her friends this. They had laughed with her.

Inside the bar they drank more and danced. She did not dance much. Only a couple of slow ones. The one song she could not resist dancing to was an old Johnny Tillotson song, and that line about the moon going behind a cloud. She held onto the young man's strong shoulders as she waltzed.

She sat at the table and watched as the young man now danced with her friend. She didn't mind that they danced with a slow grind. He could screw this girl tonight and leave her the hell alone. She just wanted to drink and have a good time. Period. That's all she ever had wanted.

The first time that she caught a glimpse of her husband sitting at the bar, it startled her so that she nearly had her heart attack right there at the table. But it was him. She had no doubt about it.

Now as she looked across the room at him, he looked directly back at her and smiled. He raised his chrome flask and tipped it toward her as he mouthed the words, "*A toast...*" It did not matter to her one whit that the man had been dead now for thirteen years. It was him. And it was real. She ignored him.

She knew that if she encouraged him he would come over to the table. He would get drunk and there would be a fight or some other explosion.

She reached in her purse for her Pall Mall cigarettes. She removed an envelope. It was a letter from her daughter. For some reason this daughter kept writing letters to her. She had not written back for quite a while.

She took the letter out now and opened the envelope. She unfolded the one page, lined, notebook paper. It was written in pencil. She read it.

*July 2, 1973*

*Momma,*

*How are you doing? Things are okay here. I wanted to drop you a line to see if you had received my other letters. You probably lost my address, if I know you. Ha.*

*Anyways, Danny is working a lot of hours and is gone a lot. Both of the kids are doing fine, but Katie is growing like a weed. She loves her little brother. Little Danny is not so little. He is a chubby baby. Katie has her father's blue, blue eyes. She is beautiful. Little Danny has my eyes, he is darker and he is a doll, too. Katie loves her little brother and she helps me with him.*

*I hope everything is okay with you. I knew that you were not feeling so well a while ago. Harry wrote and said that he and Kelly were worried that you were not taking good care of yourself. He said that you and Kelly had had another bad fight. Sometimes I wish that you had not moved all the way out there. I want you to see your grandchildren. I am sending you some pictures.*

*I don't want you to get mad, or anything, but I did not like what you said about Danny in your other letter. When I wrote to you to say that we were having a hard time, I just wanted you to understand. I know you never liked Danny. But I am not leaving him. I would never, ever do that. So please don't talk to me like he is a bad person. He is not. He has been my friend. He is my friend.*

*I know you are busy. Say hello to Tommy, Joey, and to Kelly and Harry. Please write back.*

*Maybe someday we will have the money to fly out there and visit.*

*Love, Jenny*

She folded the letter up and put it into the envelope. She returned it to her purse. Then she looked over at the bar. He was gone. She shrugged. She decided that she probably should have written back to her daughter. She needed to keep an open line of communication, just in case she ever moved back there and needed a place to stay. But it didn't matter now anyway. She drank her beer.

When she lit her cigarette, she felt the pain change in her chest. It became more difficult to inhale and the pressure increased. She sipped on her beer. She felt anxiety move up into her chest to join the pressure. She glanced around the bar.

She saw people dancing, laughing, drinking...but the noise became muffled and distant. Looking across at the bar, she saw him again. He did not look in her direction. He spoke to a small, young woman. The young woman was familiar to her.

Her husband laughed. The young woman laughed with him, then turned to look back at her mother, sitting across the room, alone at the table. She returned her daughter's gaze—she studied them both, standing at the bar, she realized how much this young woman looked like him—her father. Odd, when they were both alive, she had never noticed that fact.

The young woman smiled at her mother but did not move from the bar;

instead she turned back to her father. The woman became confused; she looked at her purse and the envelope. That daughter was still alive. The one at the bar was...dead now, for nearly ten years.

*Well, that explains that*, she thought. *They are both dead. That's why they are together.*

The woman looked away from her husband and daughter. She thought that it was not good to encourage them. If they came over to her table and her friends stopped dancing and came back to sit at the table at the same time, it would be too difficult for her to explain what was happening to her tonight.

She turned to the young man. He had spoken to her.

"What?" she asked.

"I just wondered if you were feeling okay. You've been really quiet."

She nodded at him and laughed, then looked back over to the bar. They were both looking at her now. They were not smiling at her. They were not speaking. They stood side by side, in front of the bar, and watched her.

The young man followed her gaze to the bar. Then he turned back to the table and drank his beer.

"I have to go," she said.

"The ladies room is back there," he said, pointing over his shoulder with his thumb.

She pushed back her chair and took her purse from the table. She walked past the bar and out the front door.

The humid night air made her face and body instantly damp as she walked up the sidewalk. She had not decided on any direction, she just walked. There were few cars on the side street that she walked on, and no other people. The noise from the bar had distracted her. Now she felt the palpable, solitary sense of this night. A dread began to fill her chest. She looked ahead and could see them walking in the dark, beneath a streetlight. It did not seem possible to her that she could catch up to them. She wasn't sure if she even wanted to.

It puzzled her why she had even left the bar to follow them. They did not look back for her. They did not even slow down their pace for her to catch up. She tried to jog a little, clutching her purse. But it seemed that they would always be just out of reach, no matter how fast she walked. She stood still on the dark sidewalk to catch her breath.

This time the pain slammed into her and she did fall. It landed on top of her as she hit the pavement on her back. Her head made a cracking sound as it snapped back onto the sidewalk. There it was…total, black pain. She could not see. She became blind: a darkness that had no color except the color of the pain.

Then it passed. The pain left. She looked up at the night sky. Her relief from the pain gave her an abrupt moment of clarity. There it was…the moon. *My god*! she thought. *It is huge. It is bright!*

She studied it from her position on the pavement. The bright moon came down to sit right in front of her so that she could see it more clearly. She tried to reach a hand up to touch it, but she could not move.

She looked closely. She could not see anything on the surface of the moon. She had never been able to see anything on the moon. She did not see any face or any man in the moon. She squinted. She smirked. *There is nothing there. Ha. I knew it.*

# sense of humor

He was already in bed. She came in from the kid's bedroom. He looked over the top of his book and watched her fold clothes.

"Are they asleep?"

"No. Danny wanted a story."

He waited.

"I read one to him. Then he wanted Uncle Harry to read one. I told him Uncle Harry was in bed and we were all too tired from the trip home tonight."

She stacked the clothes on the dresser and opened the top drawer. She began filling it with his underwear.

"So Katie started reading him that book about the weathervane and the horse...you know, she does pretty well for a first-grader. I told them just one more story and lights out."

Danny Cummings smiled. "That book doesn't have any words, just pictures."

"So? He doesn't know that. He loves the pictures. And besides, she does a good job making up the story."

She continued to open drawers and fill them with the folded clothes.

"He's got no luggage, Jenny."

"He said it was coming later."

"Oh...by the way..."

"Hmm?"

"Well, I got this bridge..."

She climbed into bed, and pulled the covers over her. She avoided his eyes.

"What?" he asked.

"You're not funny."

"Don't you think it's odd?"

"He's in the Army, Danny. He told us it was being shipped. You remember what that was like. He said he was just glad to be back."

"I'm just saying…it's strange."

She reached over, picked up her book from the nightstand and started reading.

"I am glad to see him," Danny said.

She did not answer. She lowered the book and looked at him.

"I mean it. I really am. I like Harry, and he always makes you laugh. I just think it is strange that we haven't heard from him for ages and now he just calls and flies in the next day…from San Francisco to Maine with no luggage? Wearing only the clothes on his back? Shit, he wasn't even carrying a toothbrush."

Jenny said nothing. He watched her as she touched her eyebrow with her little finger and stared at the bedspread. He recognized this familiar habit and her daydreaming. He thought he had said too much. She turned to him, putting her hands down, closing the book.

"I'm going to let him have those things of yours over there. The ones you don't wear."

"Sure. That's fine with me. He's going to need something. It's gonna start getting cold."

"It's only for a little while."

"I know. It's okay. I don't mind."

"And the kids like him."

"I know. He pays attention to them."

"He likes you, Danny."

"I know. And you know I like your brother. I'm just saying…"

They both turned when little Danny came into the room. He climbed onto the bed and under the covers between his parents. He rolled onto his side facing his mother and closed his eyes. She looked at her husband. They watched their son sleep. Then they each opened their books and read.

Katie came into the room, carrying a book, and she climbed onto the bed. She lay between her parents with her head at the foot of the bed, and without disturbing him, she placed her feet near her brother.

Jenny looked over at her husband, who grinned a funny-face at her, and then she threw a blanket over her daughter. They both went back to reading their books.

The boy stood barefoot on the counter top. He was wearing a white towel as a cape, a blue Red Sox baseball cap, and a pair of yellow swimming goggles. He watched as his uncle and his mother prepared the breakfast.

His sister Katie was at the table with a pad of paper and crayons. She and her father drew pictures. Her father leaned back and looked at his artwork. He picked up his coffee mug and sipped from it.

"I'm three," Little Danny said from the counter top, stretching his arms over his head in a pre-flight posture.

"Are you going to jump?" Harry asked without looking up from the green peppers he was chopping.

"I'm going to…pretty soon."

"Can you fly?"

"Nope."

"So…you're going to jump pretty soon, and you can't fly."

"Yup." He stretched his arms up over his head and held the threatening posture.

"Well…you had better wait for me to catch you then," Harry said.

He put down his knife and turned to catch the boy. Little Danny leaped into his uncle's arms. Harry made a noise to emphasize just how big a boy he had caught.

"You are growing up pretty fast. I think you flew a couple of feet there…just then!"

At the table, Katie looked at her dad and rolled her eyes.

"Harry? When you were back here for your mother's funeral, was Little Danny around then?" Danny asked.

Harry turned to his sister.

"He was. But Danny was just an infant. Harry wasn't staying with us. So he probably doesn't remember him. Remember? Sophy stayed with us when she was home for the funeral"

"I remember that Daddy's sisters were there. They looked at you as if they had seen a ghost. Remember that?" Harry asked.

"Yeah. They thought that I was Missy."

They both laughed.

"It's funny. They never even came to her funeral," Harry said.

"Probably because no one told them she had died. No surprise after the fiasco at Daddy's funeral."

"What about that?" Danny asked.

"Well…you know how at the end, when people walk down front and pass in front of the family? Well…Daddy's sisters came down in the middle of the whole thing…and turned around to Momma and started yelling at her in front of everyone that it was all her fault that Daddy died. They blamed her that he was a drunk." Harry and Jenny both laughed again, and Jenny bumped Harry with her hip.

Danny started to say something and stopped.

"Remember what you said?" Jenny turned to Harry who was scraping chopped onion onto the omelet in the pan.

"No. What? What did I say?"

"At Momma's funeral," she said to her husband, "Harry and I were sitting beside each other in the row behind Momma and Kelly. Harry kept teasing me and making me laugh. You were so awful."

"What did I say?"

"You remember…about the closed casket. You said you knew why it was closed. I asked you why, and you said because Daddy was probably still drunk and they didn't want him to ruin the party."

Jenny laughed and hit her brother on the shoulder and Harry said, "Hey…he wasn't my father. I didn't give a shit…oops." He stuck his tongue out at Katie, who made a face back at him, then returned to her coloring with her father.

"You don't know that," Jenny said.

"Do so. We're nothing alike. Never were and never will be. Besides, I look like Momma's side of the family."

Danny said, "Do you think they meant…I mean your dad's sisters…about the way your father died?"

Jenny looked up from the stove at her husband.

Harry pushed his sister with his hip. "Hey, Momma gave you a real crack, remember?"

"Yeah," Jenny said, giving Harry an exaggerated squint, "she turned around, and slapped my face. All I did was laugh at you. It hurt. How come she never cracked you?"

"She liked me better." He smirked at her.

They laughed and pushed at each other.

"She never hit you like she did me."

"She did so. She hit me just as much as she hit you."

"Not that I remember. She always beat on me when it was your fault most of the time." Jenny stood with her mouth open for effect. "I didn't even do anything."

They both laughed. On the radio, the Beatles were singing "Two of Us." Harry grabbed Jenny's hand and they did a jitterbug in the kitchen. Katie stopped coloring and watched her uncle and mother dance. She laughed at their fun. Little Danny practiced flying.

*They are good. No doubt about it,* Danny thought. He recalled the school dances and all those contests that Harry and Jenny had won together.

He walked out of his house and stood beside his wife, watching the truck back up to their barn.

"Told ya," Jenny said.

"Where's Harry?"

"I don't know."

"And our car?"

"He borrowed it."

Danny and Jenny moved out of the way as the truck backed to the barn door and stopped.

The man jumped from the cab to the ground. He carried a clipboard in his hand.

"Harold Merchant?" he asked, addressing Danny.

"He's not here."

"He lives here, right?"

"He's staying here."

"Just sign that you received this stuff. We'll unload it." He nodded toward the other man in the truck's cab.

Danny took the clipboard and signed the form. He handed it back to the man.

The man said, "Sorry this stuff was so late. We were waiting on the other end. Took several days."

They watched as the two men unloaded the truck. Boxes marked "Bathroom," "Living room," "Kitchen" and "Dishes." And several pieces of furniture.

Danny went into the house and brought out a jacket for Jenny and two cups of coffee. He offered to help, but the man said something about a union rule, so Danny stepped back.

As the truck drove away, Danny and Jenny turned to look into the barn.

"Well...I guess this qualifies as luggage," Danny said.

"There is a box there that says personal stuff. That could have clothes in it."

"The rest of this stuff…looks like…Harry's moving in."

"Maybe he just wants to store his stuff here."

"He didn't mention that."

"But…he's in the military."

"Okay. So he needs a place to put his stuff. This is fine," he said. "But he still wasn't carrying a toothbrush." Danny looked around the driveway. "How long has he been gone?"

"A while. You were down back with the kids. Are you worried?"

"Well…I still don't have any air filter covering that carburetor. The last time it backfired through the carburetor, the whole thing caught on fire. Other than that…"

"Jesus H. Christ." Dennis Witham walked over to the booth inside Cooper's Bar and Grill. "It's Harry Merchant."

"Hi, Dennis."

"I'll be damned. I ain't seen you since…high school. How the hell are you? Getting a little scarce on the old globe ain'tcha? Sorta like me," he said, rubbing his scalp.

"I'm gonna shave it."

"Yessir. I like 'em shaved. Ain't that right, Emma?" He turned toward the bar. "Hey, Emma…bring us two more beers." He sat down across from Harry. "Quiet as a graveyard in here. You'd think that the only bar in town would be full."

Emma brought two mugs of beer to their table. She said, "It's Tuesday night, Dennis. Some folks have other things, ya know."

"Emma's got the hots for me, Harry. Ain't that right, Emma?"

Emma looked at Harry. "Yeah. Dennis has the sex appeal of a wildebeest."

She walked off.

"See? She's hot. She called me a beast. You want it, Emma. You know you do." He laughed.

Harry smiled at Dennis. He thought that Emma looked several years older than they were.

"So, Harry, what are you doing back here?"

"Visiting Jenny and Danny."

"That's great. I bet they're glad to see you."

They drank their beer. Dennis swallowed his beer with several, long gulps. He slammed the mug on the table.

"Emma. Bring a couple more of these." He wiped his mouth. "And bring some of that free popcorn. And some salt."

The waitress brought over the beer and placed a large bowl of popcorn on their table. "The salt's on the table."

"You're gonna get a big tip tonight, Emma. A big one." Dennis laughed.

"Can't wait, Dennis. Been thinking about it ever since you came in the front door."

"Ooooh…"

She walked back to the bar and started wiping glasses and putting them under the counter.

"You remember Emma?"

Harry said, "Nope."

"No shit? You forgot that rack?"

"Guess so. I don't know her."

"She almost married Butch O'Brien."

"Huh. I guess I didn't know that."

Dennis turned to look back at Emma at the bar. "I give her a hard time. She's a looker for a woman her age. Remember we used to call her 'All Ass Emma?' She was older than any of us; and slept around with anyone. Didn't matter who or how old they were. I think she wants me."

"How is Butch?"

"Dead."

"Oh."

They were quiet. Harry looked at the pieces of popcorn on Dennis' greasy chin.

"Car accident. He was drunk."

"Oh."

"Alex was the first one at the scene."

"Is he still the town cop?"

"Nope. He got done a couple of years after that. He was sort of a hero you know. He shot this badass criminal guy. I don't know what ever became of him. Moved out of town and disappeared. Good shit…Alex." He drank from his mug. "Hey. You went to Viet Nam, right? Volunteered more than once, I heard… according to Danny and Jenny."

"Yeah."

They ate popcorn and Emma turned on the jukebox. The bar was empty.

Elton John came out of the speakers singing "Come Down In Time."

"He's a queer," Dennis said.

"Yeah. I heard that."

Harry drank his beer.

"You still in?"

"The military? Sort of."

"They wouldn't let me in. I have a bum leg. Let's drink to Butch; hey, and let's drink to all you guys who went to 'Nam. I'll drink to that any day. These stinkin' hippies drive me crazy. Screw that 'peace' shit. Right? Here's to the guys who went over there."

"We lost, Dennis."

"No sir…we stopped them commie bastards!"

They both drank their mugs dry. Dennis ordered more beer. Then he ordered two Jagermeisters. They toasted Emma's ass. She gave Dennis the finger. Dennis and Harry drank the liqueurs. Harry liked the sweet, licorice flavor. They chased it with the beer. Dennis ordered two more.

"Here's to…Danny and Jenny," Dennis said. "You're shister's a shweetheart. I always thought so. And Danny…he's the best. My best friend in school."

It was dark outside the bar. Harry pulled a knit cap over his ears. He and Dennis started walking across the ball field toward the bleachers behind the high school. Dennis stopped at his pickup truck and got a bottle out of the glove compartment.

"How long has the school been closed up?" Harry asked, looking at the building and thinking how small it seemed. For some reason, he remembered that there were a hundred and forty-five students in the entire school when he attended.

"Let's see…you were a year ahead of me, with Danny." Dennis had his hands in his pocket. He took one hand out and counted on his fingers. "That was '64. The school closed a while after that." Dennis's collar was up around his ears, but his jacket was unzipped and open. Harry could see his breath when he spoke. "I dunno…about two or three years after I graduated. I guess they want to open it as the new municipal building or make apartments out of it."

They climbed to the top row of the bleachers and sat down. Dennis took out the bottle he had put in his inside jacket pocket. He opened it and took a drink. He handed the bottle to Harry.

"Whooo…!" Dennis shook himself.

Harry took a short drink and passed the bottle back to Dennis. "Thanks for getting the tab in there. I owe you."

"Naaah."

They sat in silence. Harry shivered and looked across the ball field at the building where he, Danny, Jenny and Dennis had attended high school. He remembered that somewhere in these bleachers, during a ball game that they all attended together, Danny had carved, "DC loves JM."

"You working?" Harry asked.

"Ayuh. At the paper mill." He turned to Harry. "Been laying folks off lately though. Changed owners a couple of times over the years."

"Are you worried about your job?"

"Not really. The mill'll bounce back. These new owners will get the place up to speed again."

Dennis experienced strong flatulence. "Christ, Harry, was that you?" Dennis asked. Then, "Jeeesus. This is too cold. Whose idea was this, anyway?"

"I have to get back. I've got Danny's car."

"Another drink. One more. This is good Canadian whiskey."

Harry took the bottle. This time he took a long drink. Harry liked good whiskey.

He drove around the town. It was late. He drove up Elm Street and passed the apartment house they had lived in. He drove through the village square a couple of times; past Merrill's Market, the library, the barbershop; past many abandoned stores, some with poster art work from the school kids and some with the large, gaily colored ad for the Homecoming Parade last summer, hanging in the window front. He finally ended up in front of the old high school.

There was another Elton John song playing on the radio. He liked Elton John. He parked with the engine running, the heater on, and stared at the entrance of the school. Then he shut the engine off, got out of the car and walked to the front steps.

He climbed to the front door and peeked into the windows. The building was empty, but he could see a few of the old school desks pushed up against the walls. On the walls, he could see the rows of class pictures hanging down both sides of the hallway. He turned and went down the steps and around the building to the side doors of the gymnasium entrance.

He looked out back of the school toward the bleachers and then back toward the road. He remembered that if you pushed against the door hard enough, the latch would loosen and open. Danny had shown him how to do this when they were in school. Danny had used this trick when he was late and wanted to avoid passing Mr. Garner's office. Harry did this now, and the door swung open. He looked around once in the dark and then entered the building.

Inside, the familiar odor of the gym and auditorium came with strong memories, mostly of the school dances. He had not attended gym class. He had always found it too disturbing to undress with the other boys. He closed the door behind himself and walked into the building.

He walked across the gym floor and up the stairs to the front of the building. He looked out the front door windows at Danny's car parked across the street. Then he strolled through each of the rooms in the school.

He was surprised to find that many of the rooms were still set up as if they were expecting students on Monday morning. He went to the walls where the class pictures were hanging. He could not see well because of the darkness, but he did find the class picture he was looking for and pulled a chair over to stand on.

He unhooked the picture and took it over to a window where the moonlight and a streetlight made it possible to see the faces. He found his photo, and Danny's, and he looked carefully at each class member. He counted them— forty-four in his graduating class.

He took the photo to one of the desks in the classroom that used to be his history class with Mr. Garner, who also doubled as the school principal. He dragged the desk over to the window and sat there with the moonlight, looking at his friends.

The gray sky made the morning seem cooler. She sat on the granite doorstep that faced the south lawn, wearing a navy-blue hooded sweatshirt with the hood pulled onto her head and watched her children climbing and sitting on the stonewall that bordered their old farmhouse property.

She had done this before. She knew that this was play, but she was curious about her children—something about the way that they played that she could not quite put her finger on. She sat with the sun on her face. Little Danny was chasing his older sister and she slipped and fell. He tripped over her, fell and began to cry.

Jenny stood up to go to him. But Katie jumped up and went to him and getting down on her knees, she comforted him. Jenny watched this from across the sprawling lawn. She couldn't make out what they were saying, but suddenly Katie was chasing Danny, exaggerating her inability to catch him.

Little Danny, laughing hard, fell again and Katie fell carefully over him. They both lay there, spread-eagled on the lawn. She could see their breath and could hear their voices but not their words.

Harry came out of the kitchen door and walked over to where his sister sat. He also stood watching the children.

"We used to play," he said.

She looked up at him, smiled and looked back toward her children. She thought, *Yes, that is true. But we did not play like this. This is different.*

"I'm making more coffee. Come inside when you're ready."

Cupping her hand behind her right ear, she said, "What did you say?"

He repeated himself, "I said, 'I'm making more coffee! Come inside when you are ready!'"

"Okay. In a minute. Thanks, Harry."

Harry went inside.

Jenny continued to sit and watch her children. She did not smile, laugh, or speak. She thought: *My kids are playing*. Then...puzzled... *They seem so... free of cares.*

*They lived in a small, two-bedroom house on Gully Hill Road, just outside of the village of Casco when she was seven years old. There were six children: Kelly, Missy, Harry, herself, Sophy, Tommy, who was a baby, and her mother. The house was a one-story building; it had no paint, only weatherworn clapboards.*

*Their house sat alone. It sat by itself at the top of a hill that was long but not steep. There were no other houses on the road other than the remains of an abandoned, collapsing farmhouse at the foot of the hill, with a barn nearby still used by some local farmer to store hay.*

*As with most rural roads in those days, it was not paved. And she recalled that, in the spring, the hill was muddy to the point that when they walked to meet the school bus, they would have to walk along the edges of the road to avoid losing their shoes in the mud. But, this day was summer.*

*She and Harry returned home from playing in the old barn. Harry had dared her to walk across the beam above the piles of hay. He did not do this himself but taunted his little sister to tiptoe across the beam. She did it and fell.*

*The hay had caught her nicely and she spread out on her back, looking up through the cracks and gaps in the barn roof and seeing the sun peek through, flashing in her eyes. Reaching up, she removed straw from her mouth and face. She enjoyed the comfort and the scent of the hay and the barn, and she lay still. She laughed, but not aloud. It was a secret laugh. There existed this one moment of brilliance...a unit of consciousness that seemed close to peace; a kind of hopefulness.*

*Harry climbed after her and scolded her for scaring him. She nearly cried at his scolding but did not and instead stomped off home with him following.*

*This was one of those many times that Daddy had been gone for a long while. Whenever he disappeared, Uncle Lenny would come around. She did not like her uncle. He had a car and took her mother places. He used to take her sisters Missy and Kelly places, but now they were a little older and would not go with him. He gave her mother things, including money.*

*This day he was sitting in his car when she walked into the driveway. She pretended she did not see him when he waved his fingers at her.*

*"Where have you been?" her mother asked.*

*"Harry and me were playing."*

*"You..." she started, then stopped and smiled at Jenny. "Go get dressed. Put on that yellow summer dress."*

*"What for?"*

*"Your Uncle Lenny has asked to take you to the drive-in movies tonight."*

*Her stomach lurched. "I don't want to go to the movies."*

*"Get dressed. Don't be such a snot. You never get a chance to go to the movies—a drive-in movie. You should feel lucky he wants you to go and not one of the other kids."*

*Jenny hesitated. "I'm not going."*

*Her mother looked at her daughter. "You ungrateful little shit." She moved toward Jenny who stepped backwards. Harry came through the door and walked past them and into a bedroom. "You get dressed—now. Lenny is waiting in the car."*

*"Please, Momma. Pleeeese. I don't want to go. I don't feel well."*

*"Go...get ready. I already told him you would love to go to the movies. He'll buy you stuff too."*

*"Please...don't make me go with him, Momma, I don't like him."*

*In the car, she sat in the front seat with her Uncle Lenny, wearing her yellow sundress, her hands in her lap. Her mother stood at his window. Jenny could see her waist and the stained apron she wore. She could not see her mother's face until she leaned down and looked over at her daughter. She did not smile or say anything to Jenny. Then she saw that Uncle Lenny gave something to her mother... he put it in her hand and her mother made an effort to hide this gesture, slipping the item into her apron pocket.*

*The movie was a war film. Uncle Lenny brought her home early. Her mother was not up waiting for her. Nobody was awake. The house was dark. The screen door squealed and slammed shut behind her. She went to her bedroom. She slept in her yellow sundress that night but never wore it again.*

Her brother placed the coffee cup down on the kitchen table in front of her. She sipped it and looked out the kitchen window at Little Danny and Katie—still climbing and jumping from the stonewall. She held the cup to her mouth and allowed the heat to warm her nose and hands.

"They don't seem to notice the cold," Harry said.

"They're kids. Remember what that was like?"

"Yeah. Momma wouldn't let us come in until the sun went down. It didn't matter how cold out it was...get home from school and kicked us right outside until dark."

"And on the weekends it was all day long."

"I don't remember being cold. But I know that we were."

"Harry?"

"Hmmm."

"Do you remember that couple that Momma sent us to live with when I was in kindergarten?"

"Yeah."

"Do you ever think about that?"

"No."

"I do. Did she ever say why she sent us to live with strangers?"

"I never asked her."

"Do you know who they were?"

"The old hag was Mom's milk lady...she delivered the milk."

"Do you remember how long we were there?"

He shook his head and looked out the window.

"Harry? Remember when we finally did go home...all the other kids, Missy, Kelly, Kicky and Sophy...she was just a baby I think...they were already there? I mean, moved back in and everything. We were the last ones. And...I remember, it looked like they had all been living in that house for a while. And even Daddy was home."

Harry watched his sister.

She asked, "Do you ever think about what happened to us there, living with those people?"

He stood up and walked over to the coffee pot. He poured some into his cup and set the pot back down on the stove. "Nope."

She watched him as he paced around the kitchen table and then sat in his chair. She said, "They were evil people, Harry."

"I know. But that's a long time ago."

"I told Mom about it. I tried to ask her questions but she ignored most of them or just said she didn't know."

"You told her?"

"I had to. I didn't understand why we had to go there. We could have been sent to relatives like the older kids were, if she needed a place for us to go. We were the youngest, except for Sophy, Harry. We were the little ones. I still don't understand it. And Momma wouldn't say anything about it to me. When I told her what they did to us, she just sat there smoking a cigarette and said that she didn't know anything about it."

Harry stood up again and pushed his chair back. He did not look at his sister. He drank from his coffee mug and said, "I can't believe you told."

Danny walked into Cooper's Bar and Grill. There were two men sitting at the bar. He looked around the small barroom. Harry was sitting alone in a booth by the window. Harry had seen Danny drive up and park in front. He gestured to Danny to take a seat.

Danny sat at the booth facing the outside window. He could see his car parked in front of Cooper's. It had misfired when he shut it off, and popped through the carburetor. He was watching for smoke to creep out from under the hood. So far—nothing.

"Dennis is coming by. Should be here by now."

"Good."

The waitress came to the booth.

"Hi, Emma," Danny said. "How are you?"

"Okay, Danny. Don't see you in here often." She looked at Harry then back at Danny. "What'll you have?"

"Umm…a beer, I guess."

"Draft?"

"Sure."

Emma left.

Danny sat without speaking. He looked at Harry. He thought that Harry was getting drunk. Harry watched one of the men from the bar approach the jukebox and study the listing. Emma delivered the mug of beer to Danny and placed another full mug in front of Harry.

"Thanks Emma," said Danny.

"Thanks," Harry said.

"Enjoy, boys." Emma walked back toward the bar.

Danny drank from his mug and set it down on the table. He started to speak. Harry waved at someone behind Danny.

"Over here, Dennis."

"Uh, Harry…I was going to ask you to come home."

"Sure. Let's have a beer with Dennis first." Harry looked at his brother-in-law. "Is something wrong, Danny?"

"Well ain't I died and gone to Hell! Danny…don't ever see you down here," Dennis said, slapping Danny's shoulder and pushing him over in the booth to sit next to him. He turned toward the bar and nearly spilled Emma's beer mug. "Jeeesus, Emma! You're a quickie."

Emma put the beer in front of Dennis. "Well…truth is Dennis, you're a simple guy, and I know what you want before you even ask."

"All right then…let's go…"

Emma pushed him back into his seat. "Doesn't mean you get everything you want, mister. Keep your seat." She headed back to the bar, stooping to pick up a napkin from the floor.

Dennis laughed and poked Danny with his elbow. "She's got the hots for me, Danny. Ain't that so, Harry."

Harry smiled at Danny.

Dennis said, "So what brings you here?"

"Just having a beer with Harry. How are you doing, Dennis?"

"Trying to hustle old Emma."

Danny shook his head. "Some things don't change. You've been trying to get Emma since high school."

"She put out to everyone else. I'm just waitin' my turn."

"Dennis…that was just a story. Emma's a good woman."

"Story?"

"Yeah. You know…teenage boy's fantasies about older girls?"

Dennis looked troubled, then recovered. "Bullshit. You're bullshitting me." He laughed and hit Danny with his elbow.

Danny shook his head side to side. "Dennis, you need a wife. God help whoever that should turn out to be."

Dennis laughed again. He looked at Harry, then back at Danny. "Did I interrupt you guys? Just say so."

Danny thought of saying something to Dennis or just asking Harry to come home with him, but he hesitated. Instead, he looked over at Harry and smiled. Then he turned to Dennis and lifted his beer mug. "We were just going to toast to you, you shithead."

They raised their mugs, bumped them together and drank. Harry drained the remainder from his mug and pulled the full mug that Emma had delivered over in front of him. He pushed the empty mug toward the edge of the tabletop and gestured toward Emma for another round of beers.

Danny already regretted his generous mood. He thought that Jenny would not be happy if they were late. She was waiting for him and for Harry. But Harry did not know this and Danny did not tell him.

Danny was also concerned about paying for any rounds of beer. He let his mind go to his wallet and reviewed his finances. He figured he had enough for a couple of more beers, but he also knew that he should not be spending his dollars at Cooper's Bar.

Danny declined the Jagermeister that Dennis offered to pay for. Harry took the order and poured the sweet liqueur into his beer and stirred it with his finger. Then he downed the entire drink.

"Hey," Danny said, "we should be going soon."

Harry looked over at him but did not respond.

The music from the jukebox ended and no one got up to add any change to it. The two men at the bar left. Emma was wiping the bar down and putting glasses into the sink.

"Quiet as a..." Dennis started to say but didn't complete the sentence.

"Yeah. But we have to go." Danny looked at Harry and pushed against Dennis, who looked over at him and then moved out of the booth to allow Danny to stand up. "Okay, Harry?"

"Hmmm...sure."

Danny said goodbye to Dennis. He had not seen Dennis to speak to for a long while. *Small towns can be like that,* he thought. A phenomenon really. Strange. A town of just over two thousand people and most of them old friends of each other, in fact, most of them grew up together, and yet it could be months without them seeing or speaking to one another.

And, friends or family that lived miles away in other states...wrote letters and called regularly. The further away, the more people keep in touch. He shook Dennis's hand, and he and Harry left.

When she asked Harry about it, he was silent and did not look at her, but he nodded to affirm that he had taken it. She felt sadness and a deep pity for her brother. They sat alone at the table and did not speak for several minutes. Danny was already upstairs in bed. He had to work in the morning.

"You okay?"

Harry didn't answer. He looked around the kitchen.

"You want me to make some coffee?"

He stared at her.

"Harry?" She looked down at the table top, spread her hands out beside of one another on the table, and looked at them. "I…it wouldn't be a problem…see, Danny and I just don't have a lot of money right now. We kinda go from paycheck to paycheck. That money was all we had left."

Harry did not answer and he did not look at his sister. He wanted a drink.

"What about the Army, Harry?"

He looked up.

"Are they going to send you any money?"

He snickered.

"What?'

"Jenny…just…drop it." He looked away and then back at her. "I need to get to bed." Then, "Are you finished?"

When Harry left the table, Jenny was sorry that she had talked with him at all. She thought that it would have been better to just go on the way that they had been and not mention the money at all. Danny had insisted that she talk with Harry about it. She resented Danny now. And she was confused because she was also angry with Harry for putting her in this situation. She sat at the kitchen table. The house was still.

*It was Christmas. They were living in a cabin on Duck Pond Road. There were no other buildings near them. They were once again in a rural and lonely, wooded place. There was a coal stove for heat. There was an outhouse. There were two bedrooms: her parent's and the one that she and Harry shared, theirs was a woodshed really, converted into a bedroom. Kelly and Missy slept in the living room. Tommy, still a baby, and Sophy, barely two years old, slept in the bedroom with their parents.*

*Flames surged behind her father when he entered the room. He did not speak at all but scooped her underneath one arm and Harry under the other and raced back through the living room, through the fire and out the front door. He set Harry and Jenny down beside their brother and sisters, and the entire family watched as their home burned to the ground.*

*Except for Tommy and Sophy, who were with Kelly, each of them was alone. Jenny looked around at the alien scene. The heat from the burning house pressed against her body. She glanced down at her pajama bottoms and the singed cuffs. One of the pajama legs was torn.*

*She allowed her tongue to slip around her lips—they were rough and blistered. She experienced an overwhelming thirst. She tried to swallow, but her throat was tight and dry. Her feet were bare and sore and her face felt hot. She placed a hand on her cheek and felt a gleam of pain.*

*Across the lawn, her father leaned against a tree and her mother stood, arms folded across her chest, near the edge of the field, her face alight from the burning house. All of them were staring at their burning home. Jenny thought of the few gifts under the tree. Two of them were for her.*

*She thought of the tree that they had draped in homemade, paper garlands and tinsel. She, Harry, and Sophy had put the tinsel on the tree just this evening. She had draped it, one shining string at a time, to make the event last longer. They had rationed out the tinsel and she was the last one. Sophy had put it on in clumps and finished quickly.*

*Jenny had spent time re-distributing Sophy's work. She had still been putting the last of the tinsel on the tree when Harry went to bed. Missy had come over and said to her that Santa would not come until she was asleep. Now Missy came over and put her arms around Jenny. Missy held her and Jenny felt herself begin to tremble.*

*Missy wept and whispered to her little sister, "It'll be okay, Jenny."*

*It occurred to Jenny, these years later, that she and Harry had been the last ones out of the house.*

She mashed the banana and scooped it into the bowl. Adding peanut butter, she whipped it and then spread it onto a piece of bread, folded it in half and handed it to her son. He took it and ran out the door. He was barefoot. She walked over to the door and called him back inside.

"It's not summer…yet. Put on your sneakers."

The boy ran back into the house, put the sandwich on the floor and started pulling his sneakers on.

She picked up the sandwich and held onto it. She kneeled down and pulled the sneaker off his foot with one hand. "Wrong foot. Other foot…put it on that foot." She sighed, then said, "The other foot, Danny. You have to take that sneaker off that foot and put this one on that foot…here…give me that." She took the sneakers and placed them alongside their correct foot. "There…now put them on that way."

Little Danny put each foot into a sneaker, sat down on the floor, and pulled them on. She handed him the sandwich, and he watched as his mother tied his shoes for him. "Okay. Out you go. Don't go near the road. Katie will be home soon. Watch for the school bus." She yelled after him as he ran down the lawn, "But…do not go near the road."

She turned and went back to the sideboard and started cleaning up the counters.

Harry came into the room.

"I'll take him with me if you want," he said.

"Where are you going?"

"Just downtown. We can drop into the library and he can pick out a couple of books."

"Sure. Katie will be home soon, if you want to wait for her she can go too."

He nodded. "No problem."

She looked up at him. "What are you getting downtown?"

"I just need to get out."

She continued to pick up the counter. He watched her then came over and began doing up dishes. When she finished her chore she started wiping the dishes and putting them into the cupboards. They worked side by side without speaking.

Harry bumped her hip with his and said, "You're slow. I'm getting way ahead of you."

She bumped him back and they smiled at each other.

"Cabin fever?" She asked.

"I guess so." He finished the last cup and started on the silverware. "It's the first nice day. The snow's gone. I forgot how long winters are here."

"I hate doing silverware. It's…tedious," she said, without looking at him. "What else are you doing downtown?"

"I might make a phone call."

"You can use our phone you know."

"I know."

"What about the Army, Harry?"

"What about it?"

"I don't know. I was just wondering." She looked over at him. "You've been home for quite a while now. You haven't contacted any of your old friends."

"I see Dennis."

She nodded.

"You know I spent three tours in Viet Nam. You know that...right?"

"Uh-huh."

"Well..." He paused, picked a handful of silverware from the bottom of the dishpan and started washing them off one piece at a time.

"Harry, I'm not..."

"I think I've paid my dues. You know what I mean? I think I've paid my dues in a lot of different ways, Jenny."

Jenny watched his face. When he handed her the silverware, she took it and laid it on the counter. She said, "I know, Harry."

"I don't want to see anyone else. I just don't feel like looking up old friends. That's all."

He put the last piece of silverware into the strainer and wiped his hands on a dishtowel. Then he said, "I think I'll go outside with Danny until the school bus comes." He went outside.

She stood in the kitchen window and watched them toss a ball and run around on the front lawn, and then she returned to drying the silverware and putting it in the drawer.

"You can't write like that," Katie said. She took the pencil that her brother was clutching and adjusted it in his small hand until he had a writing grip on it. She placed a pad of paper in front of him and poised his small hand over it. "There. Now, take my notes." She returned, tottering on her mother's heels, to her place at the small school desk.

Danny put his book aside and watched Katie with her brother. Katie wobbled back and forth between her school desk and the table where she had placed her brother. She wore smears of blue mascara and red lipstick. She continuously pushed her mother's sunglasses up on the bridge of her nose—her hair pulled up and held by elastic. Somewhere, she had found a long white feather and had stuck it into the elastic. There was a pencil behind her ear.

Little Danny scribbled on his pad of paper. Katie colored on her own.

"Can I go now?" her brother asked, looking up.

"Not until you are done with my notes."

"I am."

"No you're not."

"Daddy…I'm all done work today. Can I go now?"

"What do you think, Katie? He's gonna be on overtime if you don't let him go."

Katie rolled her eyes, sighed and said, "Finish the filing and then you can go home."

Little Danny looked at her and then back at his father. "What's filing?"

Danny heard the car come up the driveway and walked over to the window. He watched them unload the groceries from the back of the car and walk up the driveway. They were talking and laughing. One of the bags that Jenny carried tore open and spilled onto the driveway. Both of them laughed again and continued toward the house.

Danny met them at the door and took the bags from Jenny. Harry set his on the table.

"I'll pick that stuff up," Harry said and went back outside.

Jenny waited and then said, "He wants to use the car again tonight."

She saw him watching her and took her finger away from her eyebrow. He said, "Nervous?"

She nodded her head and started playing with her eyebrow again, caught herself and stopped. The telephone was on a chair beside of them. She looked at it and then at her husband. He was looking at her.

"You want me to call?" he asked.

"We have to. Don't we?" She leaned on the table with her elbows. Her right hand went to her eyebrow, and using her little finger, moved a single eyebrow hair in circles. "I just don't like talking with him. He makes me…" she made a movement with her shoulders, "I don't know. I just don't want to talk with him." She looked at Danny, "Besides, I don't hear well on the phone."

"I know." Danny pulled the chair with the phone in it, closer to him. He did not pick up the phone. "So…what do I say? I hardly know him."

"Say, 'Hi, Kicky.'"

"Well…I think I got that part covered."

"Just tell him we need him to keep an eye out for our car around Portland."

"Should I tell him anymore? About...why? What if he asks?"

"We have to find him. He might be hurt. Or...had an accident or something. Just tell Kicky that much. If he asks…well, then tell him."

Danny dialed the phone. He held the receiver to his ear.

"Hello. Hi. This is Danny. Your Uncle Danny. Is this Jill?" He put his hand over the mouthpiece and said to Jenny, "It's Jill. She sounds so grown up." He took his hand off the mouthpiece, "I said, you sound so grown up. How old are you now? ... Wow."

Jenny watched her husband.

"Is your dad home? Can I speak with him? Thank you, Jill. Bye." He put his hand over the mouthpiece again. "He's there."

She laid both arms on the table and stretched them. She gave a long sigh. Then she brought her arms up onto her elbows and cupped her chin in her hands. She watched her husband's eyes. The morning sunlight from the kitchen window was in his face. His pupils constricted, and this made his eyes more blue than usual.

"Kicky. Hi. This is Danny." He looked over at Jenny. "Yeah...it's been a while."

Jenny made a face at him and shook her head, silently mouthing, "I'm not here..."

"She's doing fine. Actually, she has walked down to the library. She asked me to call you. I know...life is strange sometimes...time passes. Jill sounds all grown up. She says she's nine years old now...they're fine...Katie started school this year."

Jenny chewed on her bottom lip. She thought Harry was okay. She believed he was on a drunk. She did not say this to Danny.

"Well...it's about Harry...well, that's the thing...he's been living here since last fall."

Jenny made a face. Danny made a deep shrug and spread his arms out, shaking his head and pretending to hand the phone to her. He put it back to his ear.

"I don't know why he didn't get in touch. He hasn't been in touch with any of his old school friends either." He listened, lowering his head to look at the table. "He's...gone. It's been five days...my car. He has our car...no, he hasn't called. We have no idea where he is." He looked out the window. "Yeah...well...we just want to have him come home. We thought since you live in Portland, you could maybe ride around and look for the car or just keep an eye out...sure...and, Kicky...just tell him to come on home, call us, something...sure thing, I'll tell her. And thanks. Goodbye."

He put the phone down.

They were both quiet. Jenny looked out the window. Little Danny was playing in the dirt driveway with his trucks and cars. He pushed the trucks around, filled them with dirt, moved them to a different location in the driveway and unloaded small piles; a swirl of dust surrounded him and coated his clothing and the Red Sox baseball cap that he wore tilted sideways on his head. He was wearing his yellow swimming goggles. Jenny smiled.

"Well?" Danny started.

She looked over to him. "I wish we hadn't called now."

"I know."

She moved her head side to side so slowly that at first Danny thought she was turning her head. "I just don't know what else we could've done," said Jenny.

He stroked his chin with his right hand. He was trying to grow a beard. Moving his hand around on his chin and his cheeks, he could feel sparse growth in places, and in other areas, it was smooth. He rubbed his face with both hands. He watched his son out the kitchen window.

At first, Harry did not recognize his older brother. He had not seen him since his mother's funeral, and then only briefly. Harry was drunk. But he had no trouble recognizing the familiar clutch of fear he felt when in his brother's presence. It started somewhere in his abdomen, then fluttered and lurked throughout his torso and chest—like a small, wounded bird.

Kicky walked up to Harry at the bar. He sat down on a stool beside of him and looked at the young man behind the bar. He looked at Harry and then back at the bartender. "He looks like a queer," he said to Harry. "Got his head shaved and those pretty, dangling earrings and jewelry. Ain't he cute? Hey, miss, give me a beer."

Harry said nothing.

Kicky turned in his seat to face Harry. Then he looked around the barroom. It was not crowded, but there were some people dancing to the music from the jukebox. It was a waltz. There were couples at tables and at the booths in the rear of the room.

It was dark. The lighting was in blue and green. There was a single strobe light in the middle of the ceiling over the dance floor. The bartender set a beer on the counter in front of Kicky.

Kicky looked at Harry. He looked back at the bartender and then back to the dance floor.

"I always knew you were a queer," he said, shaking his head, "even when you were a little boy."

Harry did not look at his brother. He said nothing.

"Daddy knew it too." He picked up the bottle from the bar and drank from it.

Harry chose his best Truman Capote voice. He was good at this voice, especially when he was drunk. He whined, "He wasn't my father."

"Damned right."

Kicky watched two men dancing on the dance floor. "Jesus. How do they know who's supposed to lead? Look at 'em. Cuddling like…a man and a woman." He turned to Harry. "Do you dance with guys?"

Harry lightened up on the Truman Capote voice, and said, "I knew it too. When I was a little boy."

"What?"

"That I was gay."

"Gay? Is that what they call it? Gay?" Kicky laughed. "What's gay about it?"

"And they know who's gonna lead, sometimes they just know, and sometimes because they talk about it first. Simple. And I do dance with guys." He still would not look at his brother.

Kicky shook his head and drank his beer.

"How did you know where this place was?" Harry asked.

"What do you mean?"

"How'd you find me? Or do you come here frequently?"

Kicky stared at his younger brother, pausing in the middle of taking a drink, holding the bottle to his lips, then he drank slowly. Tipping the bottle with his head back, he drained it and sat it on the bar. He took a package of cigarettes from his pocket and put one in his mouth. He picked up a book of matches from the bar and struck one to light the cigarette. He shook out the match and put the matchbook in his pocket. Harry smiled.

"Let's talk in the lobby." Kicky stood and started toward the entrance.

Harry took his beer and followed his brother.

"So…" Kicky dragged deep on his Camel cigarette. "You stole their car, right?"

"No."

"Danny called me. He said you have been gone for four or five days. Took the car and just left town. Never told them anything. Never called. "

Harry shifted to one foot then the other.

"After all Danny and Jenny did for you? This is how you thank them?"

"I was going to call."

"Too late." Kicky leaned against the wall. He squinted his eyes and peered at his brother through the cigarette smoke. "I just drove around Portland and spotted their car. It's a small city. Not like San Francisco. There are only so many bars. Wasn't hard to find you, Harry."

"I'll call them now."

"I said, 'Too late.'"

"I'll take it home tonight."

Kicky shook his head. "Keys." He held a hand out.

Harry did not move. Kicky reached over and started to feel through Harry's pockets. Harry pushed his hands away and spilled his beer. Then the bottle fell out of his hand. He started to pick it up. Kicky pushed him and he fell to the floor, banging his head.

He sat up looking up at Kicky, rubbing the back of his head. The beer bottle drained out onto the floor.The bartender came out to the lobby. He looked at Kicky.

"You need to leave, mister."

"What? Could you repeat that, miss?" Kicky took a step toward the bartender.

The young man walked over to Harry and helped him stand. He said to Kicky, "If you don't leave here now, we will call the police."

Kicky walked over to Harry and put his hand out. "The keys..."

"I need them. I have to get home."

"You ain't going back there. They don't want you there, and they don't need any of your shit. You think you're a brother? You're not. You're just a drunk."

"Did they say that?"

Kicky did not answer. He stood with his hand out, palm up.

Harry mumbled something.

"What did you say?"

"I said, '*You're* a drunk—like daddy.'"

Kicky said, "Yeah? What's that? A newsflash? So...we're both drunks. Give me the goddamn keys."

Harry looked at his brother. He reached into his pocket, took out the keys to Danny's car, and placed them in his brother's open palm.

"Where am I going to stay?"

Kicky shrugged and walked out of the building onto the street.

When he came through the door, she was stacking coins on the kitchen table. She sorted out dimes, nickels and quarters into stacks and arranged them in rows. She looked up at him as he walked past the kitchen table and dropped the car keys in front of her.

He looked at the coins. She said, "For gas money."

"He's gone."

"What do you mean?"

"Kicky told him we didn't want him back here," said Danny.

"What?"

He went to the sideboard and poured out the last of the coffee into a mug.

"He asked me if I knew that Harry was a queer." Danny sipped on the coffee. "He found him in a gay bar. Our car was out front. I told him we've known about Harry since high school."

She was quiet.

He looked at her. "I think he is really gone."

"Where? I mean, where would he go?"

"Kicky bought him a plane ticket and put him on a flight back to California...I guess...or someplace..."

Suddenly Jenny began to sob. At first, Danny watched, and as she lost control, he put down his coffee and went to the table. He reached over for her and knocked over most of the coins. Jenny pushed her chair back from the table and stood. She walked into the living room and up the stairs to their bedroom. He let her go.

It was a clear night. The cool air made her cheeks and nose cold. She pulled the hood of the sweatshirt up onto her head. She looked up at the sky, spattered with stars. A new moon. She watched the sky and shivered. She heard him come out onto the front lawn and walk up behind her. He put an arm around her—and then both arms. He held her. She could smell his Old Spice shaving lotion. She turned and glanced up at him.

"Did you shave?"

"Yeah. I give up."

"I'm going to miss him."

"Yeah."

"I'm worried, Danny."

"I know."

She leaned back against his chest. She looked around the lawns at the maple trees outlined against the dark night sky. She knew from the daytime that they were already lush and full. Soon it would be summer. She had wanted to spend the summer with her brother.

"I don't care that he took our money or our car," said Jenny.

"Me neither."

"Do you think he believes what Kicky told him? About us...not wanting him?"

"I think Harry knows that you love him."

They stood quiet.

"What if I never see him again?"

They both heard the train going through town. They listened to its melancholy whistle as it approached, and then moved north in the distance behind their farmhouse. Danny thought that that was a possibility. He did not say, "You will."

# the coverture

"Did I call last week?"

"No. The week before...I think."

"Did I talk with her then?"

"I don't think so."

"Is she there now?"

"Yes. She's here. But...she's asleep."

"It's awfully early."

"Well...not really. There is a three-hour difference from San Francisco to here. Remember?"

It was silent on the other end of the line.

"You still there?"

"Yuh. You guys go to bed at eight o'clock?"

"Hey. We got kids. And, I have to get up in the morning. That job-thing, ya know?"

"I'm sorry. Just wanted to talk to someone."

"It's okay. I'm not tired. I wanna talk too," he said. He looked across the sofa at his wife. She mouthed the question, "*Is he drunk*?"

He nodded. She got up from the sofa and left the room.

He looked at his wristwatch. It was a little after eight. He said, "So...how's things?"

"I tried calling last night."

"Yeah. We were out for a while."

"Hey...Danny...tell me the truth."

"What is it?"

"Is she still mad at me?"

Dan paused. He tried to decide if Harry was too drunk to have this discussion.

"I mean…it's been a long time now."

"Have you two ever talked about any…"

"No."

"I mean, anything at all? Ever?" He regretted this question.

Harry did not respond. Dan waited. He looked across the room toward the kitchen. He saw her walking toward him. She walked past him in her pajamas and went up the stairwell. He said, "Harry? You there?"

"Yeah. Hold it just a second…" Dan could hear him pouring a drink. There were sounds of bottles and glasses. Opera music played in the background. "Gotcha. Where were we?"

"Nothing. I was just wondering how you are doing."

"How are *you* doing? You and Jenn…how are you guys doin'? How are the kids?"

"They're fine."

"Hey…I gotta…" There was a clunk on the other end of the phone. Dan held the receiver against his ear. He could still hear the opera music playing and shuffling sounds. Then, "Hey…I gotta go take a piss…don't hang up."

Dan looked at his watch. He waited. His daughter came down the stairs and wiggled her fingers at him.

She said, "I was asleep. Can I stay up, Daddy?"

Dan shook his head.

She stuck her tongue out in her pretend way. She asked, "Who's that?"

"It's Uncle Harry."

"I want a drink of water." She grinned and walked past him toward the kitchen. He watched her, barefoot, jogging tippy-toe in her Hobby Holly nightie that hung down to her ankles. He smiled.

"You still there?" Harry asked.

"Yup. Still here. Katie's just passing through."

"How old is she now?"

"Almost eleven."

"There are some things…" Harry took a drink. Dan waited. "I guess I should probably just tell you guys some things are going on out here."

Dan waited. He watched his daughter walk back into the living room. She waved to him and went up the stairs.

"You still there?"

Dan said, "Harry...what is it that you want to tell us about?"

"Well...see...I met this girl."

Dan sat up a little on the sofa. He said, "What girl?"

"We were overseas together in the service. She was a nurse in the same field hospital as me"

Dan sat up a little straighter. He shook his head. "Yeah?"

"I don't know, Danny." He took three long swallows.

"Jeez, Harry. Slow it down a bit. What time is it out there anyway? Five o'clock?" Dan shook his head again and said, "Harry, what are you trying to say? What about this woman?"

"Nothing." Silence. "Really...just...nothing."

Dan put the phone against his other ear. "Okay, Harry...don't be giving me that shit. Tell me about this woman."

Harry was mixing another drink. Dan sighed and waited.

"Hey, Danny?"

"Harry?"

"Would you...do you think maybe, you know...maybe see if she is awake? Maybe if she's awake you could ask her if she wants to talk to me? I haven't talked with her for a while. Ummm...I don't know...a long while. Have you got a drink there?"

"No. I don't. I got a beer in the frig. But I have to get up for work in the morning."

"If she's still mad about when I came home..."

"Harry. She isn't that mad about that. And neither am I. That was almost three years ago."

They didn't talk. Dan could hear Harry breathing and taking a gulp from the glass—he could hear the ice cubes rattling.

"So...what's the problem? Do you think? What's the problem do you think?" Harry sounded drunk.

"To be honest?"

"Yeah. To be honest or not to be honest...I geshh that is the question."

"I think it's the..." Dan wondered about the wisdom of this conversation. "She doesn't like to talk with you when you're drinking." There. He said it.

"Well...damn...that explains why we haven't talked in two years."

Dan raised his eyebrows and nodded his head. He wondered about going upstairs and getting her to come downstairs to talk with her brother. He decided not to do that. He looked at his watch.

"Hold on..." Harry said.

Dan looked up at the ceiling. He waited. He could hear the music still playing. He heard Harry mixing another drink. He heard a loud thumping sound. Another sound that sounded like something hit the carpet. Then it was silent.

"Harry?"

Dan waited. He waited for several minutes. He held the phone to his ear. He could still hear the music. No other sounds. He waited. He worried for a while, then decided not to worry.

He hung up the phone.

The phone rang in the dark of the room. Dan fumbled to sit up and tried to grab it before it woke the kids. He knocked it off from the nightstand and nearly fell on top of it trying to reach it from his bed.

"Hello?" he said his heart thumping in his chest.

"Danny? It's me. Harry. I just wanna say…goodnight."

"You okay, Harry?"

"Uh huh."

"What happened earlier?"

"What do you mean?"

"Never mind."

"I jesss wanna say…I love Jenny."

"I know. She knows that too."

"I love you too, Danny."

"I know, Harry. I love you too."

"You guys…I…jesss want you guys to know that."

"We know Harry. We miss you."

"You do?"

"Yes. We do, Harry."

"Maybe…maybe I can come out and visit sometime again?"

"I hope so, Harry."

"Goodnight."

"Goodnight, Harry."

She sat at the table with a glass of French red wine in a glass tumbler. The wine glasses were on the top shelf of the cupboard over the refrigerator. They were unpacked the day before yesterday and put away. The tumblers were still right on the counter in front of her, sitting in the gift box they had come in at the wedding party…so she had grabbed that first.

She glanced at her watch—nearly midnight. She thought about just having a good cry and then going to bed. But she had done that the past couple of nights and nothing had changed. Instead, she felt more exhausted and confused.

After getting out of bed almost an hour ago, she had stood in front of the mirror in the bathroom and looked at herself. She had removed her gown. It was obvious she did not have the beauty of her sister, or other beautiful women. But she was still thirty-ish, sort of young, almost slender, her breasts were too large, but well shaped, and she could see that she was not really unattractive. After all, she had passed up Stephen for her husband. That strange word hung in her mind like a broken piece on a mobile…it dangled and threw everything out of order: *husband*.

She thought of him in the next room. He snored. He slept soundly and seemed detached from events of the past few days—she did not. She stood and walked into the bedroom.

She sat on his side of the bed, looked down at him, reached up and turned on the light. He continued to sleep. He smelled of the whiskey he had finished earlier. She put a hand on his shoulder and shook him. He made a noise but did not open his eyes.

"Harry," she said. "Harry. Wake up."

He moved, rolled over, and then positioned himself onto his back. He squinted and said, "What? What's wrong?"

"I want to talk."

He looked over at the clock on the nightstand. "At this time of night?"

"Harry…can we…would you like to make love?"

Harry groaned. He rolled away from her. "Margot…I got a headache. I drank too much. I can't…not now."

She watched him. In her mind, she reviewed her options. Perhaps she could initiate something. She knew about many things that men liked. She had not performed all of these acts, but she knew what to do and she had no inhibitions really.

"Harry?"

No answer.

"Harry?"

"Hmmm…?"

"I could help."

No response. Harry shifted in bed, pulled the blankets up, but remained facing away from her.

She removed her gown and turned off the light. Naked, she climbed into bed and snuggled up against him. She put her hand on him.

"Margot. Don't." He pulled away from her.

She did not move for a while. The only sound in the room came from the toilet, it ran because of a small leak inside the tank. Harry should've replaced that little rubber thingy in the tank. He had not done that yet.

"Harry?"

"Mmm...?"

"A long time ago, when we were going out together, you said we should wait. We've waited." She paused. "We're married."

Harry did not move.

She rolled over onto her back. After a few minutes, Harry snored. She listened to the trickle from the toilet in the bathroom. One time, when she was fourteen years old, her younger sister had taken her favorite jumper without asking and wore it. She stained it with something and it could not be cleaned. They fought. She called her sister names.

That night they made up. Then they fought again, and she had thrown a can filled with crayons that hit her sister in the mouth. It broke a tooth in the front and it bled. Her mother came into their bedroom. It did not take too many words from her mother to make her feel worse than she already did. The thought that her beautiful sister would be scarred for life did not seem unreasonable to her at the time. Of course, that turned out to not be the case.

Her parents made certain that a replacement filled that space where the broken tooth gaped in her sister's smile. But that night, she had cried. She and her sister cried together. But she cried so hard that it hurt her side. She could not stop sobbing. When her sister held her, smiled and showed that gaping hole where her tooth had broken off and told her it was okay, it only made her cry worse...and harder. It hurt. So...she made a rule to not ever sob like that again.

This night, angry and hurt, she simply let the tears run freely down her face and pool in the little gully at the base of her throat. Something felt wrong about this night. A faint sound—unintelligible whispers, like the ancient voices of elders sending messages of dread—hissed through her mind. She felt something...bordering on panic; it crept up her legs, to her groin and up her belly, across her breasts, until it reached her throat. Involuntarily, her hand went up to touch the racing pulse in her neck. She thought, *Oh, my god...I've made a mistake.*

She looked at the clock: eleven minutes after three. She sat up. Harry was not in bed. Sliding her feet into her slippers, she walked out into the living room. She stood and listened. No sounds in the house.

Some light came from the kitchen. She walked over and looked in. The refrigerator door was open. It lit up the empty room. She crossed the floor and closed the refrigerator door. She leaned against it and stood in the darkness.

When she came through the door he stood at the counter chopping mushrooms and adding them to a salad. Pavarotti played at full volume on the stereo.

"I picked up some wine," he said. He spoke loud to be heard above Pavarotti. "It's that merlot that you like."

"Let's have some now." She put her purse on the table, her tote bag on the floor by the door and went to the bottle that stood on the kitchen table. "I do like red wine." Using a corkscrew that sat beside the bottle, she opened it and poured, filling each wine glass approximately half way. She handed one to Harry, and they drank. Harry turned the stereo down.

"Who gave us these?" he asked.

"My mom. She has a set just like them."

Harry finished the salad and placed it on the first shelf in the refrigerator. He opened the oven and checked inside. She came up beside of him, stooped over and looked in, holding her wine glass by the stem.

"Hey," said Harry, "it's a surprise." He closed the oven door.

"Oooh. Salmon?"

"Prepared with veggies and a special sauce."

"I love it when you cook for me."

She went to a stack of boxes beside the door that led into the living room. Opening one of them, she began removing plates and placing them in the sink. She filled the sink with hot water and suds and washed the plates, placing them carefully on the dish strainer. She was humming.

"We might as well use these new china pieces. They were a gift from my side of the family. Judy and Richard gave them to us." She held one up and displayed it to Harry.

Harry nodded approval. He sipped his wine. He did not really like wine all that much, but he drank it anyway.

They ate dinner in silence. Harry cleaned up while she did some paperwork she had brought from the hospital where they both worked. As she finished a set of papers, she looked up and into the kitchen. She could see

Harry at the sideboard by the sink. He was drinking the last of the wine in his glass.

She watched him as he finished rinsing the plates and set them in the strainer. She knew as soon as she broke the silence that it was another mistake. She felt her voice vibrate in her throat and her tongue moved in her mouth. She heard her own voice…

"Aren't you late?" she asked from the living room.

Harry did not answer.

Margot walked to the kitchen. She stood in the doorway and watched him finish the dishes. She thought, *I don't need to do this*. She said, "Aren't you late for the shift?"

He turned to her and looked at the papers in her hand. He looked back at the sink. "What are you talking about? I'm not going to work tonight."

"Are you ill?"

"Ill?"

"Aren't you feeling well?"

"I'm fine. "

"Oh."

"I've been working the day shift for a year now." She noticed the change in his voice. The tone was deeper and less friendly. A little wall began to go up. He said, "You know that."

"I know. I just thought…"

He looked at her again, then back at the dishes. He picked up a plate and dried it with a yellow towel that he took from the drawer.

"*What* did you think?"

She paused, then said, "I wondered if you were working extra shifts?'

"No. I'm not."

She shrugged, but he did not see this. She said, "Okay. It's no big deal." She started her retreat.

He put the towel on the counter and walked to the refrigerator. He opened the freezer and took out the ice tray. Taking a tumbler from the cupboard, he dropped three ice cubes into it. The Jack Daniels bottle stood beside the cupboard. He picked it up and poured a large drink of whiskey over the ice. He drank from it. Sipped. Then drank again. He poured another and set the tumbler down in front of him on the countertop.

She said, "It was a good dinner, Harry. Thank you."

"Mmmm…"

"I love it when you cook for me."

He moved over to the table and sat down without speaking.

"Remember, before we decided to marry? Remember what we said then?'

He looked at her, "What?"

"That we would become connoisseurs. We would drink French wines only and learn to prepare gourmet meals. We used to do that…experiment with meals, together. We said that would become our activity in life—we could grow old together doing…"

"I don't like wine that much."

She watched him drink the Jack Daniels.

He looked up at her. "I have to go out tonight."

"What do you mean?"

"I have to go out."

"You have to?"

"I want to."

She turned and walked back into the living room. She said, "Okay. I guess."

"I hate that."

"What?"

"I really hate it when people say, 'I guess.'"

She looked out into the kitchen. He still sat in the same position at the kitchen table. "Well, I am sorry you hate that phrase. I guess."

He did not say anything. She pushed her chair away from the coffee table where she had spread out her paperwork and stared into the kitchen at Harry sitting at the kitchen table. He did not look up from his glass.

She said, "You had this planned."

No answer.

"You had this planned for me. The dinner and the wine. Because you were going to go out again tonight." He looked up when she used the word, 'again.'

"I don't know what is wrong," she said. "It's like…I don't know what it's like. It's not like anything that I know anything about. I don't know what to do. Or what to say. I just don't understand, Harry. Please. Don't go. Talk to me. Tell me what to do. What have I done? What's wrong with me?"

He finished his drink, got up from the table, grabbed a jacket from the hook behind the door and left the house.

She knew her daughter. Something was wrong. While she paid for the brunch at the table, she kept glancing from the waiter back to her daughter, who was fussing with her purse. When the waiter thanked her for the tip, she waved him off.

"Mom. You always over do that. Tipping so much is really…show-offy."

"He's a good waiter. He deserves a good tip. I bet *he* doesn't care if I show off."

"But, really…"

"Hey…it's none of your business, now is it?"

When she started to cry, she hoped that maybe her mother would not ask her any questions. Her father would never ask her questions when she cried. He would've been quiet, kind and comforted her, but he would not have asked questions. He would have waited.

And, there were times when she would talk to him about why she was crying. Her mother always had questions to ask, even when there was nothing really wrong. So, she braced herself. She made up her mind that she would not tell her mother everything. It would be too…

"Are you going to ask me a lot of questions?"

"Damned right I am," her mother said.

"Dad would leave it up to me."

"Yes. He would. But he's dead now. So…wanna tell me about it?"

Then she told her mother everything. She cried, but not a lot. And when she finished, she was fine. She wiped her eyes with her hanky, but she stopped crying.

Her mother had gone to law school. She had never taken the bar, but she volunteered a lot for different welfare agencies, got involved in political issues and worked as a legal advocate for certain groups. Her mother made lots of noise when she talked. And she made more noise and her hands flew around in front of her face when she talked and became upset.

By the time her mother finished with her closing statements, Margot sat looking around the small restaurant. Some people looked over at her, but most simply kept on eating and ignored them.

"I want to meet with Harry this afternoon," her mother said.

"No. No you are not."

"You don't get it, Margot."

"No, I don't get it, Mom. But, I have to do this myself. You can't come over today."

The mother watched her daughter's face. She recognized the weary, hurt look around her child's eyes. Her instincts screamed at her to take this girl home with her. She did not like Harry. She had met him only days before the wedding. She had not been impressed that he was a three-time Viet Nam veteran. In fact, she wondered to herself, *What in hell was so wrong with the guy that he had volunteered three times to go over there.*

That was, she decided, a grave error on her part, to wait so long to meet him. But, she lived so far away now. It was difficult to keep up with Margot. She had always been an independent, impulsive kid. When she had dropped Stephen to start going with this guy, it should've raised all kinds of hell-bells in her head. She thought of it at the wedding—to go up to Margot and simply say, "*Hey, you're making a big mistake here. Let's go home.*"

But, of course, she didn't. And it would not have worked anyway. It was too late by then.

Stephen had been with Margot for a long while. A stable man who had a nice career going in Margot's hometown, running the local heating oil business. He had a fleet of five trucks. Never married...just like Margot...never got around to it.

"Okay, Margot. Have it your way. But..." She snapped her purse shut, opened it and snapped it shut again. She did this three times. She held the purse up and placed it on the table in front of her. She opened it one more time, removed her wallet and took out her checkbook. She wrote on it, clicked her ballpoint pen closed and handed the check to Margot. "Put this away. In a separate account."

Margot looked at the check. She started to say something and stopped. She folded it and put it into her purse. "That's an awful lot of money, Mom."

"Well...I don't expect you to go shopping with it. Besides, I'm just showing off. " Her mother smiled. She reached across the table to hold her child's hand. "You're all grown up now. I can't go home and fix your problems for you anymore. You're right. But goddamn it, I can still throw some money at you and help you to get back home if you ever need to." She gripped her daughter's hand. "Save it for emergencies. It'll make me feel better."

They shopped the rest of the day. Margot bought a small ribeye to make for dinner. Harry liked ribeye steak. When her mother got into her car, she stood by the curb, leaning into the driver's side window. A cable car went by and started up the hill. The traffic did not seem bad. Margot stood back and looked at her mother's car.

"Good god, Mom. You've had this car for..."

"About ten years or so. Your dad bought it in 1970. Nearly traded it in back in '75. Then he died. I decided to keep it."

"Ugly thing."

"Yup. I never liked maroon cars. Especially not these things...Ramblers. That's all it is. A Rambler." She grinned up at her daughter. She shielded her eyes from the sun, using her hand. "Low mileage though."

"You could afford any new car you wanted. Why this?"

"Your dad. He loved the goddamned thing. Station wagons. God, I hate station wagons too."

Margot smiled and then laughed. "And he always had station wagons. There were only the four of us." Then she said, "He always said we were going to go on a long camping trip. To...I don't know...was it Wisconsin? Or Michigan?"

"Wisconsin. I don't know why though. Something about Wisconsin. The fish, I suppose."

"Never went."

"Your sister says the same thing every time she comes over to the house. She wants to know when I'm gonna trade it in." She looked up at her daughter. "Margot. You come home if you need to."

Margot nodded, leaned in and kissed her mother on the cheek. "I'll call you."

She stood on the sidewalk and watched her mother's car disappear into the traffic, headed for the Golden Gate Bridge. She wept.

He did not call. He did not contact her at all. Several days went by. He did not show up at work. Someone at work had asked about him. She lied. She had said he was very sick.

Finally, they had asked for a note from his doctor. She gave up the lying. She did not have any answers for their questions. There was a time she had nearly called the police, but then someone at work had seen him in the city and told her. So...she waited. One day, she had almost called her mother. She decided not to and called her sister instead.

"What is this?"

"I found these."

"Well...where?"

"In a box under our bed. A metal box that had a small lock on it. But it wasn't clasped. It was closed to look like it was clasped. But it wasn't. So...I opened the box."

Her sister turned the small brown bottles over in her hand. She opened one of them and spilled the pills into the palm of her hand. She looked at them and moved them with little twists of her hand so that they tipped around in the center of her palm. Some of the pills had letters on them. She looked at the table—there were several bottles, all different sizes.

"You're a nurse. What are these?"

"There are different kinds. Some are anti-depressants, some are powerful pain pills, some are morphine-based...they're controlled substances at the hospital."

"Yeah?"

"Well, they...look...there are no labels on the bottles. They are not prescriptions that are filled for anyone."

"What do you mean?"

"He takes them."

"For what? He isn't sick...or in pain..." she looked up at her sister. "Jesus, Margot...you mean he takes them from the hospital?" She hesitated, then said, "Is he selling this stuff?"

"No. He drinks all the time. And he takes pills too."

Her sister looked down at Margot's hands. Margot held them on the table in front of her. The hands squirmed together and squeezed each other. The waiter moved toward the two women, carrying a pot of coffee. Margot reached over and brushed the pill bottles into the canvass bag she had in her lap. The waiter arrived, topped off their coffee cups and left.

"God," her sister whispered.

"I don't dare to tell Mom. Christ, can you picture that?" She leaned back and looked around the coffee shop.

Her sister imagined her mother finding this out. She held this thought briefly. She rolled her eyes, pursed her lips and shook her head.

Margot looked around the shop. There were two couples sitting at another table across the room; otherwise, it was empty.

"Genie. I don't know what to do. I worry about him. He sometimes is so stoned that he can't wake up. He acts like...I don't know." She moved her head from side to side. "He could kill himself, you know? I mean, he knows these drugs, he knows what they can do. Especially with the alcohol."

She looked at her sister. One year younger than herself, but always the stable one, the solid kid, the girl with a cool head. Genie had never made an impulsive decision in her life. "We haven't..." her voice dropped, "done it."

Her sister sat silent. She watched Margot fidgeting in her chair. "Yeah...well I'm not surprised." She smirked at her sister. "You might be the only one around who is."

"What do you mean?"

"Margot…never mind. When did this all start?"

"I think he started the drugs in Viet Nam," she said. She reached over and took her sister's hand. "Genie? There's more…"

"Oh Christ, Margot…of course there's more."

"I know. But…there is." She leaned forward and looked her sister in the eyes. "He goes out at night." She held her sister's gaze. "He's been gone for days this time. He's lost his job."

Her sister's head moved in small circles. She bit her bottom lip.

"I think it's another woman."

"Oh…no, it's not another woman…poor Margot. We have to have a talk."

Two couples came into the shop and sat at the table beside of them. Margot stopped talking. She sipped her coffee.

"Let's leave," her sister said, "and go to that little antique place on the corner. I want to look around there. I was here in San Francisco a while ago and went in there with Joyce. But we didn't have time." She drank her coffee. "Wanna?"

Margot shrugged. She finished her coffee and they left.

They walked up the hill toward the antique shop. Margot and her sister were breathing hard.

Margot said, "You know…when I first came to San Francisco, after I got out of the military, I walked a lot all over this city, looking for jobs as a nurse."

"Mmmm," her sister panted.

"I noticed…whew…it's hot…" she paused, caught her breath, then continued, "I noticed that people here seemed to have these overdeveloped…calves."

Her sister chuckled.

"It took me a while to figure it out."

Her sister said, "These damned hills."

Inside the antique shop, cool dark air gave some relief. The sisters shopped in silence. Occasionally, they would separate but always joined up to show each other some discovery. The elderly woman, who was the shopkeeper, sat near the door reading a book. They were the only customers in the place.

"You met Harry in the military, right? In Viet Nam, working in the hospital, right?"

"Yes."

Her sister held a small glass in her hand. She looked it over and did not look at Margot. She said, "Did you guys date?"

"Not really. We spent a lot of time together though. We didn't date until we met up again, here, in the city." Margot brushed her hair back with one hand and reached for the glass her sister held. She turned it over in her hand and looked at the price on the bottom. She handed it back. "Here. You can have it. It's out of my range. In fact, the whole place is out of my range."

"Did you meet any of his family?"

"No."

"Mistake."

Margot began to cry. She caught herself and said, "I'm okay."

"You know...we never got to know him at all. Until a couple of days before your wedding. You never brought him around."

"He was always busy." She rolled her eyes. "I know..."

"So...do you love him?"

"I love him."

Her sister started to say something and stopped herself. She said, "Tell me about him. What is it you love?"

Margot said, "He's so..."

Her sister waited.

"Genie...he has these nightmares."

"About Viet Nam?"

"No. About when he was a kid."

"He tell you this?"

"Well, I knew about it when we were overseas together. But as time went by and we met up again, I found out that it got worse. He won't talk about it." She looked at the storekeeper who still read her book. She looked back at her sister. "He's so lost. So...sad."

"God. Margot, you can't do this."

"He needs somebody, Genie."

"What will it take, Margot? Five years? Ten? Twenty? Thirty?" She shook her head. "You can't fix him."

"You just met him, Genie. You don't know him."

"Yes, I do."

"What does that mean?"

Her sister did not respond.

"You don't know what he's like. He can be so funny and so smart."

"And...?"

Margot stopped and looked at her sister who looked back at her.

"Margot. I don't know Harry. But I know a lot of Harry's...they are not going to be fixed by a gentle, sweet Nurse Margot. Not ever. In fact, they hurt those that love them. And if allowed to, they would destroy them along with themselves."

Margot looked away and took a deep breath. She pretended to study a small copy of an Andy Warhol photo on a tin box. She picked it up and put it down on a lower shelf. She moved over to a rack of postcards. She turned the rack and looked at the cards. Her sister moved over beside of her.

"Margot. I am not going to apologize. I love you and I want to be honest about this. I wouldn't if it weren't so serious."

Margot nodded but did not look at her sister.

"Margot?"

"It's okay, Genie."

Her sister picked out a postcard. It was a photo of Cary Grant—in drag. A black and white scene from an old romantic comedy. She handed it to Margot. "You know, he was the heartthrob of his generation. The women swooned over him. Handsome man, huh?"

Margot glanced at it and put it back in the rack. She said, "I always liked his movies." She turned the rack one more time—it squeaked. She said, "I should be going."

Her sister dropped her at the train. They hugged. Margot walked down the steps, underground, and stood with the other people waiting for the BART. When the train pulled in, she entered and found a window seat. She sat staring out the window for the entire ride.

She dropped her purse on the kitchen table and went to the sideboard. A little of the red wine remained in the bottle she drank last night. She poured a full glass, emptying the bottle. She sipped and walked over to look at the mail that sat on the counter from yesterday. As she perused through the mail, she heard voices from the pool in the backyard. She stood and walked out onto the patio.

She smiled.

As she started toward Harry, she noticed the peculiar position he was in. And then she saw the other man and it became clear to her. She and Harry had never really dated—not overseas; those nights in Saigon were not dates at all. They had not dated here either. Those beautiful nights they went out together in romantic, downtown San Francisco... were not dates. And now she understood why she had not felt her husband inside of her. Not once.

Her mother knew about annulments. Margot did not pack—she just left. Her mother and sister came by later that week when Harry was not at home. They had Margot's key, they picked up some of her things. But she left most of it. She left the wedding gifts, some still unopened.

There were only men in the band. In the entire bar, there were only men. There were sounds from the rooms in the back of the bar. The sounds were not easily covered by the rock music that came over the speakers.

The man, quite drunk, grinned up at the large, older man sitting next to him. He felt small...like a boy, sitting next to this large man. The older man wore a dark leather vest and tight, black leather pants. He wore no shirt under the vest, baring a hairy, athletic chest and arms. His sweaty, bald head reflected the colored lights over the bar. A meticulous goatee moved up and down as he chewed. Occasionally he would spit the greasy black tobacco into a beer can. He had used a large, folding knife to cut the top off the beer can.

A young man with long, braided hair, a bright red t-shirt and wearing a white suit came to their booth. He told them they could move to the rear booth. They were next.

The man wearing the black leather vest pushed the smaller man. "Move," he said, sliding out of the booth. The smaller man moved out of their seat and into the rear booth. He looked around the dark barroom. He recognized some faces. He glanced at the clock over the bar: nearly two in the morning.

The noises from the rooms behind them were the crude, vulgar sounds of inflicted pain. The sounds excited him. He drank his whiskey and waited his turn.

# empty room

She searched his face. He smiled at her and said, "What?"

A whisper came from her lips, "Nothing."

They stayed like that, her lying on the gurney, him standing by her side in the hallway, holding her hand. A nurse walked past but did not look at them. They had been waiting for nearly an hour like this.

"You want me to ask?"

"No," she answered.

"Are you scared?"

She started to cry.

"It'll be okay. I will be right out here waiting."

She wept without making any sounds.

"I just know that this is okay. I know it," he said.

She nodded.

He squeezed her hand.

The doctor came up to them. No one had spoken to them or acknowledged them until now. He said, "We'll be going in now."

Two nurses appeared and started pushing the gurney.

He walked along beside her, still holding her hand. They stopped in front of two large doors. The doctor and the nurses disappeared inside the doors and left them outside. He leaned over and kissed her forehead. She reached up and grabbed his neck, pressing him hard against her head. "Come in with me..."

"They won't let me."

"Are we right about this?"

"Two doctors…they both said the same thing. I don't want to lose you."

"I'm scared."

"It'll be okay. I promise you. It'll be okay. I'll be here."

One of the nurses returned. She did not look at the man's face. She said, "Excuse me."

He moved, letting go of her hand. He said, "I love you."

Inside of the empty room, she lay on the gurney and listened. She turned her head and looked over to the doors to the adjoining room where they would move her in just a few minutes. The sounds from this room were alien. No voices except for an occasional, brief instruction from the doctor.

She looked up as one of the nurses leaned over her and checked her blood pressure. She prepared to smile at the nurse, but the nurse did not make eye contact with her. She thought about him waiting outside the room.

She thought about her three children back home. They did not even know that she was here. They were too young to know about this. She became overwhelmed with fear. She thought, *I could stop this right now*. All she had to do was to speak. But she didn't.

The doctor leaned over her. "We're going to give you a little something."

She looked into his eyes—he looked away. Her eyes closed.

From a strange, hollow place, she heard a faint echo and the word, "*…boy…*"

They drove home. They did not say anything to each other. She looked out the passenger window. At home, he carried her bag and walked beside her, holding her arm.

Inside, she sat on the sofa. He put her bag on the floor and looked over at her. Their dog came over and nuzzled her knees. He pushed the dog away and knelt in front of her.

It took him a second in the silence to hear her gasping. She could not breathe. She could not speak. He carried her back to the car and drove too fast.

At the emergency room, he had to carry her inside. They rushed her into a small room and attached many things to her arms and her face. He watched her eyes from the foot of the small gurney. They asked him questions about her. He answered. His eyes never left her face.

It happened all of a sudden…she was gone. Then…she was back.

The young doctor said, "Talk to her!"

He went to her and said, "I love you. Don't go. Please."

She opened her eyes and looked up at him, but closed them again. The machine that made noises and measured her pulse and did other things that he knew nothing about raced and beeped and made strange patterns on a small screen.

The young doctor sent for another doctor. The new doctor came swift and bold into the small room, pushing the husband out of the way. The husband collapsed into a sitting position on the floor near his young wife. He bit on his lip and it bled. He stared at her face and watched the machine tell him how fast her heart beat in her small body. And, then, how slow it beat.

The young doctor put a needle into her arm. He said to the husband, "Talk to her."

So he did. He held her hand. He talked to her. He said her name and talked to her like they were just sitting out on their patio with a cup of coffee, waiting for the school bus to bring their children home. A breeze moved across their fields, stirring the leaves in their maple trees.

# a fine silk

I opened my eyes and peered sideways to look at Harry sitting beside of me in the back seat. I did not turn my head because it still hurt like hell up the left side of my neck and into my scalp. The medication dulled it, but the pain convinced me to not move.

It bothered me that the doctor didn't know what caused this. I thought he should know. My wife said it had to do with Harry's coming home for this last visit. I didn't care for the humor. It hurt too damned much.

"I think it's Bosco," I whispered.

"Are you awake?"

I moved my eyes, not my head, to look at my wife's face in her rearview mirror. I looked at Joey in the passenger seat. His eyes roamed over my face.

"Yeah. A little."

"How are you feeling?" she asked.

"You mean as long as I don't move? Awful."

"You think it was Bosco?" Harry whined, using his Truman Capote voice. He used this voice when he was drunk.

"Yeah."

The three of them broke into song:

"'*I hate Bosco, it's very bad for meee...*'"

Harry said, "Hold it! Hey...hold it!"

"What?" asked Joey.

"I gotta pee."

Joey said, "Jesus, Harry...again? You just pissed twenty seconds ago."

"I can't help it."

"Slow down on those screwdrivers. That would help."

Harry was the only one drinking.

Jenny drove at a slow speed. She pulled over into a picnic area—no one around—in November. We were deep into the Maine countryside, off from Route 302. We had turned off from Route 11 a few miles back, near Raymond.

Harry climbed out and wandered over to a tree. He stood, back to us, weaving and pissing.

Joey and Jenny started again, " '*I hate Bosco, it's very bad for me. Momma put it in my milk to try to poison me. But I fooled Momma. I put it in her tea...*' "

Harry climbed back into the car, banging his head on the top of the doorframe. He finished the jingle with them, " '*...now there is no Momma to try to poison me.*' "

The three of them tittered.

"Dan...?"

I debated not responding. I replied, "What?"

My wife watched my face in the rearview mirror. "We decided to go to the graves on our way back home."

"Sure." I didn't really want to go to their parent's graves. My condition aside, this sounded like a mistake. Hell, I never visited anyone's grave. I always figured they weren't there. A pile of bones maybe. It's really a visit with yourself in my book. I went back to a half-sleep. My head and scalp throbbed.

They stood beside of the graves. I opened the car door and sat there letting the breeze come in. I could see their breath as they stood there. I looked up, the dark sky brooded and threatened. But...I needed the cool air.

The cemetery sat on the western edge of the small village, bordered by tall firs and pines on the west—their bittersweet scent played on the breeze—the pond to the north, the village to the east, and the road to the south...running east to west.

A crumbling stone wall, clogged with ferns and vetches and mats of dead leaves, ran parallel to the road and offered a separation that allowed a small vehicle entrance to the graveyard. The graveyard itself appeared untended. Mounds of sand and piles of rocks littered the boundaries. Tall, straw grasses that had not been mowed since summer now lay matted and yellowed. Naked, leafless shrubs, and dead flower stems stood out against the gray horizon. Some plots still had plastic flowers—faded and now exaggerated on their late-autumn graves.

"Why is there a hump there?" Jenny pointed at a place where the sandy soil of the earth came to a rise under her mother's gravestone. A thought occurred to me about that, but I kept it to myself.

Joey kneeled and pulled up grass around the graves.

Harry shrugged.

"Looks like someone put a flag on Daddy's grave. He was a veteran," Joey said.

"Ha. Right. A flag for Daddy," Harry said.

"He was a veteran. He was in World War II," said Joey, standing up, still looking at the graves.

No one spoke for several seconds.

Jenny said, "Well…he was not in the war. He never left the states."

Harry sniggered. "They wouldn't let him hold a gun."

"You don't know that," Joey said, looking at Harry.

"Hell…you never even knew the man. What do you know?" Harry whined, pitching the Capote voice up a notch. "And he wasn't *my* daddy."

Jenny looked back at me. I would've rolled my eyes, but I hurt too much.

"Don't start in on that," Joey said.

Harry ignored him.

I watched them stand with their shoulders up, their backs turned to the wind that came off the pond and across the hill in the cemetery.

Joey looked over at Jenny. "Does anyone come over to put flowers here?"

Jenny said, "I don't know. I think Kicky does on Memorial Day and maybe at other times." Then she said, "I guess I should sometimes."

Jenny looked away and across the cemetery hill toward the pond.

"It's cold," Harry said.

Jenny said, "Let's go over to Missy's grave." She started toward the car.

Missy, an older sister, had been buried in an even smaller cemetery a few miles away. Jenny put the hood of her blue wool jacket up over her head and strolled toward me.

Harry and Joey still stood by the graves. Then Joey turned and started back to the car. Harry followed. They walked single file down the short, dirt path. Jenny, in the lead, reached the car first.

"Good idea," I mumbled to her as she approached my open door, "you know…visiting the graves."

She didn't look at me. She closed my door and climbed in behind the steering wheel, closing her door behind her. Joey and Harry each got in and slammed their doors. No one spoke as Jenny drove through the small village.

"Remember the village on Parade Day?" Jenny was looking at Harry in the rearview mirror. Her voice trailed off, "It seemed so big to me then."

Harry looked out his window. He didn't answer.

I left my door open again, this time I took my jacket off, but I was still warm

"This cemetery is really small," Jenny said. "I forgot it was so small."

Inside the cemetery, Missy's grave came right up against the narrow dirt road. There would be no room for another vehicle to come down that path, but there were no cars around. This small, rural cemetery looked as abandoned and neglected as the one we just left. The three of them stood beside the small gravestone.

The wind did not come through this grove of pine trees as it had by the pond. I peered between them at the gravestone. I saw the dates: 1943-1963. Missy had left two young kids behind when she died.

Jenny wept quietly.

Joey and Harry were staring at the grave stone. They did not speak.

Jenny spoke as though she were talking to herself, "Missy was a good person. Her life stunk. She had to put up with Uncle Lenny. Then she married that animal—John. He owned her when she was still just a kid. He was a pervert too. He and Uncle Lenny should've both been shot." She said, "Momma should've done something."

Harry and Joey did not say anything.

Joey stood looking down. He shifted from one foot to the other.

"Hard to believe it's been so long…so many years, I mean," said Joey. He reached down and brushed moss from around the dates carved into the stone. Then he stood up straight. Stretching his back, he glanced over at his older brother. He looked away toward the main road and up at the sky.

"We should've brought warmer clothes. Hell—it was in the seventies when we left San Francisco. I forgot how cold it is back here."

Harry, his hands in his pockets, looked around the small cemetery. He looked back at the grave. He did not speak. He was no longer weaving.

"Sometimes we get snow before Thanksgiving, remember?" Jenny said, looking up at the sky. "Maybe we'll have some snow for you two yet."

I watched Harry. He stood staring at Missy's grave. He seemed small. Harry still wore glasses; but these glasses were too large and teetered off the bridge of his nose. He pushed them up with his forefinger. It seemed to me that his face had shrunk. He had no hair left on his head. He looked old...skeletal. He looked like death.

I thought, "*He's dying.*"

The cold air smelled of snow. I knew the scent. A damp, clean smell that stirred childhood memories of sliding, skating... playing hard in crystal-fresh snow... itchy, wool-knit caps and the smell of wet mittens.

Time does stop. It really does. I know that everyone of us felt it. One of those moments that become suddenly still and motionless and then...the instant is gone.

The Japanese have a word for a unit of consciousness: nen. This sensation fell between those units of consciousness; a place outside of time. Or maybe my temperature just climbed.

I watched a single leaf that dangled from an otherwise bare, maple tree, just behind Harry. The leaf spun in a slow movement, one way—then the other. It clung to the tree. There, beside the leaf and tucked in between the worn, wooden slats of the decaying fence that surrounded this side of the graveyard, a spider web hung, moving gently in the air. The spider was long gone, of course, but a large moth, tangled and caught sometime ago, now dead, still dangled in the silk that the creature had left behind.

Suddenly, Harry made a noise and reached down, grabbed the flowers off from Missy's grave and flung them at the woods.

"I hate plastic flowers," he said not using his Truman Capote voice. "Don't ever put plastic flowers on my grave."

The second story bedroom of our old farmhouse in Cold Brook Mills had a register in the floor that allowed the heat from downstairs to come up into the bedroom. This kept the bedroom just tolerable in the freezing temperatures of January. But at least it made it possible, covered with heavy quilts, to use the upstairs in the winter. It also provided an opening to the downstairs.

The kids, when they were little, dangled and dropped toys and other objects through the grating: little lessons in eye-hand coordination and gravity. It also functioned as a communications port. All conversations from downstairs were easily heard upstairs, and vice-versa—even when the grating is shut.

Jenny slept. I remained motionless in my bed, having found the precise, relatively painless position for my neck.

"Don't leave them lying around, Harry."

"I didn't," Harry said.

"I found them in the bathroom. Keep them in this," said Joey.

"Do they know?"

"Yes. They know."

"Does Jenny know?"

"I said they know. Both of them."

I heard noises.

"Keep the needles in this can and keep it covered. I told them you would be careful."

"Want a drink?"

"Sure…wine." Then Joey said, "Harry…are you even paying attention?"

Silence. Some clinking noises of glasses and bottles.

"Harry? You need to be careful of body fluids."

"I know that…" Then, "Here…"

It was quiet. I could hear them moving around in their room, directly off from the kitchen. The room with the register in it. I closed my eyes.

Thanksgiving dinner. Turkey, ham, turnip, mashed potatoes, cranberry sauce, peas, squash, apple pie, pumpkin pie, chocolate cream pie… Lot's of food. Everyone came. Someone said a little prayer at the table. We all went around and spoke of what we were thankful for.

Harry said, "Family." Jenny said, "All my favorite people are here." Joey said, "I'm thankful that we can all be together. All of us. This is an important day for me. Very important." I read something from the Dhammapada as a sort of grace.

I carved the turkey and served. My head and neck still hurt like hell. Jenny drank too much wine. She laughed. Joey laughed. He drank too much. But he drank vodka. Harry drank also. I noticed that Harry was not drunk.

I would have joined them, but I could not drink…so I watched them. Kelly's daughter—Jenny's niece—Emmie, and her husband, who lived nearby, left first. Emmie was pregnant and she became tired easily. Katie and Joe left early; Joe had to leave the next day for Virginia. Mary went to her friend's house for the evening and Danny stayed late.

After everyone left, Jenny, Joey and Harry continued to drink. Finally, I went to bed. I left the window open a crack.

Later, when I awoke, the room was cold. I closed the window and went down stairs. It was after two in the morning. All of the lights were still on. A note on the table said that Mary was staying all night at her friend Jocelyn's house. Harry was in bed, asleep. Joey was asleep in the living room chair with the television on.

Jenny was sprawled out on the couch. I woke her. She was drunk. I helped her upstairs. She fell into bed. I turned out the light and stretched out in the dark. I felt warm again, but I did not get up to open the window.

I shifted onto my side and tried to close my eyes. They opened. I gaped into the darkness for as long as I could, but still I could not sleep.

The night air climbed right through my jacket. I had not bothered to put on a shirt. I took a glass of wine out onto the patio with me and sipped on it. I walked down onto the south lawn and turned to look back at the house. Everyone inside was asleep. The brightness of the moon twinkled off the frost that glazed the trees and grasses of our fields. *How bright, bright, bright the moon.*

The frosted lawn crunched beneath my feet. I stood and stared at the lofty silhouette of our barn against the night sky—how many times had I, with Mark, an old friend, climbed onto that treacherous barn roof to do repairs?—then over at the huge maple tree beside of our house, naked now, stripped, dormant, and poised for a long, cold winter. This was my favorite place in the whole world. And this was my favorite view of my favorite place in the whole world.

We bought the farmhouse more than twenty years ago. Our first child, Katie, was born that year. I had a dream one night, shortly after we moved in. I dreamed that I was an elderly man, alone, in the upstairs bedroom. There was no one else around. The house was empty and barren except for me in my bed. I believed that I would grow old and die in this house.

It was the only house my children would ever remember living in as kids. They would all grow up in this house. But Jenny and Harry had never lived in any place for very long. Jenny and I had counted once: eighteen moves by the time she had graduated high school—fifteen of those moves before she had entered high school. This house was the most permanent fixture in Jenny's life. It was...a home.

I thought about Harry. He had never had a home. He and Jenny had had houses and apartments and places to sleep and eat...but they had not ever had a home.

I thought about waking Harry up. I wanted to ask him if he understood. If he understood the damage his parents had inflicted on them. If he could possibly find it in himself to talk to his sister about their life together. To talk about what it was that tied them—kept them so close—but mysteriously distant...and hurt.

I knew some of it. But, I also knew that it was not important for me to know more. It was important that they confirm for each other what had happened, to make it clear, to sort out the child's stuff in the grimness of their memory. And...to forgive those things that can be forgiven.

Then I saw him. He stood on the patio where I had stood only moments before. Trembling—ghost-like in the glow of the night. He was looking at me. He motioned to me. I could see his breath in the moonlight.

I wrapped my arms around myself, careful of the wine glass and walked toward the house. I looked down at the ground to see where I was going. But when I got to the patio he was not there. I went inside the house, but it was quiet and dark. I looked in the bathroom, and the living room. Nothing.

I sat at the kitchen table and thought about going to the room that he and Joey were sharing, but I did not do that. Instead, I finished my glass of wine and went upstairs. I thought about Harry standing on the patio. I was certain it was him. But...I also knew that I was not well. The possibility that I had not seen Harry began to take over as I fell asleep. Harry might have stood there; he might not have stood there.

Mary played Bach on her piano. I pushed up from the sofa and looked over at her. Harry sat in a chair nearby. His eyes clung to Mary's face. His face had some color. He held his eyeglasses in his lap. I did not see Joey or Jenny.

Outside, a soft, slow snow fell past the window. Our dog slept on the floor beside of Mary.

I walked out into the kitchen. No one was in the house. There was a pot on the stove. I lifted the cover: beef stew. It simmered on low heat. I went into the bathroom and sat on the toilet. I hung my head, it throbbed, so I lifted it and looked around the bathroom.

Outside the bathroom window, the sun was shining. The wind blew through the trees across the field. The trees bent deep with the strong gusts. I sat for a long time but could not accomplish anything other than a dribble of urine.

I stood and pulled up my pajama bottoms. I started to leave and noticed the spray bottle of bleach I had prepared. It sat beside of the toilet on the floor. I shrugged: *Too late. Should've used it before I sat down.*

We went to the movies. A vampire film. Tom Cruise had a young girl as a sort of adopted vampire daughter. I wore my neck brace. But I was so zonked on pain medication—and pain—that I kept falling asleep in the film. I awoke to brief glimpses of eerie, surreal scenes of the living dead who looked vaguely familiar.

Coming out of the theatre people stared at me. Harry said, "Can I borrow that?" People laughed. I smiled.

We stopped at a Mexican restaurant and had tacos and drinks. I drank some cold ale. I felt a little better. I drank some more. I noticed that Danny and Mary were with us.

We left the Mexican restaurant and went to another place. We had more drinks. Jenny drank red wine. I drank two more Geary's ales, very cold, and I felt pretty good. We left.

Leaving this restaurant, a small band was setting up to play later in the evening. Harry, now drunk, said to them as we passed to the exit, "You guys stink!" Outside, everyone laughed at Harry's comment because the band had not played yet.

Laughter came from the kitchen. The door was closed but I could hear voices. Harry, Joey and Jenny. There was music from the radio. I rolled over and closed my eyes.

I thought of my father. Later in his life, after his stroke and the dementia had set in, he used to sit for hours in his old swivel chair. He had loved to watch reruns of his favorite, old John Wayne movies. He would ask me who the people were. I would say, "Well…that's Ward Bond…and that is Walter Brennan. That guy is Dean Martin…Richard Widmark…that's The Duke…Maureen O'Hara…"

One time, I had visited him while Mom was gone with my sister. I fell asleep on the sofa during *The Searchers*. I had woken up and looked over at Dad—he was staring at me—his eyes, strange, with tightly constricted pupils, black…empty and menacing. It had startled me.

When I had spoken to him, he just continued to stare at me, and I realized then that he didn't know who I was. I wondered, *What is that like, to not know your own child?*

I awoke now but could not keep my eyes open. So I surrendered to a disturbed sleep, the voices still loud from the kitchen. I was hot and sweaty. I kicked off the blanket.

"Because it is in the past."

"No. It's not in the past. It's right now, Harry. It's happening to me right now," Jenny said. "Listen to us...it's happening to us, right now, Harry. In the present."

Harry and Jenny were sitting alone in the living room. They were oblivious of me. I watched them through half-closed eyelashes, curled up on the sofa; my head felt better. I looked outside. It was dark.

"Momma left us with them and she didn't even know them."

"She knew them."

"Well, Jesus, Harry, that would be even worse!"

"I mean, she knew who they were."

"Yeah. She knew that the woman delivered milk."

"She needed a place for us..."

"You heard Uncle Marty...she could've left us with them. She left all the others with family."

The television was turned off. I pretended to sleep.

"Harry...she did lots of things that you won't even talk about."

"If Daddy..." Harry mumbled.

"Daddy was never around. That was part of the problem. But Momma *was* around...and she did nothing...in fact, she did a lot of things that were really bad."

"Like?"

"She used to give us to Uncle Lenny and take his money for starters."

Harry was silent.

Jenny continued, "She caught John with Sophy once. Right after Missy's funeral. She blamed Sophy! She was, what?...ten years old or something? She knew exactly what he was and she practically gave Sophy to him after Missy died. She let him have her."

"She kept the family together. She..."

"What family? If that's what a family is like, I don't want to be a part of one. She beat us, Harry. Lots of people have bad lives, but they don't do what she did." She took a breath, sighed, shook her head, then said, "When we were little, she used to call us in from outside to make us watch porno movies with John...as a family! That was our family, Harry."

"Daddy..."

"Momma, Harry, Momma!"

Through my squinting, I could see that Jenny was leaning towards Harry, sitting on the edge of her seat.

"Jenny...it's over. It's all over now. It doesn't do any good to keep bringing it up."

"What do you mean, 'keep bringing it up?' We've never...talked about any of this. And it is not over. I'm...no, *all* of us...we're all still caught up in it. This whole family is...trapped in this. We're all...dying." She stopped.

Harry left the room.

"...excuses for her," Jenny was saying.

"Do you want the pasta for tonight? Chicken Marsala? Or what?" Joey asked.

"The chicken," Harry said.

"Chicken," Mary said.

Harry, turning to Jenny, said, "Enough, Jenny. No more talk about the past, okay?"

I opened the door and walked into the kitchen.

"Hi, Dad," Mary said.

I smiled at Mary.

Jenny said, "Are you feeling any better?"

"A little, I guess."

I went into the bathroom and washed up. I found the spray bottle of bleach and sprayed the toilet and the bathroom sink. I wiped them clean with paper towels and then washed my hands with the same spray. I had read somewhere that this was a good precaution.

I splashed cold water on my face and dried it with a clean towel. I did not feel feverish anymore, but my neck and head were still locked in pain.

At the table there was laughter. As I came back into the room, Harry and Jenny were doing a graceful waltz around the kitchen table to Don McLean's "Vincent" playing on the radio. They moved as smoothly together as they had in high school when they won those awards. We all watched, smiling.

We had Chicken Marsala that night and Mary played for us. I watched her fingers on her instrument. She played the Bach Suite No. 1. It was a gesture of love that Mary gave all of us as she touched the keys. I looked over at Harry sitting next to Jenny. Together, they watched Mary.

Harry watched Jenny's face as she studied her daughter. He looked over at me. I smiled at him. He looked back at Mary. Joey sipped on a white wine.

At the airport, Jenny sat between Harry and Joey, their arms draped across her shoulders. I took their photograph. Joey was laughing. Jenny laughed also. Harry smiled.

I said, "Jeez…I'm sorry, Harry, about this visit. I missed most of it. This thing I've got just won't let up."

Harry said it was okay. We all hugged. I hugged Joey and thanked him for getting Harry out to visit us.

Jenny and Harry held onto each other for a full minute. Then Harry and Joey walked down the ramp to get onto their plane. I put an arm around Jenny. We stood like that for a long while after Harry and Joey had disappeared into the plane.

We did not talk much on the hour drive home. In the darkness of the car, Jenny cried.

"What in the hell is this?"

I felt much better. The pain that I had had over the past four weeks or so had subsided, and this day…not a trace of it.

I looked up from my book. Jenny was holding a can in one hand and a cover in the other.

"Let me see," I said, taking the can.

Danny came over and looked inside. He said, "Looks like needles. You know…for injections."

I smiled. I looked at Jenny and then at Danny. "Well…looks like Uncle Harry left us with a small gift."

"What…?" Jenny asked.

"You haven't touched these have you?"

"No."

"Give them to me." I took the can and the cover.

We sat at the kitchen table with the can of needles sitting on the floor by the kitchen door. We talked about our options. Danny thought of taking them to the local hospital and letting them dispose of them. Jenny wanted to bury them. I pointed out the window at the snow-covered ground.

Finally, Danny and I took the can outside. We put some gasoline in the bottom of the can, took it down behind the barn, placed the can in the snow and set it on fire. Danny stood several feet back from the smoke. He had a scarf held up to his face. He said something.

"What?" I asked.

He mumbled again.

"What?"

"I said," he took the scarf from his face, "can we catch anything from the smoke?"

I laughed. We walked back up to the house.

We didn't see Harry again. He called a few times. I took most of those calls because Harry was drunk. Harry told me that he loved Jenny. He told me that he loved me too. He told me, during one phone call, that when he went out with that man, on several occasions, a few years ago, he knew that he would get sick. He told me he knew it—and that he knew it would kill him.

# the point

He watched the boxcars creeping past his windshield. Lost in the clanging signal, flashing red lights and the clacking and rattling of the cars on the rails, he shivered, shook his head and rolled his window up all the way. April—end of winter and still gray and cool outside.

He made himself look away from the train. Out his driver's side window, across the road, he observed the old Congregational Church, its worn, white clapboards scraped and prepared for painting, left like that for the past two summers. He bent his head to gaze up at the steeple.

The church steeple displayed itself, towering above the treetops, easily seen from any of the hills coming into this valley town. Its only competitor had been the mill's chimneystack—and that was gone now.

When he was a child, the churches in town rang their bells every Sunday morning. The bells were silent now. Instead, the church used an amplifier and speaker to send out church music. *A poor substitute for the bells,* he thought.

In its day, Cold Brook Mills was one of those postcard scenic Maine villages. After the mill closing, the town showed its poverty. Empty, abandoned storefronts and homes began to deteriorate. The village square lost many of its buildings. Spike's Garage, in the center of town, disappeared and in its place came a Cumberland Farms convenience store and gas station.

He sniffed. He found himself holding his breath. He let it out and breathed deeply. The railroad cars wobbled by one by one—*Canadian, Boston to Maine, St. Lawrence and Atlantic, Bangor and Aroostook*—graffiti spread along their sides that included messages of love, hate, and raw, vulgar works of spray-paint art. The train no longer pulled into the mill to deliver or pick up paper or paper pulp, but they did still stop to switch tracks and drop off or pick up boxcars.

Dan Cummings hit the steering wheel with his palm. His nose ran. He wiped it from his moustache with his shirtsleeve. His mind raced. He understood that this was evidence of the fury of his emotions, but he could not stop his mind long enough to focus on their argument.

He thought, *I can't do this anymore with her.* The boxcars continued to pass slowly. *It's just not fair.* He felt exhausted and hurt.

She had slept on the couch last night. They had at least been in the same bed before that, even though they had avoided touching each other during sleep. He knew her well enough to know that she had not been sleeping well either.

It irked him that he needed her closeness even when he was angry. And he knew that this was true for her as well. They both knew it about each other. And yet this thought upset him all over again; he thought he had never felt so exasperated and hurt as he felt at this moment. His chest felt tight with emotion.

*Goddamnit.* He hit the steering wheel again. Then he glanced in his rearview mirror. *Shit.*

Dennis Witham was waving from the car behind him. He blew his horn at Dan. Dan watched in the mirror as Dennis opened his car door, slammed it and limped toward Dan's passenger side door.

"Hey..." Dennis said, knocking on Dan's passenger window, "open up."

Dan reached over and unlocked the car door. The door stuck, Dan pushed on it and it squeaked open. Dennis opened it wide and climbed in, slamming the door shut behind him.

"How the hell are you?" Dennis said. He reached up, pulled his knit hat off from his head and set it on his knee. The hat had "New England Patriots Superbowl Champions" printed on it.

Dennis was nearly bald. What hair he had was gray, it stuck out from behind his ears; his whiskers were a salt and pepper stubble. He shook himself and looked at Dan.

"That friggin' train is gonna stop right in the middle. We'll be here a while," he said and nodded his head toward their rear, "what with that tractor trailer parked up our ass." He stared at the train that was slowing. "Damn, am I ever sick of this weather. Supposed to be a nice spring day today. Seems like winter gets colder and longer every year."

He paused and looked at Dan. "Ain't seen you to talk to for...hell, I dunno...months!" He thought for a second. "No shit...months. How the hell are you anyway?"

Dan looked over at his friend. "Okay." He noticed that Dennis had only a couple of teeth left up top. He was suddenly grateful that he had all of his hair...gray as it was and most of his own teeth.

He found himself wondering how he was showing his age. He reached up with his right hand and ran it across his beard...also gray, and thought again about shaving it off. But Jen often told him it made him look distinguished, and he was still vain enough to want to keep it.

Dennis looked around the interior of the car. He said, "What happened to the New Yorker?"

"Got a kid in college, Dennis. Had to downsize."

"Yeah. But you bought one of those foreign cars."

Dan shook his head. He looked straight ahead. "Yeah. One of those foreign cars that doesn't break down as much and lasts a lot longer. That's what I needed." Annoyed, he added, "Besides, they're built all over the place nowadays."

"How's Jenny?"

Dan hesitated, then said, "She's doing okay."

The train stopped. Then it shook hard, like an angered beast, and clanged, shifting to a rear movement. The cars began to creep in reverse and then came to a complete stop.

"See. Told ya," Dennis said. "Son of a bitch."

Dan was thinking of Jenny. His sympathy for her only frustrated him more. He had left her at home, crying in their bedroom. She told him to get out. She told him not to come back.

He pulled himself up in his seat and leaned on the steering wheel. He was so pissed he could not carry on a conversation. He watched the train struggle to move backwards.

"You see that shit on the news?"

Dan made a noise.

"Can you believe those assholes? I'm telling ya, there's gonna be another war. Well...good. But as far as I'm concerned, they could take care of this bullshit with one fell swoop...boom! Just blow the whole damned country right out of the East and into the Arctic region. That'll cool the bastards off...quick." He glanced at his friend. "See how they like taking a shit in the cold, huh?"

Dan shrugged. He remembered the military. He had other thoughts about war.

They were quiet. The train had not moved.

"Hey, did you hear about Alton?"

"Yeah."

"Damn. Sure makes you stop and think, doesn't it?"

Dan took another deep breath and let it out. "Yeah. It sure does."

"I went over to see him before he died. He was smoking while I was there. Still smoking...dying of lung cancer." Dennis was shaking his head. "Good shit, Alton. I always thought he was a really good shit. He'd give you the shirt off his back."

Dennis nodded. That was true. Alton had been a good shit...and he would've given you anything he had if he had thought you needed it.

"Where you headed?"

Dan said, "Nowhere special. Just..." he realized his mistake and said, "picking up some stuff at Danny's house." He didn't think his son was home, but that didn't matter.

"Wanna get a coffee after this train takes a dump?"

Dan pretended to study his rearview mirror. He just needed a second to think. After a few seconds, Dennis turned in his seat to look back toward his own car, and then back at Dan.

Dan said quickly, looking at Dennis, "Uh...sure. I can't be long though. I have to...get over to Danny's house and pick up some stuff."

"Hey. I can give you a hand."

"Well...if he's home."

Danny's black Ford Ranger sat in his driveway, backed in as usual. Dan pulled in beside of it. Dennis opened his door and got out. Dan watched him and then got out on his own side. His son was walking across the driveway toward them, his boots crunching in the gravel. He looked like he had just gotten out of bed.

He wore a dark colored flannel shirt over a black t-shirt. Dan often wondered where he got his size; he was a well-built man, bigger than his father. It still surprised him that his son was a grown man.

"Little Danny..." Dennis held out a hand to the young man.

"Hi, Dennis. Haven't seen you in a while."

"Same thing I said to your dad."

A large dog wandered out and welcomed each of them with his tail wagging and his tongue hanging out. He nuzzled Dennis in the groin. Dennis pushed him away.

Dan walked up to his son. “How you doin’?”

“Good, Dad.”

“Ellie?”

“Still pregnant with the other Danny. She’s at work.”

“Thought I’d pick up that...lawnmower, if you can spare it.” He caught his son’s eye.

“Sure. It should fit in your trunk. But you might want to wait for the rest of the snow to disappear.” Danny gave his dad a small grin.

They walked toward the shed at the rear of Danny’s mobile home.

Dan squinted at his son. “I’ll tinker with it in the meanwhile.”

Then Danny looked closely at his father. “How’s Mom?”

His father shrugged. “She’s home.”

“How’s she doing?”

“Well...” he looked toward the road and then back toward the shed, “she’s having a rough day. She’ll be okay.”

Danny looked at his father and put his hands in his jeans pockets. He glanced back toward Dennis who was still standing by the truck playing with his dog. Dennis threw a stick and hooted at the dog when he chased it down the driveway.

“What’s up with Dennis?”

“Nothing. I ran into him earlier.”

“So...is Mom...?”

“It’s nothing, Danny. She just has these days, you know?”

“I know. But you seem different. You look tired.”

They stopped in front of the shed door. Dan turned toward his son. “It’s okay, Danny. It’s okay. Really.”

He watched his son search his face, then turn to open his shed door.

“You really want this lawnmower?”

“No. Not really.”

Danny smiled at his father again. He pulled the lawnmower out of the shed, into the wet grass and onto a patch of snow. He looked at his father. He smiled, “Got stuck with Dennis, huh?”

“I don’t mind. He’s an old friend. Just not good timing, ya know?”

They started back toward Dennis and the dog. Danny yelled to Dennis, “His name’s Martha.”

“Listen,” Dan said, pushing the lawnmower, struggling in the mud and snow, “have you heard from your sister?”

"You mean Katie? Last night. She and Joe are home today. Why don't you drop by there later? Maybe Mom, too."

"I think I might."

"You know, Dad, you should check to see if Mary is off today or tomorrow. Maybe she could swing by and see Mom. Mom always cheers up with Mary around."

Dan smiled at his son's suggestion. Their youngest one did have a way with her mother. But Mary would not be likely to get any time off from school right now. It was a busy time of the year at the college, and she rarely came home to visit these days.

Dan stopped; suddenly he felt overwhelmed. He had a memory of the kids with him and Jenny, together on a camping trip to the ocean near Eastport, just a few years ago. He had allowed Danny to take Mary in one of the canoes out into the bay, and he had taken the other with Jenny and Katie.

They had come upon some seals on a rock, sunning themselves. Mary had nearly tipped the canoe over, trying to get closer, with her brother yelling at her to sit still and stop moving around so much. He and Jenny had laughed, watching them, awkward in their lifejackets, with Little Danny trying to paddle from the back of the canoe and Mary in the front, banging and slapping the water, attempting to get closer to the seals.

Dan thought of Katie. He had thought of calling her. He knew Katie and Joe would be home. He did not like to bother Katie about this stuff with her mom. Katie could be impatient. She worried and was not always able to separate out her own emotions to deal with her mother's.

Dan realized that this was what he was having trouble with himself. It occurred to him that he should not bring the kids into this at all...at least, not right now. This confused him. He needed comforting himself.

He looked up toward Dennis...he could rule his friend out. Dennis would never be noted for his tactful empathy. And yet, the kids should have their own lives. He needed to leave them alone.

Or—should they be involved with their mom? Well...not the marriage stuff, that was between Jenny and himself, but the rest of it? Their mother's history was certainly no secret to them, even though it had rarely been discussed. Dan realized how few friends he did have. In fact, he had made a point over the years of not having many friends. And he did not regret this. He doubted seriously that that would be the kind of support that he would pursue regardless.

"Dennis is gonna wear Martha out. He's as hyper as he is."

Dan watched Dennis with his son's dog.

"You okay?"

Dan nodded and looked at his son. He said, "Fine." He pushed the lawnmower over to his car.

Dennis flung the stick and Martha took off up the driveway after it. Dennis said, "Hey…lickity-split…Arthur is a hot shit dog."

Danny looked at his father then at Dennis, "It's Martha. His name is Martha."

"What the hell…you named a boy dog Martha?"

"Yeah. After the Beatles' song, Paul's English Sheepdog, Martha."

"Well, shit…that's dumb. He's a boy."

"Yeah. But I didn't have a female dog, and I liked the name Martha," Danny said.

"Danny likes to be…paradoxical," said Dan.

Dennis said, "Ayuh. But he's a boy dog."

Dan smiled at his son, lifting one shoulder to shrug toward his friend. Dennis stopped playing with Martha. He looked at the dog but did not throw the stick again.

Dan dropped Dennis off at his car in front of The Village Store. He drove up to his own house. Looking at the lawns and the maple trees, he did not stop but instead went on by and turned around in his neighbor's driveway and headed back down the street.

He looked at the maple trees again and made a mental note that they would need cutting back; some of them would need to be taken down. The ice storm in 1998 had done serious damage to the old maples. He wondered what Jenny was doing.

His anger flared again. He tried to remember what had started it. But when he put his mind to that task, it just raced. He tried to slow down…he thought of the train: the boxcars…the noise…the painful slowness and his impatience. It seemed to have started over something simple and then escalated until they were screaming at each other.

Although they had rarely fought over the years, he noticed this happening more frequently in the past several months. Dan drove through the village, under the railroad underpass, and headed out of town. He thought that he would drive by Kate and Joe's, just to see if they were around. He would not bother them, he decided. He would just see if they were at home.

He drove up behind his daughter's sports utility vehicle and parked. His old Tercel was lost in the shadow of the SUV. He and Katie bantered some about the SUV and whether or not it was too much of a vehicle. Of course, he secretly admired it. It was new. His was old. It was large. His was...well, a lot smaller than the SUV. He comforted himself with the rationalization that he was conserving gas and space on the planet.

She blew him off when he brought that subject up. They shared common politics, most of the time. At least, he thought they did. He sometimes didn't dare to ask about her politics. She was a bright, articulate, and out-spoken young woman. She was a feminist, most of the time, and he thought that most of the time he was a feminist as well.

He and Jenny prided themselves on the way they had brought up their children to be appropriately outspoken. When it came to his kids, he preferred to keep their relationship affectionate and simple. He shut the Tercel's engine off and climbed out of his car.

"Hey, Dad." Katie opened the kitchen door and he walked inside.

"Joe home?" he asked.

"Down to the Home Depot picking up some plumbing stuff. Got chores today." She nodded toward the open doors under the kitchen sink.

"Ooops."

"Nah...he loves this stuff. He needs to tinker on something all the time, or he's not happy. So how's Mom?"

Dan noted that Danny had immediately raised the same question.

"Home. She's okay, I guess."

She looked at him and then walked to the kitchen table and sat down. She reached behind her and grabbed a clean coffee mug from the counter top.

"Here," she said, handing him the mug. "Get yourself a coffee."

He walked over to the pot and poured a cup. He added one sugar and a spoonful of powdered cream, then he walked over to sit down at the table with his eldest child.

She sat and waited as he sipped on his coffee.

"Ouch." He pulled his mouth away from the steaming mug. "Hot."

She was silent. She watched him and sipped on her tea.

"So...how's Mom?"

"Not so good. We had an argument."

"About what?"

"I don't know. Really, I don't think it was about anything. But damn if it didn't turn ugly."

"Well, what were you talking about?"

"I honestly don't know. And you know...when I try to think about the fight, I just go blank. I can't remember what I said or what she said." He stopped, and then said, "Well, that's not exactly true. I do remember some of the words. They were..."

Katie watched her father and did not speak.

He regretted talking this much.

"But it'll be okay...we just have this once in a while...lately."

"So you aren't going to tell me about the fight?"

"Katie, it is so difficult for me to even think about it." He looked at her and then down at his cup. He didn't want her to see his face right now. He stood up and walked out of the kitchen and into the living room. He stood inside the doorway, his back toward Katie. He said, "It'll be alright..."

Katie said, "What did you say?"

"I said, 'It'll be alright.'" He turned and looked across the kitchen at Katie sitting at the table; he held his mug with both hands. "You know, I don't really want to bother you with this stuff. Your mom and I fight sometimes. That's all. You know, we've been married a long time...it's just a fight."

Katie was quiet. She sipped on her tea.

Dan walked across the kitchen and sat at the table again. He looked up at Katie. She avoided his eyes.

"Katie..."

"It's okay...you don't have to talk to me about it if you don't want to."

"Katie...it's...hard. She is so defensive...paranoid, even...at times. I want to be able to be honest with her when we talk...and we will talk again. Someday." He set the mug on the table. "And, she will be upset if I tell her I brought you kids into this."

"I think you underestimate her. She has to know that it's our business too. It is, you know. You're our parents."

Dan nodded but was quiet. She was right.

They sat for several minutes without speaking.

"So...Joe has some stuff ahead of him today, huh?" He looked toward the sink.

She made a face and nodded.

He said, "I saw Danny this morning. I had Dennis Witham with me when I dropped by earlier."

"Dennis Witham? What the heck was he doing with you?"

"I haven't seen him to talk to in a long time. He just pulled up behind me at the railroad crossing and we got stuck there…there was this trailer truck halfway across the road behind us… and he got into the car and…well…"

"I don't know him very well. I know who he is. You guys used to be friends…right?"

"Back in school. We sort of grew up together."

She was quiet again.

"I should be getting going."

"You know…" she said, looking up at him, "it really pisses me off."

"What?"

"Well…you just breeze in here and drop this on me and then leave."

He watched her.

"See…I worry. You can't just do this. You can't just come in here and use me for a sounding board then not talk to me and leave. This has been happening a lot. I worry about both of you."

"What are you worried about, Katie?"

"Jesus. What do you think I would be worried about? You. You just keep…I don't know…pretending that she's okay. She's not okay. You need to talk to us. Tell us what's going on."

"I know…"

"Are you getting divorced?"

He paused and looked up at her. "No."

"No?"

"I don't think that will ever happen."

She wiped tears from her cheeks and reached for a box of tissues on the counter. She pulled out a clump of tissues. "Shit. Damn." She threw all but one of them onto the table in front of her. Then she threw the box onto the floor.

"I'm sorry, Katie. I shouldn't have come in. I should've just left this alone."

She stood abruptly and put her hands straight down at her sides. He recalled this posture when she was a little girl making a stand for herself. "No. You came in here to talk to me. That's what you should do. Talk to me."

He looked down at the tabletop. He said, "I will."

She waited for him to look up at her. He lifted his head and stood up. He went over to her, put his arms around her and hugged her to him. She sniffled. He patted her on the back with his right hand.

He said, "But not right now. I just can't right now. It's too complicated. Mixed up…"

They stood like that for several minutes. Dan thought he needed to get out of his daughter's house before Joe got home. He needed to be alone.

She watched him turn around in Peter's driveway and drive slowly past their house. She turned and went up the stairs intending to go back to bed. She stopped on the stairway and stood like that for several minutes. She backed down the stairs and went into the kitchen.

Standing in front of the table, she picked up her glasses and held them in her hand. She looked at them and put them back down on top of a placemat. She saw her cat watching her. She stared at the cat who continued to watch her from her place on the floor, then she looked away and sat in one of the kitchen chairs.

"Are you hungry?" she asked the cat, but she did not move. The cat continued to watch her. Suddenly, she started to tear up. She wept. Her hands moved across the surface of the kitchen table in small, circular movements, and then she brought them up and placed them over her face and sobbed.

When she awoke, she lifted her head from her forearm, that was still damp from her crying. The cat was on the table, curled up and asleep near her. She reached over and stroked her cat. The cat made a small, curling movement with the tip of her tail but did not open her eyes.

"I don't know what is the matter with me," she said to the cat. "I don't know what to do anymore."

The cat opened her eyes and looked at her, then went back to sleep. Her tail moved again.

Jenny said, "I'm just so tired."

She stood up and went to the sink. It was full of dishes. She stared at the dishes for several minutes, then turned on the faucet. She ran hot water over the blue Dawn dish detergent that she had squirted into the pan. She watched the suds grow. She kept squirting the Dawn into the hot water until the suds were pouring over the sides.

She stopped and began washing each dish in a slow motion. She did this for several minutes until all of the dishes were rinsed and sitting in a pile on the counter beside the sink. She decided to let them dry there and went into the bathroom.

Picking up clothes from the floor, she began to load the washer. The cat sauntered into the room and jumped up onto the dryer and made a noise.

"You're hungry, huh?" She put the clothes she held into the washer, then picked up the bag of dry cat food and poured some of the small nuggets into the cat's dish. She watched as the cat hunched over the dish and began crunching on the food. Jenny watched her cat eat—the cat's tail swished back and forth and she purred, settling into a sitting position.

Jenny decided that she was hungry also. She left the laundry room without starting the washing machine and went to the refrigerator. She pulled open the door and bent into the opening. She examined the contents. Then she started pulling items out of the refrigerator, setting them on the sideboard.

She stopped and went to the wastebasket and brought it over to the counter. She began throwing out most of the contents of the refrigerator. After several minutes of this activity, she stood up suddenly from the refrigerator, stretched and watched as her cat rubbed against her shins. She reached down to pat the cat.

"Good kitty. Oh! Damn..." She turned and went to the laundry and began putting clothes into the washing machine. She added detergent and turned on the machine.

She stood there and briefly reviewed her routine in her head then walked back to the kitchen, sat on the floor and continued to clean the bottom shelves of the refrigerator.

She remembered her dream from last night. It just came to her out of nowhere and entered her waking day. It intruded. It was not unwelcome...but it was not invited either. She stopped and sat down on the floor.

In her dream there was a phone call. It was from her brother, Harry. But Harry had died several years ago. This was an important call. She told the operator she could not take the call because she had a hearing impairment and could not use a phone. The operator in her dream said, "*It's okay. You'll be able to hear this call.*" Jenny said, "*Hello?*" And Harry was there.

They talked. They laughed about things that they talked about. She could not recall the conversation, but it had been pleasant and filled with happy memories. The conversation was not a long one, but it was clear; she had no trouble hearing him. Harry was with her.

Jenny sat like that on the kitchen floor and revisited her dream. The cat returned and climbed onto her lap, putting her paws up onto Jenny's chest, pressing and pushing against her, her claws making gentle pricks on Jenny's skin, as she purred.

She wanted to tell Danny about her dream. They often shared their dreams, discussing and interpreting them with each other. She missed him. Their argument had left her with a deep fatigue and an anger that was not proportionate to the substance of their fight.

It was the words that hurt. They had both flung hostile and hurtful words. Danny could be so gentle and easy that when he did lose his temper, it always frightened her...not physically frightened, he was never like that, but she would fear his leaving her.

She had forced these rare arguments in the past, to this same point...where she seemed to expect him to abandon her...to leave and not return. She still felt the hurt, and she was angry that he had hurt her.

In reality, when Harry had been alive and did make phone calls home, she could've talked with him, but did not. She thought, *Danny did... it was Danny that spent late nights on the phone with Harry. Danny listened to Harry, drunk or sober, and made excuses for me.*

There were real reasons...it had hurt too much to talk to Harry...especially when he had been drunk, which was most of the time. Harry never wanted to talk for real. Not about their lives...not about what really happened. He telephoned drunk, and she did not believe it was the real Harry that she would talk to...just the drunken Harry, who was not her real brother. But Danny would listen.

*It was easier for Danny than for me*, she thought, *he was not his brother*. Danny could feel Harry's "lost-boy" feelings but not like she felt it. And the few times she had tried to talk to the Harry that was real...her real brother, he would not speak of the unspeakable. He would not acknowledge any of it.

Then...he would be drunk again. He would leave her and be drunk. Then...he died and left her alone with their nightmares.

When he drove under the railroad underpass and entered Cold Brook Mills, he continued out Main Street. He turned off Main Street and headed toward the other edge of town and Cold Brook. He passed the house where he had grown up. It had been restored as an apartment building.

He continued past the cemetery and came to the small bridge that crossed Cold Brook. He turned right onto the narrow road to the interior of The Point, where the Androscoggin River merged with Cold Brook.

He had not been into The Point for many years. He tried to recall when he had last visited this spot. He could only remember it as a place he and Dennis had hung out, with Alton and some other friends from school. Usually playing hooky, smoking cigarettes or cigars, but sometimes camping in the summer, swimming, fishing...

It was no longer a road. Barely a trail really. He could see old tracks where a four-wheeler had gone through. And maybe a jeep. There were large puddles, and there were still some patches of snow in the woods. Much of the wood's floor was bare, the grasses and leaves flat and wet from the melted snow.

His car was not going to make it in. He could not back out. He finally stopped and backed carefully into a grove. He got out, checked the ground and then backed further into the area. He shut off the engine and sat there for a few minutes. He realized that the sun had come out and it was warming up.

He opened his door and got out. He started walking into The Point, the muddy trail made squishing sounds as he walked around large puddles. He stopped and removed his jacket. He had worked up a sweat.

He walked until he came to the clearing that led to the spit where the brook and the river merged. He paused and looked around. It was still a clearing but partly grown up. It seemed smaller to him.

Someone had built a campfire near the brook's edge. There were some partially burned pieces of wood, enclosed in a rough circle of rocks. *Not recently*, he thought, *maybe last fall.*

He found some old fish line caught in the brush. A crow flew over and made noise. He looked up and followed the large, black bird as it opened its wings, slowed and landed in the top of a young oak tree across the brook. The large black bird spread his wings as he swayed on the slender branch and caught his balance.

The woods were bare and stark, no foliage yet, except for the evergreens—tall, eternal, a dark, bold green against the blue of the sky. It was quiet. He could hear the brook gurgle, further down beyond the spit.

He turned and walked to the other side of the small peninsula and stood staring at the river. It was a little cleaner now than when he was a kid and came here to swim and fish. The closing of the paper mill several years ago allowed the river to heal and clean itself. But the closing had hurt the town. For a while, there had been persistent rumors that the mill would reopen. Then one summer night, a few years after the closing, the mill burned.

The town had turned out that night to witness the burning. His father had been ill that summer, but they had all walked uptown to watch the volunteer firemen—most of them former mill workers or the children of former mill workers—fight the fire.

After a couple of hours, Jenny and his mom had stayed with the kids, and he had walked home with his dad. He put him to bed and sat on the porch, watching the glow of the fire across Water Street on the other side of the river until Jenny, his mom and his children returned. His father had died two years later.

The fire damaged the mill but did not destroy it. Still, the town had suffered with the closing of the paper mill and the fire convinced everyone that it was over. The mill would never reopen. Some people had moved away and found other jobs; some in other paper mills in other small towns. Some had not moved and instead found ways to live on less and remain in their homes, in their hometown.

Dan felt fortunate. The mill's closing had not directly affected him and Jenny. Dan still worked for the newspaper. He had only worked at the paper mill on a part-time basis over the years to make a little extra.

Dennis had tried to move away but had moved back after a few months. His bad leg, his age and lack of education limited his employment opportunities. Now Dennis did odd jobs around town, worked at the dump part-time, and in the winter, he rode with the snowplows.

Dan thought of Dennis. He smiled and turned to look again at the brook. Dennis and he did not see much of each other these days. They were different. But Dan still thought of Dennis as a friend. He knew that Dennis felt the same way.

As kids, they had found much in common. Mostly mischief. And Dennis always made Dan laugh. But it was best this way. They could not talk much about things because they would not agree. In fact, they would disagree strongly, Dan was certain about this. They were grownups now.

Dan walked to the end of the point where the river and brook flowed together. He looked to his left and found the large oak tree that had been cut years ago to drop across the brook as a crossing near the sandbar. He moved around some fallen trees and across a small sandy area to the oak tree. He noted that a smaller tree, a maple, had been cut and dropped almost parallel to the oak, probably as a replacement. The oak tree was still solid but rotting into the brook.

He stepped up onto the oak tree and walked across to the other side. He strolled through the woods and came to the fields behind the Verrill farm. The old barn still visible above the trees. The weather vane with the pig was gone though.

He stood at the edge of the field and looked around. It surprised him that it had changed so little. Although he had driven past this area many times over the years, he had never stopped to pay attention to it. He thought of his dog Jack. And he thought of the mallard he had shot that day when he was a boy.

He turned and headed back toward The Point. He was breathing hard and sweating. As he neared the brook, he stopped and sat, leaning against one of the huge old pine trees. The sun shone directly in his face. He closed his eyes.

*He walked through the papermill with Dennis. It was busy. People moving things, pulling large carts of paper pulp. He and Dennis talked and laughed. The mill was noisy and the machinery hummed.*

*As they walked into the pulp room, he smiled at how busy the mill was. He looked ahead and caught a glance of his father. His father had not seen him, and as he turned, he moved out of sight behind a panel. Dan thought,* "Oh, god. It's Dad."

*He became aware that he was inside of a dream. But this only made the sensation more intense...as if his mind were somehow challenging his awareness of the dream. Then, it became more real.*

*He thought,* "I'm going to have to get through this. I will speak to Dad and see what happens." *And he and Dennis moved closer to where his father was standing, talking to another man.*

*Dan became excited and anticipated the flood of emotions that he knew would soon envelop him. He stopped where his father was talking and laughing with the other man. He said,* "Hi, Dad." *His father turned and looked at him. His father smiled and walked toward him. They did not speak.*

*When his father got close to him, Dan reached out for him and hugged him close. He thought how young his father looked, how handsome and how blue his eyes were. He could smell the scent that was his father—that unique scent that parents have that is such a comfort to their children. Dan realized that he and his father had rarely hugged.*

*And so, in his dream, he determined to hold onto his dad, close, for as long as this dream would allow them to be together. He took it all in and savored it. He felt his father's strong, broad shoulders through the flannel shirt that he wore. He smelled the familiar Old Spice aftershave—and the bristle of his father's beard scraped across his cheek*

*And then when it was time to go, he pulled back from his dad. His father smiled at him, holding him by the shoulders at arms length, but still did not speak. Dan started to weep. His father held onto his hand as Dan started to walk away from him.*

*Dan thought,* "I have to let go." *He did...and walked away with Dennis. Letting go of his father's hand he said,* "Goodbye, Dad."

Dan awoke. A woodpecker across the brook, hunting insects in a dead tree, made a loud, "*Tock, tock...tock, tock, tock.*" Dan looked for him but could not see him.

A crow cawed and moved in the top of a young poplar, stretching his wings, attempting to balance himself as the branch swayed.

Dan sat thinking about his dream. He had only dozed for a few minutes, but it seemed like much time had passed. The warm sun shined down on him. Then he stood, walked to the sandbar and started across the oak tree bridge. He stopped to watch a cormorant, perched on a rock in the brook, his large wings spread in a strange, contorted position, to dry in the sunshine. Dan still felt sleepy.

As he reached the other shore, he looked to his left and saw that there was an elderly man sitting on a rock near the end of the small peninsula that jutted into the water where the brook and the river merged. The man had his back to him. He did not want to stop, and so he decided to move quietly toward the road leading out of The Point.

"I used to fish here," the old man said without turning.

Dan stopped. "Yeah. Me too."

"Still any good?"

"I don't know. I haven't fished here in years." He shook his head. "I haven't been here in years."

The man was quiet. Dan started to leave. Moving around a large puddle, he stopped, turned and looked over at the man who sat with his back to him. He stood watching him for a few minutes. The man wore farmer jeans and a light-colored t-shirt. His nearly bald head still displayed some wisps of white hair. Dan moved so that he could make out this man's profile.

Dan said, "Alex?"

"I am," said the man.

"Alex...the cop?"

"I was a police officer...once," said the man, turning toward Dan.

Dan grinned. He felt a surge of surprise and pleasure. He searched his memory and recalled that Alex had moved out of town while he was away in the military. He had not seen him since. He walked back toward Alex.

Alex stood. He steadied himself with a walking stick. Dan thought he was still a good-size man, though certainly smaller than Dan remembered him to be. His face was familiar. The rather large nose and the dark eyes and complexion, a familiar face, now furrowed, but taut and firm. Yup...this is Alex, but Dan thought, *There is something different about Alex. Of course, he is much older now, but...his eyes...maybe they always had been...*

Dan put a hand out for Alex to shake. "I'm…"

"I know who you are," said Alex taking Dan's hand. "I knew your dad. His brother and I were friends. Used to play poker together. Sometimes your dad would be there. Nice man, your dad. He wasn't much good at poker though. Sorry to say."

"Yeah. That's right. Neither am I." This surprised Dan and his grin became wider.

They shook hands. Dan noted that Alex had a firm handshake and that his hands were large. Alex's hand felt bony and hard. Dan let it go. He thought of his dream.

"He still around?"

"My dad? No. Dad died about ten years ago."

Alex nodded.

"My uncle is still alive. I don't see him much. He isn't well."

"You're Danny."

"Yup," Dan smiled at Alex.

"You married that little girl…her father killed himself."

"Jenny."

"Yes. Jenny."

Alex was quiet. He was looking at Dan's face. His eyes held Dan's eyes. Dan found that he did not want to look away.

"How is she?"

Dan hesitated, then surprising himself, he said, "Well…" he paused again and decided, "she's having a hard time these days."

Alex did not respond.

They stood for a while and then Alex turned toward the rock he had been sitting on. He motioned to Dan to follow him. Alex sat down. Putting his walking stick on the ground beside of him, he reached for a thermos.

"Sorry," he said. "I need to sit down."

He unscrewed the top of the thermos and poured some tea into the cup. He handed it to Dan.

"Thanks." Dan sipped on the tea and handed it back to Alex.

Several minutes went by; they listened to the sounds of the woods and the brook as it merged with the river downstream from where they sat. Dan watched Alex as he drank the tea

"I'm not surprised," Alex said.

At first Dan did not know what he meant. Then he realized Alex was referring to Jenny.

"I remember her face," Alex continued. "She asked me, 'What about my dad?'"

Dan sat quiet.

Alex said, "You know…there are some things you don't forget. Those kids…well…that family…those parents… There was a poverty there that had nothing to do with them being poor. They were not there for their kids; they were souls adrift, lost, and their kids suffered for that." Alex sat facing the water, he turned to glance at Dan. "A parent's suicide is the ultimate betrayal. The ultimate child abuse."

Dan nodded, mostly to himself. Realizing that Alex could not see him, he found a stump near where Alex was sitting. He sat down and leaned forward toward Alex, placing his forearms on his knees. He looked down at the ground.

"Where did you go, Alex?" he asked, turning his head up to see him.

Alex turned to him. "I moved out of town. Annie and I, after Phoebe graduated college, decided to do something different."

"I haven't seen you around."

"We were nearby. I came through town once in a while, but we didn't stop much."

"What kind of work did you do?"

"I went back to college on the G.I. Bill, and later I became a pastor of a church up near Bethel. Just a little place. Something I had always thought of doing. Annie and I loved it. Spent most of our time doing things in town. Church suppers. Picnics. Funerals. Weddings. Births." Alex smiled. "Lots of fun. Lots of life."

"How is Annie?"

"She's fine. She's in a nursing home though. But, she's fine."

Dan said, "I'm sorry." He watched Alex. "How about yourself? How are you doing?"

"I'm doing great. The doctor just diagnosed me with Alzheimer's. That's the bad news. The good news, I guess, is that it's early and it's a slow onset…*he* says. Seems fairly quick to me. But by the time it's full-blown, I won't even know it."

"I'm sorry."

Alex looked at him. He said, nodding his head, "An interesting disease. There is a saying that the motion of …" he waved an arm around him to include the forest, the brook, the creatures and more, "all of this…is in returning. This disease is certainly that."

Dan grinned. He looked down the river and then back at Alex. Alex was staring at him. Again, Dan became caught in those eyes.

Then Alex said in a quiet voice, "This child who dreams? Well, he dies—from the same disease as the man." He moved his head to one side to peer at Dan from another angle. "Paraphrasing Greene, I think. Goes something like that. Been rereading some of the good old writers lately. Running out of time. Can't waste it on crap." Again—a long pause.

The trees made a shush sound with the gusts that moved through them. Dan thought of the many quiet, peaceful times he had spent here at The Point as a boy—camping, fishing and reading.

Dan thought, *I am still Danny...I'm still that boy. I will always have that boy inside me that dreams and plays and laughs and cries...*

"I'm eighty two years old, Danny. I am amazed. I am not a whit smarter than I ever was. I thought I would be. When I was younger, I thought I would be smarter when I got older. But...I'm not. I am wiser though. Which has nothing to do with being smart."

Dan was quiet.

"You were a good kid."

Dan looked at Alex and said, "I'm sorry for giving you such a hard time as a boy. Seems like I was always getting into some kind of trouble."

Alex laughed. "You were not a kid in trouble. I got a big kick out of you and that other Dennis kid...now that Carver boy...he had a problem."

"After prison, he got married and brought up a couple of kids, you know. I think they did all right."

"Good. He deserved a life. But that boy tried awful hard to be bad."

Alex started to hum. A random humming—no melody. It startled Dan, but he sat quietly. Then, without turning to Dan, Alex said, "Things changed fast during that time. The town and the people. It changed. I remember thinking at the time that things were changing."

"Drugs. The sixties...the war."

"Hmmm."

"How did you happen to go into the ministry?"

"Well...see...I don't really know the answer to that. But I had thought about it for a long while. Old Burpie had brought it up to me once many years before. Planted the seed, I guess...I don't know why. As the town cop, I suppose I thought of myself as more of a...well, not a cop. But, I liked helping folks."

He paused and shifted his position. "The job had challenges that gave me opportunities to help others. It felt right to me. That is the way it should be. Then one day, after old Dummy died, I looked around and decided that things really had changed. And I wanted to do something else."

Dan waited. He realized that Alex was no longer talking just to him.

"I started searching. I was still a young man. I guess that was it really. I just got extremely curious." Alex sat up straight. He was looking past Dan at some point just above Dan's head. He seemed alert suddenly. "I learned something from Dummy. A word..."

Dan now wondered where Alex was going with this.

Alex caught Dan's gaze. "I know...you're wondering about Dummy. He was deaf and dumb, but he was hardly dumb. Dummy was a self-educated man. He read avidly and studied. His younger sister had taught him to read and write when he was a boy—before he went completely deaf. He kept diaries...my god, you should've seen the notebooks he had in his little apartment on Water Street. Notebooks full of...everything...his daily life, incidents that happened in our town. We were all in there...all of us."

Alex shook his head and laughed again—loud—and, Dan thought, full of abandon. His laugh filled the woods, and Dan found himself with a great smile of his own at Alex's uninhibited amusement.

Alex continued, "But, strangely, or surprisingly maybe, he studied the Bible and religion in general, I guess you could say."

Dan leaned forward. He could not take his eyes from Alex's face.

"That pack he carried," Alex started, "remember the canvas pack over his shoulder?"

Dan nodded, now completely fascinated.

"He had his notebook in there. He also had books that he carried around. And sometimes, I think he put his lunch in there."

Dan grinned.

"I went through his stuff after he died. I went through all of his notebooks. I tried to give them to his family, but they did not want them. I took them. All of them." Alex continued, "And I read every one of them. And Dummy had books! God. I never saw such a pile of books. Stacked around his apartment on the floor. Up the walls. On chairs. Everywhere!" Alex laughed again, "Ha!"

"What kind of books?"

"All kinds really. Some biology books. Science. History. Some literature. But mostly about religion. All kinds of religions. I had never heard of some of them." Alex shook his head. "I was dumbstruck." He smiled at this word.

"Struck by Dummy. Struck dumb."

Alex was beaming at his pun. Dan smiled at him.

Alex became quiet. Then, "Anyway…I was flipping through all of this and I came across a word. Now mind you, Dummy was able to read and write, but his handwriting was horrible…and his spelling? I struggled with it. Sometimes, especially the older he got, the writing just became a running together of words. Rambling. Very difficult to read."

"What was the word?"

"Hamartanein. Greek, I think. Scribbled into a page. But Dummy had circled it and underlined it and just made it…stand out…special-like." Alex cleared his throat, his face relaxed and brightened; he still smiled.

"Now, I can't say why…but the word got under my skin. I suppose it was in some context of the diary I was reading it from. But it seemed important to me to find out what this word meant."

"What did you do?"

"I had no clue what the word was. I didn't know the language even. I showed it to Phoebe, and she thought it was Latin or Greek. I went searching and found myself immersed in the Old Testament and other ancient religious texts, some of them were Dummy's books. I discovered a lot I was ignorant of, but I could not find this word." He paused.

"I became sort of distracted by all of this studying, and I ended up, somehow, getting into the ministry after finishing college. I loved the work. But it was not exactly what I was searching for, as I later discovered. Then one day I was…actually, I think I was in the library at Bates College, going over some books on religion…and there it was. The word…'Hamartanein.'"

Alex glanced at Dan and then away again. He said, "I apologize. This is why they call us 'preachers.'"

"No…I want to know what happened. What did you find out?"

Alex paused, then continued, "Well…I was actually looking for something else: an ancient, Christian form of prayer—hesychast. Ceaseless prayer—Paul mentions it in I Thessalonians. Instead, what I stumbled onto was a specific type of Japanese meditation that had its origins in ancient China and India. This is a type of sitting meditation and this ancient meditation, this prayer, you could say, well…it is a word that means: a devoted effort to hit the mark; to be on the point—to become one with the process of living.

"As I continued my research, that very same day, I found hamartanein. And it turns out that hamartanein...translated into English, is the word—sin, and means to *miss* the mark or to be *off* the point."

Dan let this thought settle. The drift of a warm breeze passed through him; but this breeze originated somewhere in his solar plexus.

"So this changed everything for me. It suddenly all fell into place. It was as if someone had reached inside my soul and turned it inside out. I saw it from the inside out. These two words, they went together, even though they came from different sides of the world. Worlds apart, you could say. When we miss the mark, ...when we sin...well, we are off the point. And, there is a method—a way—to focus on living our lives in the present."

Dan was silent. He thought how strange this all seemed. He looked at Alex. He looked around the forest, the brook, the river...suddenly, they no longer seemed familiar. His surroundings seemed mysterious, bright and extraordinary. Dan felt a peculiar shift, perhaps in the way the sunlight came through the trees and reflected off the water, into the surrounding woods.

Alex was quiet now. They both sat in the stillness of the woods. Then Alex sighed and sat up straight. He reached for his walking stick and used it to stand. He looked down at Dan. With his stick he pointed up the brook toward the quiet reeds and lilies in the small cove.

"It has been described as being like a boat on a lake. The lake is sometimes calm, and other times...not. The point where the bow breaks the water...that is the present instant...the wake of the boat is behind us, where we have been. And by looking back at the wake behind the boat, we may be able to see what direction we have come from, and we may discern the general direction we are headed in, but that exact point where the water breaks at the bow...that is our present action...and to be on the point, we must pay attention to that precise instant...the present moment."

He looked around the woods then back at Dan. "This is not my teaching. See...the great teachers all tried to teach us the same thing."

"And...we make choices."

"Yes."

"Those choices...they are at the bow?"

"Of the boat...that instant where the bow breaks the water. Yes. Tiny ones sometimes, but choices that we act on in any case."

"And they determine our course."

"Yes."

Dan was still. He did not look at Alex. He thought about Jenny. He thought about Jenny's parents. The way that they had hurt and damaged their children.

"The further off the point," Danny began, "then the more…afflicted."

"A kind of suffering…in the extreme, a person can live in a sort of…hell."

Dan suddenly lost his thought. He moved his head side to side. "I don't get it…"

Alex watched Dan's face.

Dan said, "It's hard to hold onto it…the thought, I mean."

"Yes. It is. Because it is the present. And that is impossible to hold onto. In fact, that is what I discovered. That to practice this…well, we have to learn about letting go."

Dan stood up. Alex walked toward the water. Together they walked over to the end of the spit. They stood watching the merging of the brook and the river.

Alex was a long way away. He muttered something.

Dan said, "I didn't hear."

"This is about being in the present, not committing sin, that is, not missing the mark." Alex spoke as if he were alone in these woods, as if he were discussing this with the forest and the creatures around him. "Not *holding onto*, but *being in*…paradoxically, we *get* this by learning to let go of it."

Dan did not respond. He thought about Jenny and their painful argument. He looked closer—inside, and he found that he was no longer angry. He looked over at Alex.

They were silent. The woods remained silent as well.

Dan said, "So…what did you do?"

"Well…I continued as a pastor. For a while anyway, and I devoted myself to this new practice. But, I don't think people were liking my sermons after a while," he said, grinning at Dan, "it was no longer about religion, you see."

"What do you mean?"

"Religions try to teach us. But they often miss the mark and they sometimes can be dangerous. They are not inclusive, they are exclusive. They exclude…they separate people. No…it's about a kind of forgiveness: that things are just as they are. And we have to let go. In order to live complete lives, we have to learn to let go. Our whole lives are about letting go."

Alex stepped toward the river. Dan followed him. Alex leaned on his walking stick and looked downstream.

"God is not a religion, son. Religions are made by man." Alex spoke in a soft voice now. He turned and looked directly at Dan. He did not seem like Alex anymore. He was a stranger. A friendly, strange man that talked to him now.

"See…I believe that in the end, when we're all alone and finished…" he paused, took a breath, sighed and said, "when all of our faiths, our religious beliefs…when all of our moralizing is over? Well then, all we are truly left with is how we have lived our lives. We are what we have done."

Dan could not pull his eyes away from Alex.

Alex turned and started walking out the road.

Dan made a face and looked at the ground. He stood like that for a while, then looked up, watching Alex's back as he walked slowly out the road. Then he jogged to catch up to Alex.

Dan and Alex walked out the road. A rabbit scurried across the path in front of them. They paused when the rabbit stopped in the middle of the road. They waited until the rabbit hopped into the deep grass on the other side of the narrow road.

They continued. They did not talk on the way out. Alex was slow but surprisingly strong in his stride.

They came to where Dan had backed his car into the grove; they kept walking. The day had turned into a warm, sun-filled afternoon. As they came upon Alex's small pickup truck, they paused by the front hood. Dan noticed the truck was old, the dark paint had faded, and some rust showed through in places.

Dan had been thinking. He asked, "Can everything be forgiven? I mean, aren't some things just…I don't know…unforgivable?"

"Don't get stuck on one meaning of a word, Danny. It might turn out to be someone else's meaning." He paused. "If you are always looking back at the wake of the boat, you aren't on the point."

Dan shook his head.

"You're a good kid, Danny. Don't worry about it. It's not that important."

Dan thought of his dream. He thought about his dad. He thought about Jenny. He looked at this old man standing across from him. He reached out and embraced Alex. They held onto each other for several seconds. Then they let go of each other.

Alex poked him on the right foot with his walking stick. It startled Dan. In fact, it hurt a little. He thought, *It* is *important. What does this mean?*

Alex climbed into his truck. Dan had an impulse to stop Alex; he wanted to ask him that question; he was certain he would never see Alex again. Alex started his truck and waved at Dan—just a small gesture—as he drove off.

Dan returned to his car. He sat on the hood and looked around the small grove. His right foot still stung from the poke Alex had given him. He recalled that he, Dennis, and Alton had pitched a tent near here one time during a summer vacation.

They had spent the afternoon preparing a campfire for the evening. They fished, swam, then they had played a game of Stretch...this was a boy's game. He thought of his daughters...no girl, sensible as they were, would ever be caught playing Stretch.

The game required each boy having their own jackknife, and facing each other, they would toss it a reasonable distance, if it stuck into the ground, blade first, the other boy was required to stretch his foot to that spot, and then, if he was successful in that stretch, it was his turn to pick up the knife and toss it to another spot for the other boy to stretch...until, well...until one of them could not stretch...senseless, really.

Dennis had tossed his knife a little too hard. It sliced deep and stuck into Dan's right foot. Dennis and Alton ended up taking turns carrying him piggyback out of The Point to his home.

The rest of the afternoon and evening was not spent in their camp. Dan went to the emergency room, Alton and Dennis went home to face their parents. The injury was serious enough to Danny's foot that he spent the summer in a cast. Dennis had not come around much that summer. Danny had spent the summer alone at home that year.

It was that summer that Dan had made a discovery. One early morning, lying on top of his sheets, sweating from the humid night in his bedroom, he had heard his parents arguing. They were angry. He had reached over to his bedroom door without getting out of bed and cracked it open. He could not see them, but he could hear better. Their words were harsh and hurtful.

Dan remembered feeling sad and...afraid. How could they hurt each other so—if they loved each other? And then his father said something that had caused young Danny to lay rigidly in his bed. He had called his mother a bad name. And something about him—Danny. Dan could not remember the exact words, but he realized that something had happened between his parents before he was born, and it had something to do with their first born child...himself.

He had spent those days reading and writing stories and making up games. He did not like board games and he did not like cards. But he had played solitaire until he could stand it no longer.

Then one day while his parents were at work, he had climbed out of bed and hobbled into his parent's bedroom. He had started to just sort of look around. He thought about shooting the shotgun out the bathroom window…just for fun, but decided not to.

Then he had gone over to his father's top dresser drawer. This drawer had always been full of little treasures. His father had had a little packrat in him.

That day he had found and fooled around with the different pocket knives his father had collected, opened and closed them, felt their sharp edges with his finger—thought about his foot—and had put them back. He had found the French playing cards that his uncle had sent his dad from overseas. They were a constant fascination to Danny. And then he had found a large envelope that he lifted from the drawer.

He had opened it and found a document, studied it and found his name, and handwritten on the reverse were the names of his parents. It was a birth certificate: his. He had examined the birth date. Then he had found another document in the same envelope. It was a marriage certificate: His parents'. He had scrutinized this document also and found that they had married just two months before his birth date.

For a long while after that summer day, young Danny had tried to reconcile the argument he had heard and the hurtful words between his parents—and the discovery he had made about himself that day. A small secret but significant to his sense of belonging in this life.

He had grappled with this information. His imagination had taken him to disturbing places. And…only for a while…Danny had wondered if his parents had ever really wanted him to begin with. He knew better, and it did not overly disturb him as the years went by. He knew that his parents loved him.

But now, sitting on the hood of his Toyota Tercel, thinking of Jenny, he wondered, *How do we ever belong in the world if we do not belong to our parents?*

The morning air was cool, despite the warm sun. *A better beginning than the other day,* Dan thought. He poured the coffee into two cups. He picked them up and walked out onto the patio.

"Here you go," he said, handing the mug to Jenny. She was wearing a gray, hooded sweatshirt with the hood up. "You too cold?"

"No. It's nice out here. Just not warm enough." She wrapped both hands around the warm coffee mug.

He sat down on the wicker patio seat, placing himself near her right ear as always, so that they could have a conversation with minimal difficulty. They sipped on their coffee.

The sky was a bright blue. The trees across their southern lawns were starting to bud. Dan looked over at the large maple tree that stood beside their house for a closer view of the buds.

There was a black bird sitting near the top branch. It seemed that the blackbird observed them from his lofty perch. The buds were full and ready to produce copious green leaves that would fill the huge tree…but, not yet…a few more warm days and warm nights and they would come forth, one quiet morning when he was not paying attention. And then they would just be there, and he would think, as he did each spring, *When did that happen?*

The warmth from the sun intensified. Jenny pulled the sweatshirt off over her head. He watched as she fixed her hair and put her glasses back on. Then he turned and looked up at the sky. Closing his eyes, he took a deep breath. He recognized the familiar, spring scent that he thought of as the thawing of the earth.

"I had a dream the other night." She reached out and took his hand.

Dan opened his eyes and turned toward her, shifting in his seat. He thought of the dream he had had of his father. Now they would tell each other about their dreams.

"I dreamed that Harry called me on the phone. And…I could hear him."

He waited, watching her face.

She told him about her dream. He listened and thought about what Alex had tried to talk to him about that day on The Point.

He said, "I know this is hard," he searched her face, "but we should talk about this. Do you ever think about why you have been like this for so long?"

She watched him. "What do you mean?"

He tried a different way to approach this. "Did you ever talk to Harry about what happened? Did you two ever talk about your childhood…your parents?"

She shook her head. "I will never forgive them. Never. Don't ask me that."

Dan paused. He sat back in his chair. He sipped on his coffee. He recognized the old stubbornness.

They did not talk for several minutes, and then Dan said, "You know who I ran into the other day?" He thought about how strange that day had been for him.

She looked over at him.

He said, "Alex."

"Alex? You mean Alex the town cop?"

"Yeah."

"He must be old now. When?"

"The other day, when we had that…argument."

She was silent.

"I wasn't going to mention it because…well, I have been thinking about how to describe it. To myself, even."

"Did you speak to him?"

"Jenny?" He ignored her question.

"Yes?"

"It's too late to talk to Harry. Do you think that you could talk to someone else?"

She shrugged.

"Maybe…" he hesitated. "What if forgiveness wasn't something you gave to your parents. What if it were something that you experienced for yourself?"

She squinted, looked away and made a face.

"What are you holding onto? It feels like you are clinging to something that is dragging you to the bottom."

She shook her head. Her eyes welled up.

"What is it? What is it that you hold onto?"

There was a long silence—then, "They were my parents. My daddy and my momma." She mumbled something. "Hate." She her shook head, and said, "No." Then whispered, "Anger."

He waited, then said, "It's okay. It doesn't matter how long it takes. We can do this together."

# Epilogue

## shikantaza

The loon hopped once, then dove deep. His legs and webbed feet moved efficiently through the water, taking him deeper into the darkness of the lake. He remained under the water, chasing a fish; it was too large, and he retreated. He came back to the surface without food.

When he broke the surface, the water rippled. The spring plumage now complete, his checkered, black and white back glistened in the sun. He came to an abrupt alertness. Moving his black head from side to side, he scanned the lake for signs of danger or friends; he looked for his mate.

His red eyes moved to the land. He avoided land. He could not move well on land. Often his fishing would bring him up close to the land surface. He could not judge well, ascending after a long, underwater hunt.

This time he was close to the land. He looked carefully. An inquisitive creature, if something moved on the land, he would sometimes move closer to examine the movement. Rarely, he would encounter a human. Sometimes this would result in a mushy food item. Usually it did not.

More often, his curiosity was simply returned; then he would turn and move back to the deeper waters…a large loon, and a strong swimmer, with a neck as thick as a large water snake. He did not know this, but he was getting old—nearly six years in age.

He gave a call—a yodeling, resonating cry that reached the full length of the lake in both directions. He waited. There was no response. He called again. This time he heard her and he swam in her direction. He called again. She responded, her cry as melancholy as his own. It was as if they could not stand to be parted.

He moved through the water to the end of the lake where the sun came down. There was a small cove, filled with yellow and white lilies, lily pads, frogs, mallards, sometimes Canadian geese on their way back home, a beaver and his family, and always turtles and sun-fish. The loons nested here, along the land, near reeds and cat o' nine tails. They would rest, then return to fishing later in the night.

The elderly woman moved toward the lake. Her slight size and good health allowed her a robust stride. She crossed the small lawn to the bank of the lake. In her hand she carried a paper bag. She approached the bank of the lake and opened the bag. She reached inside and tossed scraps of food into the lake.

The loon moved over to the banking. He hesitated. He watched the woman. He gestured with his head in a dipping motion, then with a familiar move, he came up to the woman. His mate joined him and they fed on the scraps. The woman watched and smiled.

She spoke, "There now…"

She moved toward two seats that faced the lake, with a small table separating them. She chose one of the seats, and placing her hands on either arm of the chair, she lowered herself, adjusting her position until she was comfortable. She sat watching the lake.

There were no bugs this evening. The breeze and warm sun kept them down. She sat like that, the sun warm on the side of her face that turned toward the west. A breeze moved her fine white hair, her hands quavered and her lips moved—but she did not speak.

From the cottage behind her, an elderly man approached the woman. He also had thinning, long white hair that matched a full moustache. He walked with a wobble, not so robust as the woman, and when he reached the chairs, he moved in front. He looked down at his wife. She gazed up and put a hand to her forehead to see him in its shadow. He smiled at her, and teetered, as he lowered himself into the seat.

They watched the two loons from where they sat. They did not speak to each other.

A loon is naturally curious. The elderly woman and her husband knew this, and they had encouraged the loons' curious nature and nurtured their trust over time. These two loons became familiar with the elderly lady and her husband.

When the loons had returned from the Atlantic coast each spring, they sought out this same location and found the couple waiting for them. They had become friends, of sorts, as animals and humans sometimes do.

On some evenings, they would sit and watch each other. The elderly couple from their vantage point in front of their cottage, near the loons' nest in the cove, and the loons from their place on the lake, close to the land.

Now the male moved through the water, flapped his wings, gained speed, his webbed feet dragging, then he lifted off from the lake's surface. His mate followed him.

The woman reached over to touch the man's hand. Her own hand, deeply creased and touched with brown spots, trembled. But as she reached out for his hand, resting on the small table, it was not there. She turned to look up for him, but he faded—a smile for her as he faded away—and there was really only the warm sun in her face, setting in the west...his chair, empty. She knew this...she had merely forgotten for a moment.

So, she just sat there. She sat alone. She raised her hand, placed it on her cheek, and with her little finger, she fooled with the tiny hair of her eyebrow as she watched the changing surface of the slate-colored lake.

The loons circled from high above. The male, his thick neck extended and drooping, his broad, webbed feet trailing behind—with deep wing beats—he moved as strong in the air as he did in the water. His mate flew east toward the far end of the lake. He let her go and circled once more over the cottage and the small cove and the woman. His large, red eyes moved over the scene below. And from the other side of the silent cove, a flock of black ducks flushed lazily into the orange-lemon sunset that blazed across an indigo sky.